Taylor, The Journey Home

Harold J. Fischel

ISBN: 0692341811
ISBN 13: 9780692341810
Library of Congress Control Number: 2014921396
Harold J. Fischel, Howell MI

I dedicate this novel to all who work tirelessly to free those who have been wrongfully convicted. Because the accused lack the means to finance a proper defense, they become victims of a system of justice that does not protect their constitutional rights.

Author with his Labradors

Harold J. Fischel, a graduate of Washington & Lee University and the NYU School of Law, has lived and worked on four different continents. His family fled the Netherlands shortly after the Nazi invasion, moving to Curacao and Aruba before settling in the United States in 1952.

After law school, Fischel served the US Army in Germany, later retiring as a captain. Since then, he again lived in the Netherlands, before returning to the United States to work for the US subsidiary of a Chinese company.

Fischel is now retired and living in Michigan with his wife, Jan, and their two beloved Labrador retrievers. He has two daughters, five wonderful grandchildren, and two great sons-in-law.

Chapter 1

"Hey, Taylor, come quick."

"What's the matter, Mike?"

"Quick, look over there. That's the new girl walking down the hall. Man, what a dish! She's really something; man, look at that body."

Taylor turned around to look. "You ain't kidding, she's really hot."

"That's all you can say? Look at that face. That girl is gorgeous! We haven't had a girl like that at Pentonville High before."

Taylor smiled, and as he continued to walk towards his homeroom he said, loud enough so Mike could hear him, "Guess I'll have to check her out."

Mike turned around and caught up to Taylor. "You gonna hit on her?"

"Why not? You just said she's the best-looking chick here in school."

"But, what about Valerie?"

"What about her? We're not going steady; so I can still see what this babe is all about."

"You son of a bitch."

"What's up with calling me that?"

"Because of the way you treat girls. Valerie is crazy about you, and you think nothing of just dropping her because some hot chick moved into town."

"Oh, come on. I never made Valerie any promises. Our relationship never was that serious and you know it."

"Yeah, I know. You just skip from one girl to the next the same way I would a new coat. I could never get away with it, but you can because you're the school's big jock and everybody likes you."

Taylor's good looks and athletic ability had already made him one of the most popular and sought-after kids in school. But being the star quarterback of the high school football team literally propelled him to stardom, and he knew it. Pentonville was a small town with only one high school. Everybody in town took great pride in the football team. Taylor was their hero. The high school girls adored him, and Taylor knew how to take full advantage of his status.

His mother worried about this. She constantly reminded him of their social position in town and the dire consequences if a boy with his family background were to get a girl pregnant. Taylor took his mother's warnings very seriously, but this didn't stop him from enjoying himself and dating every pretty girl in town. His friends even took bets as to who Taylor would select for his next short- lived romance.

Taylor had just started dating Phyllis Demeo. Phyllis' family had moved to Pentonville less than a month before the start of her junior year. She was a tall girl, with a beautiful face and a body that made her one of the sexiest girls in school. A lot of the girls already disliked her, solely because of the effect she had on boys, especially if the boy happened to be *their* boyfriend. But if they were honest about it, they had to admit that she was nice and had a quick smile for everybody.

This afternoon, Taylor and Phyllis were driving around in his car, going no place in particular. It was a beautiful day, and Taylor put the top down. Phyllis stretched her arms as if reaching for the sky and said, "Let's go someplace for a walk. It's much too beautiful to waste a day like this. I'm not ready to go home and do my homework. Do you realize that this is the first afternoon since we have been dating that you don't have football practice?"

"I know a great place we could go," Taylor said. "We could take a walk along the Penton River behind my house. It's beautiful this time of year."

"You have a river behind your house?"

"Yes, the back of our property runs along the river. I think it's the most beautiful part of the river."

"Then what are we waiting for? As they say in the movies, 'Take me to your river'."

Taylor made an illegal U-turn right in the middle of town and headed towards his house. When they arrived at the imposing entrance to the Marx estate, Taylor avoided the paved driveway and took the dirt road that led to the river.

Phyllis was a little apprehensive. "Hey, wait a minute. Where exactly are we going?"

"Don't worry; we're going to the river. It's just a little further down this road." Taylor parked the car at the end of the dirt road. They got out and walked to the river. When they got to the narrow path, which stretched along the river bank, Phyllis stopped and looked around.

"You're right, this is incredibly beautiful! Does your family own all of this?"

"Yeah, my grandfather bought this land years ago. He had the house built for my parents as a wedding present."

"I didn't see your house. Where is it?"

"When we entered the gate, I turned onto the dirt road. If I had stayed on the paved road, we would have come to the house. It's set back about a quarter-mile from the main road, almost in the middle of the property. Come on. Let's take a walk along the river."

After a while Phyllis took his hand, and they walked silently for about two miles before turning back towards the car. Just before reaching the spot where they had entered the narrow path, they sat down on a fallen tree trunk.

"I would just love to dive in," Phyllis said, looking at the clear water racing by.

"What's stopping you?" Taylor asked, with a mischievous smile on his face.

"Bathing suits!" Phyllis exclaimed.

"Well, that's not stopping me." Taylor jumped up quickly, stripped down to his shorts, and dove into the river. Phyllis, totally surprised, watched in amazement as he surfaced in the middle of the river.

Taylor laughed and called out, "Come on, your turn! You suggested it."

"Yeah, but I wasn't serious."

"Come on, don't be a prig, jump in!"

At first, Phyllis had no intention of undressing in front of Taylor and going into the water, but Taylor kept after her. Finally, Phyllis gave in. She looked around to make sure they were really all by themselves and called out, "Don't look!"

When Taylor turned his head away, she stripped down to her panties and bra and bravely plunged in. Taylor peeked anyway. Seeing her gorgeous body made him more determined than ever to make out with this girl. After they had swum around for a short while, Taylor swam over to Phyllis and reached for her. Her first impulse was to pull away, but then she changed her mind and let him kiss her. Taylor put both arms around her and tried to pull her tightly against his body.

"Come on, Taylor, don't!" She tried to push him away, but the feel of his muscular body pressing against her aroused an unexpected desire. As he tightened his grip around her she stopped struggling, and soon she was kissing him back. She opened her lips and his tongue pushed deep into her mouth; she could feel his chest rub back and forth against her breasts. It didn't take long before his hands started caressing her breasts. As he gently stroked her nipples, they became hard inside her bra. She tried to object when he reached around her back to undo her bra, but his kiss smothered her objection.

He pulled her bra off and took her breasts in his hands and said, "They're gorgeous."

She could feel him getting hard. She knew that she had beautifully shaped breasts. Although she was hesitant to go along with what was happening, she loved the effect her body was having on him. Taylor pushed her slowly to the river bank. When his feet touched the ground, he took her in his arms and carried her to the tree trunk they had been sitting on. He put her down and stood for a moment to look at her. Her figure was beautiful, and her bikini panties didn't hide much of where her long legs flowed into her slender hips. Her breasts were small, but firm and curved up, and her nipples were still swollen and hard as a rock from Taylor's touch in the river. Phyllis smiled; she enjoyed the look on his face as he looked her over.

"Okay, that's enough. Now turn around so I can get dressed." But Taylor had other ideas; he leaned over to stroke her breasts. Phyllis told him not to, but she didn't pull away from him. He bent down and started kissing her breasts. His lips closed around her nipple and he softly sucked on it. When he felt a tremor going through her body, he knew she was getting excited. He reached for her hips and tried to pull down her panties.

"No, no, let's not," Phyllis said, as she pushed his hand away. In her heart she was aching to have him make love to her, but she dared not. "Just come sit next to me here on the log and kiss me. I love it when you stroke my breasts; really I do, but I don't want to go any further." They sat on the tree trunk and while he kissed her, his hands were holding her breasts and his thumbs were rubbing back and forth over her nipples. His hands slipped down to her legs and he started massaging the inside of her thighs.

"Taylor, I said no! We've gone too far already. Let's just get dressed and start walking back to your car." But Taylor had no intention of stopping. He let his hand slowly slide up, and before she could protest, his hand was in her panties and his finger was stroking her.

Phyllis tried to push his hand away. "Come on, Taylor, I really don't want you to touch me there!"

"Relax. It's okay. You love me, don't you?" His finger explored further, and his stroking became more urgent. A wave of excitement went through her and she stopped trying to push his hand away. With his free hand, he pushed down his shorts and reached for her hand, which he pushed between his legs.

Phyllis protested, "No, I don't want to."

Taylor kissed her and held her really tight while he whispered, "Come on, baby, please."

Her hand reached for his penis and she slid off the tree trunk, pulling him with her. She slipped out of her panties. Breathlessly, she whispered, "Taylor, quick, I want you in me."

"I didn't bring any protection. We can't." Her breathing was very fast, and he could feel her hot breath as she pushed herself on him.

"I don't care, I want you. Please. Hurry!"

Taylor pulled away. His mother's warning was preventing him from doing what his body was telling him to do. "Without protection, we'll get into trouble."

Phyllis sat up and stared at him. Then she buried her head in her arms and started sobbing violently.

"Please don't cry. Come here and I'll hold you. We can still make out. We can have oral sex; we just can't risk having intercourse without protection."

Phyllis jumped up and ran for her clothes, left in a pile on the river bank. Without bothering about her wet panties or her bra, which was lost somewhere in the river, she dressed herself as quickly as she could. Then she sank to her knees, sobbing violently.

"What's the matter?" Taylor asked. "It's not that I don't want you. Look at me, I am totally aroused. You have a great body, and I'm dying to have sex with you. It is just too risky to go all the way without protection. Next time, I'll bring condoms. Come on, let me go down on you and you'll see that I do love you."

"You don't understand, do you?" Phyllis sobbed. "My God, I was ready to give myself to you. I don't know what happened, what came over me. I have never even touched a boy's penis or let anyone finger me!" Again, she burst into heavy sobbing. After a while, she continued, "You must think I am some kind of slut. You probably brought me here because you thought I would go down on you. One of your jealous little girlfriends must have told you I was a pushover for football players. Oh my God, what happened? How could I be so stupid? No, I don't want

8

oral sex with you. I don't want sex! I don't know what happened. I don't let boys touch me. I am not that type of girl. Take me home, please!"

Taylor didn't really understand the sudden change. He got his clothes and started to get dressed. "Sure, I'll take you home. Don't act like I was trying to rape you or force myself on you. Most girls love to make out with me. I certainly never forced you to do anything. You're nice, but I certainly don't need you! Besides, what are we talking about here? It's *you* who wanted to go all the way. *I'm* the one who stopped *you*!"

Phyllis looked at him, tears still streaming down her cheeks. "You're right. I have no right to blame you for anything. I don't know why or how, but I was out of control, and ready to submit to something I would never dream of doing. I shouldn't even have let you touch me like you did. I guess I have to thank you for stopping me from making the biggest mistake of my life. You can't imagine how dirty I feel right now. So please, just take me home! If you have any feelings for me at all, I beg you to try and forget what happened. It was a moment of insanity which I will regret for the rest of my life."

Taylor didn't get it. He was sure that she was upset that he wouldn't have intercourse with her. He couldn't understand why they couldn't have settled down and had oral sex. He'd had oral sex with girls who were quite willing to go all the way if he had wanted to. They didn't make a big fuss when he refused to go all the way without protection.

He drove her home. They sat silently for the entire trip. When they arrived at her house, she ran from the car without saying good-bye. She never spoke to him again. Taylor found her behavior rather bizarre, but it didn't really bother him that much. There were lots of pretty girls who were more than willing to go out with him. His friends continued to bet on which girl he would pick for his next fling.

Chapter 2

Taylor opened the curtains. A slight trace of fog still hung over the large circular driveway in front of the house, but Taylor could tell that it was going to be one of those clear, crisp days that were great for football. He was excited. Today was the day of the big game. Pentonville High and their archrival, Crestwood, would be fighting for the state championship. He had gotten up early so that he could give Ginger, his big golden retriever, a nice run in the woods before leaving for the game. The wooded trails behind the house were great to let Ginger run free. Taylor slipped quietly out of the house and ran at a leisurely pace down the trail, which ran through the middle of the property. Ginger followed, barking happily. The Marx property covered more than two hundred acres and resembled a triangle with the top cut off, the bottom running along the Penton River. Taylor decided not to make his usual stop to let Ginger jump in the river. He was in a hurry to get back to the house and get ready for the game.

Once back at the house, he was in and out of his room in record time. He was on his way to the garage when his mom called him back. "What did you eat for breakfast?" When he confessed that he had only eaten a small breakfast bar, she repeated her usual admonition, "You can't play football on an empty stomach." He knew she was right. Rather than argue, he quickly returned to the kitchen and sat down while his mom prepared his breakfast.

"Helene tells me that Phyllis, the pretty girl you were dating a while back, lives across the street from her. According to Helene, Phyllis was crying when she got out of your car. You haven't dated her since; what happened?"

"Nothing, Mom. We went swimming and made out a little. For some reason, she got upset and insisted that I bring her home immediately."

"You just made out and nothing happened? I've heard that before! Girls don't come home crying when nothing happened. I told you to stop it! You're going to get yourself in a heap of trouble."

Before Taylor could respond, his father walked into the kitchen. "Come on, Sue-Ann, leave the boy alone. He's a healthy teenager, and teenagers make out."

"Yes, but Helene told me that the girl was crying when he dropped her off."

"Tell Helene we hire her to clean the house, not to babysit Taylor."

"Henry, you have to stop protecting the boy. He'll get us all in trouble if he keeps fooling around with the girls."

Taylor was not in the mood to once again hear his parents argue about his social life. "Dad, are you coming to the game today?"

"Of course. I wouldn't miss it for the world. I'll even try to drag your mother along." Taylor took that as a signal that he could leave. He gulped down the fried eggs and bacon, quickly drank a large glass of fresh-squeezed orange juice, and was out the door.

It was about a twenty-minute ride from the house to the high school. Taylor was tempted, despite the chill in the air, to put the top down. The car, a restored 1957 Chevy Bel Air convertible, had been a present the year before for his sixteenth birthday. Taylor suspected that this outrageously expensive present had more to do with the fact that he had been selected to be the starting quarterback in his sophomore year than it had to do with his birthday. His father made no secret about being proud of his only son, "the quarterback."

When Taylor entered the locker room, Greg Mattum, the lanky wide receiver, was already there. The two of them had practiced for several hours the day before, and Greg had dropped more balls than usual.

Noticing that he looked rather glum, Taylor walked over to Greg's locker and said, "When things get screwed up during dress rehearsal, the show itself goes fine."

"Easy for you to say," Greg moaned. "This is my final game against Crestwood, and we're playing for the state championship. Hell, my family and everyone in town will be there. I'm a senior; I won't have a chance to redeem myself if I screw up like I did in practice."

"Come on, Greg." Taylor sounded pretty self-assured. "You'll do fine. Just run your patterns and when you turn to look back, the ball will be right there, in your chest. Just squeeze that baby and run for the goal line."

"Listen to the man." Big Daddy Timmons, the 290-pound lineman, lumbered into the locker room and joined the conversation. "I'll keep those Crestwood puppies bottled up so our boy with the golden arm can throw some beauties right at you, Greg." That remark didn't do much for Greg's mood, but it drew cheers from the other players. They laughed as they bragged about how they were going to beat those wimps from Crestwood. Taylor relished the way they described the long touchdown passes he would throw, and when he prepared to take the field, he was cockier than ever.

When the Pentonville team came on the field, the crowd roared. The stands were filled to capacity, and there was hardly any standing room left along the sidelines. Bud Simmons, a deputy from the local sheriff's office, had trouble keeping the people from standing too close to the playing field. Teddy Buskin, the owner of the local Ace Hardware store, switched off the music that had been blaring over the P.A. system, and started introducing the members of the Pentonville team. When he came to Big Daddy Timmons, the senior all-state lineman, the crowd cheered loudly. The cheerleaders ran onto the field to give a cheer for Timmons. But when he announced, "And our quarterback, Taylor Marx," the crowd really went wild.

Once again, the cheerleaders ran onto the field, this time to lead the crowd in their favorite cheer "Taylor, Taylor, he's our man, if he can't do it, no one can!"

For the home crowd, there was plenty to cheer about that day. At the start of the game, Pentonville seemed pretty shaky. The first two passes Taylor threw were dropped by Greg Mattum. In the huddle, Taylor tried to calm Greg. "You're trying too hard. Just let the ball hit your chest and then squeeze it. I promise it will be right there. Let's try the same route one more time; you'll do fine."

When the ball was hiked, Taylor took it and rolled out of the pocket. But when he looked downfield, he saw that Greg had slipped and fallen. Taylor yelled at Big Daddy, "Hold them! I need more time! Greg is down!"

"I got 'em!" Big Daddy shouted, as he strained to hold off two defenders. Taylor turned and raced to the opposite sideline. The defensive end caught up to him and Taylor turned again, evading a huge defensive lineman. Taylor looked downfield. Greg was back up and racing for the end zone. Taylor felt a defender's arm close around his middle as he was being pulled down. With a burst of strength, Taylor pulled loose. He saw that Greg had almost reached the end zone and he propelled the ball in his direction. The crowd was quiet while the ball spiraled in the air. Everybody held their breath! Greg turned, and the ball hit him squarely in the chest. The defender didn't have a chance. The crowd roared as Greg held the ball above his head in the end zone. The Pentonville players slapped each other on the back as they returned to their bench.

Big Daddy signaled the team to approach him. When they had formed a circle around him he said, "Okay, Greg has shaken off the jitters, and our boy Taylor has once again shown what he can do. We're ready! Let's go and maul those puppies!"

By the end of the first half it was 21 to 13 in favor of Pentonville. In the second half the Crestwood team fought hard, trying to catch up. Their offense was good, and they scored 32 points against a badly organized Pentonville defense. However, they were no match for the Pentonville offense. Big Daddy Timmons anchored the offensive line, and Taylor completed one pass after another. By the time the game was over, he had thrown six touchdown passes and rushed for two more. Pentonville had won the state championship. The town couldn't stop celebrating. They toasted their football heroes at a huge bonfire later that evening.

Taylor was selected as the best football player in the state, and was later named a High School All American.

Chapter 3

Van Beuren Textile, the children's clothing company founded by Taylor's grandfather, Timothy Van Beuren, had been losing business to cheaper imports from the Pacific Rim countries. This seemed to have little effect on Taylor Marx's life. But one day, when baseball practice had been cancelled and he arrived home early, he found his parents sitting in the library. His father was acting rather strangely, and it looked like his mother had been crying. Taylor realized that his father was drunk. Taylor hesitated. Should he leave them alone and quietly slip into his room? Or should he ask what was going on?

Before he could decide, his mother called out to him. Between sobs, she explained that the Van Beuren company had suffered heavy losses for several years. His father had borrowed large sums of money from the bank in an attempt to keep the factory afloat. The previous week his father had been in New York City to present new designs to Darling Stores, the big national children's clothing chain. Darling Stores was the last major customer Van Beuren had been able to hang on to. That morning his father had received the news that Darling Stores had placed large orders with

MyLin Clothing manufacturers, a Chinese company. Van Beuren would not be getting any orders for the coming season. In the clothing industry, news travels fast. Late that afternoon his father was notified by the bank that they were canceling all of Van Beuren's credit facilities and calling in all loans.

Taylor was stunned. He knew that his father was having difficulties competing with the cheaper imports, but he had no idea of the extent of the problems.

"Oh, Taylor!" his mother sobbed. "We'll lose the factory." Taylor tried to absorb the situation. The secure cocoon within which he had been living was suddenly torn apart, and he felt naked.

He clearly remembered the day his father took over management of Van Beuren Textile from his grandfather. Timothy Van Beuren, his grandfather, was a legend in Pentonville. He'd arrived in town as a penniless eighteen-year-old. To prevent being locked up for vagrancy, he took a job as an assistant to Miss Anna, the local seamstress. After several years of delivering dresses to local dress shops, he noticed that Miss Anna's designs were out of date. Her customers had started to prefer the more fashionable dresses sold by the big New York City fashion houses. He'd mentioned this problem to Clair Blain, the spunky young lady he had a crush on.

Over dinner one night, Clair asked, "Have you thought about children's clothes? Children's clothes are not quite as fashion-oriented as women's dresses, and I love designing them." It didn't take long for

Timothy to persuade Miss Anna to switch to children's clothes, and to let Clair design them. Within ten years, Timothy bought out Miss Anna and changed the company name to Van Beuren Textile. A decade later, the company had become a major manufacturer of children's clothes, employing over one thousand people. And yes, Clair became Mrs. Van Beuren.

In the days after Taylor learned about the financial problems of Van Beuren Textile, his carefree life rapidly fell apart. His mother, concerned about his father's drinking, asked him to skip school and drive his father to several meetings. She made him promise that he would stick close to his father all day.

The first meeting was at the bank. After that, they went back to the factory to meet with the board of directors and the legal advisors. Sitting in on all those meetings was a strange experience for Taylor. He was totally out of his element. His father had never involved him in any business discussions, and it was hard for him to follow the conversation. It frightened him when one of the board members started yelling at his father. The man demanded that the company CFO make full disclosure of exactly how much money his father had borrowed from the company.

Mr. Hendricks, the CFO, gave a rather confusing report. When he was asked to elaborate, he admitted that he didn't have the exact figures. Many of the transactions had taken place before he joined the company less than a year ago. The same board member who had raised his voice before about the loans, now started complaining about some specific expenses. He claimed to have repeatedly objected to these expenses. He said that he had pointed out that these were not legitimate company expenses, and that they should have been booked as private expenses of Henry Marx.

The only agreement to come out of the board of directors meeting was that the company would formally file for bankruptcy protection the next morning. After the meeting, everybody left. Only Taylor, his father, and John Phillips, the family lawyer, remained in the big board room. Neither Taylor nor John Phillips could prevent Henry Marx from going over to the bar and pouring himself a generous glass of scotch.

"Damn them all. They knew all the facts. Nobody ever complained! All they were concerned about was their compensation, and all the perks I arranged for them. Did any of them ever do anything positive for this company? Hell, no!" He quickly drained his glass and poured himself another. "They only worried about what I could do for them. Where were they when our costs went through the roof, when the union would not give me an inch in the negotiations, and when those bastards in Washington did absolutely nothing to stop all that cheap Asian crap from stealing my market? Hell, they encouraged it! Make more trade agreements, open up the borders. Who gives a shit about the American manufacturers?" The whisky was getting to him, but he kept on drinking.

"Calm down, Henry," John Phillips said. "When push comes to shove, you have to expect everyone to try and cover his own ass. The moment the bankruptcy papers are filed, the IRS will be all over this place, and all of those guys will claim a complete lack of knowledge. They will say that all details were carefully hidden from them, and they didn't participate in any decision which the IRS questions. It's human nature. They'll all run for the hills. If it helps their case, they will gladly pin your hide to the wall. From what I heard in the meeting, you have enough problems of your own, so let's not worry about what the others may or may not do. We have to talk. Taylor, please leave the room. Your father and I have to go over some matters before tomorrow's filing."

"Mom asked me to stay with Dad," Taylor responded.

"That's okay, but now your father and I have to talk in private; you can go and wait in his office." Taylor looked at his father to back him up, but his father signaled, with a wave of his hand, for him to leave.

Once in his father's office, Taylor rushed to the phone to call his mother. He explained to her that the meeting had been rather nasty, and that John Phillips had asked him to leave the room while he talked to his father. His mother said it was okay to leave his father alone with John. She proceeded to ask him a lot of questions about what had happened in the meeting. Since Taylor had not understood all the details of what was discussed, he could only give her some general information. He explained to her that over the years, his father had borrowed large amounts of money from the company. As he under-stood it, they were saying that the IRS would consider this money as income. He also heard them say that his father would have to pay taxes and fines for not declaring this income.

An alternative scenario would have the board demand that he pay back the loans with interest, so that creditors could claim the money as an asset of the company. Several board members also claimed that many of Henry's personal expenses had been paid for by the company. They pointed to the dress-ing rooms, with showers, that had been built around their pool several years ago.

Chapter 4

Van Beuren Textile was never given the opportunity to reorganize under Chapter 11. The financial situation was so bad that the company was quickly forced into liquidation. Pentonville was in shock. Besides being by far the biggest employer in the county, Van Beuren had always been relied on to sponsor all major events in town. Many people lost their jobs. The high rate of unemployment in the area that followed Van Beuren's collapse caused quite a bit of resentment against the Marx family.

When the news spread that Henry Marx had been indicted for financial manipulations, people in town celebrated. Most of them blamed him for bankrupting the company. People enjoyed gossiping about how the many lawsuits, claims from the IRS, banks, and other creditors had left Henry penniless. They gloated over the fact that the Marx estate, and all those fancy cars, were about to be put up for auction.

Taylor had started skipping school. Even though most people didn't hold it against him that he was Henry's son, he felt uncomfortable facing them. His friends, especially the coach and the guys on the football team, tried their best to rally around him, but

Taylor didn't know how to justify his father's actions. In a way, he felt guilty. He had benefited greatly from his father's manipulations, which now caused such grief among his friends' families. Taylor tried acting normal towards his father, but it was obvious that any support he expressed was not very sincere.

The only person Taylor could discuss his feelings with was John Phillips, the family lawyer. John pointed out that, although using company money to support his rather extravagant lifestyle was morally, and even legally, wrong, his father had never purposely tried to hurt people. On the contrary, he had always been overly generous and understanding. Many of the people who now condemned him had come to him when they needed help. He had always responded, either financially or in other ways. John explained that he always had great regard for Taylor's father, and was proud to be his friend. He couldn't abandon this friendship, not now, when Henry needed it most. John Phillips had no trouble putting his heart and soul into Henry's defense. He explained to Taylor that it had been important for him to let Henry know he was still proud to be his friend, that he wanted to be his lawyer, and he would stand by him during this horrible time.

"Taylor," John said, "I know you are aware that your father has a drinking problem, but you don't know why. You're old enough for me to tell you now. When Van Beuren Textile first started feeling the effects of cheaper imports, your grandfather forced your father to buy his shares in the company for a decidedly unfriendly price. Your father financed this forced purchase by mortgaging his home and taking a substantial personal loan from the bank. On top of this, your mother continued to spend money like water. As an only child with an adoring father, she was used to getting whatever she wanted. After she married your father, she continued her extravagant lifestyle. And you, my young friend, are a replica of your mother growing up. All this is a hard lesson for you, but I hope you have learned from it.

"Now, before you get the wrong idea about why the company failed, I want to impress upon you that, although your father's financial problems and the resulting drinking problem probably hastened the collapse of Van Beuren Textile, it was not the cause of it. You'll hear your grandfather saying that he was smart enough to change to children's clothes when they couldn't compete with dresses. To me that is just a cheap shot from an egotistical old man.

"Van Beuren Textiles can only produce clothing, and the domestic apparel manufacturers are all in trouble. The only ones who can survive are those with a strong brand. Your grandfather never tried to establish a brand. He was happy to make generic house brand children's clothing. Your father tried, but it was much too late to build a strong brand, which would have given him some added value to his product. Now go home and give your dad a hug. He desperately misses his son, 'the quarterback'. He is so proud of you."

When Taylor drove up to the house, he noticed that his mother's car was gone, but the front door was open. He went inside and Ginger, his dog, came running down the stairs. Rather than jump all over him as she usually did when he came home, Ginger kept running up and down the stairs, as if she wanted him to follow. He followed her, and she led him to the guest room at the back of the upstairs hallway. Ginger sat down in front of the guest room door and kept barking. Taylor opened the door and entered the guest room. He noticed someone lying on the big double bed. When he approached the bed, he saw that it was his father. His father lay fully dressed, staring at the ceiling. He had a pistol in his right hand, and there was a big, ugly hole in his right temple. The bedspread was covered with blood. Taylor froze. He couldn't get himself to approach the bed. He knew he should check to see if his father was still alive, but he didn't dare go any closer to touch him. For what seemed like an eternity, Taylor just stood there, looking at his father lying in a pool of blood. He felt like he was going to throw up.

Ginger's incessant barking brought him back to reality. He felt a strange calm come over him. His hands were ice-cold and it felt like he had involuntarily urinated, but he knew exactly what to do. He grabbed Ginger and backed out of the room. He closed the door and ran to his room to call 9-1-1.

Even before the ambulance arrived, police cars were filling up the driveway. Taylor met the first officers to arrive at the front door and told them to go up the stairs to the guest bedroom. Holding tightly onto Ginger, Taylor stayed downstairs. Soon the house was filled with police and EMT personnel. Taylor, all the while clutching Ginger tightly by her collar, was led into the living room and asked to tell the officers what happened. As best he could, he explained how he'd arrived home and how Ginger led him to the upstairs guest room, where he discovered his father lying on the bed.

"Did you touch anything?"

"No, I didn't."

"At what time did you arrive home?"

Taylor didn't know the exact time that he got to the house, but he explained that he came directly from John Phillips' office. One of the policemen left to call John Phillips, apparently to verify that Taylor had been there. Taylor asked if they could tell John to come over as soon as possible.

"Why, do you need a lawyer?" the officer asked.

Oh no, Taylor thought, *they don't really think I had anything to do with this, do they?* "He's our friend!" he blurted out.

As soon as he arrived, John Phillips took control of the situation. He called in a doctor to give Taylor some strong sedatives and to be on hand once Sue-Ann, Taylor's mom, arrived. He had given the police officers the license number of her car to help find her, and to tell her to return home as soon as possible. Under no circumstances were they to tell her what happened.

When the police told Sue-Ann that she was needed back at the house, she immediately thought that something had happened to Taylor. When she stormed into the house and saw Taylor standing next to John Phillips, she looked greatly relieved. That relief didn't last long. John sat her down and slowly proceeded to tell her what happened. Taylor steadied himself for her reaction. He was prepared to see her break down in tears, but he was not ready for the complete breakdown he had to witness.

Sue-Ann started screaming and yelling, "It's not true! You're lying! No! No, get away from me, you liar!" When the doctor tried to give her a sedative, she violently pushed him away. John forcefully grabbed her, holding both arms tightly while the doctor quickly gave her an injection. After a few minutes she started calming down. The tall, beautiful woman was almost unrecognizable as she sat slumped over, sobbing in her chair. "It's my fault, it's my fault!" she cried. With the police still in the room, that was about the last thing John wanted to hear.

"Sue-Ann, calm down. You weren't even here," John said in a low but firm voice.

"We fought. We argued about his drinking. I hid the liquor and he demanded that I give it back to him," she sobbed. Taylor went to his mother and tried to comfort her. He put his arms around her and gently stroked her long, blond hair. She continued to sob while she explained what happened next. He discovered where she had hid the bottle of scotch. She dared him to take a drink. When he did, she called him some terrible names and stormed out of the house. She kept repeating that she didn't mean all those terrible names she had called him. She had wanted to tell him she was sorry. The strong sedative took effect, and she slumped deeper into her chair.

Henry Marx's apparent suicide made national headlines. The death of the CEO of a major textile company shocked Wall Street. The bankruptcy of Van Beuren Textile had already had an impact on the financial world. Shareholders lost their entire investment. America First Bank took a major hit. The vice president in charge of the southern region was replaced, and the manager of the Pentonville branch was under investigation. All this publicity forced the local district attorney to launch an investigation into the circumstances surrounding Henry's death. It was not clear if it was a homicide or a suicide. Taylor and his mother were named "persons of interest."

Chapter 5

Taylor and Sue-Ann left Pentonville almost immediately after the funeral. John Phillips had seen to it that Henry's death was ruled a suicide, and that Sue-Ann and Taylor were spared the harassment of further investigation into their possible involvement. The funeral itself took place in a nearby town called Breston, where Henry had grown up, and where his family still owned a plot in the local Jewish cemetery. Complications were avoided when it became clear that Taylor's grandfather, Timothy Van Beuren, would definitely not attend. As such, there was no objection to a rabbi presiding over the funeral services.

The bankruptcy had taken most of the family's possessions. Sue-Ann and Taylor packed their few remaining personal items into the Chevy, which was in Taylor's name and couldn't be touched by the creditors. Taylor took Ginger to John Phillips' house, and tearfully gave to Jake, John's six-year-old son. Jake was ecstatic, and promised to take very good care of Ginger, and play ball with her every day.

Taylor and Sue-Ann headed for Miami, the retirement home of Timothy and Clair. At first Taylor had vigorously objected to moving in with his grandparents, but John Phillips explained the hard truth to him: financially, there was no other solution.

Sue-Ann didn't see it as a problem. She was an only child, and having no siblings to turn to, she longed to be with her parents. To an outsider, it would not appear to be such a bad deal to be forced into moving in with Timothy and Clair Van Beuren. Their house was on a large bay, and had over four hundred feet of waterfront. The stately two-story house had five bedrooms; Sue-Ann and Taylor would have their own space. Even though he was getting along in age, Timothy still enjoyed his Porsche Carrera and his speed boat, which he always referred to as his cigarette boat. All that should have been attractive to a young man like Taylor. But Taylor knew that his grandfather blamed his father for the loss of Van Beuren Textile. He never passed up an opportunity to remind everybody of his disgust for his deceased son-in-law.

That fall, Taylor entered high school in Florida as a senior. His scholastic achievements during the final month of his junior year at Pentonville High were terrible. But his teachers fully understood his situation; they recommended that he not be held back. Thanks to his grandfather, his reputation as a star quarterback preceded him, and the family expected him to be the quarterback for his new high school's football team. It was difficult to foresee how differently things would turn out.

When Taylor walked into Coach Nielson's office to sign up for football practice, he was made to feel less than welcome. The coach made it very clear that it was by no means a given that Taylor would make the varsity team. Although it was unusual to have a senior try out for the team, he said he would make an exception because Taylor had been a High School All American at his previous school. Taylor didn't understand why the coach acted that way. He knew he was a very good quarterback, and would be an asset to any team.

The next day, when Taylor was suiting up for the promised tryout, Andy Beckworth came into the locker room and walked over to talk to him. Andy explained that even though he was a starting pitcher on the baseball team, and a pretty good all-round athlete, Coach Nielsen had never given him much of a chance to play quarterback. No matter how well he did in practice, he'd spent most of the season sitting on the bench, barely qualifying for his letter.

When Taylor asked why, Andy explained the situation. Coach Nielson had twin sons, Abe and Charley, who had been playing on the varsity football team since their sophomore year. Abe was the quarterback, and Charley was the running back. Both were good athletes. Coach Nielsen was convinced he could groom them to become star athletes on a college football team. Andy also mentioned that Coach Nielson fully expected both boys to receive a full scholarship to some major university.

"So you and I really don't stand much of a chance," Taylor said. Andy just nodded.

Taylor had a lot of difficulty adjusting to his new surroundings. In Pentonville he had been part of the so-called "popular" kids in school. As the best known high school jock, he was readily recognized by almost everyone in town. In Florida he knew no one, and he felt isolated. The situation at home didn't help. His mother continued to swallow large amounts of sedatives. As time went by, she became more and more withdrawn. She blamed herself for his father's suicide. The fight they'd had and the names she'd called him seemed to bite deeper and deeper into her conscience. She couldn't get over the fact that she had never had the chance to tell her husband she was sorry.

In one of those rare moments when she paid any attention to his presence, she would say, "Taylor, I never meant what I said. I only tried to stop him from harming himself with all that drinking."

Andy had been right about Coach Nielson. Taylor's reputation as a quarterback, widely broadcast by his grandfather, made it impossible for the coach to keep him off the team, but that was as far as he got. No matter how well he performed in practice, he was rarely called upon to take a couple of snaps during a game. The few chances he did get were a disaster. He never seemed able to evade the defenders rushing at him. He was either sacked or had to throw the ball away prematurely. His failure on the football field, even more than the horrible grades he was getting, caused some major arguments between him and his grandfather. Timothy, who felt that he had never failed at anything in his life, viciously derided his grandson for his failures.

The most stinging remarks were, "You are just like your father. When push comes to shove, you can't do it. Why don't you fight back like I did in my day?" When Taylor's grandmother tried to intervene on Taylor's behalf, it only made the situation worse. His grandfather would start shouting about how he knew his daughter should never have married that man. Clair frequently reminded him that it was he who'd brought Henry into the company.

"You raved about the fact that he was a brilliant accountant, and how lucky we were that he agreed to join Van Beuren Textile. It was *you* who courted him so you could get him to marry your daughter and keep your precious company in the family forever. It's a wonder you didn't force him to change his name to Van Beuren!" The result of all the arguing only made the relationship between Taylor and his grandfather worse.

During this time, Taylor did get a lot of help from Andy Beckworth, who made sure to draw him into his circle of friends. He always tried to include Taylor in their activities. One day, during lunch, they were sitting in the school cafeteria discussing the previous Saturday's football game. Taylor had been sacked pretty badly during that game, and he'd left the field with a mild concussion. Several of the guys sitting around the table were critical of how Taylor, in their opinion, had gone down much too easily. Andy objected, but rather than continue to argue with the other guys, none of whom actually played on the football team, he suggested to Taylor that the two of them go out to his car for a smoke.

When they were seated in the car, Andy told Taylor something that he had suspected, but only got confirmation of after Saturday's game. Benny Rivas, the burly center, was worried about the extent of Taylor's injury. He asked Andy how Taylor was doing, and seemed greatly relieved when Andy told him that Taylor was doing fine. Benny proceeded to confess that it was all a setup. He let the opposing lineman through to get at Taylor. It had been the same all season.

When Taylor was the quarterback, Coach Nielson instructed the offensive linemen to fake any real resistance. "Just let the opposing team get at Taylor as fast as possible." Any lineman who disobeyed this instruction could be sure to sit out the next game. Coach Nielson's motive was obvious. He would do anything to prevent Taylor, or anyone else, from challenging Abe's position as the starting quarterback. Andy wondered why Taylor had not figured out what was going on.

"Couldn't you see that you got no protection whatsoever?"

"Now that you tell me all this, sure, I should have noticed. But Coach had me convinced that I was lousy, and I was trying so hard to complete the play that I didn't notice our line faking it. What about you? When did you first notice something suspicious?"

"Just like you, I never got any real protection. And when I did get a pass off, it was never caught.

The few times I was allowed to take a snap or two, Coach said my timing was off. With hardly any play time I never really got into my rhythm. When I asked Coach for some more play time, he just brushed me off."

For a while the two of them sat in the car and discussed bold plans as to how they would expose Coach Nielson. Then reality set in. To expose the coach, they would have to implicate their teammates. Obviously, everyone would deny it. The end result would most likely be that they would be labeled as two pathetic losers who couldn't face the truth that they were not good enough to play on this high school team. Rather than become pariahs among their classmates, the two of them decided to stick it out for the last few games of the season, and hope for better times on the baseball team.

Baseball did bring relief. Andy quickly established himself as the ace on the pitching staff and Taylor, with his powerful throwing arm, became a regular at third base. Baseball was never as big a deal as football, but the star players did attract their share of pretty girls. Andy broke up with a girl he had been dating since tenth grade and started going steady with Caroline, a pretty blond junior who starred on the gymnastics team. Both Caroline and Andy kept urging Taylor to become more sociable and start dating more often. Taylor preferred to be by himself. Finally, Caroline managed to arrange a double date with Maria Valera, a good friend of hers, who was also a member of the girls' gymnastics team.

There was no way Caroline could have foreseen the forces she set in motion. The attraction between Maria and Taylor was instant, and soon they became inseparable. In Pentonville, Taylor had had his fair share of girlfriends, but this was different. He not only felt a strong physical attraction for Maria, but, as time went on, he become more and more emotionally dependent on her. He just had to be around her. When they were not together, he would constantly call her on her cell phone.

Physically the two couldn't have been further apart. Taylor was almost six foot four, two hundred ten pounds, with short, light brown hair, strong masculine facial features, and sad eyes. Maria was five foot three and one hundred and fifteen pounds. She had a dark complexion with long, jet-black hair and big black eyes, which always seemed to sparkle with joy. She had a beautiful figure, which got lots of attention from boys who drooled over her at gymnastics meets. Maria made no secret of the fact that she was crazy about Taylor. Her obvious show of affection made him feel good about himself. That was something he had not experienced since that fateful day his father died.

Andy noticed Taylor's heavy dependence on the relationship. Knowing that Taylor's situation at home made him vulnerable to a girl's attention, he tried to persuade him to back off a little and occasionally date other girls. Taylor would have no part of it, and Andy turned to Caroline for help. Caroline's talk with Maria backfired. Instead of listening to her good friend, Maria was offended, and it nearly broke up their friendship. The end result of that well-meant interference by Andy and Caroline was to drive Taylor and Maria even closer together. Taylor started spending more and more time over at Maria's house. Soon he developed a good relationship with her parents. Maria's three younger brothers loved to play catch with Taylor, and they would beg Maria to take them to the high school baseball games to see Taylor play.

All this was in stark contrast to the reception Maria received the one time Taylor took her over to his house. When she was introduced to his grandfather, he all but ignored her. He left the two of them standing on the patio while he walked down to the waterfront and got into his boat. As usual, Taylor's mother was in her room, and in no condition to come downstairs to say hello. Unfortunately, his grandmother was not at home. Betty, the housekeeper, did her best to salvage the situation by offering to prepare cold drinks and snacks and bring them out to the patio. Taylor was happy she made the offer, but politely declined. He had intended to show Maria around the house. Instead they quickly got back in his car and returned to Maria's house.

The relationship between Maria and Taylor became more and more physical. On weekend nights they started frequenting the large parking lot adjacent to Bayside Beach, also known as "Lover's Lane." As long as every body's head was showing, the cops rarely bothered to check what was going on inside the cars parked at Bayside Beach. They just made sure that their presence kept any criminal elements away. One night, shortly after eleven, Taylor and Maria pulled up in his Chevy. They found a spot close to the water, and Taylor quickly closed the convertible top of the Chevy.

The movie they had just left had been a romance and contained some steamy love scenes. It had excited them sexually, and both of them longed for some physical contact; they could sense that the feeling was mutual. As soon as Taylor closed the last clamp tightening down the roof, Maria slid into his arms. After some urgent kissing, Taylor's hand started caressing her breasts. One by one he undid the buttons on her blouse, and his hand slid to her back to unhook her bra. Rather than wait for him to fumble around trying to get the thing unhooked, Maria pulled away from him and quickly took off her bra, leaving her breasts exposed. Her firm breasts curved up, and her nipples were hard and swollen. She leaned towards Taylor and pulled his head to her chest. Before Taylor could bend down to kiss her breasts, a strong beam of light was pointed at them. Maria let out a shriek, and Taylor immediately threw his arms around her to cover and protect her.

"What the hell?!" Taylor shouted.

The person who was shining the flashlight in their face responded with, "Both of you, get out of the car." Taylor tried to push Maria to safety under the dashboard. At the same time he tried to quickly start the car and get the hell out of there.

"This is Officer Kinney," the voice behind the flashlight said. "I repeat, get out of the car." By now Taylor's eyes had adjusted to the harsh light, and he could see the cop car parked alongside his. In the dark he could make out two policemen standing on either side of the car.

"Okay, officer, I'm coming out," Taylor said, "but please put out that light so my girl can get dressed."

When they were both standing next to the car, Taylor and Maria were checked for any weapons they might be carrying. After one of the officers had checked the inside of the car, they were asked for their identification. Maria was sobbing uncontrollably, and the officers allowed Taylor to hold her for a moment to calm her down. Taylor handed his driver's license to one of the officers, and asked if he could reach into the car to get Maria's purse so she could retrieve her license. One of the officers shook his head no and said that he would get it. After looking at Taylor's license, the officer asked him what he was doing in Florida.

Taylor responded, "I live here." Only then did he realize that his license still listed his Pentonville address. He had never bothered to get a Florida license.

"Sure you do," the officer responded, "and that's why you drive a car with out-of-state license plates?" He had also failed to register the car in Florida.

The cops turned to Maria. Looking at her license, they asked, "You, young lady; you're seventeen, right?" Holding tightly onto Taylor's hand, she nodded yes. "What are you doing out at this hour with this gentleman from out of state?" Maria tried to explain that they went to school together, that he was her steady boyfriend, and that her parents knew that they had gone to the movies that evening.

"Sure, he goes to school here," one of the officers laughed. "One hell of a commute every morning." The other officer was in no mood to stand there and make fun of these two kids. He asked Taylor to explain his out-of-state driver's license and the car's registration. Taylor explained that he had been living with his grandparents since the death of his father and that, as Maria said, he did go to the local high school. He was asked for the name and address of his grandparents.

"If it weren't for those out-of-state plates on your car, we would never have bothered with you kids," the more serious officer said. "But now that we have, we are required to bring the young lady home. And you, Mr. Marx, will have to accompany us to your grandparents' home so we can further establish that what you told us is true."

At first Maria's father refused to open the door for the police. He relented when he was informed that his daughter had been caught parked with Taylor in Lover's Lane. After getting over the initial shock of having the police arrive at his door in the middle of the night, he gave Maria an angry lecture about how she had disgraced the family with her promiscuous behavior.

"Decent girls don't do things like that. That's the last you're going to see of that boy. I'll not have him in my house ever again." His wife, although fully agreeing with her husband, tried to shush him.

"Please calm down, you'll wake the boys, and the neighbors can hear you. Isn't it bad enough that we have the police parked in front of our house at this hour of the night?" She quickly thanked the police for bringing Maria home, and told them how much she and her husband would appreciate it if they didn't file a report.

The situation was not much different at Taylor's house. His grandfather tore into him as if he had committed a major crime. Although he readily verified Taylor's story for the policemen, he testily told the officers that it was too late at night to discuss the driver's license and car registration. His lawyer would see to these issues in the morning. After the officers left, he continued his tirade against Taylor.

"That's what you get when you start hanging around with a girl like that. Next thing you know she'll have you knock her up so she can get you to marry her. Don't you get it? The little bitch is after my money. You will stop seeing that girl! I will not have a member of my family hanging around with those immigrants. It's bad enough that you have to go to school together. Next thing you know I'll have a spic grandchild!" he shouted.

The next morning, he instructed his lawyer to take care of the car registration and sell the car as quickly as possible to cover all the costs and the fines for the late registration. Taylor's grandmother had to step in to make sure that Taylor could keep his car and be permitted to take a drivers' test in order to get a Florida license.

Despite the strong resistance from the home front, Taylor and Maria continued their romance. They hung out together before and after school, and their friends became masters at covering for them when questions arose about their whereabouts. The positive thing that came out of this was the fact that Maria, who took her schoolwork very seriously, egged Taylor on to do better in school. The result was a sea change. From barely passing or not passing at all, Taylor's grades shot up to A's and B's. All doubt about graduating vanished.

But the incident in Lover's Lane kept hanging in the air. Without discussing it, they both knew that, but for the arrival of the police, they might have gone further than Maria's firm rule: "Anything below the belt is strictly off limits." The subject was more or less off limits until, one evening, it came up while they were sitting in a booth at a local pizza place. Several members of the football team walked in with their dates. They gave Taylor a casual hello, and the group sat down at the large round table in the middle of the restaurant. Taylor remarked that Benny Rivas appeared to have a new girl.

"Yes, that's Doris, and they're already sleeping together," Maria said.

"How do you know these things?"

"Girls talk too much, and they spend a lot of time gossiping about what they know about their friends. Come on, don't act so naïve. You know that most of the couples in our school sleep together. Andy and Caroline do, and I bet you everyone thinks we do it too."

"You think?" Taylor looked doubtful.

"I know," she replied. Maria looked at him, thought for a moment, and then asked, "Have you ever done it? Maybe back there in Pentonville?"

Taylor laughed. His first impulse was to deny it, but he didn't want to tell her a lie, so he tried to evade the question. "Let's not go there."

"Come on, you didn't even know me then, so how could I be angry or hurt if you did? It's what guys do when girls let them do it."

Taylor looked at her and became very serious. This was Maria. He had never lied to her, and they had never kept secrets from each other. He wanted to keep everything open between them so he said, "Yes."

Maria didn't seem shocked, or to attach much emotion to it. In a very casual tone she asked if he was sorry that the cops interrupted them that night at Bayside Beach. He felt awkward discussing the subject with her, but she pushed on. "Come on, you didn't answer. Are you?"

"No, I'm not sorry. I'm okay with our agreement that we don't touch below the belt. Why'd you bring it up?"

"Because I never did it, and I'm curious. Deep down, do you wish I would let you go all the way?"

"Look, I really love you, and I would never ask you to sleep with me if I knew you didn't want to.

Of course, I'm tempted when we make out, but I would feel very uncomfortable if we went any further knowing you didn't want to."

"I love you, you big goof, and I'm glad you feel that way. The first time you do it with someone who really loves you, it's going to be great, I promise. And it's going to be with me. Maybe we'll be traditional and get married first."

"Fat chance that we can get married soon. As long as your father and my grandfather are around, that can never happen."

"Give it time. My dad will turn around. It's just that he is desperately afraid of the police, and it really scared him when they came to the house in the middle of the night."

Taylor asked her why her dad would be so fearful of the police. Maria hesitated, but Taylor and she had never kept any secrets from each other, and she trusted him completely. She told him that when she kept asking her dad why he never agreed to go visit his family in Argentina, he was forced to explain to her that he and her mother had stayed in the country illegally after graduating from college. Maria and her brothers were born in the States and could freely travel back and forth to Argentina; they had their own passports. Her parents could never join them. "Swear never to tell anybody about what I told you."

"Of course, but I don't think that after all these years it will make any difference."

Chapter 6

Three month later, Maria's parents were arrested and accused of being in the country illegally. Because they had three young children at home, they were not kept in jail. They were allowed to continue their lives "as normal" pending the extradition hearings. Maria confronted Taylor. He vehemently denied telling anyone about her parents, but she refused to believe him. Taylor was desperate; he was determined to find out how, after so many years, the authorities found out. He was convinced that it had to do with the census, which had been conducted the year before. He was sure he could prove this to Maria. But when he came home that evening, his whole world caved in. His grandfather, who usually ignored him, greeted him at the door and invited him to join him in the library. There he told him what he had done. He said that after the incident at Lover's Lane, he had been well aware that Taylor was continuing to see "that girl."

In order to protect Taylor from this unsuitable relationship, he'd hired a private investigator to check out the Varela family. He just knew that about "those types" of people, you could always find some dirt.

And bingo, last week the investigator came to him with the beautiful news; the girl's parents were illegal immigrants. It seems they came to the United States from Argentina on student visas to study at the University of Miami. After graduation, they decided to stay. That was over twenty years ago, but that didn't change the fact that they were in the country illegally.

Taylor ran from the room screaming. He raced across the patio to the waterfront and threw up all over the dock. A couple of minutes later he reappeared, brandishing a boat hook. He raced to the library. His grandmother and Betty had to practically sit on him to prevent him from attacking his grandfather. Even though he could have broken loose, he couldn't get himself to hurt these two women. After a while he allowed them to lead him into the kitchen, where they sat him down. His grandmother sent Betty to Taylor's room to pack a suitcase. Next she called the downtown Hilton to reserve a room in her name for her grandson. When Betty came downstairs with a suitcase and a big travel bag, Clair called a taxi to bring Taylor to the Hilton.

As they walked out to the taxi, his grandmother said, "You can no longer stay here, and I'm sure you don't want to. Don't worry. I'll take care of you. It will be hard, but try to get some sleep, and I'll see you in the morning."

Taylor lay awake all night worrying what would happen to Maria in event the court decided to have her parents sent back to Argentina. He also worried about how long it would take before it leaked out that it was his grandfather who was responsible for this horror.

The next morning, his grandmother met him for breakfast at the hotel and handed him an envelope with money. "Until we can figure out what to do, you'll be living here, in the hotel. Your car is parked in the parking lot. Here are the keys."

Taylor stayed holed up in his hotel room. He ate very little, and the little he did eat, he ordered from room service. He continually tried to call Maria, but she didn't answer her phone, nor did she respond to the numerous messages he left on her voice mail. He was desperate; he had to get hold of Maria, to once again explain that he had nothing to do with her parents' arrest.

Andy Beckworth called to find out why Taylor had not been in school the last couple of days. Andy tried to avoid talking about the possible deportation of Maria's parents, but he did tell Taylor that people knew it was Taylor's grandfather who had informed the authorities. According to Andy, it was not clear how he got word that Maria's folks were illegally in the country. After hiding three days in the hotel, Taylor drove out to Maria's house to try and talk to her.

Before he could get out of the car, her father came running out of the house and shouted for him to go away. "You bastard! Haven't you people done enough to hurt us? How dare you show your face around here!" Taylor tried to get out of his car to explain that he had nothing to do with his grandfather's actions. Mr. Varela wanted no part of it, and physically pushed him back into the car. Taylor could do nothing else but drive away. He decided to go to school in the hopes of seeing Maria there.

Before he reached school he had dialed Maria's cell phone at least a dozen more times, but each time he reached her voice mail. All he could do was leave the same message over and over. "Maria, I love you, please call me. You know I had nothing to do with the horrible thing my grandfather did!" Maria was not in school that day, and Taylor walked around all day long like a zombie. The school was buzzing with the news, but each time Taylor approached a group discussing the fate of Maria's parents, everyone immediately lapsed into silence. Even Andy carefully avoided him that day. It seemed like forever, but the day finally ended, and Taylor headed for his car. When he reached the parking lot, he saw it immediately. His top had been sliced, and the whole car was smeared with black paint. He walked around the car to assess the damage. Thankfully his tires were intact, but to his horror, the black paint on his trunk spelled out, "Coward-Informer fuck you." He got into his car; the inside had not been touched. As he reached for his keys he noticed that his cell phone was blinking. His heart was pounding as he retrieved the voice mail message.

It was Maria. "How could you do this?" she sobbed. "You know I trusted you completely… getting my parents out of the way could solve nothing." Taylor was devastated; Maria's message hurt more than what had been done to his car. Slowly he drove off. He went directly to the hardware store and bought a couple of cans of spray paint to cover up the offensive words on his trunk. As he drove back into town towards the Hilton, he worked himself up into an uncontrollable rage. Damn that nasty bastard who happened to be his grandfather. Damn Maria's father for not giving him a chance to explain. Damn all his so-called friends at school for immediately thinking the worst of him, and damn Maria for believing he could be guilty of such a heinous act. Damn her for not sticking with him when they needed each other most.

When Taylor reached the Hilton he went straight to his room, packed his bags, and checked out. With tears streaming down his face, he drove north. He had no idea where he was heading. All he knew was that he had to get out of town; he had to get away.

Chapter 7

The rain splashing against the window woke him up. Taylor remembered that he had left the sliding doors leading to his small balcony open. He jumped out of bed and rushed to close them. For a while he stood behind the glass panels and watched the outlines of several boats bobbing up and down in Mobile Bay. The sun was starting to come up, and, despite the sweeping rain, he could see people getting the boats ready to sail out. He made himself some coffee and sat down at the table in the small kitchenette, which, despite its modest size, took up most of the space that served as his living room. While sipping his coffee, Taylor reflected on what had brought him to this small waterfront village in Alabama.

On the day he checked out of the Hilton, he kept on driving till he reached the Florida Panhandle. Impulse made him turn west, in the direction of Alabama. He knew they might start searching for him, but he was sure the police would not be involved. He had not committed a crime. He was eighteen, free to go wherever he wanted. However, the classic, torch-red 1957 Bel Air convertible, covered with black paint smears, was easy to spot, and he feared it would help his grandparents find him. He had stopped along the way to buy some masking tape, with which he tried to cover the cuts in his canvas top. It helped to keep the material together, and prevented it from tearing even further, but it looked like hell, and called even more attention to the car. In a small town north of Pensacola he stopped at a gas station, and asked if anyone knew of a good place to sell his car. The owner came out to look at the car and asked if it was stolen. After Taylor showed him the registration and identified himself by means of his license, the man expressed interest in buying it for himself.

He looked the car over carefully and asked, "How much?" Taylor didn't have any idea of what the car was worth.

"I'll need enough to buy another set of wheels that look a little more presentable than this thing. I don't have the money to have it painted and buy a new top, but it runs really well."

"I could screw you on the deal," the gas station owner laughed. "But I have to be honest; this baby is worth a hell of a lot of money. It does not have the original engine, and it looks like a lot of other parts have been replaced, but it's still worth a pretty penny."

Before he got deeper involved, he wanted to know more. What exactly was Taylor doing in this neck of the woods, and why on Earth was he in such a hurry to sell the car? Taylor thought it could do no harm to tell the man that he had been involved in a nasty family fight, and that his grandfather, whom he had been living with, was a real bastard. No way was he going back there.

"Well, according to your license, you're eighteen, so I guess they can't make you return. If you're serious about this, come back in the morning, and we'll see what we can do. Make sure you really want to sell this car; it's a classic, and you should really think about that before selling it."

"I know it's special, but I do have to sell it. Is there a place near here where I can check in for the night?" The gas station owner directed Taylor to a Best Western Motel about ten miles up the road.

The next day, the gas station owner took Taylor to the local Pontiac dealer. To Taylor's amazement, he was allowed to select a sleek-looking black Pontiac Grand Prix. The gas station owner bought it for him in exchange for his Chevy. While the dealer was working on all the paperwork necessary to get the two cars registered, the gas station owner took Taylor to lunch.

"Where are you heading to next?" he inquired. Taylor admitted that he had no plans whatsoever. He just wanted to get out of Florida. The gas station owner proceeded to tell Taylor about his son, who had been a cook in the army. After leaving the service, he'd found it hard to find a job. He didn't want to work for his father in the gas station. Finally, with the help of his father and his father-in-law, he had bought a small restaurant in Battles Wharf, Alabama, his wife's hometown. Running the restaurant was very demanding. The young couple worked day and night, trying to make a go of it. It didn't help matters that the waitress they'd hired had disappeared one day without a word, taking most of a week's receipts with her. Even though they desperately needed some help, that experience left them suspicious of strangers. They were afraid to hire someone new.

Would Taylor be interested in going to Battles Wharf and see if they would take him on? Taylor didn't have the slightest idea as to where Battles Wharf was. He had never even heard of it. The gas station owner assured him that it was actually quite close, and that it would not take him long to drive there. Before Taylor headed for Battles Wharf, the gas station owner made a few calls to his son. After his son talked to his wife, he called back to say that they agreed to meet with Taylor to discuss the possibility of hiring him to work for them in the restaurant.

Taylor hit it off almost immediately with John and Marcie Fidderman, the young couple who owned the restaurant. John Fidderman didn't look at all like his father. He was of average height and quite pudgy, but he had a great smile and a nice, outgoing personality. The people who frequented the restaurant really liked him. Marcie, his wife, was a good three inches taller than he was. She had a pretty face, but was more than fifty pounds overweight. She liked to joke that most of that weight was in her substantial bosom, ignoring the fact that her more than generous behind accounted for a large part of the weight she had put on since high school.

Taylor had never worked in a restaurant. Actually, he had never had a real job. But he learned quickly. The three of them became a team. As business improved, they were able to hire more help, and soon the restaurant employed two part-time dishwashers and three part-time waitresses. Taylor found a cute little apartment facing the bay, and he settled into a comfortable, but dull life in Battles Wharf.

As he poured himself a second cup of coffee, Taylor mulled over an incident that hastened his decision to leave Battles Wharf. The day before, John had approached him to warn him that he had heard that a man had been in town to inquire about a young man named Marx. John knew all about Taylor's past, and the two of them discussed the possibility that Taylor's grandfather had hired a private eye, and that they were close to finding him.

Taylor knew that there was no way they could force him to move back, but he didn't want to suffer through another confrontation with his grandfather. Who could tell what the old man would do next if he didn't get his way? Taylor fully realized that John could have made up the story about this man, hoping that Taylor would flee town. That would put an end to the affair Taylor was having with Marcie. In either case, this incident helped make up Taylor's mind that it was high time to move on.

The need to leave Battles Wharf had been brewing for quite a while, but Taylor had been putting it off, thinking he could handle the situation. From the moment he had started working at the restaurant,

John had been his close friend and confidante, but it was Marcie who had taught him all about the restaurant business. As time went on, some of Marcie's remarks had started making Taylor uncomfortable. He realized she was hitting on him. It started rather innocently, with Marcie asking about his relationship with girls and why he hardly dated. When he did go on an occasional date, she asked too many details. She had the habit of standing very close to him when John was not around. Her remarks were full of sexual innuendo that was hard to misinterpret.

What really shook Taylor was the day he was bent over, cleaning a table in the dining room, and Marcie remarked, "Nice butt. Bet a girl would like to get hold of that, and more!" When he looked up, she smiled at him. It was clearly a come-on smile. Taylor ignored the remark and quickly headed for the kitchen. Marcie followed him, and when he stopped to put some dishes on the large aluminum counter, she came up behind him. She started rubbing her hand over his back.

"Come on, Taylor, there's nothing wrong with me admiring your butt," she said, as she dropped her hand down and slowly stroked his behind.

Taylor warned her, "Marcie, don't do that." He turned around to face her and was shocked when Marcie kept her hand down and reached for his crotch.

"You know you like this," she said, as her hand closed over his penis and she massaged it through his pants. Taylor quickly pulled away and left the kitchen.

Two weeks later, he was sitting in the dining room, folding napkins, when Marcie came over to him. She stood behind him and, as she bent over him, rubbing her big breasts back and forth against his back, she asked, "Have you changed your mind yet, Tiger? You and I can have some real fun together." Taylor got up and pushed Marcie away.

"Come on, Marcie, you're going to cost me my job. John is my friend, and he's been good to me, but if he were to find out what you're doing, he'd throw me out. You know damned well I have no place else to go."

But Marcie stepped right back and once again reached for his crotch. While stroking him rapidly she said, "John isn't here today, so we're alone, and he'll never know. Hey, come on, I really want you!"

Again Taylor pushed her away, this time rougher than before. He glared at her as he said, "What you're doing is really unfair. Of course you're getting me excited, but I can't afford to lose this job."

"I told you John will never know, and if he did find out, I wouldn't let him fire you."

"He'd be furious. Of course he'd fire me!"

While tugging at his belt, Marcie said, "I said I wouldn't let him fire you, so he won't!" She pulled Taylor towards her and put one hand behind his neck to pull his head down so she could kiss him while her other hand pulled the zipper of his pants down. Her fingers quickly pushed his shorts aside and her hand closed around his penis, which was becoming harder by the minute. They stood like that for a while until Marcie suggested they go upstairs to the apartment she and John lived in. Taylor followed her up the stairs. He felt a little funny when she pulled him into the bedroom she and John shared. Marcie wasted no time getting undressed. Taylor watched as she took off her shirt and unhooked her bra. Her breasts were huge, and gravity had gotten the best of them. She sat down to take off her pants and before walking over to the bed, she pulled off her panties. Seeing her stark naked, heading for the bed, Taylor wasn't sure if he wanted this. Marcie pulled the covers off the bed and stretched out on top of the sheets, waiting for Taylor to join her.

"Hey, what are you waiting for? Get those clothes off and come over here and make love to me." Taylor hesitated. Even though his life had changed drastically, he was still reluctant to have sex without protection.

"Do you have a condom for me?" he hesitantly asked.

"Don't be stupid. I won't get pregnant; I can't have children. Or are you afraid I'll give you some kind of disease? Don't worry, I'm clean."

"I'm not worried, just asking if you were protected." While he was undressing, Taylor tried to understand why he was doing this. He was angry at what had happened to him, angry at the circumstances that forced him to leave Pentonville, angry at the way the coach had treated him, and angry at his grandfather. But most of all, he was angry about being accused of betraying Maria's parents. Marcie couldn't be blamed for any of it, yet he felt this urge to physically vent his frustrations on her. He finished undressing and looked over at Marcie. Lying there naked, she looked much heavier. Her thick thighs touched all the way from her knees to her vagina. For a moment he wondered how this would work, but he had gotten this far, so he stepped to the bed and laid his large frame on top of her. He forcefully buried his head between her enormous breasts.

Marcie rubbed his penis and quickly got his erection back up. Using his legs, Taylor pushed Marcie's legs apart and felt along the inside of her thighs until he reached her vagina. He started stroking her. Marcie spread her legs as far as possible, pushed his hand away, and deftly pushed his penis inside of her. She wrapped her legs around him and Taylor started to move faster and faster, thrusting wildly. Holding her tightly in his powerful arms, he must have hurt her. But Marcie didn't mind his anger; she enjoyed it. She climaxed at least three or four times before he came. When it was over, they were both covered with sweat. For a while they laid next to each other, panting heavily.

Marcie finally caught her breath. She sat up and nonchalantly said, "Thanks, that was great. You really know how to please a girl. We'll do this more often." When Taylor looked at her questioningly, she added, "Remember who does the hiring and firing around here."

By *often*, Marcie meant a couple of times a week. When she couldn't corner Taylor alone in the restaurant, she would come by his apartment. Marcie became more and more obsessed with Taylor's big, powerful body, and the ways in which she wanted him to satisfy her sexual desire. She kept coming up with new positions she wanted to try.

One time she called out, "Come on, Taylor, push harder! I want to feel your anger, like the first time you had me. I want to feel your power and anger inside me. Push harder. Make it hurt!" Marcie started groaning, which was followed by, "Hey, you know I like it nice and rough. I love it when that big, strong body of yours takes me till it hurts. John is always so damned timid and careful not to hurt me that I almost fall asleep when we're supposedly having sex. Shit, he's so weak and flabby that he couldn't make it hurt if he tried. With you a girl knows she's being screwed. I love it!"

For several months Taylor thoroughly enjoyed the situation. He had no experience to compare it with, but he thought sex with Marcie was the greatest. He was only vaguely aware that his frustration with all that had happened to him was being projected onto Marcie. He tried not to think about the fact that he was having wild sex with another man's wife. Since she controlled what went on at the restaurant, he didn't worry about John and getting fired. That is, not until he overheard a bitter argument between John and Marcie. Afterwards he saw John sitting in his car, parked behind the restaurant, trying to keep his head low so no one could see he was crying. At that point, Taylor realized it was time for him to move on. The situation was getting out of control, and his sexual exploits with Marcie had to stop. Because he had no place to go, he didn't leave immediately.

The day after Taylor received John's warning about the private eye, the restaurant didn't open until twelve. Rather than wait till noon to talk to John, Taylor called him and asked if they could meet as soon as possible; he had something important to tell him. John agreed to come over to Taylor's apartment. Taylor told John that he planned to leave Battles Wharf before his grandfather found out where he was living. John knew the real reason why Taylor was leaving, but at first he didn't let on that he knew. Instead, he thanked Taylor for being a good friend and helping them make such a nice success out of the restaurant. He said he was sure Marcie would understand that Taylor couldn't risk being harassed by his grandfather, and that it was best for him to leave town. Actually, John had known for quite a while that Marcie was having an affair with Taylor, but he didn't know how to handle it. He loved Marcie deeply, and didn't want to cause irreparable harm to their relationship by confronting her. The one time he had confronted her with his suspicions, they had fought bitterly and he had backed off.

Suddenly, John broke down and started sobbing. He looked at Taylor with tears in his sad eyes. "Thanks for leaving; Marcie and I will somehow have to figure this out." John had always treated Taylor like a friend rather than an employee, and Taylor didn't know what to say. Instead he just put out his hand, and John took it. "It happened before, while we were in the army," John said. "I'll just have to deal with it."

Chapter 8

Taylor left Battles Wharf two days later. In order to avoid coming even close to Florida, he headed west. John had offered to call a few of his army buddies to see if they could help find Taylor a job. Taylor assured him that this was not necessary, he was sure that he would be okay. He had not spent all the money his grandmother had given him, and, during the time he'd worked in the restaurant, he had added to his savings. Upon leaving, John had given him an additional month's salary in cash. There was no immediate need to find a job.

Taylor had heard a lot about New Orleans, and since he was very close, he decided to take a look. When he arrived in New Orleans, he checked into a hotel and got some maps to help him explore the city. His first stop was Harrah's Casino, which was located within walking distance from his hotel. He quickly decided that gambling was not for him. Not understanding all the different gaming opportunities offered, he was bored and left the casino to explore the rest of the town.

After exploring the town for two days, he wound up on Bourbon Street. He had walked all the way from

Decatur, via Chartres, through Exchange Alley and Royal, until finally finding what he was looking for; Bourbon Street. By this time, he was a little tired and hungry. He decided to skip looking for the restaurant which the people at his hotel had recommended. He settled for the first place that looked attractive. The restaurant was fairly crowded, but he had no trouble finding a place at the bar. Although he rarely drank, he ordered a drink and was busy looking through the menu when a tall blond slid onto the stool next to him.

When he looked at her she asked, "Buy a girl a drink?" This was something new for Taylor. He had never met a "professional" before, but he could guess what she was up to. He found it somewhat exciting.

He had not really talked to anyone for the last couple of days, so he thought, *Why not?*

"Sure," he replied. "What will you have?"

"Bourbon, straight up," she replied. After Taylor had asked the bartender to give the lady a bourbon, straight up, she asked his name.

"Chris," he lied. "What's yours?"

"Mary," she said. *Sure,* Taylor thought, *like mine is Chris.* Mary went on to ask what Chris did for a living. She wanted to know if he was a tourist or in town for business. Taylor said he was from New York, worked in a restaurant there, and was in New Orleans on a short vacation. Mary was a good conversationalist, and Taylor enjoyed talking to her. After a while, Mary said that there was a really good band playing in back of the restaurant. Did Taylor mind if they went to listen? Taylor forgot all about eating dinner and followed

Mary to a courtyard in back of the restaurant, where tables were placed around a small bandstand. They found an empty table, ordered fresh drinks, and listened to the music. Mary knew the band quite well, and she told Taylor all about them and their music. The table was quite small, and accidentally, but most probably on purpose, Mary's legs rubbed repeatedly against Taylor's.

Looking at her face, he decided that although she was not pretty, she did have something cute about her. Before they sat down he had noticed that she had incredibly long legs, which seemed even longer because she was wearing a tight little mini skirt. While he listened to her explain about the reputation of the bass player, he couldn't help staring at the curvature of her breasts. The low neckline of her sweater didn't leave much to his imagination. Her nipples pressed against the soft material of the tight sweater. She was not wearing a bra. After a couple more drinks, Taylor was on the verge of being tipsy. Mary asked if he wanted to go home with her. Of course Taylor knew she was a professional, but he found it awkward to ask what he would have to pay. Besides, he was not quite sure that he wanted to do this.

Mary noticed his hesitation. "Don't worry, you can afford it. For the old farts it's five hundred or more, but for a hunk like you, I'll be happy to do it for a hundred."

Taylor was still not sure. He had always laughed about men who had to pay for sex, but he quickly convinced himself that this was not like that. Mary and he had spent a nice evening together, almost like a date. He thought of her as a really nice person. Although she dressed a little too provocatively, she certainly didn't look like some floozy. Physically she was very attractive. Her body reminded him of Phyllis, the girl he had dated back in Pentonville.

Mary's apartment was a modest little studio two flights up from a noisy jazz club. As soon as they got in, Mary pulled the coffee table aside and pulled out the couch, which turned into a rather narrow double bed.

"You get ready while I slip into the bathroom," she said. When she reappeared, she was wearing a very transparent negligee with an ever-so-brief pair of panties, and, of course, no bra. Taylor was sitting in the La-Z-Boy recliner in the corner, a little sleepy from all the liquor.

"What's the matter?" she asked. "You want me to help you undress?"

Taylor got up quickly. "No, no, I'm okay." Rather than wait for him to awkwardly pull off his clothes, Mary went over to him and expertly had him out of his clothes in no time. She stood in front of him, admiring his body. Her negligee fell open, and she started rubbing her breasts against him.

"I'm a lucky girl tonight; I don't often get to make love to a buck like you with a body to die for." She put her arms around his neck and pulled him tightly against her body. Her hips swayed back and force as she rubbed against him. "You don't have to kiss me if you don't want to," she murmured in his ear.

Ignoring the fact that she was a prostitute, Taylor buried his tongue deep in her mouth. He pushed her slightly away from his body so he could stroke her breasts. Her breasts were small, but curved sharply away from her slim body. Taylor had never seen such large nipples. They were bright red, and felt like hot little rocks when he fondled them. He leaned down to kiss them. Her hand reached down and she gently started stroking him. He followed her lead and slowly lowered his hand until his fingers touched her between her legs.

Mary pulled him over to the bed, but before lying down, she said, "Rules of the house; you must wear a condom." Before he could tell her that he was fine with that, she had already put one on him and pulled him onto the bed. When Taylor stretched out on top of her, Mary spread her legs and helped Taylor enter her. She pushed her heels into the mattress, gently moving her pelvis back and forth expertly, in the same rhythm as Taylor's movements. He kissed her on the lips, and Mary closed her eyes. His hands reached for her breasts and his fingers stroked her big nipples. Taylor felt Mary's body tighten up, followed by a slight quiver.

She opened her eyes and smiled. "Hold me just a little bit longer." This was quite different for Taylor, much different from the wild, thrashing sex he'd had with Marcie.

When Mary stopped rubbing the back of his neck, Taylor rolled over and laid on his back, fully expecting her to tell him to get dressed and that it was time to leave. Instead, she snuggled against him. Like lovers, they lay silently in each other's arms. After a while, Mary asked if he wanted to stay the night. He almost ruined the tender moment by asking how much extra that would cost. Luckily he shut up and just held her tightly in his arms.

The next day, they both pretended as if nothing special had happened. They both had felt this strong need for affection, which had been missing from their lives for a long time. At the same time, both realized that this was not the real thing.

As he was getting dressed, Mary said, "Here, you must have dropped this." It was the hundred dollar bill he had given her the night before.

"No, that's yours. That's what we agreed on."

She winked at him and smiled. "Consider it on the house."

"No, I insist," Taylor said, trying to hand the bill back to her.

"Shut up and don't spoil this!" Mary said, as she gave him a firm kiss on the lips and pushed him out the door. Just before she closed the door, Mary said, "Go home to Maria." Shocked, Taylor turned around.

"What are you talking about?"

"Honey, you talked in your sleep. When you held me you called me Maria, and I wished to God that I was her. You really love that girl. Go home to that girl. I bet she misses you as much as you miss her."

"I can't go home. She doesn't miss me!"

Back at his hotel, Taylor checked out and once again hit the road without a definite destination. He had mixed feelings about the night he had spent with Mary. Part of him felt a little ashamed that he had slept with a prostitute, but he really liked Mary, and in a way it was less degrading than having an affair with Marcie.

Chapter 9

As she had done for the last three days, Clair Van Beuren drove over to the Hilton to check on her grandson. When she arrived at the hotel, she went straight to his room. She knocked on the door, but there was no answer.

She knocked again and called out, "Come on Taylor, open up. It's me, Grandma!" After a couple more tries, she hurriedly went down to the reception desk to ask if they could call his room. The clerk at the reception desk informed her that her grandson had checked out late in the afternoon the day before.

"Did he leave a message for me?"

"No, madam."

"Do you know where he was heading?"

"Sorry, he just left in a hurry, and I didn't feel it was my place to question him as to why he was leaving. I had no idea you didn't know he intended to leave. I would have been happy to warn you if I had."

Not knowing where to start looking for Taylor, Clair went home and confronted her husband.

"Damn you, it's all your fault!" She made it clear to him that she would hold him responsible if anything happened to her grandson. If he didn't immediately take some action to find Taylor, she would leave him for good. Relations between Timothy and Clair had been strained ever since their daughter and grandson moved in. After the arrest of the Valeras, they had fought constantly, and the word *divorce* had crossed their lips quite a few times.

A week went by, and still no word of Taylor's whereabouts. Fearing that Taylor might do something drastic to himself, Clair decided to reach out to Maria, in the hope she would have some idea about where Taylor might be.

With the help of Andy Beckworth and a counselor at the school, Clair managed to arrange a meeting with Maria. Maria entered the counselor's office in a defiant mood. It was obvious that she had no interest in speaking with Clair. Sensing that Maria was in no mood to be civil towards Clair, the counselor calmly but firmly took control of the meeting.

"Sit down, Maria. Mrs. Van Beuren has something very important to tell you. I know you'll really want to hear this." Clair started explaining how her husband, in his determination to keep Maria away from his grandson, had hired a private investigator. She stressed that it was the investigator who had discovered that Maria's parents were illegally staying in America. She repeated over and over that Taylor had nothing to do with it. For emphasis, she went into great detail about how Taylor had attacked his grandfather. She gave a vivid description of how Betty and she had held him down in order to prevent him from severely injuring the old man. After she finished,

Maria just sat there with a totally bewildered look on her face. Then she became completely hysterical.

"Oh my God, I didn't know, I didn't know! I'm so sorry. If anything happens to him I'll kill myself! How could I send him away like that? Oh, why didn't I trust him?" Tears were streaming down her cheeks. Suddenly she threw herself in Clair's arms, and, with her head in Clair's lap, she continued to sob uncontrollably. It took Clair a good ten minutes, with the help of the counselor, to calm Maria down enough so that they could discuss the situation.

The counselor suggested that Maria talk to her parents, and explain that Taylor had nothing to do with his grandfather's betrayal of them. Regardless of what his grandfather had done, it was important that they not blame Taylor for it. It took Maria several days to muster the courage to speak to her parents. When she did, her mother sided with her. The two of them persuaded her dad to meet with Clair.

Friends and family were surprised when the Valeras became deeply involved in the effort to find Taylor. Initially the trail led to a small town in the Panhandle. A private investigator discovered that the Chevy had been sold there. The gentleman who bought the car from Taylor claimed that Taylor had left in another car and told him he was heading for Mexico. The gentleman vaguely recalled that Taylor was traveling with two Spanish-speaking friends who were on their way home. Weeks went by, but no one discovered any further clues as to Taylor's whereabouts. In the meantime, a close friendship developed between Maria's mother and Clair. Clair had often thought about leaving Timothy, but she had no way of dealing with her daughter. Sue-Ann had become more and more reclusive, and only left the house in order to see her psychiatrist. When Sue-Ann's condition deteriorated even further she had to be institutionalized, and Clair was free to move out of the house.

The extradition proceedings against the Valeras continued. It was Clair who arranged for Juan Pereira, a well-respected immigration lawyer, to represent them. Even though the Valeras had been model citizens for over twenty years, Pereira couldn't prevent the court from ruling that they had to be sent back to Argentina. He did, however, arrange that they could immediately apply for family reunion status once they were back in Argentina. Because their teenage daughter, who was a United States citizen, would be in the US, they would be given priority, regardless of any quotas.

The Valeras left for Argentina with their two sons to live with relatives. Maria, who wanted to finish her senior year with her classmates, chose to stay in the US. She had arranged to stay at a friend's house, but Clair wouldn't have it. She had come to adore this spunky young girl. The feeling was mutual, and the two of them had become very close. Maria called her Clair, but it could just as well have been Grandma. Clair came up with the following solution. She would move into the Valera's house, take over the mortgage payments and other expenses. That way, Maria could remain living in her own home. Maria's father was happy with the idea that he would not have to sell the house on such short notice, and that it would be theirs on their return. He did, however, have some doubts about Clair, at her age, being able to keep up with a teenage girl. This argument was quelled by Maria's mother, who told him that Clair had more energy, and was more attuned to teenagers, than she was.

Regardless of all the promises, it took over a year for the papers, which would allow the Valeras to return to the US, to make their way through bureaucratic channels. In the meantime, Maria graduated at the top of her high school class. Her parents missed her graduation and her valedictory speech. Clair cried through the entire ceremony; she was so proud of her little girl. Maria received a partial scholarship from the University of Miami, and with Clair's financial assistance, she was a freshman in college by the time her parents arrived back in Florida.

Clair never did move back into the big house on the water. She bought a small penthouse apartment on the other side of town. Sue-Ann's condition became so bad that the doctors advised Clair that she should be moved to another institution, where she could receive around-the-clock care. A short time later, Timothy died of a massive heart attack while trying to pull his boat ashore.

Chapter 10

After he left New Orleans, Taylor headed for Dallas. He had made quite a few stops along the way. But the possibility that it was actually true that an investigator might have been asking questions about him in Battles Wharf made him head for a big city. There he hoped to get lost in the crowd. It turned out that Dallas was not a good choice. Finding a job proved to be very difficult. The main problem was that he had no education to speak of. His only work experience was the year he'd worked in the restaurant. Eventually, he got a job as a busboy, but this hardly paid the rent on the two-room walk-up apartment he had rented in a rundown part of town.

One day he read an advertisement from a cleaning service; they were hiring extra people to work a night shift. The hourly pay was almost three times as much as he was making as a busboy, even if he added in the tips.

Cleaning large office buildings proved to be easy work. He didn't mind working nights; his social life was non-existent anyway. The neighborhood around his apartment was less noisy during the day than at night, so he could sleep all day if he wanted to. This routine went on for almost three months until, one day, Taylor failed to see a pail at the top of a staircase. He tripped over the pail and tumbled head over heels down a full flight of stairs. His screams brought the night watchman running. The man questioned him as to where it hurt, and decided not to move him, in case his back or neck was broken. The night watchman called 9-1-1, and the EMTs arrived within a few minutes. Taylor was strapped onto a stretcher and transported by ambulance to the hospital. There it was determined that he didn't have a broken neck, and there was no danger of paralysis. He did, however, have a broken back, and several broken ribs. Since Taylor had no one at home to take care of him, he had to stay in the hospital until he recovered enough to be able to walk.

As soon as he got out of the hospital, bills starting pouring in. Taylor knew little about his rights as an employee, but he knew enough to expect his accident to be covered by workman's comp. Unfortunately, this became his first experience with corporate greed. He knew that no matter how bad the financial condition of Van Beuren Textile might have been, his father would never have treated his employees the way the cleaning company treated him. When he tried to collect some compensation for his injuries and have his medical bills paid under workman's comp, he learned that the cleaning company had listed him as an independent contractor. Apparently he had agreed to this by signing one of the many forms they handed him when he applied for the job.

By the time he had sold his car and exhausted all his savings in order to pay his medical bills, Taylor had no money left over to hire a lawyer to fight the unethical, and probably illegal, practices of the cleaning company. He avoided having to declare bankruptcy when the hospital declared him a hardship case and reduced his bills to the amount he could pay after selling all his assets.

He was lucky to find a job as a telephone operator, one of the few jobs he could manage to do in his physical condition. In order to rebuild his broken body he joined a health club, and worked hard at rebuilding his physical strength. The trainer at the club took an interest in him. With his help, Taylor not only regained the strength in his back and arms, but he further developed his already impressive physique. While working on his own body, Taylor learned a lot about physical therapy and responsible body building, without the use of steroids or any type of hormones.

Once he was fully recovered, Taylor went back to the restaurant business. This time he was hired as a waiter in a nice club. He made new friends, and moved to a nicer apartment. He was even able to save up some money. But despite the fact that his life had become a lot better, Taylor decided that he really didn't like life in the big city. He started making plans to move on.

The opportunity presented itself when the hostess in the club he was working in told him that her brother, whom she spoke to occasionally, ran a gym in a small town on the Oklahoma border. Taylor told her that he loved working out in a gym, and that someday he hoped to work in one. He confided in her that he was not happy living in Dallas, and he asked her to inquire if her brother would hire him. She called her brother and gave Taylor a nice reference. Taylor was hired sight unseen. He had no idea what he would earn or what exactly his duties in the gym would be. Nevertheless, he quit his job, packed his belongings, and sent them ahead, care of Bobby Barnes, owner/operator of the local gym.

When Taylor went to say good-bye to Liz, the hostess who helped him get his new job, she invited him to her house for a farewell dinner. Liz had prepared a very nice meal. After dinner they had drinks, and talked for several hours. During the time Taylor worked at the club, he and Liz had become pretty good friends. Sitting in her living room and chatting with her made him realize that he was going to miss her; she was a very nice person.

They were reminiscing about some funny incidents that happened at the club when Liz said, "The young waitresses at the club are not happy that you're leaving."

"What makes you say that?" Taylor asked.

"Come on, don't act so innocent. You know darn well that most of them have a crush on you. The rest of the staff enjoyed watching the way they were always coming on to you and you were completely ignoring their advances. I even heard them fantasizing about you when they were gossiping in the kitchen."

Taylor was a little embarrassed, and he made light of what Liz was saying. "You're trying to make me stay by using those girls as bait."

"No, I'm dead serious! I probably shouldn't say this, but I, too, have had one hell of a crush on you since the first day you started at the club."

Taylor didn't quite know how to handle Liz's remarks. "You're just trying to make me feel good and tell me I'm not being run out of town because everyone dislikes me."

"No, Taylor, I'm telling you that even a homely spinster like me can dream about a guy like you. It doesn't hurt to fantasize about something that can never happen."

"Stop putting yourself down! You're a nice-looking woman. What makes you think you're not attractive?"

"Because I'm a realist."

Taylor didn't react immediately, but then he said, "Can I stay with you tonight?"

Liz was hurt. "Don't joke like that. It's not fair to make fun of me when I talk honestly with you."

"I'm not joking. I'm serious."

Liz had a questioning look on her face, but Taylor thought he detected a slight smile when she said, "Really?"

Taylor stood up. "Yes, really."

Liz got up, took Taylor's hand, and led him to her bedroom.

Chapter 11

B obby Barnes met him at the bus station and took him over to the gym. What a disappointment that was. Taylor didn't know what he had expected, but definitely not this. The gym was located in an old warehouse. The conversion to a gym had been very rudimentary and had taken place a long time ago. The locker rooms and showers were dingy and could have used some fresh paint. The main exercise room was filled with a lot of equipment, but most of it looked like it had seen better days. Bobby must have bought all the equipment second or even third hand.

"Well, what do you think?" Bobby asked when they had finished a tour of the premises. It was obvious that Bobby was proud of his gym, and Taylor didn't have the heart to express his disappointment. Instead, he asked what his job would consist of. Bobby explained that they all did everything together; no one had a specific assignment. By all, Bobby meant the staff, which consisted of only three persons: Jason Cox, Kelly Hunter, and Bobby himself. Taylor would be number four. Taylor would be expected to help the customers use the equipment, clean up, and put things away. When necessary, he would help at the bar, although that was mostly Bobby's job.

The gym was not open on Monday mornings, so Bobby suggested they grab some lunch while they waited for Jason and Kelly to arrive. During lunch, Bobby mentioned that his sister had spoken very highly of Taylor.

"She said you were a very nice person, and made me promise to take good care of you. I tell you, that's not like her. Usually she only bitches about the people she works with. I avoid talking to her; she's always so bitter about everything that it depresses me."

After lunch, they went back to the gym. Bobby introduced Taylor to Jason and Kelly. Kelly was a big woman, with a muscular, body builder's physique and masculine facial features. She was easily forty-five, if not fifty. Jason was not anything like that. He was small, five foot six at best, freckled face, and a huge smile. Taylor judged him to be in his late twenties, early thirties at the most.

Jason welcomed him with a, "Hi, roommate." It seemed that Bobby had arranged for Taylor to room with Jason, whose apartment was within walking distance of the gym.

After the appearance of the gym, Jason's apartment was a pleasant surprise. It consisted of a large living room, a kitchen with dining area, and two big bedrooms. The bathroom left something to be desired, but it was still better than what Taylor had had in his first apartment in Dallas. Since Taylor's clothes and other belongings had arrived ahead of him, Jason had placed them in the smaller of the two bedrooms. Jason was a jovial fellow, and Taylor was sure this arrangement would work out fine.

Taylor was surprised at how many members Bobby's gym had. Not everybody came to exercise; the bar was a popular hangout. Membership fees were very modest. Bobby kept the place running on his bar receipts. The money he paid Jason, Kelly, and Taylor depended heavily on how well the bar had done during the previous week.

In the ensuing month, Taylor's life revolved totally around the gym. When it wasn't crowded, he could be found sitting at the bar, chatting with one or two of the customers. The use of steroids and growth hormones would occasionally come up for discussion. Taylor steadfastly refused to get involved with those drugs. He was happy that Bobby always backed him up. Bobby didn't allow the use of any drugs, regardless of whether they were banned or not, on his premises. Although no one really knew what Kelly did privately, the club was known to be clean.

Taylor's rather uneventful life at the gym was interrupted by Bobby's announcement that his sister was coming to visit. "I don't understand it," Bobby said. "She's never given a damn about what I was doing, and now she says she's coming to see my gym. I don't know, but I have this sneaking suspicion she's coming to see you."

To Taylor, the news that Liz was coming to visit was less than welcome. Sleeping with her was meant as an act of friendship. He felt sorry for her, and wanted to make her feel better about herself. He never considered that she would attach a deeper meaning to it. How was he going to explain to her that he considered her a good friend, but nothing more? Would she be able to accept that? Or would she feel hurt, maybe even abused? It could become messy, even screwing up his relationship with Bobby.

At first neither Bobby nor Taylor recognized Liz when she got off the bus. Her hair was a couple of shades lighter and cut into a very short, trendy style. She was wearing makeup, and was dressed in a fashionable red pant suit. When she saw them, she hurried over to where they were standing and threw her arms around Bobby. Next she gave Taylor a big hug.

She turned back to Bobby and gave him another big hug and said, "I'm finally here to see that gym of yours. I'm so proud of you; you always wanted to own your own gym."

On the way to the gym, Bobby whispered to Taylor, "I don't know what's going on, but she doesn't look, or act, like the sister I know."

At the gym, Bobby introduced his sister to Jason and Kelly. She was an immediate hit with them. The stories she told of the times Bobby got into trouble when the two of them were growing up had them in stitches. Except for three of the regulars sitting at the bar the gym was empty, and Liz asked Bobby if Taylor could leave to show her where he lived. Taylor was not quite ready to be alone with Liz. He asked if Jason could also come along. Bobby wanted Jason to stay in case some members showed up to use the gym. Liz and Taylor were left alone to take the short walk to his apartment.

When they got to the apartment, Taylor gave Liz the "grand tour" of the place. He tried to stretch it out as much as possible while formulating, in his mind, how he was going to explain to Liz that he wanted to be her friend, but not her lover.

Liz noticed his discomfort and said, "Don't worry, I won't ask to stay here tonight." When Taylor tried to say something, she put her finger to her lips. "Hush, let me talk. Not that it wasn't wonderful, but I don't want to repeat that night. You did a lot more for me than sleep with me. You made me realize that if a gorgeous hunk like you wanted to have sex with me, I couldn't be that bad. So right after you left, I marched myself to the beauty parlor and had a complete makeover. Next I took a good look at my wardrobe and decided it had to go. I asked Melissa to go shopping with me."

"You mean Melissa Salinger, the girl at the club you used to criticize because she was always shopping for clothes?" Taylor asked.

"Yes, Melissa helped me a lot. We had a ball shopping, and I got all new stuff. That girl is really up on the latest fashion trends. In my new clothes, people started treating me differently, or maybe I acted differently. Anyway, Kevin Fergusson, you know him, he's the assistant manager at the club. Well, he started hanging around my hostess station and we talked a lot. Guess what; he asked me out! We had a great time, and the next week I invited him to my house for dinner. We've been going out together for several months now. He treats me like a princess, and I'm nuts about him."

Taylor was delighted. He congratulated Liz on her good news and told her how happy he was for her. He didn't mention how relieved he was to have escaped a rather awkward situation. He didn't need to mention it; Liz was well aware of how worried he had been about her visit.

Two days later, before boarding the bus to take her home, Liz kissed Taylor on the cheek and whispered, "I'm desperately in love with Kevin, but I still have a big crush on you. You'll always be my hero."

Four hours later, she was dead. A twelve-wheeler, loaded with gravel, broad-sided the bus, killing Liz and seven other passengers. She died instantly.

Chapter 12

Jason was in the habit of dating female gym members. When he spotted an attractive single girl, he would work with her on the exercise equipment. Next he would offer to buy her a drink at the bar. At closing time he would explain that he lived quite near. Why not go over to his place for a nightcap? When Jason entertained these ladies in the living room, Taylor would excuse himself and withdraw to his bedroom. In his room he had his own television and stereo. Although Jason never asked him to leave, he felt more comfortable going to his own room rather than staying and witnessing Jason's efforts to get a little more intimate with his date. Jason couldn't understand why Taylor didn't invite some of the women from the gym to come to their apartment.

"What's the matter with you? Are you still grieving about Liz's death?"

"Of course, I still feel terrible about her death, but that's not it."

"Then what's the matter; don't you like girls? The women at the gym are all over you, but you just go around helping them with the equipment, oblivious to their advances. Believe me, most of them don't need any instruction; they've been coming to the gym for a long time. They just want your attention."

Taylor just laughed it off. His experience with Marcie had made him hesitant to get involved with any woman he met at the gym. He really liked his job. He was afraid that if he got involved with one of the customers, she might want to get serious. If he refused, she could get him in trouble with Bobby. Anyway, he didn't find any of the women very interesting. He was much more interested in talking cars with some of the guys from the local classic car club.

One night, as the gym was closing, Jim, one of the classic car club members called Taylor to come outside and see the Corvette he had just bought. The car was a beautiful, almond-beige 1962 Convertible.

"She has the original 340 HP engine and 4-speed transmission," Jim proclaimed proudly. Taylor walked around the car. The red interior was in showroom condition. Taylor was a little jealous. Owning a car like that might have been possible back in Pentonville, but now it was forever out of his reach. Jim took him for a spin. The sound of the powerful three hundred and forty horsepower engine made Taylor even more jealous.

"Hey, you want to buy my 1979 Corvette?" Jim asked. "I'll take you over to my house to see it."

Taylor laughed. "Way out of my league." But he was happy to go see the car anyway. Even though he knew that he couldn't afford it, Taylor fell in love with the car. The blue paint had a few spider marks, but the rest of the car was in good condition. The interior and carpet had recently been restored, and the engine had been replaced. The chrome see-through T-tops made the car look very special.

"Think about it," Jim said. "I have to sell her in order to pay for the new one; I'll let her go for a bargain price."

During the next few days, Taylor kept talking about the car. First Jason had to hear all about it, but Jason couldn't understand why Taylor was so excited about what was, in reality, just a used car. Kelly did understand; she owned a pretty beat-up Pontiac muscle car. She told Taylor that if she could afford it, she would buy a car like that in a heartbeat. Like Kelly, Bobby was also interested in the car. When Taylor saw Bobby talking to Jim, he was asking a lot of questions about the car. Taylor was sure that Bobby was going to buy the car.

The next day, at Bobby's request, Jim brought the car to the gym. "Come outside and see what we got," Bobby said. Taylor, convinced that Bobby had bought the car, followed him outside. Standing next to the car Bobby said, "What Jim is asking for this car is very reasonable. If you really want it, I'll countersign a car loan for you."

Taylor was stunned. He knew Bobby liked him, but even though they got along pretty well, Bobby was very bossy. He always made it pretty clear that the gym was his, and Taylor didn't consider him a close friend. When Taylor finally realized that Bobby was very serious about his offer, he went over and grabbed Bobby's hand to thank him.

In his enthusiasm, he shook it so hard that Bobby cried out, "Hey, big fellow, watch out! I'll need this hand to sign for the loan. Wow!" He smiled. "You don't know your own strength, do you? Maybe you should lay off the weights for a while."

When Taylor ran inside to tell Kelly the good news, he couldn't stop his eyes from tearing up. What Bobby was doing for him made him feel like he had really become a part of the gym. He realized that he had become closer and more dependent on the friendship of Jason, Kelly, and of course, Bobby, than he ever intended to.

Jason loved to joke that he knew two different guys named Taylor. One was Taylor before the Corvette, and the other after he got the Corvette. Indeed, Taylor seemed to blossom after he got the car. He took more time off from work, and was often seen touring around with his friends from the classic car club. His new, happy personality made him immensely popular among the regulars at the gym.

Chapter 13

One day, a new face appeared in the gym. It was a burly guy, wearing expensive sports clothes and an ostentatious gold chain around his neck. He didn't apply for a membership. He just hung out at the bar.

On one quiet day, he was once again sitting at the bar. Bobby had taken the day off, and Taylor was tending the bar. The rest of the bar was empty, and Taylor went over to speak to him. They got into a conversation, and the man told Taylor he planned to open a new gym in the strip mall that was being constructed on the other side of town. Taylor didn't particularly like hearing that, but he showed no emotion one way or the other. The man was a customer, and Bobby had very strict rules about customers always being welcome in his bar. The man elaborated on how luxurious his new gym would be. All new equipment, a complete sports bar-type restaurant, and great locker room facilities. He might even add a sauna; it would be nothing like Bobby's old gym. Soon it became clear why the man was telling Taylor all this.

"Why don't you come work for me?" the man asked. "I'd make it well worth your while. You're obviously an attraction for women. I'm sure a lot of female members would follow you to my new gym." Taylor politely declined. He said he was quite happy where he was. The man urged him to think about it. He knew about the car loan that Bobby had co-signed.

"As a signing bonus, I'll pay off that loan; you'll no longer be obligated to Bobby in any way. The money would be much more." He kept on urging Taylor to reconsider. "It's more than likely the new gym will have a serious effect on Bobby's gym membership. It could very well put Bobby out of business. Taylor, you should think about your own future." Before he left, he gave Taylor his business card and told him to contact him; not if, but *when* he changed his mind.

Bobby was taken completely by surprise. He had never heard about any plans to open a gym in the new shopping mall that was being built. Taylor wasn't sure if he should tell Bobby that he had been offered a job in the new gym. He finally did tell Bobby about the job offer, and the grim predictions the man had made about the future of Bobby's gym. Bobby said that if Taylor decided to take the job, he wouldn't hold him back. Bobby pointed out that he couldn't match the salary the guy could offer, and that the man was right. He wasn't at all sure that his gym would survive the competition.

The idea that someone thought that he could buy him away from Bobby's gym made Taylor mad. He would never consider abandoning Bobby *or* the gym. No matter how much that guy offered, he would never take the job! He had, however, been thinking about the possibility that a new, more luxurious gym would cause their gym to lose a lot of members. He urged Bobby to fight back with an aggressive renovation plan. He pointed out that before the new gym could be completed, Bobby could install new equipment, put a real ceiling into the main exercise room, and pay some attention to the locker rooms. New showers couldn't be that expensive, and there was plenty of room to build a nice sauna. Taylor's enthusiasm got to Bobby. He agreed to fight back. He even proposed a major expansion to the bar, the addition of several pool tables, and a few pinball machines.

Financing the renovation was the only thing holding them back. The solution to that problem came when Taylor remembered that Fred Osterhouse, a buddy of his from the classic car club, knew an influential person at the local branch of the Unified Trust and Savings Bank. This person turned out to be none other than Fred's stepfather. Fred agreed to discuss the renovation plans with his stepfather. After getting a positive response, Fred introduced Bobby to his stepfather. From then on, things progressed rapidly. Although it had to be highly mortgaged, as Bobby had little money of his own to invest, the renovated gym was a big success. When the new gym in the strip mall opened, Bobby's gym retained most of its membership, and actually gained some. The new gym drew its membership from the affluent new subdivisions, with their health-conscious yuppies.

Chapter 14

The changes at the gym didn't have much effect on Jason and Taylor's lifestyle. They continued to room together. While Jason managed to date almost every single female at the club, Taylor spent most of his time with his friends from the classic car club.

One night, while they were watching the late news in their apartment, Jason told Taylor that his latest flame had a girlfriend she wanted Taylor to meet. As usual, Taylor brushed it off, but Jason insisted.

"Come on, don't be such a fruitcake. It won't kill you if we just take the two of them out for a movie and some pizza. Besides, it's high time that you start keeping some female company. You don't want the people at the gym to think that you're gay or something, do you?"

Taylor wasn't too keen on the idea of dating someone who had some connection to the gym, even if it was only through Jason's girlfriend. But he didn't always want to say no. He knew Jason was trying to be nice. His girlfriend was probably nagging him to death about arranging a double date with her girlfriend. Taylor knew Carolyn, Jason's girlfriend. She had become a regular at the gym. Taylor thought she was a lot nicer than some of the other girls Jason had been dating. More out of friendship than anything else, Taylor agreed to the double date.

The gym closed early on Sunday nights, and Jason had arranged that the girls would meet them at the Cottage Inn. Jason's girlfriend was short and slightly overweight, but she had a very pretty face. Her long blond hair reached to her shoulders. By the way she dressed, she managed to call attention away from her wide hips and focus all eyes on her ample bosom, which she happily displayed by wearing extremely tight sweaters. Her friend, Dottie, was much taller. She wore a lot of makeup, and her low cut jeans and small tank top revealed much too much of her midriff. Her breasts almost popped out of the tiny tank top. She had a nice body and didn't mind showing as much of it as possible, while still claiming to be fully dressed.

Upon seeing Dottie, the first thing that went through Taylor's mind was, *Oh, no, a real floozy. How do I get out of this gracefully?* But since this was Carolyn's friend, he didn't want to embarrass her or Jason. He decided not to back out of the date.

After they finished eating, they went to the movies. Jason had selected a real guy movie, and the girls were a bit bored. After the movie, Taylor was ready to call it a night, but Jason suggested that they go back to his place for a nightcap. He told them that he had just bought some great new CDs he wanted them to hear.

Back at the apartment, Jason prepared some snacks while Taylor got everyone a drink. Jason came over to help Taylor carry the drinks, and softly, so the girls couldn't hear, asked, "So, how do you like Dottie? Hot-looking broad Carolyn got for you, right?"

Taylor was rather blunt in his response. "You must be kidding! She looks and dresses like a tramp. I don't want to spoil your evening, but if it was up to me, I would dump her as soon as possible."

"Come on, she's not so bad. That's the way girls dress nowadays. She's got a great body and wants to show it; nothing wrong with that! Besides, I have big plans. I'm horny as hell, and I think Carolyn is getting that way too. Please don't spoil it."

"Don't worry, I won't spoil your little party. We'll just watch some TV in my room while you and Carolyn do whatever. Just don't be too loud; you may give that little tramp the wrong idea as to why she's here."

As he had promised the girls, Jason put on his new CDs. He and his date settled on the big couch to listen to the music. This left the two rocking chairs for Taylor and Dottie. As the evening progressed, Jason kept refilling their glasses with generous servings of liquor. Each time he sat down he moved closer and closer to Carolyn. When Taylor saw Jason's hand inside Carolyn's skirt, slowly sliding up her leg, he knew it was time to leave the two of them alone. He asked Dottie if she wanted to watch some TV, and invited her into his bedroom.

Taylor turned on the TV and directed Dottie to the only chair in the room while he sat on the bed.

After a while, Dottie got up and took the remote from Taylor. After aimlessly flipping through the channels, she sat down next to him on the bed. "I didn't like the movie much, did you?"

Taylor agreed with her. "No, it wasn't really my type either."

Dottie moved closer to Taylor and placed her hand behind his head, slowly rubbing his neck. Then she pulled his head towards her and said, "Don't you want to kiss me?" Taylor knew that she never expected to hear no for an answer, and he was warming up to her. Looking at Dottie's exposed midriff for most of the evening, and watching Jason's hand disappear between Caroline's legs had not left him unaffected. The large amounts of liquor Jason had been serving were also taking effect.

He put his arms around her and kissed her. Dottie opened her lips. He could feel her tongue explore the inside of his mouth. She bent back onto the bed and pulled Taylor on top of her. Her arms were tightly around him, and she moved her legs so his would be between them. Taylor didn't resist when she took his hand and rubbed it over her breasts; he could feel her nipples getting hard. When she could feel Taylor getting aroused, Dottie's breathing increased rapidly. She pushed Taylor onto his side and he felt her pulling his zipper down. Her hand reached in his pants and she pushed his shorts aside. Slowly, she started stroking him. Taylor knew he had to stop this; it was going too far.

But when he tried to pull away, Dottie quickly took off her tank top. "Hurry up, take off your clothes," she said, breathing audibly.

"No, we shouldn't," Taylor said, as he rolled to the far side of the bed. Again Dottie rolled on top of him and put his hands on her breasts.

"Don't tell me you don't want to touch these babies," she said, as she rubbed his hands over her bare breasts. He could feel her nipples getting even harder. Before Taylor could protest any further, she slipped out of her jeans. Naked except for her thong, she flung herself at Taylor.

"I have no protection!" he told her.

"We don't need it. I'm on the pill," she said, as she pulled off her thong. Completely naked, she held out her arms to him. "Those two in the living room are screwing by now, and I want to get laid too! Please come here, I'm too excited to stop now. I have to have you."

Taylor wanted to stop, but his young body betrayed him. He quickly slipped out of his clothes. Eagerly he got on top of Dottie, who was ready to let him enter her. It didn't take long before a strong quiver ran through Dottie's body and Taylor held her tightly as he, too, came.

Chapter 15

More than a month after the four of them went on that double date; Dottie came into the gym and went straight to Taylor. He had not seen her since that night at the apartment. He had made it clear to Jason that Dottie was a little too fast for him. He didn't want to get too deeply involved with her.

Jason thought that Taylor was being a little too prudish and said, "Come on; a little sex doesn't mean that you became deeply involved with that girl."

Taylor hadn't told him what happened that night at the apartment, but Jason had heard from Carolyn that Dottie had managed to get Taylor, who everybody suspected to be a virgin, to have sex with her. Despite Jason's opinion that having sex would not necessarily lead to a deeper commitment, Taylor persisted in his refusal to allow him to arrange another double date with Dottie.

Dottie found Taylor at the weight machines, helping a customer adjust the tension. "I have to see you outside," she hissed. Once outside, she wasted no time telling him she was pregnant.

"I thought you were on the pill!" Taylor said defensively.

"I was, and I wasn't. I must have skipped a few times."

"Are you sure?" This news scared Taylor.

"Of course I'm sure! But I'm not about to have this kid. I need money to have it taken care of."

"An abortion?" Taylor asked.

"Yes, I want to have an abortion! But that costs money, and I don't have any."

Of course Taylor knew that young pregnant girls often resorted to having an abortion, but this was not part of his world. He took some time to absorb what was happening. How could it be possible that the one time he went to bed with this girl she became pregnant? He had always avoided unprotected sex, and now he was faced with this problem, which he had always been so careful to avoid. He knew that he couldn't just tell Dottie to go away and solve her own problems. Even though she had lied to him about being on the pill, he felt responsible.

"How much do you need?" he asked.

"Don't exactly know, but I don't want to be butchered here in town. I'll have to go away and try to have it done in some hospital. I don't know where to go, but I'll find out."

Taylor explained that he had no ready cash available, but he would see what he could do. "You can sell that fancy car of yours," she threw at him.

"Sure, and use my fancy car loan to pay for your abortion."

Taylor wasted no time consulting with Jason, and later with Kelly, as to how he could best go about getting some cash to pay for Dottie's abortion. Kelly responded pretty heatedly.

"How do you know it's yours? That fucking tart probably screws around with every Tom, Dick, and Harry. There is no way she can know that you are the one who got her pregnant."

Jason pointed to the timing, but Kelly would have none of it. "Hell, you don't really know how long she's been pregnant. Maybe she knew she was pregnant before she got you to fuck her. Look here, Taylor. I'll help you the best I can, but first find out what that slut is up to."

Jason defended Dottie. He said that Carolyn would have told him if Dottie was known for sleeping around. He was sure that Carolyn would never have set Taylor up on that blind date if Dottie had a bad reputation, and he suggested that they go speak to Bobby about some cash advance or something. Taylor begged him to keep Bobby out of this.

Taylor, Jason, and Kelly, between the three of them, raised enough money to allow Dottie to leave town and look for a hospital where she could have an abortion.

Dottie tried to check herself into a hospital rumored to do abortions without parental permission. But when they found out that she was not even seventeen, they immediately contacted her parents. Her parents did consent to the abortion, but they also contacted the police. They wanted to have Taylor charged with statutory rape.

Questioned by the police, Taylor freely admitted that he'd had intercourse with the girl. He insisted that it was consensual. He didn't go so far as to explain that she damn near raped him. The magistrate judge assigned him a lawyer, but since he had admitted to having slept with a minor, there would be no trial. The judge scheduled sentencing a month later.

Bobby was outraged when he heard about it. He wasn't angry because Taylor had sex with Dottie. He considered that quite normal. No, he was angry that Taylor talked to the police without first coming to him.

"That asshole of a lawyer they assigned to you should have objected to that so-called confession they got from you. That was the one bargaining point you had to help reduce your sentence."

Bobby promptly dismissed Taylor's court-appointed lawyer and put his own lawyer on the case. The new lawyer talked to the prosecutor, and managed to keep Taylor out of jail. Because of Taylor's previously clean record, and the fact that it would have been difficult for him to guess Dottie's real age, the prosecutor agreed to ask for just a suspended sentence, with some community service thrown in. The judge agreed. She took special note of the fact that it was Dottie who had initiated both the date and the sexual encounter. But the lawyer couldn't prevent Taylor's name from being placed on the sex offenders list.

Even after Taylor's mild sentence, the incident would not go away. Dottie's mother was a big-shot real estate broker in town. She was also head of the local school board. Determined to clear her daughter's name by smearing Taylor's, she floated one nasty rumor after another about him. Because of her stature in town, most people believed those rumors to be true. The situation got so bad that Taylor decided to once again move on. Bobby tried everything in his might to talk him out of it. He even enlisted the aid of the members of the classic car club. But Taylor could no longer take the nasty stories and the whispering that went on behind his back. As he had done three times before, he packed some of his belongings into his car and drove off, destination unknown.

Chapter 16

Maria looked great in her cap and gown. Her parents, both brothers, and Clair sat in the front row as she proceeded up the podium steps to accept her university diploma. This time she was not the valedictorian, but there was loud applause when the president of Miami University called out "Maria Josephina Valera, magna cum laude."

To the embarrassment of her brothers, her father jumped up and shouted loudly, "Brava, Brava Maria." He ignored his sons' protestations and continued cheering. He leaned over and kissed his wife. Next he went over to Clair and kissed her on both cheeks. "Thank you, thank you so very much," he said, while giving her a big hug. "You have single-handedly turned our worst nightmare into a wonderful dream come true."

An emotional Clair replied, "I couldn't have been more rewarded than by the wonderful times I have been allowed to share with your daughter. You can truly be proud of our little girl."

After the ceremony, they all went to have lunch at the Capitol Grille to further celebrate Maria's graduation. Maria had been accepted to medical school.

She hoped to become a surgeon. During lunch, Clair surprised everyone by announcing she was moving back to Pentonville.

"Why leave us?" Maria's mother asked.

Clair explained that she'd always felt she had some unfinished business in Pentonville. Recently she had heard that the old factory buildings, left over from what once had been Van Beuren Textile, would once again be sold at auction. Initially, they had been bought by a private investment fund, which tried to produce some new type of form-fitting underwear for men. But most men felt uncomfortable in the tight-fitting garments, and the venture closed down within two years. Clair had contacted John Phillips to find out how much she would have to bid to buy the buildings. He reported back that the only group interested in making a bid consisted of a consortium of builders, who planned to demolish the buildings and build a retirement village on the grounds. According to John's information, the demolition would be quite costly. The consortium's bid would be very low.

Armed with this information, Clair was off to New York City to see the famous dress designer Fay Regal, whose troubles she had read about in the Wall Street Journal. For years Fay had managed a very successful brand of women's sports clothes and casual wear under the brand name Regal Design. She even branched out into men's casual wear. According to the article in the Wall Street Journal, she had recently come under fire for the conditions in the factories in

India where her clothes were produced. Newspapers carried stories about child labor, which they described as being tantamount to slavery. Rumor had it that many under-aged workers had been killed in a factory producing clothes for Regal Design. To make matters worse, American unions organized protests against several department stores that featured Fay's line of clothes. Sales plummeted, and Fay was in financial trouble.

When she met with Fay, Clair made the following offer: she would purchase the factory in Pentonville and produce Fay's clothing line there. Fay and she would be full partners in this venture. Clair would handle production, and Fay would continue to handle sales and design. Fay loved the idea. She agreed with Clair that it would solve her problems by allowing her to sell her clothes as products made in the USA by union labor.

Clair went to Pentonville to arrange the purchase of the factory buildings. She didn't want anyone to know that it was she, a Van Beuren, bidding for the factory. She was afraid it would drive up the price, so she had John Phillips handle the bidding for her. They got it for a song.

Next, she negotiated with the unions that she would accept a closed shop contract in exchange for their full support in getting production started. To cover the startup costs, she bargained for some deep concessions in the first year to help her cash flow. The important part she had played many years before in starting the original Van Beuren Textile Company was well-known, and the older union leaders urged the members to accept her conditions.

When she finished explaining why she was moving to Pentonville, Clair proudly announced, "The first samples were finished last month. We are ready to start actual production by the end of this summer."

Maria clapped her hands. "I hate to see you move so far away, but boy, am I proud of you! What an amazing achievement to get the factory up and started again. I wish to God Taylor could be here to hear this."

The mention of Taylor's name dampened the mood. It was good that Maria's younger brothers were full of questions about the factory. They managed to bring the conversation back to Clair's amazing venture. They wanted to know how big the buildings were, and how many people worked there. Could they come and visit? Clair assured them that they would always be welcome. Maybe she could even arrange a summer job for them in Pentonville. Maria wanted to know if Clair would keep her apartment in Miami. Clair said that it was already sold; she needed the money to complete the startup of the factory. She had arranged to rent it back on a temporary basis until such time that she could permanently move to Pentonville.

After lunch, Maria went with Clair back to her apartment. They were out on the balcony when Clair said, "I'll miss this place, and the view of the city from up here, but I know I've done the right thing. The people of Pentonville deserve to have decent jobs, and I just couldn't leave some abandoned factory buildings as the sole remembrance of what once was Van Beuren Textile."

Maria gave her a big hug. "Yes, you did a great thing. I hope that someday I'll have the courage to do something really important." She looked up at Clair, who despite her age was still several inches taller than she. "Have I ever told you how much I love you?" They stood together for quite a while, silently looking out over the city below.

When they went back inside, Maria burst out crying. "Grandma, I miss him so!" she sobbed.

"I know, dear, so do I. But you must move on. We've searched everywhere, but Taylor doesn't want to be found. You're a beautiful young girl, and you have your whole life ahead of you. He's my grandson, and I pray for him every day, but you can't spend the rest of your life waiting and hoping that he'll return. No matter how much you love him, you cannot sacrifice your life waiting for him."

"But it's my fault; I drove him away!" Maria sobbed. "I should have trusted him and let him explain."

Clair took Maria's tearful face in both hands and gently turned it up towards her. Softly but firmly she said, "It wasn't your fault. We can only blame his grandfather, my husband. The Timothy I knew was kind and warm-hearted. He was a generous and charming man; I never knew he could be that cruel and bigoted."

Chapter 17

Taylor bounced around from town to town until his finances became critically low. When he heard that there were good jobs available in Galveston, he decided to go there. Once in Galveston, it didn't take him long to get hired as kitchen help on one of the offshore oil rigs. Work on the oil rig went on 24/7, and Taylor spent long, boring hours in the kitchen. He did, however, get three days off every other week. He enjoyed the free time he got to spend on shore. His car brought him into contact with other classic car enthusiasts, and he soon developed a whole new circle of friends. He tried to get promoted to a better job on the oil rig. When that didn't seem possible, he found a new job as bartender in a popular waterfront bar. The money, due to many extravagant tips, was good. Soon he was able to pay off his car loan and buy some new furniture for his apartment. He also had a lot of work done on his car. To his regret, the car never won any prizes in the car shows he entered; it had not been restored to a level to be classified as "showroom condition." But Taylor enjoyed the atmosphere around the shows, especially talking about cars with the other owners.

Mr. and Mrs. Gonzalez were part of the regular group of customers who frequented the bar Taylor worked in. Mr. Gonzalez was not part of the group of classic car owners Taylor hung around with, but he did own a brand-new Porsche. He loved to talk cars with Taylor. Because he was quite generous in buying drinks for people, Mr. Gonzalez was well known and very popular with the bar crowd. He was not too tall, but he had a big barrel chest, which was always partially exposed. He had the habit of keeping the top buttons of his shirt unbuttoned to show off the heavy gold chain he wore around his neck.

As the evenings progressed and his alcohol consumption started to take effect, his deep voice would grow louder. Mrs. Gonzalez, by contrast, was always soft-spoken, and beautifully dressed in the latest fashion. Had it not been for the fact that she had married Mr. Gonzalez long before he'd made his fortune, she could easily be mistaken for a trophy wife. Her gorgeous body belied the fact that she was in her late fifties. She made sure that the expensive clothes she wore showed off every inch of that body. Her face was too perfect not to have undergone several surgical corrections.

On this particular night, Mr. Gonzalez was drinking more than usual. He was loudly chatting with a group of friends seated at the end of the bar. In the meantime, Mrs. Gonzalez was sitting at the other end of the bar, nursing a drink and talking to Taylor. At one point she excused herself and headed to the ladies room. When she returned, Taylor noticed that she had undone the top button of the silk blouse she was wearing. When she bent over the bar to reach for her drink, he could look all the way down her cleavage. She smiled when she saw him look at her breasts. He realized she had gone to the ladies room in order to remove her bra. She moved a little forward on the bar stool and gave Taylor a clear view of her breasts. Unabashedly, he took in this enticing view.

Mrs. Gonzalez smiled approvingly. "Hope you like them; these babies cost well over ten thousand bucks."

Taylor blushed. He was a little embarrassed, but he tried not to show it. Mrs. Gonzalez and her husband were very good customers, and he had been taught that bartenders don't judge the customer. Customers are always right, no matter how bizarre their behavior. There are only two things they can't do: start a fight, or insult another customer. Clearly, Mrs. Gonzalez was not guilty of either. Taylor glanced around to see if any of the other customers could see or hear what was happening, but the bar was practically empty. Her husband's group was out of earshot, and no one else was sitting near them.

Mrs. Gonzalez sensed his uneasiness, but continued anyway. "What good is spending all that money if nobody gets to look at them, right?"

Taylor hoped that this was a rhetorical question, because he really didn't know what, if anything, he should answer. Without saying so, he had to admit that Mrs. Gonzales did indeed have a pair of beautiful breasts. They looked nice and firm, and didn't droop. They could easily belong to a gal in her twenties.

Mrs. Gonzales took a big swallow from the drink she had been nursing and said, "Taylor, why don't you give me a refill? By the way, call me Betty. That Mrs. Gonzalez stuff might be nice and polite, but it makes me feel old."

"Sure, Betty; you and your husband are good friends. I would love to call you by your first name. Give me a minute and I'll get you your refill."

It was almost closing time, and Taylor felt that he had neglected the other customers sitting in the booths. He quickly made the rounds to see if anyone wanted another drink before closing. When he returned to give Betty her drink, he was surprised to find that she had gotten up and joined the group gathered around her husband.

Pretty soon the bar closed and Betty walked up to where Taylor was wiping down the bar. "Taylor, can you do us a big favor and drive us home? Pedro is drunk as a skunk, and I also had a few too many drinks."

This request was something new. Her husband, Pedro, always drank a lot, but that never seemed to prevent him from driving home. Taylor looked over to where Pedro was sitting and saw that the man was drunker than usual. Because Betty claimed not to be in the best of shape either, he thought it would be a good idea to drive the two of them home.

"Sure, it will be my pleasure to give you a lift, but we'll have to figure out how; my car is a two-seater."

"Don't worry; we're not in the Porsche. We came in the Caddy. You can drive us home in it, and we'll switch cars in the morning."

Despite her claim that she had drank too much, Betty sounded quite lucid; but Taylor decided to go ahead and drive them home anyway. "Give me a moment to finish cleaning up and I'll be right out."

Taylor had never been to the Gonzales' house, and he was impressed by the neighborhood Betty directed him to. He was even more impressed when he drove up to their house; it was huge. Betty pushed the garage opener and directed him to pull the car next to the Porsche and the Lexus, which were parked in the garage.

Pedro Gonzales was passed out on the back seat of the Caddy, and Betty asked Taylor to help bring him into the house. Taylor had no trouble picking the man up, even though he weighed over three hundred pounds.

"Just put him down over there on that couch by the fireplace," Betty said when they got inside. Taylor gently put Pedro down and headed back toward the garage.

"I'll return the car in the morning."

"Thanks for doing that for us, Taylor. I couldn't have handled him all by myself." Betty walked with him to the garage and said, "For being so kind, you deserve a kiss." Taylor expected a slight peck on the cheek. Instead, Betty took hold of his upper arms and firmly kissed him on the mouth. When she pulled back her head, she looked at him teasingly and continued to stroke his biceps. The black T-shirt, which was part of his bartender's uniform, was a tight fit, and showed the full extent of his big biceps.

"You must be a weightlifter," she said.

"Yeah, I love working out in the gym. I've been doing it for years."

"Hmm, they feel wonderful," she said, as she continued stroking his arms. "I bet those muscles ripple all the way down your back."

Taylor pulled away from her and opened the door to the garage. "I'll be here around ten to return the car, or is that too late?"

"No, ten would be perfect. Good night, Taylor, and thanks again."

The next morning, at ten sharp, Taylor pulled up to the curb in front of the Gonzales house. He went to the front door to tell them that he was there with the car. Betty saw him come up the walk. Before he reached the front door, she opened it and called for him to pull the car into the garage. As Taylor got back into the car, the garage door opened so he could pull in.

"Coffee?" Betty asked when he came in from the garage.

"Yes, that would be nice, thank you. How is your husband feeling?"

"He's fine. He often drinks too much, but he recovers in a hurry. He left an hour ago to go fishing with his friend." When Taylor finished his coffee, Betty got ready to drive him over to pick up his car.

"It's not at the bar. Last night I asked the guys at the bar to bring it to my house."

Betty smiled. "Great, then I'll just bring you to your house."

They pulled up in front of Taylor's apartment and Betty asked if she could come up to see where he lived. Taylor hesitated. Based on her actions the night before, he thought it might be a bad idea, but he really didn't know how to refuse without offending her. She was acting pretty normal that morning, so maybe her behavior the night before was due to too much alcohol.

"Sure, come on up," he said, as he pointed to the stairwell that led to his second-floor apartment. His apartment was sparsely furnished. His furniture was all new, but he really didn't have anything special.

Nevertheless, Betty seemed to like what she saw. "A real bachelor's pad! I like it."

Taylor expected Betty to leave after she had looked around, but instead she said, "Aren't you going to offer a lady a drink or something? You're not being a good host, young man."

"Sorry, what would you like?"

"It's early, but a Bloody Mary would be great." When Taylor handed Betty her drink, she once again reached out to stroke his muscular arms.

"These muscles are so gorgeous; can I see your back?" Taylor pulled away.

"Betty, please don't."

"What's the matter, am I too old for you?"

"No, of course not! I think you're beautiful, but it isn't right. Your husband—"

She cut him short. "Don't worry about him. Right now he's having fun on our yacht with his friend, and by *friend*, I mean his little boyfriend."

When she saw the look on Taylor's face, she laughed. "Don't look so surprised; it so happens he likes boys better than girls." Betty put her drink down and unbuttoned Taylor's shirt. She reached in and, with both hands around him, started stroking his back. "This feels so good!" she said, as she rubbed the muscles on the side of his back.

This time Taylor didn't pull away. He felt himself getting hard. He realized he wanted Betty from the moment he saw those beautiful breasts. Betty moved her hand from Taylor's side and pulled his zipper down. She slipped her fingers inside his shorts. Taylor took her in his arms and kissed her.

Betty pulled away and said, "We'll be more comfortable in the bedroom."

Betty undressed quickly, but Taylor just stood there with his shirt off and his zipper down, looking at her.

"Like what you see?" she asked.

Taylor walked over to her. She had the sexiest body he had ever seen. Dottie and Mary had nice bodies, but nothing like this. Betty's naked body exuded sex. Even if he had tried, Taylor couldn't resist her. He started kissing her, and his hands were all over her body. The breasts she was so proud of felt very real, and she pushed his head down so he could kiss them. His hand slid down over her perfectly flat belly, and his fingers found their way between her legs. She stopped him.

"Hold on, we have to get rid of those pants first." When he stepped out of his pants, Betty pulled off his shorts.

Completely naked, they rolled onto the bed, and Taylor couldn't control his excitement. His hands went up and down her smooth legs and slid up her firm thighs while he was kissing her breasts. Betty expertly guided him to the spots she wanted touched. She pulled him on top of her, and his big frame covered her completely. With both arms around him she massaged his back muscles and stroked the hard muscles along his sides. She slid down so her hips were at the same level as his. One of her hands went between his legs, moving back and forth in a deliberate, slow rhythm. At the same time her other hand took Taylor's hand and pushed it between her legs. When she was ready, she slowly pushed him inside her.

It was over too quickly. Betty sat up in the bed. "I guess our stud here doesn't have much experience with the girls, right?"

Taylor wisely decided not to contradict her and murmured, "I'm sorry."

"Hey, cut that crap! I love your innocence; it gives me that extra kick when a strong, young buck like you paws wildly at my body before he explodes in me. A body like yours makes my juices flow. Man, I have wanted you so badly since the first day I saw you in the bar. It's a wonder it took me so long to get you into bed."

She reached over and started playing with his muscles. Touching his back and strong legs got Betty going again. Taylor stretched out to let Betty massage his body. "Wow, like I said, these muscles really get my juices going," she sighed. "Turn over so I can get at that tight butt of yours." Cupping Taylor's butt in her hands made Betty want more, and she said so. "Stay where you are, I'm just going to wash myself."

When she returned from the bathroom, she was still completely naked. Smiling at Taylor, she once again asked, "Like what you see?" Betty raised both her arms above her head and did a pirouette. "Can you guess how old I am?"

Taylor was not about to spoil a good thing. "I'd say you're around forty."

"You're such a sweetheart." She put her hands on both sides of his face and gave him a long, hard soul kiss. With her lips less than five inches from his she said, "Stud, you're really hot. I think I got me the best hunk of male flesh in all of Galveston." She climbed onto the bed and rolled over onto her back and spread her legs apart. She grabbed Taylor by the nape of his neck and pulled him towards her. "You came first, so now it's my turn." As she said that, she pushed his face down in between her legs. She started telling Taylor exactly what to do, but he interrupted her.

"Don't worry, I *have* done this before." Still a little embarrassed by his earlier performance, Taylor was determined to please Betty. His efforts were rewarded quickly. Betty's pelvis started moving back and forth and her breathing increased rapidly. Her movements became so wild that Taylor had a hard time keeping up with her. Then Betty let out a loud screech, and her movements relaxed. She sat up and pulled Taylor's head against her chest.

"Wow, that was something else! You weren't bluffing when you said that you knew what to do. My hunk turns out to be a great girl pleaser."

Even though Betty was old enough to be his mother, Taylor was hooked. He knew the relationship was all wrong, but Betty kept pursuing him, even buying him expensive presents. Each time he decided to break it off, Betty called and he would be anxious to have her come over.

During the time he spent in Galveston, Taylor kept in contact with Jason. One day Jason called to tell him that Bobby was seriously ill. He had a brain tumor. Tests indicated that the tumor was malignant. Bobby had to be operated on as soon as possible. Taylor called Jason almost every day to hear how Bobby was doing. The news went from bad to worse. Like the others at the gym, Bobby had never taken out health insurance, and his medical bills were piling up. Eventually the gym had to be sold to help pay for Bobby's treatments. The new owners kept Jason on, but Kelly had been fired.

Although Bobby was out of the hospital, he could no longer care for himself. The operations he had undergone had left him partially paralyzed, and his speech was also affected. Bobby had been placed in a nursing home. Jason was frantic. The conditions in the home where the state had placed Bobby were abysmal. There was no money to move him into a better place. Taylor decided to take leave from his job to go see what he could do to help.

By the time Taylor arrived, it had been discovered that the cancer had recurred and spread to other parts of Bobby's body. The doctors gave him only a few more months to live. Jason and Taylor agreed that they couldn't let their friend spend the remaining months of his life in that horrible place. They decided to pool their money and move Bobby to a private nursing home. This proved much more expensive than they had anticipated. Taylor once again called on Fred Osterhouse to help him secure a car loan. With the cash from the car loan and a good part of their monthly income, Jason and Taylor managed to move Bobby into one of the best nursing homes in the state. Taylor went back to Galveston. He knew when he said good-bye to Bobby that it would be the last time he would see him alive.

The call came several months later; Bobby had passed away. Taylor once again asked for a few days off and went to help Jason make funeral arrangements.

The funeral was attended by a large crowd of people, consisting mostly of members and former members of the gym. All too frequently Taylor heard, "If I had only known."

Taylor had to hold himself back in order not to answer, "If you had cared enough to ask why he had to sell the gym, you would have known." He did like hearing the stories of how Bobby had helped many people who told him their sob stories while sitting at his bar. Taylor knew Bobby had helped some people through rough times, but he had never realized the extent of Bobby's generosity.

The man who had offered Taylor a job in his new gym approached Taylor. "What can I do to help?" he asked. Taylor was in no mood to help the man feel good about himself and he politely brushed him off.

After the funeral, Taylor and Jason went back to Jason's apartment to go over the final bills. Neither of them was left with much, but everything was paid for. They felt good about the fact that they had seen to it that Bobby's final days were as comfortable as possible.

Later that evening, Kelly came by. Her eyes were red and swollen. "He was so young, so very young," she lamented. "Why does God take the good guys so early?"

Chapter 18

Taylor had intended to drive non-stop back to Galveston, but the emotions of the funeral the day before had left him feeling drained. At dinnertime he pulled into a motel. After checking into his room, he walked over to the nearby truck stop to order something to eat. The place was crowded and noisy, but Taylor found a quiet booth in the back and sat down for dinner. The waitress came over and, after serving him a beer, she rattled off the specials of the day. Taylor settled on a double cheeseburger with onion rings.

The couple in a nearby booth was sitting very close to each other. When Taylor glanced at them, he could see that the man was fondling the girl's partly exposed breasts.

"Hey, what the hell are you looking at?" the man snarled at Taylor. Taylor ignored him and concentrated on his cheeseburger. "I asked what you were looking at." Obviously the man wanted to pursue the issue.

"Nothing really," Taylor replied. "I'm just sitting here, trying to enjoy my dinner."

The man didn't want to let it go. He got up and approached Taylor in a threatening manner. "Why don't you mind your own business?" he demanded.

Noticing that the man had had a little too much to drink, Taylor replied calmly, "I am minding my own business, now sit down and let me eat my dinner in peace."

The man stepped closer and said, "Why don't you step outside and I'll teach you to mind your own business." The girl in the booth tried to get the man to sit down, but he wouldn't listen.

Taylor started to get annoyed and got up to face the drunk. At six foot four, with the arms and chest of a body builder, Taylor was an imposing figure. Grudgingly, the man decided to follow the advice of his girlfriend and sit down.

The incident made Taylor lose his appetite. He called for his check and left. Before he returned to his room, he moved his car to a safer parking spot in a well-lit area of the parking lot. He was dead-tired, and fell asleep as soon as he laid down.

The next day, Taylor was eating breakfast when the police entered the motel dining room. They announced that they wanted to speak to everyone who had been at the truck stop the night before. When asked, Taylor confirmed that he'd had dinner at the truck stop. They asked him not to leave until they could get a statement from him. When Taylor inquired why, they told him that in the early morning hours a trucker had discovered the body of a young female, lying close to where his truck was parked. The police immediately recognized the victim as the mayor's daughter, and all hell broke loose. The police showed Taylor a picture of a pretty brunette. They asked if he had seen this girl at the truck stop and if she had been in the company of anyone. Taylor looked closely at the picture, but he couldn't recall seeing her. He explained that the truck stop was very crowded and that he had sat in the back. After talking to the police, Taylor went back to his room to finish packing his bag.

Before he finished, there was a knock on the door. The police wanted him to come with them for further questioning. Taylor tried to explain once again that the girl might have been at the truck stop, but he definitely didn't see her there. The police told him to come with them anyway. Before he knew what was happening he was shoved into the back of a squad car and taken to the police station. Despite his protests, he was put into a holding cell and made to wait. After a while, a detective showed up and told him that if he wanted to, he was allowed to make one telephone call. Earlier, when they'd booked him, they made him empty his pockets and they had taken away his cell phone. The detective offered the use of the phone in his office. Taylor could have taken this opportunity to make a call, but he had no idea whom to call. He didn't even understand why he was locked up. He declined the offer of the telephone call, but did ask the detective why the hell they had him locked up.

Instead of giving an explanation, the detective called two policemen to escort Taylor into an interrogation room. The room was pretty bare. Taylor was placed on a straight-backed chair behind a shabby old card table. The detective remained standing. He was joined almost immediately by another detective, who hastily read him his Miranda rights. Taylor remembered Bobby's admonition from way back, and he was determined not to answer any questions. The detectives kept pushing for an answer as to where he had been the night before.

All Taylor would offer was, "I was asleep in my room."

One of the detectives finally gave Taylor a clue as to why they were holding him. "We have a witness who saw you running away from the area where the girl's body was found."

"Bullshit," was all Taylor replied. The detectives kept pushing him, but all they could get out of Taylor was, "I told you before, after dinner I went back to my room in the motel and I went to sleep."

The detectives kept it up for more than two hours; finally, they had the guards return Taylor to his cell. The next morning he was forced to put on a green shirt, which they had recovered from the trunk of his car. He was led up several flights of stairs to what appeared to be a lineup. Taylor knew that he looked like hell. He had not slept all night, and he was not given a chance to freshen up and shave before they took him to the lineup. He hadn't even brushed his teeth. He was told to go stand between a group of men, all about his height and wearing green shirts. That's where the similarity ended. Taylor had a much more powerful build than the others, and he was the only one wearing his hair long. The glaring light made him squint, and he was glad when told to turn to his left and next to his right. He couldn't hear or see what was happening beyond the large glass window in front of him. He stood there for what seemed like ages, but finally he was marched back to his cell.

In the afternoon, he was allowed to clean up before he was led before a magistrate, who asked him if he wanted a lawyer. When Taylor answered affirmatively, the magistrate asked the lady from the prosecutor's office why it had taken this long before Taylor was offered counsel. She assured the judge that the detective had asked, but that Taylor didn't seem interested in having a lawyer. The judge was clearly irritated by this answer. Although he ruled that Taylor could be held over for trial, he was willing to review his decision after Taylor had a chance to confer with counsel.

All this time Taylor kept asking himself, *Why is this happening to me? What have I done to deserve this?* He thought of calling Betty to ask for help, but then he thought that maybe this was God's way of punishing him for once again having an affair with another man's wife, even if this time, the man had boyfriends of his own.

Chapter 19

Lou McGregor was ready to retire. He had been practicing law without much real success for over forty years, and he was ready to call it quits. He never expected to be appointed to a murder case this late in his career. Initially he had tried to refuse. But when the judge personally approached him and pointed out that he was the only one available to handle this type of case, he relented.

Taylor was not impressed with Lou when the latter introduced himself as his court-appointed lawyer. The man weighed over three hundred and fifty pounds. Although he had a big frame, most of that weight had settled around his belly and thighs. Taylor, always careful about his own physique, was slightly repulsed by the man's disheveled appearance. His big belly had forced the lower two buttons of his shirt to come undone; his jacket was at least one size too small. He had a square, bulldog-shaped face, fleshy cheeks, and big, bushy eyebrows. He still had most of his hair, but indications were that he didn't frequent the barber too often.

"Hi. I'm Lou, and I'm going to take care of your defense." Without seeming to care about a more detailed introduction, he went right on. "Do you know what they want to charge you with? It looks bad! They're throwing the book at you. The coroner confirmed that the girl was strangled to death after she had been raped." He went on to explain that one of the waitresses at the truck stop had seen a man matching Taylor's description run away from the exact same area where the trucker later discovered the body.

Taylor looked Lou straight in the eye when he responded, "I left the truck stop early that evening and went directly to my room. When exactly does she claim to have seen me?"

"If I remember correctly from the report, she claims it was about three in the morning. She finished the late shift and was on her way to her car."

"It's dark at three o'clock; how in the hell can she know who or what she saw? Or is that parking lot back there fully lit?" Taylor asked. Lou said he had no idea, but that he would check it out.

"The trouble is that the police picked you up based on her claim that she saw a white Caucasian man, over six feet tall, with a powerful build, run away. She stated that she was within a hundred feet when she first saw him. The next day, she picked you out of the lineup."

"Shit, I don't care what that dame says, it was not me."

"It doesn't help any that when the police ran a check on you, they discovered that you are on the sex offenders list."

"That was a fucking technicality!" Taylor shouted. "They pinned a statutory rape on me, but it was all a bunch of horse shit. That girl looked much older, and besides, she started the whole damned thing."

"All they care about is that you have a felony conviction for a sex offense on your record, and this involves another sex crime."

"Whose side are you the hell on?" Taylor wanted to know.

"Hold on; don't get mad at me for telling you the truth. They had enough evidence against you to convince the judge to hold you over for trial. It doesn't matter if I believe you or not; it's what the jury believes when they put you on trial for murder and rape."

Lou asked Taylor to think carefully. Was there anything he could think of that would help prove he had been in his room all night long? Maybe a late-night movie he had watched? No, Taylor couldn't think of a thing. He did think of the drunk who'd confronted him during dinner, but that didn't help. He left the truck stop early, and that couple had no way of knowing if he headed for the motel or not.

"You do realize," Lou said, "that a conviction in this case could lead to the death penalty."

"Thanks for cheering me up," Taylor said. "There is no way I'm going to hang for this. I didn't do it; I never even saw the girl. They're just going to have to dig deeper, and they'll find out that they have the wrong guy. What about a lie detector test? Get them to give me one. That will clear me!"

Lou let Taylor rant on for a while about how they couldn't possibly convict him merely on the fact that some woman thought it was he she saw running away in the middle of the night.

After his initial interview with Lou, Taylor was taken from his holding cell to the county jail, which was more than fifty miles out of town. This made it more difficult for Lou to keep in contact with his client, and he didn't make any extra effort to see Taylor more than was absolutely necessary. In the meantime, the pressure was increasing on the prosecutor's office to get a quick conviction in the case of the murder of the mayor's daughter. The mayor had made several inflammatory remarks about the "drifter" who had murdered his daughter. To stir things up further, the mayor's other daughter gave several interviews in which she tearfully explained what a wonderful person her twin sister had been. She was sure that this awful man had kidnapped her and dragged her out to that truck stop, a place she would never have gone to by herself. In the interviews, she never missed an opportunity to refer to her sister's killer as "that monster."

The inflammatory rhetoric even reached into the county jail. Several of the inmates made threatening remarks. They were heard saying that a bastard like Taylor should be shot, but not till after he had been castrated. Luckily, Taylor was man enough to take care of himself, or surely he would have been attacked. After Taylor made friends with the ring leaders in the jail, the threats stopped. He managed to convince most of the prisoners that he was innocent, and that he had absolutely nothing to do with the girl's death.

After Taylor had been in the jail several weeks, a new prisoner was placed in one of the cells near him. The guy's name was Jim. He had been arrested for dealing drugs. One day, in the exercise yard, he came up to Taylor and said, "So, they claim you killed that Morgan girl, right? Well, I don't know if you did it or not, but she sure wasn't the goody-goody they say she was."

Taylor interrupted him to try and explain, once again, that he didn't kill the girl.

"I don't really care if you did or not, she was just a slut." This caught Taylor's interest, and he wanted to know more.

"What makes you say that?" he asked.

"Because I used to sell her drugs. She bought all kinds of shit from me."

"Did you see her the night she was murdered?" Taylor anxiously inquired.

"Nope, I cut her off a long time ago; she never had enough dough to pay for the stuff. I don't know how she got herself killed, but I sure as hell don't think she got raped."

"What makes you say that?" Taylor asked.

"That girl would fuck anybody in exchange for a fix," Jim said as he walked away.

Taylor immediately contacted Lou in order to tell him what Jim had told him. It took several days before Lou was willing to drive out to see him. When

Taylor finally got to tell him what he considered a major piece of information that would really help his case, Lou quickly dashed his hopes.

"Makes no difference, even if it is true," Lou explained. "They claim that you murdered and raped the girl; her reputation is not really relevant to the charge. The judge would never let me bring it in. Besides, even a slut has the right not to be raped, and certainly not to be murdered."

"For Christ's sake, Lou, can't you even use this information to try and find out who the hell killed her?" Taylor just couldn't accept that what Jim had told him would not be of great help to his defense. Lou, however, was convinced that if they tried to find out if Jim's accusations were correct, it would stir things up even more, and that would not help Taylor's case. The girl was, after all, the mayor's daughter. Lou tried to explain that if he dug up the fact that she was not the nice girl everyone thought she was, the mayor would put even more pressure on the DA to get a quick conviction. Taylor was not buying it; he couldn't understand why Lou couldn't go to the police with the information that this girl was a drug addict. Maybe that information would help lead them to her real killer.

"Look here," Lou said, "If you want me to save your life, let me handle this! I've been working my balls off for you, and I finally talked the DA into letting you plead guilty on all counts in exchange for a life sentence."

"Are you fricking out of your mind?!" Taylor shouted. "Can't you get it through your head? I didn't do it! No way am I going to plead guilty!"

It was at this time that Lou broke the news that the prosecutor had come up with some additional evidence. It seemed the desk clerk at the motel was willing to testify that Taylor's car had been moved that night. He told the investigators that he had noticed the car when Taylor checked in. He had even gone outside to check it out because he loved classic Corvettes. Early the next morning, when he went off duty, he noticed that the car was parked in a different spot. That clearly contradicted Taylor's claim that after he'd left the truck stop, he went straight to his room and went to bed. The prosecutor was ready to show that at some time during the night, Taylor must have left his room and gone somewhere in his car.

"Jesus," Taylor exclaimed. "Yes, I did move my car. When I first drove up I parked it close to the front of the motel. But when I left the truck stop, I decided to move it closer to a light post. The spot I had parked in when I arrived was very dark, and I didn't want anyone fooling around with my car in the dark. Shit, I didn't think that was really important, so I never mentioned it to the cops."

"Well, the prosecutor thinks it is very relevant. He thinks it will help prove that you did leave your room at some time during the night. They have more; seems like the witness who claims to have seen you running from the scene also described that person as wearing a green shirt. They found a green shirt in the trunk of your car and made you wear it during the lineup in which she identified you."

Taylor was starting to feel scared. Were they really out to get him, and if so, why? And why did Lou not seem willing to help him? "No matter what, there is no way they'll get me to plead guilty."

Lou spent a long time trying to convince Taylor it was best to accept the plea he'd managed to arrange for him. Taylor would not buy it. Nothing on Earth could persuade him to plead guilty to something he didn't do.

Chapter 20

She placed her hand on the Bible and raised the other, ready to be sworn in as the first witness for the prosecution. Taylor glared at her, hostility projecting from his eyes. So this was Maureen Brown, the woman who claimed to have seen him in the parking lot.

"Do you swear or affirm that the testimony you are about to give is the whole truth and nothing but the truth, so help you God?"

"I do."

"Please state your full name and occupation."

"Maureen Clara Brown. I'm employed as a waitress at the Clear Valley truck stop on Highway 50."

This was the first time Taylor saw her. She was a tall, large-boned woman, with an angular body and a somber face which showed signs of many years of hard work. Judy McKinney, the assistant prosecutor, stepped really close to the witness and smiled encouragingly at her. She asked Maureen to explain in detail what she had been doing the night of the murder. When Maureen got to the part where she got ready to leave the restaurant and head for her car, Taylor observed one of the jurors lean forward to pay extra attention to what was coming.

Taylor had tried to evaluate each one of the jurors as they were chosen. Regardless of the outrage the murder of the Morgan girl had created, Lou never asked for a change of venue. The jurors were all local townspeople who had known the mayor's daughter. During jury selection, Taylor urged Lou to challenge a school teacher who admitted to having Kitty Morgan in his class for the past two years.

Lou could see nothing wrong with that, but Taylor insisted. "They might as well put her twin sister on the jury and you wouldn't find anything wrong with that."

"You don't understand," Lou tried to explain. "Unless they have already decided, they can sit on the jury. All we want is that they are willing to listen to the evidence and that they are willing to consider that there is some reasonable doubt that you are the one who killed that girl."

"From what I hear back in jail, there isn't a soul left in this town who doesn't believe I was the one that bitch up there on the witness stand saw running away that night."

"I told you it would be a tough case, but you insisted on a trial."

Maureen continued her testimony. "When I was about two-thirds through the parking lot, this man came running from behind a big, red truck and took off in the direction of the diesel pumps."

"Can you describe this man?"

"Yes, he was tall, over six feet I would guess."

"Any other features you can describe for us?"

"He had a powerful build, and he was wearing a green shirt."

"Did you get a look at his face?"

"Yes, I did."

"Do you see this man in this courtroom today?"

"Yes."

"Please point him out."

"That's him, sitting at the table next to Mister Lou."

Taylor wanted to jump up in protest, but Lou held him back. "Shut up and sit down," he hissed. "Don't make this any worse than it is."

"Had you ever seen this man before?" Judy McKinney asked.

"Yeah, I saw him earlier that night in the truck stop."

When Judy McKinney pushed her to go into more detail, Maureen continued. "He was having dinner in the back of the restaurant, not too far from my station. I saw him get up and pick a fight with a young man sitting with his girlfriend in the booth opposite his. I think they were arguing over the girl."

After Judy McKinney announced that she had no further questions, it was Lou's turn to question Maureen Brown.

"Maureen, was there anybody else besides you who might have seen this man?"

"I don't believe so."

"You have told us that you had finished the late shift and were on the way to your car, is that correct?"

"Yes, sir, it is."

"And at what time was that?"

"It was about three in the morning."

"And how far were you from this man when you first saw him?"

"I don't know exactly, but I would say one hundred, or maybe one hundred fifty feet."

"But it could be more, right?"

"Yeah, maybe, but I could clearly see him."

"Now, Maureen, think carefully. It was three o'clock in the morning. It was dark. The man was more than one hundred feet away. Are you sure the man you saw was my client?"

"It wasn't dark; that part of the parking lot is lit by those yellow sodium lights." The answer took Lou by surprise, but he tried to act like he expected that answer.

"Of course, Maureen, we know that, but that is not the same as seeing someone during daylight."

"I saw him plenty good," Maureen shot back.

"You have stated that you saw his face, but he was running away from you."

"He sort of glanced around and looked at me. I know it was him."

Taylor was livid over the fact that Maureen had testified that it was he who had started the argument during dinner that night. "How could she say I started it? She has no idea what happened. Couldn't you stop her from saying that nonsense?"

"I might have been able to challenge her, but I didn't want to call any more attention to that supposed fight. If I challenged it because she was just guessing what was happening at your table, she could have insisted that she clearly saw you start a fight about a girl. That would really have looked bad for you."

"Put me on the stand. I've got to tell them it was that drunk who, for no good reason, challenged me to a fight."

"You're crazy," Lou told him. "You go on the stand and she'll grind you up."

If the rift between Taylor and Lou wasn't bad enough at this point, the issue of Taylor wanting to testify on his own behalf really set them at odds. Taylor was too inexperienced to know he could request that the judge replace Lou, but he did threaten that unless Lou put him on the stand, he would go directly to the judge and request to be heard.

On the stand, Taylor testified that he was on his way from a friend's funeral back to his job in Galveston. He had intended to drive non-stop to Galveston, but had gotten very tired and decided to stop for the night at the Clear Valley Motel. He explained that he had walked over to the truck stop next door for a quick dinner. Next he went into detail as to how the drunk sitting in the opposite booth, for no real reason, started to pick a fight with him, and even challenged him to step outside. He went on to explain why the desk clerk had seen that his car was moved to a different parking place. He described his Corvette, and why he felt safer having it parked under a street light to prevent parts being stolen from it, or vandals damaging the paint. He did follow Lou's strong warning not to try and mention anything about Kitty Morgan he had learned from Jim.

Next it was Judy McKinney's turn to cross examine him. Taylor was totally unprepared for her assault. Her rapid questions made him hesitate when answering, which she in turn exploited to attack his credibility. Lou was dismayed and sat at his table, staring at the blank pages of the yellow legal pad in front of him. He failed to respond when Judy McKinney's badgering became excessive.

Since the defense had brought up the character issue, Judy jumped all over Taylor's previous conviction for statutory rape. Taylor tried to explain the mitigating circumstances, but Judy was a real pro. She took his explanation that it was Dottie, who looked much older than sixteen, who had actually instigated the sexual encounter, and she turned his explanation against him by making it look like he was a coward who refused to take responsibility for his actions.

To patch up some of the damage from Taylor's crucifixion on the stand by Judy McKinney, Lou called Jason, and later Kelly, as character witnesses. Lou's plan had been to show what a clean life Taylor had lived. There was no indication in his past to suggest that he could be guilty of the cruel act of which he stood accused. Lou had Jason and Kelly paint a picture of Taylor as a clean-cut young man who lived a relatively quiet life and was often willing to help others. But again, Lou was no match for Judy McKinney. She managed to inject enough innuendo in her remarks to make it appear that the gym was basically a den of iniquity.

By the time the case went to the jury, Taylor feared they might find him guilty and that he could be facing the death sentence. Maybe he should have taken Lou's advice and pleaded guilty in exchange for a life sentence. But how could he possibly admit to having done the disgusting things they were accusing him of? This couldn't really be happening to him. *God, please let me wake up from this horrible nightmare!*

Chapter 21

G reg Evans, the foreman of the jury, was in a hurry to get this trial over with. He had planned a fishing trip with his friend, Edwin Barker, and being called up for jury duty had already seriously delayed their schedule.

"Okay, folks, this shouldn't take too long. It's clear the bastard did it. Now let's quickly go around the table so I can get your vote on the record."

"Hold on, Greg. Not so fast." It was Catherine Mitchell who spoke up. "We never heard any proof that he actually killed her. All we know is that Maureen saw him run away from the spot where the body was found. I would like to hear what the others have to say about that."

"I knew I would have trouble with that dame!" Greg hissed under his breath. The two of them had never gotten along. Greg was the owner of Thomson's Lumber, which he bought when Arthur Thomson, his boss, died in a car accident. Catherine Mitchell was the one whom Greg sarcastically called, "that sweet old lady from the bank," who tried to persuade Frances Thomson, Arthur's widow, not to sell.

"Come on, Catherine. You heard how Judy summed it all up. That guy left his room and went cruising around town in that fancy car of his, looking for girls. He came upon young Kitty Morgan who, in her innocence, was persuaded to go with him for a ride. What happened next is not difficult to figure out. The guy has a history of going after young girls."

"I still would like to hear from the others what they think about Judy's theory." Catherine turned to Timothy Myers, the young nursing assistant.

"Timmy, what do you think? Do you think he killed her?"

"Yeah, I think so. Miss Maureen saw him there, and what else would he be doing there at three in the morning?"

Carter Brooks, the pharmacist, spoke up. "For my part, we have a clear-cut case here. He picked her up someplace in town, raped and killed her."

"Do you really think you could rape a girl in a Corvette?" Catherine asked.

"No, he probably didn't rape her in the car," Greg chimed in. "He brought her to that quiet parking lot, behind the truck stop, where he raped and killed her. Before he could dispose of the body, he heard Maureen coming and ran away."

"Then why didn't he leave town right after that?" Catherine wanted to know.

"Simple," Greg replied. "He snuck back into the motel without the desk clerk seeing him, but he was not going to take a chance of being seen leaving at three in the morning with his suitcase and all.

141

Remember, he was registered under his own name. He never figured our police would put two and two together so fast. His plan must have been to slip away quietly in the morning, without provoking suspicion. Hell, those types are sure they can get away with anything."

They went around the room once again and everyone, except for Catherine, was convinced that Taylor was guilty.

"Look, what we have here is only circumstantial evidence. At best we know that this guy was seen at the scene of the crime."

Carter Brooks, holding up his notes in which he had written down parts of the prosecution's summation, didn't agree. "Judy was very clear that what you call circumstantial evidence is enough for us to conclude that he did it and find him guilty."

"But we don't have any forensic evidence that he actually killed her," Catherine replied.

"Here we go. Now we have to listen to Catherine using those big words of hers to explain to us that we don't really know what happened." Greg Evans did little to hide his dislike of Catherine.

Ben Weston, the school teacher, had been quiet during most of the discussion, but now he wondered out loud why a good-looking guy like the defendant would rape a girl. "A guy with his looks could get almost any girl he wants; why would he resort to rape?"

"Come on, Ben, you know why. It's power. It's this sick need of these bastards to exert power over women. That's it for me; that's why he did it," Greg said.

The group sided with Greg, but Catherine would not give in. Greg called for a vote, and it was nine to one, with Catherine the lone holdout. Rather than give up, all nine started arguing with Catherine. Greg was very belligerent in his attacks on her theories, but Carter Brooks was sympathetic towards her views. He just felt that the evidence presented was enough to convict. Catherine was not to be persuaded, and she requested that they go over the part of the transcript in which Jason and Kelly described what type of person Taylor was.

When Lou heard that the jury had requested parts of the transcript, he was hopeful they might be deadlocked, and that at least one person didn't agree to convict. He told Taylor not to get too excited, but there was some hope.

After the jury had gone over the transcript, they discussed the testimony given by Jason and Kelly.

"What faith do you expect us to put into the testimony by that would-be playboy and that dyke?" Greg asked Catherine.

"Name calling is not going to help you convince me," she threw back at him. "What makes you say such nasty things about those two friends of his?"

"Look at that one fellow," Greg continued, but Catherine interrupted.

"His name was Jason."

"Yeah, Jason; he freely admitted that he picked up every girl he could in that gym of theirs and proceeded to have sex with them. Then he tries to persuade us that his roomy stood by and lived a celibate life. Come on, Catherine, how gullible does he think this jury is? Did you really buy that? And then that woman, did you see those muscles? She had a better build on her than my guys in the lumber yard. For Christ's sake, look at the facts. First, this guy works in one of those gyms, and next, he moves on to some waterfront bar in Galveston. And didn't you notice he didn't produce one family member or other decent person to vouch for him? Or do you call those two characters he calls his friends respectable citizens?"

Catherine felt pushed into a corner, but she didn't have much to fight back with.

Chapter 22

As the jury filed back into the courtroom, Taylor felt his stomach turning. His hands were ice-cold. The formalities seemed to take forever. The judge carefully quizzed each juror individually. Had they been sequestered during their deliberations? Had any outside person tried to approach them during that time? Had they discussed the case with anyone other than the other jurors? Had anyone other than the final ten jurors participated in the deliberations? Taylor thought that the process would never end, and he felt the bile slowly creeping up his throat. A sharp pain ran all the way down his chest, and he almost wished he was having a heart attack and that sudden death would get him out of this horror.

Then the words finally came, "Have you, the jury, reached a verdict?"

"Yes, Your Honor, we have," Greg responded.

"May I have your verdict, please," the judge said, and the bailiff took a paper from Greg and handed it to the judge. Taylor stood trembling next to Lou as the judge read "We the jury, find Taylor Mathew Marx guilty of murder in the first degree in the case of Katherine Alice Morgan."

Strangely, Taylor felt almost relieved that the tension had finally come to an end, and he had heard what he had suspected for a long time. He was no longer listening while the judge read the rest of the verdict, which also found him guilty of the charge of first degree felony rape. The judge asked each juror if this was his or her verdict, and they all responded that it was.

Taylor was in a daze while Lou explained to him that the jury would now start deliberations on his sentence. After the Morgan girl's family and others had had a chance to express their grief and hatred for Taylor, the judge clearly outlined the parameters for sentencing. They could choose the death penalty for the crimes of which they had convicted him, or they could choose a sentence of life imprisonment, with or without parole.

Again Greg thought it was a no-brainer. Of course they would ask for the death penalty. Once again he found Catherine in his way.

"I think we would be better off by asking for life in prison," she said.

"Do you still think that maybe he didn't do it?" Carter Brooks asked. "If you really have your doubts, you should not have voted with us for conviction."

"Of course I believe he did it, but I feel that Kitty Morgan had a lot to do with what happened."

"How so?" Carter asked.

"It's not normal for a girl to just hop into a stranger's car, no matter how nice that particular car may be. We never discussed it, but Kitty was not quite the lovely little maiden Judy and her family described. Some of you must have heard other things about her, including rumors that she was on drugs. Timmy, you hang around with the younger folks in town; what have you heard?"

Tim readily admitted having heard that Kitty went around with some questionable characters, and that he thought she probably used drugs.

"That does not excuse the fact that he raped and killed her," Greg hotly responded.

"I couldn't agree with you more," Catherine calmly said. "But in my mind that makes him less of a monster. I studied him carefully all during the trial. He may be a big, powerful guy, but there is something soft about him. He's not the type to deliberately go out to rape women. If you ask me, he has terrible judgment, and gets into situations he can't get out of."

Greg jumped all over this explanation, but it struck a chord with several other members of the jury.

They argued back and forth until Carter Brooks started siding with Catherine. "Life in prison is no cake walk; it may not be the same as death, but just the same, it is a very hard sentence." This finally persuaded Greg and the other death sentence proponents to come around and agree that life in prison would be acceptable punishment.

When the judge sentenced Taylor to life in prison, without the possibility of parole, Lou leaned over to congratulate him; he felt that they had achieved a major victory. Taylor, although happy that he didn't have to face being put to death, didn't find too much joy in having to spend the rest of his life in jail for something he didn't do. At the beginning of the trial he had been confident that there was no way they would find him guilty based on the single fact that some woman thought she had seen him run from the scene of the crime. As the trial progressed, he became less and less sure. Eventually, he was just hoping against hope that the jury would acquit him.

Night after night he lay awake in his jail cell, imagining what it would be like to be put to death. When he did manage to fall asleep, it was often only to wake up in a cold sweat after a recurring nightmare about being strapped down to receive a fatal injection. At times he considered calling his family and asking for help, but after what had happened, he couldn't face his mother and grandmother. He was sure his grandfather would only blame him, and not believe he was innocent.

Directly after sentencing, Taylor was brought over to the state penitentiary to start serving his sentence. He heard that his car, which initially had been held for any possible evidence against him it might contain, was repossessed by the finance company when they failed to receive payments on the loan. It was the last remaining vestige of his life before his arrest that fateful day at the Clear Valley Motel.

The cell they put him in was even smaller than the one in the county jail, and he had to share it with another inmate. The man's name was Patrick Turner.

If Taylor had a formidable stature, he was nothing compared to Patrick. Patrick was huge. He stood six foot eight and had shoulders that made Taylor's look puny by comparison. The loose-fitting prison garb couldn't hide the muscles in his back. The fact that they both loved to lift weights and develop their body created an immediate bond between the men.

Up to the time he'd heard that Pat was in jail for the cold-blooded killing of his wife, Taylor had been happy to have Pat as his cellmate. Pat made no secret about how he killed his wife. He picked her up and threw her from the balcony of their twelfth-story apartment. The idea that Pat was capable of such violence scared Taylor. Without Pat's knowledge, he asked to see the warden in order to request a move to a different cell. The warden flatly refused his request. He made it clear that this was not some luxury hotel where you could request a room change. Here, he, the warden, assigned the prisoners to a cell, and that was final. Taylor asked if maybe there was some way in which he could appeal this decision. The warden just laughed him out of his office.

Except for apparently having no regrets about killing his wife, Pat turned out to be a really nice guy. As time went on, Taylor got to appreciate the fact that Pat was always in a good mood. He went out of his way to cheer Taylor up when he was having one of his bouts of depression. They soon discovered their mutual talent for football. Pat had been drafted by a professional team and might have had a career in football, had he not badly injured his right knee during his first training camp. Pat suggested that Taylor help him organize football games during the time the inmates were allowed in the exercise yard. The games soon became a regular thing; Taylor would captain one team, Pat the other. You didn't play unless selected by either captain. Deciding who got to play football was not the only thing Taylor and Pat controlled. They also protected some of the younger inmates who were in danger of being assaulted by some of the older "lifers."

The role of protector came about when Taylor and Pat were returning from their turn in the weight room. After they worked out with the weights, the guards allowed them to take a shower. When they entered the shower room they heard someone crying. They looked into the big room, which contained about twenty showers, and saw a group of five inmates huddled around a young man lying naked on his stomach. The kid was crying, and both Taylor and Pat noticed that he was bleeding from his rectum. Without hesitation the two of them jumped on the five men standing over the boy, and they proceeded to beat them to a pulp. At one point, Taylor had to actually restrain Pat, or he might have beaten one of the men to death.

The guards knew why they had beaten the hell out of those five men, but that didn't prevent them from putting the two of them on report for fighting. They were each given a week of solitary confinement. As Pat later said, in his usual upbeat manner, "That was well worth it. Those bastards had it coming. I would do it again, even if they put me in solitary for a month."

Even before they returned from solitary, the whole jail knew about what Taylor and Pat had done. From that day on, they were accepted as the enforcers, and no one dared touch one of the youngsters for fear of what the two of them would do. Even the guards started relying on the duo to keep order.

Chapter 23

The football games had become more and more competitive, and on this particular day, Pat's team was leading by four touchdowns. "We're really kicking your butt today!" Pat laughingly called out to Taylor. Taylor, ever the big competitor when it came to football, didn't seem to think it was that funny. His teams usually relied on a passing game to score points. Taylor's strong arm and accurate passes normally accounted for almost all their points. Pat's teams, on the other hand, mostly ran the ball. With Pat blocking, even the lighter men became good running backs.

Pat's team had just scored again, and he held back a little to allow Taylor's team to return the kickoff all the way to the thirty-yard line. Taylor was determined to score on this drive. He sent three receivers into the end zone while he handily evaded the opposing players rushing at him. His pass was perfect. It hit Joey Pierro, who was standing in the far corner of the end zone, right in the chest. But as had happened repeatedly that day, Joey couldn't hang on to the ball. He dropped it. Taylor burst out in anger.

He ran up to Joey and gave him a harsh dressing down. "How could you drop that ball? I threw it right on the mark and you screwed up again. With guys like you we'll never win a game!"

Pat quickly called a time out and signaled Taylor to come to the sidelines. When they were out of earshot of the others, Pat said, "Are you crazy, yelling like that at Pierro?"

"That fool has dropped at least five passes today. Two of them when he was standing all by himself in the end zone!"

"You call *him* a fool, but the only fool I see on this field is the one standing right in front of me."

"What are you talking about? Those passes I threw at him were perfect, right on the mark!"

"I'm not talking about your passing; I'm referring to you losing your cool with that kid. You have no business yelling at him like that."

"Why not? He's a clumsy idiot; he keeps dropping perfectly good passes."

"Did you take the time to teach him how to catch those perfect passes of yours? The kid has never played football before. He's new in here, and is trying to fit in. You yelling at him certainly won't help him. This will probably be the last time he tries to join these football games."

While Taylor was digesting Pat's lecture, Pat called out to the rest of the players in the exercise yard, "Okay, men, let's call it a day. Ask the guards if we can go directly from here to the showers."

Later that day, when they were back in their cell, Taylor asked Pat, "Hey, buddy, you still mad at me for yelling at Pierro?"

"Not really mad, but I don't like what you did."

"I'm sorry. I won't do it again."

"The last thing that kid needed was you, a so-called big man on campus, giving him a dressing down in front of all the other inmates. That's just plain cruel. It's not exactly on the same level as the abuse from those five slobs we caught sodomizing that kid in the showers; this was mental abuse."

"I certainly didn't mean to abuse Pierro by yelling at him for dropping all those passes."

"I realize that, but just the same, it amounted to abuse. You have to understand your body, and that great throwing arm of yours, are God-given gifts. You did nothing to deserve having them. Yes, I know, you worked hard to add all those muscles, and practiced hard throwing a football, but just the same, your body and arm were gifts of nature. So you have an obligation not to lord it over others with less spectacular endowments. You were lucky. You could walk into a place like this and know that you would easily be a match for almost any slob who wanted to do you harm. Pierro is not so lucky. He's five foot five and maybe one hundred and twenty-five pounds; he can easily fall victim to any bully. And today, my sorry-assed friend, you were that bully."

To show that he didn't consider Taylor a purposeful bully, Pat smiled as he continued. "You really have to watch these things. I'm not one to preach that we are our brothers' keeper, but I do know we have a duty not to pick on those we can intimidate because of our size, or some other advantages we may have. By the way, I'm not taking anything away from Pierro. He may have a small physique, but that kid is fast. I was watching him; he was in the end zone in no time flat. Tell you what; you teach him a little about catching a football, I'll teach him some broken field running, and we'll create our next star of the exercise yard football league."

Before falling asleep that night, Taylor lay on his bunk thinking about what Pat had said. He had called lording your ability over others bullying. Was he a bully back in Pentonville, when he was the star of the high school football team? He knew he didn't do it on purpose, but maybe he did that stuff without thinking, like today during football. What Pat had said made a lot of sense. He made up his mind to reach out to Pierro and make sure the kid would continue to join them in the football games. He didn't fully understand how Pat could be a self-confessed killer and still be so considerate of others, but he liked having him as his cellmate.

Chapter 24

C lair was livid. She'd just found out that Fay was negotiating with a factory in the Dominican Republic to produce part of the new spring collection. She grabbed the phone and called Fay in her New York office. Tina Coleman, Fay's private secretary, answered the phone.

"Sorry, Fay is in a meeting and I cannot interrupt."

Clair really exploded. "What do you mean, you can't interrupt? You march yourself right into her office and tell her Clair is on the phone!"

"I really would love to do that, Clair, but she gave me instructions. Absolutely no calls during her meeting."

"This is not just some call, Tina. It's me, Clair, and I demand to be put through."

"Clair, really, I can't."

"Yes you can, and you will. Don't make me ask again."

Tina was about to cry. "Please, Clair, she'll fire me if I interrupt."

"Who is she meeting with that is so important that I cannot speak to her? What I have to ask her is very urgent."

"Clair, please, I can't. She told me not to tell you who she's meeting with. Please, please understand, I can't." Clair realized that she was getting no place and hung up. For a while she sat in her office, thinking what she should do next. There was no way she would allow Fay to have part of their collection produced by another company. An offshore company to boot! Didn't that woman learn anything the last time she tried to have her stuff produced cheaply? Clair called John Phillips.

John came right over. After Clair gave him all the details of what she had heard, he sat back and put his hands, fingers intertwined, in his lap.

"I was afraid someday something like this could happen. It's partly my fault; I approved the legal construction of your company, even though it didn't adequately prevent Fay from taking some independent action. We didn't have much choice, really. The negotiations were not between two strictly equal parties. Her side held a lot of aces."

"What do you mean, not equal! She was in deep trouble and about to lose her shirt when I came to her rescue and offered her a chance to recover from the mess she had gotten herself into."

"Yep, you sure did. Without you she would have surely lost everything."

"So why were we not equal during the negotiations? I even thought we held the stronger hand."

"True, we held a strong hand, but they had to pony up a lot of the cash to help buy the factory and get the production started. You also put in a huge amount of capital; more than they did. But we had to agree to a very high evaluation of her brand name. They agreed to equal ownership of everything, with you controlling production, and Fay sales and design. Unfortunately, I couldn't prevent Fay from retaining exclusive control of a small part of the brand name. I would never have agreed to that, but her lawyers played a rough game. When you explained your plans to Fay, we had not completed our purchase of the factory. Fay and her lawyers took advantage of this and contacted several private investment funds to see if they would be interested in the venture. They got a couple of positive responses and used those as a hammer to gain concessions I normally would never have been willing to make."

"If they could have gone ahead with one of those investment funds, why did they choose to work with us?"

"You're quite a dynamic person, Clair, and armed with the Van Beuren name, they felt you were best suited to get the factory up and running."

"I'll show them I'm dynamic enough to stop that bitch from getting her way and screwing us!" John smiled. Clair must be really angry; as long as he had known her, he had never heard her swear. "Exactly what rights did she retain?"

"It was a very narrow field. It covered the right to independently produce and market items that had never been part of her collection before. I'll give you an example; if she would start designing men's shoes, that would not be covered by our contract. She would have the right to have them produced and to market them without involving you."

"So it all depends on what she is having made down there in the Dominican Republic?"

"That's right; it may well be some type of leather goods. She would not be the first to have a leather product produced in the Dominican Republic."

Clair wasted no time trying to find out what it was that Fay was having made in the Dominican Republic. She tried calling Fay again, but once again she couldn't get past Tina. Next she started calling several other people in the New York office to ask them to give her some more information as to what exactly was being produced in the Dominican Republic. To her amazement, no one knew any of the details. She spoke to Sharon Butler, the office manager and Fay's close friend. Sharon claimed not to know any more than Clair. She said that Fay had been very secretive about the project, and had kept her completely in the dark as to what was going on. Clair knew Sharon as a straight shooter, and she had no reason to believe that Sharon was lying. She discussed her failure to get more detailed information with John Phillips. He suggested she should go to New York and confront Fay in person.

"No, I'm going to the Dominican Republic to find out for myself."

Sharon had told Clair that Fay had held frequent private meetings with a man named Thomas Scott, who was the factory manager of Del Estero Enterprises, located in La Vega in the Dominican

Republic. Clair knew little more about the Dominican Republic than that it covered most of the eastern part of the Caribbean Island of Hispaniola. She bought a first-class ticket, and within a week she was flying to Las Americas International Airport in Santo Domingo.

Her inexperience showed up right away, on arrival, when a customs official asked for her passport. The man was extremely polite, but he insisted he had to see her visa. Before Clair could explain that no one told her she would be required to obtain a visa, the man standing behind her in line pointed to a sign that read Tourist Cards. "It's no big deal," he assured her. "You just go over there and pay ten bucks and you'll be fine." Relieved, Clair moved to the other line, and, as the man had said, she had no trouble obtaining a Tourist Card, which allowed her to enter the country.

Clair had wanted to make sure she had a nice place to stay while in the Dominican Republic, and she had booked a hotel before she left the USA. Outside the airport there was a long line of waiting taxis. A uniformed attendant directed Clair to the first one in line. The ride to the hotel took less than twenty minutes.

After checking in and grabbing a quick snack, Clair went over to the concierge desk to inquire about transportation to La Vega.

"That's a long ride, madam," the elderly gentleman in a beautiful linen suit told her. "Is that your final destination in our country?" When Clair answered affirmatively, he questioned why she didn't fly into

Puerto Plate International airport in the north. "That is closer to La Vega, and probably offers a better connection from the USA."

"I didn't know that. I'll do that next time." When Clair said that the long ride didn't matter she, had to get to La Vega, he offered a better solution than the long taxi ride.

"Why don't I book you a commuter flight to Santiago City? From there you can take a taxi to La Vega." Clair thanked him for the suggestion, and asked him to go ahead and book the first flight out in the morning. He volunteered to arrange a car and chauffeur to meet her at the airport in Santiago City. That seemed like a good idea, and Clair told him to also book that for her.

When Clair entered the arrival hall of Santiago City International, she spotted a young girl holding a sign reading "Ms. Van Beuren." She walked up to the girl and announced "I'm Ms. Van Beuren."

"Hello, I'm Angela; I'll be your driver."

Clair smiled and gave herself a little admonition; she had not expected a female driver, and certainly not one quite so young. *Men are not the only ones with preconceived ideas about women,* she thought.

Angela guided her to a side entrance and they walked across the road to an area reserved for waiting limousines. "Over there, that's our car." Angela pointed to a fairly new black Cadillac sedan. As they approached the car, Angela said, "If you sit up front with me I can point out some of the important places along the way." Clair liked the idea; this way she could chat with this pleasant young girl during the ride to La Vega.

"Do you know how to find Del Estero Enterprises in La Vega?" she asked.

"Sure, that's not a problem. A lot of business-men from the USA come to visit Del Estero. I've taken quite a few of them there. A few months ago I brought a lady to that same factory. You should have seen her; she wore beautiful clothes. I think she might have been pretty, but she wore much too much makeup."

That certainly describes Fay in a nut shell, Clair thought.

Angela turned out to be quite a talker. During the drive she told Clair all about her life. Her father had been a chauffeur, doing the same work she was doing now. He died early from cancer of the liver. She inherited his car and quit school in order to support her mom and younger sisters. The car she inherited was quite old, and due to her young age, people were hesitant to hire her. Business was terrible, so she had to change things. Instead of looking for another job, she went to the local Cadillac dealer to trade the car in for a brand-new one. The dealer was very reluctant, and was not willing to get the financing approved. When she told him she was willing to pay the full list price, he put more effort into helping her finance the car, and the loan was eventually approved.

Next she had a printer make up a "car with chauffer for hire" poster, featuring the car with her standing next to it, dressed in uniform. The uniform made her look a lot older. These posters were widely distributed at the airport. Since then, there was not a day that went by without her having a customer or two. Once she had established herself as a trustworthy driver, she discarded the uniform.

With Angela happily chatting away the drive went by quickly, and soon they arrived at Del Estero Enterprises. The factory was much bigger than Clair had expected. She was happy Angela knew exactly in which of the many buildings they could find Thomas Scott. The receptionist asked if she had an appointment.

"No," Clair said. "Just tell Mr. Scott that Clair Van Beuren from Pentonville is here to see him." Thomas Scott responded quickly, and immediately had her ushered into his office.

"Ms. Van Beuren, how nice to meet you. What a surprise. I was not expecting you." Then he quickly added, "Did we slip up and miss a scheduled appointment?" Clair assured him she had come without first contacting his office.

"Anyway, it is nice to finally meet you. Fay has told me so much about you and your operation in Pentonville. Now that we'll both be working on Fay's clothes, we should keep close contact."

If you only knew, Clair thought to herself.

After some polite talk in his office, during which he repeatedly stressed his admiration for Fay and her designs, Thomas offered to show Clair the factory. The buildings were nice and bright, with big windows to allow the sunlight in. The machines looked like they were maintained well, but they were of an older vintage than those Clair had in her factory. In contrast to the machines, the workers were considerably younger than those in the factory in Pentonville.

Thomas Scott gave Clair an extensive tour of the factory. Unaware of Clair's real reason for visiting his factory, he proudly told her all about the products they were producing for Fay. When they finally got back to his office, he was surprised to hear that Clair intended to leave again that same day.

"It's been a long day for you, and you have already done a lot of traveling for one day. Are you sure you won't stay here tonight? We have an excellent hotel here in La Vega; you'll be very comfortable." Clair assured him that she would be fine. She had to get back to the factory, and she was sure she would be able to catch some sleep on the plane. Upon leaving, Clair asked if she could take a few samples with her.

"Of course, I'll have several sets packed up for you. After you leave, I'll call Fay and tell her about your visit. I'm sure she'll be pleased you got to see our operation here in the Dominican Republic. Some people in the States have such a misguided view of what we do here."

"Yes, they do," Clair said. "When you call Fay, say hello for me, and tell her I'll be in her office in a few days to discuss the samples you gave me."

Before she'd left Santo Domingo, Clair had asked the same friendly concierge who had helped her the night before to help her change her ticket for the flight home. She was now scheduled to fly out of Puerto Plate. Angela, who had waited for Clair to finish her meeting, agreed to drive her up to Puerto Plate. When Angela dropped her at the airport, Clair gave her a big hug and handed her several hundred dollar bills.

"Oh no, that is much too much!" Angela tried to give some back.

"Do an old lady a favor and please accept it. It's my way of telling you how pleased I am to see a young girl take charge of her life and succeed against all odds." Her eyes were moist when she added, "My Maria is a fighter, like you." Clair turned away quickly and headed for the check-in counter.

Back in the States, Clair first headed back home to Pentonville to show the samples to John Phillips. After giving him a short recap of her visit to the Del Estero factory, she spread the samples on his desk and asked, "Do these fall in or outside of our agreements"? John studied the samples. They were brightly colored unisex sweat suits.

"Fay has never designed something like this before, but I think that by the doctrine of migration we can argue that sweat suits have become part of her clothing line, and are not a stand-alone product."

"So I can stop her?" Clair asked.

"I'm pretty sure you can, but do you want to?"

"Of course I want to. If I don't stop her now from excluding us from these new items, she'll put all the efforts of her design team on this type of product and keep all the profits for herself. She'll let us muddle through producing some old models."

"How do you plan to stop her? A lawsuit will take time and it will be expensive. From past experience we know that she has some pretty sharp lawyers working for her. Don't forget, the success of your factory is dependent on her design team, and certainly on her brand name. If you break up the partnership, both of you might lose."

A hard look came across Clair's face. "Don't worry, I have a plan."

Chapter 25

The plane landed at La Guardia airport in New York City. When they reached the gate, Clair glanced at her watch; twelve noon, right on time. She was sitting in 1B, very near the exit door, and as soon as the door opened, she grabbed her roll-on and hurried to catch a cab. She had scheduled a two o'clock meeting with Fay, in their Seventh Avenue office, and she wanted to eat some lunch before that time. Luckily, there were several cabs waiting when she walked out of the terminal building. Clair got in the first one in line and gave the cabbie the address of her favorite little restaurant on 45th Street, right off Seventh Avenue.

After lunch, Clair took a short walk up Seventh Avenue, to the building where their offices occupied the top two floors. Tina came out to meet her at the reception desk.

"Hello, Clair. No hard feelings I hope?"

"Dear, you were only doing what you had been instructed to do. Don't worry; I understand the pressure you were under."

"Here, let me take your coat." Tina took Clair's heavy coat over one arm while she led Clair into Fay's private office. The office was huge, and beautifully furnished. Fay was sitting behind her aluminum and glass desk in front of a big picture window. To the side of her desk was a sitting area with a massive leather couch and two big leather chairs. The oval glass and aluminum coffee table in front of the couch was covered with design sketches.

Fay got up and extended her hand as she walked towards Clair.

"Good to see you, Clair. How was your flight?"

"The flight was fine," Clair answered curtly.

Turning to the two men sitting in the leather chairs, Fay said, "Clair, let me introduce you to my attorneys, Christopher Collins and his partner, Adam Wright. Gentlemen, this is my partner, Clair Van Beuren."

Clair greeted the two lawyers and reminded them that they had met before, when she came to New York to sign the partnership agreement.

Fay, never known for great diplomacy, started right in. "I assume you have come here to tell me that I should have told you about the Dominican Republic." She paused for a moment and stared at Clair. "Well, as the gentlemen here will explain to you, what I'm doing in the Dominican Republic does not concern you, and is in no way connected to our partnership."

Clair smiled at her. "With all due respect for these two learned gentlemen, I'm here to tell you that you are wrong."

At that point Adam Wright entered the conversation. He lapsed into a long explanation as to how their contract excluded any new items Fay might develop.

"Mr. Wright, we can let the court decide if those sweat suits fall in or out of the original agreement. But, fortunately for me, I do not have to go to court to stop Fay from producing these new items in the Dominican Republic."

"You really think you can stop me?" Fay laughed in that annoying self-assured style of hers.

"No, Fay, I don't think so, I know so," Clair threw back at her. Adam Wright looked at her with a questioning look.

"Would you like to explain that?" he asked.

"Actually, I have to correct myself," Clair said. "I can't stop you, but others will." This caught the interest of both lawyers. Clair went on to explain, "I don't know how, but news of the planned production in the Dominican Republic has quickly spread all over Pentonville. It's the talk of the town. I have heard that Sam Hall, the shop steward in our factory, contacted his local union leaders, and they are meeting as we speak. The union people are furious that Fay has once again chosen to move production of her clothes off-shore. I have heard they are planning similar boycotts of Fay's clothing brand as they did when Fay got herself involved in that mess in India."

"You, you are behind those plans. I just know it; you put them up to it!" Fay looked threateningly at Clair, but Clair remained unperturbed.

"Fay, dear, before you go around accusing me of that, you'd better be able to prove it. In the meantime, if you allow another boycott of your brand name to develop, you'll be back to square one. Only this time, it will be worse. You won't have me to bail you out."

Now it was Christopher Collins who spoke up. "That nasty little plan which you dreamed up to stop Fay is not very realistic. A boycott of Fay's brand name would seriously impact the factory. If she goes down, so will the factory. Those folks working in your factory rely for one hundred percent on the production of Fay's clothing line. Personally, you might be rich enough to survive without the factory, but those union people are smart enough not to jeopardize the jobs of their members."

"You seriously underestimate me, Mr. Collins! I have with me a letter of intent from Ashley Reynolds to have her entire collection made by us in Pentonville. It will, of course, require a major expansion of our facilities. This will require a large infusion of capital. Thank goodness you and Mr. Wright were kind enough to make us aware of several large hedge funds willing to invest in our factory. Excuse me, *my* factory." Both Wright and Collins sat silently and waited for Fay to respond.

Fay was totally in denial. She kept insisting that a boycott couldn't hurt her. She kept on shouting that it was she who put Clair in a position to buy the factory, and that without her designs and brand name, Clair and the factory were nothing. "Let those bastards organize a boycott, I don't care! I'll show them who Fay is. They can't blackmail *me* with their lousy boycott."

Adam Wright turned to Clair. "Mrs. Van Beuren, I assume you came here not solely with the intention of notifying us of an impending boycott. Do you have a proposal for us?"

"Yes, I do." Clair opened the briefcase she was carrying and took out a large file, which she placed on the table, right on top of the design sketches.

"Unfortunately, Fay has proven to me that I cannot trust her. She does things behind my back. More importantly, she is willing to do things at the expense of my employees in the factory." She pointed at the papers she had placed on the table. "Here are several contracts drawn up by my legal advisors. I intend to leave New York with these contracts signed by Fay. I will not accept any changes, additions, or deletions. I'm sure you gentlemen will want to read through these contracts before you advise Fay to sign them. I will be staying at the Marriott Hotel, where you can reach me to advise me when I can pick up the signed contracts. In no event will this be later than six o'clock tomorrow night." With that, Clair strode out of the room, retrieved her coat from Tina, and took a taxi to her hotel.

Later that day she called John Phillips. She told him all about the meeting and how she had demanded that they give her a signed contract or else.

"You are one tough lady," John said admiringly.

"Not really," Clair replied. "I'm just trying to be a good factory owner. We let those folks down once before, and I couldn't bear to see them suffer again."

Two days after arriving in New York, Clair boarded the early plane out of La Guardia, the signed contract safely in her briefcase. The contract was rather simple. Silver Point Holdings, one of the larger hedge funds originally interested in purchasing the factory buildings together with Fay, would purchase Fay's interest in the factory. Clair would keep a controlling interest. As a separate transaction, the investment funds would buy all the rights to Fay's brand name and give a minority interest to Clair. Fay was given a very lucrative contract to run the design team in New York. To keep her fully dedicated to the success of the clothing line, a large part of her compensation would consist of a percentage of the profits. What Fay had lost in power was more than adequately compensated by the money she received for her share of the factory and the rights to her brand.

Chapter 26

Pat had been thrashing on his bunk for quite a while, and Taylor heard him murmur what sounded like, "Sue, please don't, don't...." This was not the first time that Taylor had been woken up by the sound of Pat's violent movements. He got up and went over to Pat's bunk and gently shook the big man's shoulder. Pat woke up with a start. For a moment he stared at Taylor with wide-open eyes. Then he quickly rolled over and lay facing the wall. He was sobbing.

"Pat, what's the matter? What happened?" Taylor asked anxiously. The sobbing subsided, and Pat turned to face him. "Nothing, just a dream," Pat said, but the forced grin on his face made Taylor feel uneasy.

The dreams, which so badly disturbed Pat, started occurring more frequently. One day, on the way back from the weight room, Taylor asked Pat about them. Pat's violent reaction caught Taylor completely off guard. It scared the hell out of him.

"Just leave me alone!" Pat yelled at him. "It's none of your fucking business. If you ask me one more time, I'll beat the crap out of you, you fucking know-it-all!" Still slinging threats at Taylor, emphasized by some choice swear words, Pat turned away and started for the showers. When Pat abruptly turned to face him, Taylor considered running back to the weight room to avoid a further confrontation.

"Just kidding, buddy. Don't look at me like you just shit in your pants; it was just a little joke. Can't you take some funning?"

Taylor tried to smile. "I didn't think it was that funny. You really scared the hell out of me."

"Sorry, buddy, didn't mean to scare you. But this place is so dull that I need a laugh once in a while."

They didn't discuss the incident any further, but when Pat had another one of his dreams, Taylor felt that he needed some advice on how to handle the situation. He decided to talk to the prison chaplain, Father Flynn.

Although he had started gaining a little weight lately, Father Flynn was well preserved for his fifty-odd years. He had one of those bulldog faces which seemed to transmit the message "Trust me, I'm on your side." He visited the prison often and the prisoners, regardless of their religion, turned to him to discuss their problems. In order to be more accessible to the inmates, Father Flynn would frequently join them in the exercise yard. Occasionally he would even join in one of the football games.

It was on one such occasion that Taylor approached him to discuss Pat's dreams. Taylor waited until he was certain that they were out of earshot of the others before he told Father Flynn about Pat's violent movements during these dreams.

"His reaction when I asked him about those dreams scared me, and, to be honest, I'm still a little leery about sharing a cell with him. Don't get the wrong idea; I like the guy a lot, and he has never harmed me. But his reaction that day in the hallway was really strange."

Father Flynn took the story very seriously. He had gotten to know Taylor as one of the more caring men among the inmates. He also knew that he was not the type to make up stories, certainly not just to change cellmates. During subsequent visits to the prison, Father Flynn went out of his way to talk to Pat. He also devoted a lot of time digging deeper into Pat's background. First he reviewed the records of Pat's trial. He discovered that there had never even been a trial. Pat pleaded guilty and received a life sentence. The circumstances surrounding Pat's wife's death were never contested.

Father Flynn decided to conduct his own investigation, and started a search for any possible witnesses. No one had actually seen Pat throw his wife from the balcony. There was only his confession, in which he freely admitted that he did it. The police never had to question him; it was Pat who called them to tell them he did it. Believing that there had to be more to the case, Father Flynn dug deeper. He visited Pat's hometown and questioned many of Pat's old colleagues from the company he worked for, but he couldn't discover anything unusual. They all told him that Pat had been a great colleague, a bright guy who talked a lot about football and spent too much time building his muscles in the gym. He had more luck when he went back to the apartment building where Pat and his wife had lived. Here he heard from several sources that Sue, Pat's wife, was a great gal, but she did have a gambling problem. It was common knowledge in the building that Pat often had to pony up large sums to cover her losses. "That's probably why he finally killed her," was what the neighbors told Father Flynn.

The simple explanation offered by the neighbors didn't satisfy Father Flynn. Pat's frequent nightmares and his violent reaction to Taylor's questions made Father Flynn believe there was more to Sue's death than just a man reacting to his wife's gambling debts.

As Pat's nightmares became worse, he was more inclined to discuss his lack of sleep with Father Flynn. Finally, Father Flynn talked him into accepting a temporary transfer to the prison infirmary to be evaluated. The psychologist who was initially assigned to Pat's case decided that she couldn't determine the cause of his nightmares. She referred Pat to a psychiatrist.

Not long after Pat moved into the prison infirmary, Father Flynn received an urgent call from the prison warden to meet with him in his office. The meeting was also attended by the psychiatrist who was treating Pat. The resident prison physician was also there. The psychiatrist explained that he'd had many sessions with Pat, and after they'd made some progress, he asked Pat if he was willing to submit to hypnosis. Pat didn't object, and that produced some surprising results. It convinced the psychiatrist that Pat's upbeat and friendly demeanor hid some very deep sorrow, and that he harbored a deep hatred for someone other than his wife.

"If we don't get to the bottom of this and treat this fellow, he is very likely to explode in anger someday, and may kill again."

"I can't have this time bomb in my prison," the warden said. "The potential risk to my guards and the other inmates is too big."

Turning to the prison doctor, he asked, "Doctor, can we keep him in your infirmary until we can think of some treatment for this man?"

"Thanks a lot, Warden. That way you can spare your people at the expense of *my* staff."

Father Flynn didn't care where they kept Pat, as long as he got some constructive treatment as soon as possible. "Let's not start any fights over where we have to place Pat. This man is a human being in need of help. I would rather we concentrate on getting him some immediate treatment." He turned to the psychiatrist. "Do you have any suggestions?"

"Yes, I do. It is quite radical, and, without his permission, it would be illegal. As a matter of fact, it will be frowned upon in legal circles, even if he agrees to it."

"I won't participate in anything illegal," the warden said.

"I didn't say it would be illegal, I said we would need his consent. Of course, we would have to be able to prove that he didn't agree under duress, or some promise of favorable treatment while in jail. We will have to show he clearly understood what he was getting into."

"If we managed to do all that, what is it you would propose to do with him?"

"Father, I would give him a hefty dose of Sodium Pentothal."

"What the hell is that?" the warden interrupted him.

"The real name is thiopental sodium. You have probably heard of it referred to as 'truth serum.' It's used for narcoanalysis in psychiatric disorders. I won't bore you with a detailed explanation as to how it works. Just think of it as a strong sedative; the patient may lose his or her inhibitions and talk more freely. However, patients do not lose self-control, and you cannot force them to tell you something against their will."

"We use it as an anesthetic during surgery," the doctor said, "but I don't see how you would use it in this case."

"Now that I have gained his confidence, I could ask Pat for his permission to give him an injection of sodium pentothal. After it takes effect, I would ask him the details surrounding his wife's death. It's likely that we'll learn nothing new, and that he'll just repeat the story that he threw her off the balcony. But it's worth a try; he might offer up some new facts that will give us a better understanding of his anger."

After a hefty discussion, it was decided that if Pat gave his unqualified consent, the psychiatrist would go ahead with the sodium pentothal injection. To fully protect Pat's rights, in case he would reveal additional information that might incriminate him, they agreed that only the psychiatrist and Father Flynn would be present. That way anything he did say couldn't be used against him.

The warden laughed. "He's confessed to killing his wife and is in here for life. What in the hell else could we use against him?"

The results of the psychiatrist's experiment were beyond anyone's expectations. Under the influence of the sodium pentothal, Pat related, piece by halting piece, how he arrived home one day and found his wife, drunk, standing on the balcony of their apartment. When he approached her, she bent over the railing and tumbled over. He tried to grab hold of her, but he couldn't save her from falling to her death twelve stories below.

Now that he had the facts, it was clear to the psychiatrist why Pat confessed to the crime he didn't commit. He explained it to the others. "He blamed himself for not preventing her from jumping to her death. This sense of guilt took complete control over him, so much so that his mind turned the facts around, and he claimed to have killed her."

The warden was not convinced. "If what he told you is the truth, your theory might be right. But who's to say that he wasn't lying? You told us that serum doesn't always solicit the truth. I still think he pushed her. He gave us no reason whatsoever as to why his wife would voluntarily jump off that balcony. Are we to believe that she was so drunk that she lost her balance?"

"I believe him," Father Flynn said. "But I do agree with the warden that we are missing the motive for his wife's behavior. Why would she voluntarily jump, or become so drunk as to lose her balance and fall?"

Chapter 27

Father Flynn was convinced that there had to be more to the story, and he returned to Pat's hometown to do some further investigation. One of Pat's closest friends, Benny Steward, whom Father Flynn had not spoken to during his earlier visit, was able to tell Father Flynn all about the couple. Benny expressed his doubts about Pat's confession to the police. This made Father Flynn even more determined to dig deeper, and he visited the racetrack where Pat's wife did most of her betting. He hung around the track for two days incognito. Finally he came in contact with Jimmy Carson, who claimed to be a "sometime" partner of the bookie with whom Pat's wife placed most of her bets.

Carson was a closed-lip tough guy, but under heavy pressure from Father Flynn, Jimmy finally gave Father Flynn what he was looking for; a reason why Pat's wife could have intentionally jumped off the balcony. Armed with this information, and the account Pat had given while under the influence of sodium pentothal, Father Flynn was able to piece together the full story surrounding Pat's wife's death.

Father Flynn wasted no time hurrying back to the prison to inform the others of his finding. He told them the following: "Pat and Sue were high school sweethearts. They were the golden couple. He was captain of the football team, and she was the gorgeous homecoming queen. They were married right after they graduated from high school, and went off to college together. Pat quit school after his junior year; he was drafted by a professional football team. Sue followed him. They were banking on a successful professional football career for Pat. Their hopes were quashed when Pat injured his knee. He was dropped from the team even before the season started. Sue took a job to support the young couple. She stood by Pat while he went through severe bouts of depression. Things started looking up when Pat landed a job with a public relations firm. He made some quick promotions, and his disappointment in not succeeding in football soon faded away.

"At about the same time, Sue started gambling. What started as entertainment became an addiction. She lost considerable sums of money, which Pat always managed to cover."

Father Flynn continued. "That part of the story was told to me by Pat's friend, Benny Steward. The next part is what I concluded after hearing a lot of gory details from Jimmy Carson, who told me his former "partner" is a real low-life.

"The losses kept coming, and Pat kept paying until finally Sue no longer dared tell Pat how much she had lost. Most of the money was owed to Willie

Baker, a local bookie. Willie kept pressing Sue to get the money from Pat.

"When she refused, he made her a proposition. 'You sleep with me, and I'll forgive the debt.' Sue flatly refused, but Willie kept pursuing her. He threatened her; she either had to pay up, or give in to his sexual advances. When Sue continued to refuse, he started making threats regarding Pat's safety. Sue had heard stories about Willie's connections to the underworld, and she feared that something might happen to Pat. She gave in and slept with Willie. Sue had hoped that this would be a one-time occurrence, but Willie forced her time and again to sleep with him, each time threatening to go to Pat and tell him that she'd had an affair with him. Sue saw no way out of this situation, and, in her desperation, decided to kill herself. She drank a full bottle of whisky and stepped onto the balcony of their apartment. At that moment, Pat entered the apartment and saw Sue on the balcony. Expecting nothing unusual, he went out to the balcony to say hello to her. It was then that he noticed that she was quite drunk.

"Sue, what in the hell is the matter with you?" he asked.

Sue leaned against the balcony railing and sobbed. 'I didn't want to do it, really I didn't. Willie forced me!'

"'Forced what?' Pat asked. Before Pat could stop her, Sue bent over the railing. Pat lunged to grab her, but barely got hold of her dress as she plunged over the side. He tried to hold on, but the dress slipped from his fingers. He could only watch as Sue fell to the ground."

Father Flynn went on. "Now that we know that he is not guilty of murder, we have to see to it that he gets out of this jail as soon as possible."

"Hold on, it's not that easy," the warden said. "We first have to get hold of the DA's office in the town where Pat was convicted, and get them to agree to review his case in light of this new evidence. We'll have a hell of a time persuading anybody that the story you just told us is really factual. With all due respect for the work you did, Father, I myself still have some doubts. The people you spoke to didn't have firsthand knowledge of much of what they told you. And a lot of the detail is pure speculation on your part."

"I have no doubt that we'll succeed in getting the DA to review the evidence." Father Flynn was very sure he had gotten the truth.

"Do we really want to try and get him freed quite so quickly?" the psychiatrist asked. The others looked up in surprise, and the psychiatrist went on to explain. "If we succeed too quickly in getting him released, he'll be free, but he'll be penniless, and in no way able to pay for the medical help he urgently needs. If he stays in jail, the government foots the bill, and I, or another psychiatrist, can continue to work with him until he's fully capable of accepting what really happened. And have you considered this? Once out on the street, this man might find out what we think Willie really did. Now he just thinks Willie caused the excessive gambling. When he finds out that Willie might have forced his wife to sleep with him, I'm willing to bet he'll really be guilty of murder."

Father Flynn had not thought about the consequences of getting Pat released as soon as possible. After listening to the psychiatrist, he agreed with the others to wait a while before starting to work on Pat's release.

With Pat in the infirmary, under doctor's care, Taylor felt very lonely. True, in the past he had tried to switch cellmates, but now that Pat was gone, he missed his companionship. His new cellmate was a morose old man who had already spent ten years in jail on a previous conviction. Without Pat around, Taylor lost much of his authority among the inmates, and he started keeping more and more to himself, even giving up on the football games.

He was about to forsake his beloved weightlifting when one day a guard game to get him from his cell. "Marx, come with me. You have a visitor."

Must be a mistake, Taylor thought. He knew no one would come to visit him; even so, he was required to follow the guard out to the visitor's area.

Chapter 28

Through the thick glass windows he saw her sitting at a small table in the visitor's room. Her short, grey hair perfectly in place, her back kept perfectly straight. Despite her advancing age, she still looked like the woman he remembered from years ago.

Taylor stepped slowly to the thick glass separation wall with its long row of telephone receivers in front of low, backless stools. Clair looked up, and when she saw him, she quickly moved over to her side of the glass separation. She picked up one of the phones. Taylor sank down on one of the stools and burst into tears.

"Grandma, Grandma, I didn't do it!" he sobbed. Clair tried to reach out to him, but the glass separation prevented her from touching him.

"Calm down, honey. It's okay. I'm so glad we found you." She, too, had trouble containing her emotions. Clair was the first to calm down. "Taylor, honey, why did you run from us? We tried so hard to find you." Before Taylor could answer she continued, "It's okay. I'm here now. No matter what happened, we still love you."

Taylor felt an overwhelming need to tell his grandmother what happened; to have her believe him when he told her that he was totally innocent. He tried to tell her everything at once, but he talked so fast that his story was very confusing.

Clair tried to slow him down. "Go slow; of course I believe you. First, let me take a close look at you. I missed you so very much!" Taylor wiped away his tears and looked up at his grandmother.

"Oh my, you're all grown up. My boy has become a very handsome man," she said proudly. The sparkle in his grandmother's eyes seemed to calm Taylor down, and he slowly started explaining what happened that night at the Clear Valley Motel.

When he was about halfway through his story, the guard came over to them. "Sorry, folks, time is up. Taylor, I have to take you back to your cell."

"Come on, George, just a few minutes more," Taylor begged.

George was the young prison guard who had always expressed admiration for Taylor's accurate passes during the football games. He had been reprimanded more than once for stopping by Pat and Taylor's cell to talk football. "You know I'll catch hell for this, but go ahead. I'll give you a few minutes more."

Taylor finished telling Clair what happened, and how no one would listen to his explanation. "Grandma, what I'm telling you is the God's honest truth. I swear it is, but nobody will believe me. I should never have run from you the way I did," he continued. "It's really all my fault for running away." Once again Taylor burst out in tears.

"No, Taylor, it's not your fault. Timothy, your grandfather, did this to you, and I stood by and did nothing to stop him. Honey, I'll do anything to make it up to you. I love you so much. I should have been strong enough to stand up to that man. Of course I believe you!"

Taylor looked at her sadly. "It feels good to finally have someone believe me, but there is really nothing you can do. The jury convicted me. I had no way to prove that I didn't do it."

"Taylor, don't ever give up hope. I'm a rich woman, and if it takes my very last cent, I will get you out of here! As soon as I get back home, I'll talk to John Phillips; he'll know what to do."

Taylor wanted to believe her, but he knew that it would be next to impossible for him to ever leave the place. Still, he felt a lot better; someone finally believed in his innocence. Clair wanted to take Taylor in her arms and give him a big hug, but of course that was impossible.

"Hey, Taylor, we've got to go now," George said, and he hastily escorted him back to his cell. On her way out, Clair tried to speak to the warden, but she was told that the warden was not available to speak to visitors. She left quietly and took a taxi back to the airport.

On the plane back home, Clair reflected on how in the intervening years Taylor had become a grown man. His muscular build surprised her, but his tall, handsome looks reminded her of his father, the man who, many years ago, had caught Timothy's eye and eventually swept Sue-Ann off her feet. Poor Sue-Ann; she never recovered from the loss of her father's company and her husband's messy suicide. Clair doubted that Sue-Ann would ever be well enough to leave the mental institution to which she was confined. She mourned over Sue-Ann's condition, but now it was time to worry about getting her grandson exonerated from the crime he never committed. She was convinced that Taylor was incapable of doing the things he was convicted of, and she firmly believed that John Phillips would know how to prove his innocence.

John Phillips carefully researched all the possibilities, and concluded that Taylor deserved a new trial for many reasons. The main point John wanted to base the appeal on was the ineffective assistance of counsel. Lou's failures were many, and it was John's opinion that those failures had prevented Taylor from getting a fair trial. Lou had failed to stress the total lack of any corroborating evidence. Even more important, he never attempted to have a DNA exam. The fact that the coroner concluded that Kitty had been raped should have alerted Lou that it was more than likely there was some evidence of semen. That would have required Lou to request his client undergo a DNA test to show that the DNA found on the victim didn't match Taylor's. Or did Lou fail to explore this issue because he believed Taylor to be guilty, and was afraid this would definitely prove it?

Clair didn't place any limits on the budget she gave John to prove Taylor's innocence. Since money was not an issue, he hired the top law firm in the county where Taylor was convicted to help him process the appeal. In addition, he hired Daniel Harris, a well-known expert on DNA issues, to pursue the possibility that DNA had been found on the victim.

Chapter 29

On her third visit to the penitentiary, Clair had a surprise for Taylor. In order to break the news gently she said, "I brought someone very special to see you." Taylor was hesitant, and looked at her questioningly.

"Who did you bring?"

"Maria is here to see you."

"No, no, you can't do that! I don't want her to see me in this place! Grandma, please, I can't! Look at this horrible prison outfit I'm wearing. No Grandma, please don't do this. I just can't face her."

"I understand your feelings, but you can't deny her this visit. That girl has prayed day and night for you. During the long years we searched for you, it was *she* who never gave up hope. When many a presumed sighting turned out to be a false alarm that led us on a wrong trail, it was *she* who gave me the strength to continue. Taylor, you owe it to her to let her come in here and see you."

When Maria entered the visitor's room, she and Taylor just stared at each other. Neither one managed to utter any kind of greeting. Taylor felt his heart pounding when he looked at this beautiful girl he still deeply loved, even though he had been mad as hell when he left Florida.

Clair broke the silence. "Come over here, Maria. We can talk through these telephones." Maria came over and sat next to Clair. With her palms pressed together in front of her face, she said, "It's you, it's really you. You're alive and well. Thank you, God, for giving me this day! I can see you healthy in front of me!" With tears still rolling down her cheeks, but with a huge smile on her face, she looked at Taylor. "Come, let me look at you. I didn't know what to expect, but you look great! Grandma assured me that you were fine, but I had to see for myself."

Taylor sat quietly looking at her; he didn't know what to say. Clumsily he muttered, "Grandma?" This broke the ice, and Maria burst out in that catchy laugh of hers. "That's right; she has become my grandma. We'll just have to share her."

Taylor had trouble adjusting to the situation. Without admitting it to himself, he had longed to see Maria again. But now that she was there, sitting behind the glass partition, he didn't know how to react. She looked so grown up, not anything like the girl he had known so long ago in Florida. But as she spoke, her mannerisms, her voice, and especially her eyes, reminded him of that girl he had left behind. He studied her face carefully and thought, *It's really the same face, only a little bit more mature.* She was even more beautiful than he remembered. *Does she have a boyfriend or fiancé?* he wondered. She could even be married, but he didn't dare ask.

"When Grandma told us the full story, and I heard that you had nothing to do with exposing my parents, I could have killed myself for acting the way I did."

"I understand, there was no way for you to know," Taylor replied. He felt guilty about his strong emotions when he left town. Carefully, he inquired about her parents.

"They are doing great," Maria said happily. "It took more than a year, but they got their immigration papers and came back to Florida. My brothers went with them to Argentina and attended the international school there. They didn't miss a beat, and once back at home, they graduated with their old classmates. They are in college now. Kevin, the eldest, graduates this year."

"Did you go to Argentina?" Taylor wanted to know.

"No, I didn't. I stayed and finished my senior year."

"You stayed all by yourself?" Taylor asked in amazement.

"No way; I had a guardian angel to take care of me." Taylor didn't understand what she meant by that, and Maria continued. "Your grandma became my grandma, and she hovered over me for a full year." Maria went on to explain how Clair moved into her parents' house and lived with her until she left for college. "In case you have not figured it out yet, I want you to know this lady here is a saint." Maria reached over to hug Clair, and Taylor could clearly see the deep affection between the two.

All too soon, George appeared to announce that it was time to leave. When Taylor turned to look at him he said, "I know, just one more minute. Taylor, I swear someday you'll get me fired." In the few extra minutes George gave them, Clair quickly explained that John Phillips had started working on an appeal, and that he had already hired other lawyers to help prepare the brief.

As she stood up to leave, and before she hung up the phone, Maria said, "Taylor, don't worry, we'll get you out. I'll be back soon to see you."

After Clair and Maria left, George took Taylor back to his cell. "Wow, who was that gorgeous babe?" George asked.

"Oh, just a friend of mine from way back," Taylor replied nonchalantly.

"Must be close to your granny, huh? I saw them walk in arm in arm from the parking lot."

Clair and Maria made frequent visits to the penitentiary, and when Clair couldn't make it, Maria came alone. She claimed not to mind missing classes at her medical school. All lectures were posted on the university's website, and she could follow them later on her computer. During a rare occasion when Clair came by herself, Taylor tried to explain away his conviction for statutory rape. Naturally, he didn't cover all the details, but he did explain that Dottie definitely didn't look sixteen, and it certainly was not his idea to have sex with her. Clair said she understood, but considering his honorable behavior while dating Maria, she thought he would have been more careful. They dropped the subject, and never discussed it in front of Maria.

During the many visits that followed, Taylor told them all about his life on the road, and, in turn, he found out about their lives in his absence. As was to be expected, the death of his grandfather didn't greatly upset him, but he was sad to hear that his mother had to be confined to a mental hospital. He relished the stories about Clair and the factory, and was full of questions about the people he had known in Pentonville. When he finally found out that Maria was not married, and didn't even have a boyfriend, his heart momentarily stood still. He had not dared to ask, but when she volunteered this information, he felt a wave of gratitude come over him.

On a visit when Maria came by herself, Taylor quizzed her about the kids in their high school. Did they know he was not the one who disclosed her parents' illegal status?

"Of course they found out," Maria assured him. "As soon as I knew, I told all our friends of my mistake; word got around very quickly. It was Andy Beckworth who discovered which group had gone out to spray your car. When he told Benny Rivas which boy had sprayed those hateful words on the back of your car, Benny cornered the kid in back of the gym and beat him to a pulp. That caused quite an uproar. The boy was injured badly enough to require a couple of days of hospitalization. At first, they wanted to suspend Benny, or even expel him from school. The student body, and most of the teachers, wanted no part of that. Benny became somewhat of a hero instead. He was never charged with assault, and the kid's parents were smart enough not to sue."

Maria turned very serious. "Taylor, I was so stupid to chase you away. I'm so sorry. I loved you so very much, and believe me, I still do."

"No, you had no way of knowing. I should have stayed to explain things."

At that moment George came back into the room. "You two ready to say good-bye? I'm getting some heat from my supervisor. He says that it's time for the young lady to leave."

Taylor could hardly believe how drastically his life had changed since the day his grandmother had first come to see him. He actually started believing that, somehow, they would manage to get him freed. He reflected on how lucky he was to have Maria come back into his life. He had often daydreamed that someday he would see her again, but he thought of it as merely an illusion that could never become reality. And there she was, as beautiful as ever, talking about sharing his grandma. Better yet, she still loved him. He realized how badly he had missed her.

Sadly, it was not all good news that came to Taylor during those days. While he was working out in the weight room, Father Flynn came in and asked him to follow him to the warden's office. A visit to the warden's office usually meant trouble, and Taylor wondered what he had done wrong. He asked Father Flynn if he should get permission from the guards to leave the weight room, but Father Flynn assured him it was okay to just follow him.

"Sit down, Taylor," the warden said when Taylor and Father Flynn entered his office. Taylor knew the warden as the strict disciplinarian who always went around with a scowl on his face. Now the man looked almost sympathetic.

"Taylor, I have to tell you some sad news about Pat. I know you two were close, so I don't want you to have to hear it from the other inmates as the news spreads around." Taylor braced himself for the worst. "Pat passed away sometime during the night."

"How can that be? He was one of the healthiest human beings I know. Except for his bad knee, there was nothing wrong with him."

"Physically, yes. You're right, he was healthy, but unfortunately he had severe mental problems. Of course you know we were treating him in the infirmary for his problems; you were the one who reported his nightmares, so you know all about that. During his treatment, Pat told us things that may have affected the circumstances surrounding his wife's death. These facts may or may not have been true. Even though Father Flynn made a thorough investigation, we'll never know the full extent of that. In any case, by submitting him to a procedure meant to stop those terrible nightmares, we upset his mental balance. We couldn't let him continue in that state. In order to make him function well enough to work with his psychiatrist to overcome his demons, he was kept under heavy sedation.

"For a while it looked like he was doing better, but Pat had other plans. Three times a day, when the nurses brought him his pills, he would swallow one and somehow manage to hide the others. He saved those pills, which were strong sedatives, with the intention of swallowing them all at once at a later date. Last night he secretly swallowed at least thirty of those pills. The nurse found him dead this morning."

It was hard to believe. Pat, that big hulk of a man with that friendly personality, dead by his own hands.

Pat's family and all his former friends refused to have anything to do with him after he confessed to killing his wife. Nobody came forth to claim the body. Father Flynn raised the money for his funeral, and services were held in the prison chapel. As a special exception from prison regulations, the warden allowed Taylor and a few other inmates to help the guards carry the casket out to the waiting hearse. From there they were allowed to follow the hearse to the graveyard, and witness the casket being lowered into the grave. At Father Flynn's request, the guards didn't carry their weapons to the gravesite, but the prisoners did wear chains around their ankles.

After the funeral, Father Flynn had permission from the warden to take Taylor back to the chapel for a talk. The two of them sat down in the back of the small prison chapel, and Father Flynn turned to Taylor. "Mind you, if you'd rather not, you certainly do not have to talk to me about Pat's death."

Taylor did want to talk to him. "Father Flynn, we all know that Pat confessed to the murder of his wife, but when I got to know him I thought he was a great guy. Except for that one time, when he threatened me after I asked about his nightmares, he was a great friend. He helped me a lot when I felt depressed about being locked up in this place. Sometimes I felt separated from the others, and that included Pat. They did what they're in here for, but I didn't! As I've told you many times, I really didn't kill that girl, and I do not feel I belong in here. But until a short while ago I considered all of them as part of my world. I thought I would have to spend the rest of my life in here with them. Now that Pat is gone, I miss him, and I feel more separated from the other inmates. Father Flynn, tell me, was Pat a good man or not?"

"You mean do I think he sinned by taking his own life?"

"Yes; that, and the fact he killed his wife."

"Pat took his own life while he was under such severe emotional strain that he couldn't make rational decisions. Under such circumstances, we should not hold a man responsible for his actions. As for killing his wife, as the warden told you, I investigated the circumstances surrounding his wife's death, which would make me answer yes, Pat was a good man."

"What exactly did he talk about during his treatment that so upset him?"

"I'm not at liberty to tell you the details, and if I were, I would not burden you with that information. No one can say for sure if what Pat told us was the truth, or merely the product of a deeply disturbed mind. All I can tell you is to pray for your friend. No matter what, we have to pray for him."

There were more changes in store for Taylor. He was moved to another cell block away from the lifers, and he was assigned to kitchen duty. This made him a trustee, a status rarely granted to an inmate sentenced to life behind bars. At first, no one would tell him why this was happening, but Taylor kept on asking. Finally, the deputy warden explained that a member on the board of the state's correctional facilities had heavily leaned on the warden to make sure Taylor was kept out of harm's way. It seemed some influential lawyer had approached this board member with the information that Taylor's conviction was being appealed, and they were working on getting him a new trial.

Chapter 30

Taylor was busy in the kitchen helping the cooks get ready for the evening meal when a guard came to get him.

"Warden wants to see you in his office."

"What's up? Is there news about my new trial?"

"I haven't the slightest. I was just told to go get you."

Taylor was ushered into the warden's office, and the guard closed the door behind him. *Unusual,* Taylor thought to himself. Normally the warden never spoke to inmates without an armed guard present. *Even though they call me a trustee, how do they know I won't attack the man?*

As if reading his mind, the warden said, "Sit down, Marx. I've asked the guard to leave us alone because I want to talk to you about a confidential matter. Lately we've been experiencing too many fights among the prisoners, and I've been given orders from higher up to improve security, or else. The 'or else' means I'll be ordered to put the offenders in solitary more often, and for longer periods of time. I think that would be counterproductive. I have another plan."

Taylor looked at him questioningly. "And this concerns me?"

"Yes. During the time you and your former cell-mate Pat organized those football games among the inmates, we had an unusually calm period here in the penitentiary. Do you think you could do that again?"

"I really don't know, sir. Pat was a professional football player, and he taught those guys a lot about how to play the game. I'm sure you must remember his enthusiasm for the game, and how difficult it was to say no to Pat. When that big guy got excited about something, he knew how to motivate others to join him. I also heard there are a lot of new guys in my old cell block. They never participated in those football games; that was before their time."

The warden nodded his head in agreement. "I know it will be a challenge, but I think it's worth a try. The guards told me it was not always Pat who was the leader out there in the exercise yard. Most of the members of my staff are of the opinion you have a lot of influence among the inmates. I would really like you to give it a try. I'm not saying it will work, but are you willing to try?"

"Sure, I'll give it a try, but I don't see how I could organize a game. I now exercise with a bunch of trustees in a different area."

"I can arrange to have you once again exercise with the men from your old cell block. Of course, you'll have to get used to the fact that there will be several extra guards present to prevent anyone from attacking you; not all the men like trustees."

Taylor's arrival in the exercise yard was not received well. Most of the men thought of him as a spy sent to inform on them. After several days of observing who was who, Taylor went over to a group of men who had played football with him before.

"You guys want to see if we can get that football thing going again?" He was disappointed when they turned him down flat.

"Why don't you go back to your kitchen, Mister Trustee?" an inmate named Willie replied. Willie was a short, stubby guy, built like a tank. Pat had coached Willie on the moves of a running back. He turned out to be a good broken field runner. With his powerful legs, he could run through anybody brave enough to try to bring him down.

"That's bullshit, Willie. You know darn well this is not the type of place where I can go wherever I want. I was put here and I'm bored just standing around, so I want to know, do you want to play some ball?"

"Isaiah over there tells us they put you with us to spy on us."

"Isaiah must know more than I do. You guys must be pretty damned important if they sent me here for the sole purpose of spying on you."

Willie wasn't buying it and replied, "Don't know, but that's what the man says." Taylor knew he was getting nowhere with Willie, nor with any of the men who'd played football with him before. He decided to confront this new guy, Isaiah, obviously the new leader.

The next day Taylor went up to Isaiah and said, "So, you think I'm a spy?"

Isaiah was somewhat surprised by the directness of Taylor's approach, but he calmly answered, "Yeah, I said that. What of it?"

"I'd like to know where you get your crazy ideas. If I'm a spy, I must report what you're doing. Well, that's easy. I'll just tell them you just stand here and talk big, but you don't move your fat ass during exercise period."

This obviously annoyed Isaiah. "Look, white boy; you looking for trouble?"

"What's this white boy shit?" Taylor shot back at him.

"You heard me. You ain't black and you ain't Hispanic, so you're obviously the white face around here."

"So you got something against whites, do you?" Taylor wanted to know.

"Look here, pal, just get off my ass! I know damn well what's going on. Almost every inmate here is either black or Hispanic. The warden and the guards, except for a few Uncle Toms, they're all white, so they sent you to see what the colored folks are doing. Right?"

Taylor stepped close to Isaiah. He was several inches taller, and his body-builder physique was in sharp contrast to the extra pounds Isaiah was carrying in the wrong places. "If you want to start a race war between us, I'm not interested. Don't take the wrongs from outside these gates out on me. You got the wrong guy for that."

"So, what the hell are you doing here?"

"If you look in the mirror, you'll know. You don't exercise; you don't move a muscle if you can avoid it, and look at you. I don't know if someday you'll be eligible for parole, but if you are, I wouldn't plan for that day. With your physical condition, you'll die long before you're allowed out. "

"So now you're a doctor, sent to take care of my health?"

"Look, Isaiah; let's keep things straight between you and me. I won't lie to you. Yes, I was placed here for a purpose, and I'll tell you why. When I was in this cell block, we played football during exercise time. We enjoyed it. It gave us something to look forward to. It kept everybody in pretty good shape. Believe me, the way my cellmate Pat played, it was no game for sissies. We beat up on each other pretty good. The games were fair, but we did play pretty rough. It felt great to get rid of all that stress from sitting in a cell all day. That might sound stupid to you, but it's a lot better than standing around spouting off your hatred for this unfair world we live in. I know your type. You like instigating fights so your buddies can be sent to solitary, proving that it *is* all about race in here."

"You talk nice, Mister Know-it-all, but how are you going to play your game of football with guys who only know city streets and never had a field big enough to throw a football?"

"That's why that lily white warden, who you are so sure is out to make your black ass miserable, sent me to teach you how to play."

"Oh, sure, he sent you to save our souls because he loves us so much, and you think you can teach us to play football?"

"Nope, I really doubt that he loves us. As a group, we inmates are not exactly what a mother wishes for; and it's Father Flynn, not the warden, who is here to try to save a few souls. As for teaching you how to play football, yeah, I can do that."

"Man, you must be kidding! If I could play football, I would've gone to college and made millions playing pro ball."

"You're big enough, but I'm not saying I can make you a pro, or even bring you close to college level. But I can teach you enough so we can have a decent game for our own enjoyment."

"You teach *me* to play football? Man, that's funny!"

"I don't think it's so funny. I think you could be pretty good at it. I would guess that before you put on all those extra pounds, you were quite the man. I bet you had a lot of muscle up here before it all slipped down to your waist," Taylor said, pointing at Isaiah's chest.

Before Isaiah knew what he was up to, Taylor called out, "Hey, Willie, ask the guard for a football and come over here. Isaiah doesn't believe you can run right over any man here in the yard who would try to block you." Willie got a ball and walked over to where Taylor and Isaiah were standing.

"What's this I hear, Isaiah? You think you can stop me?"

"I said no such thing," Isaiah said. "It's this guy here. He claims he can make football players out of us."

Willie was quick to agree with Taylor. "He's pretty good, but not like that fella Pat. That guy was like a giant. He actually played pro ball. He could teach good, too. He taught me how to hold the ball and run right around people, or just put my shoulder down and run right over them. Man, we had some good times! This fella here ain't bad, either. Let me tell you, he has a mean arm."

Taylor thought that if he didn't grab this opening, he might not get another chance. "Okay then, let's do it! Willie, collect some of the guys who played before, and we'll try to put together two teams. Let's teach these new guys how to have some fun."

The first few attempts at putting two teams together were a disaster as far as playing football was concerned. But most of the men had some good-natured laughs at their own failures. Everybody enjoyed the way it helped kill the endless boredom of life in the penitentiary. As time passed, Taylor and the so-called old group did manage to teach the new men enough about football so that they had some decent games. In order to keep up with the others, Isaiah wanted to lose some weight. He enlisted Taylor's help to get some extra time in the weight room. He relished telling everyone that Taylor was his personal trainer.

The warden was enthused about the resumption of the football games during exercise time, and he couldn't stop praising Taylor for his assistance. The praise the warden showered on him was nice, but it didn't make Taylor happy when once again he was called on for assistance.

This time he was still in his cell when the warden sent for him. "What am I here, the prison snitch?" Taylor asked when he heard what the warden wanted him to do.

The warden tried to set his mind at ease. "No, this is not like being a snitch. We have a serious problem. Drugs are being smuggled into this compound, and we cannot discover how it's done. If we catch any of the inmates with drugs, the punishment will be quite severe. So, it would be very beneficial for the men if we stop the importation of these drugs before they are distributed."

"If you rat on the person who's doing it, that's like being a snitch," Taylor pointedly mentioned.

"Okay, call it what you want. I consider it of the utmost importance to stop drugs coming into this prison. Think of it this way; helping to put a stop to it is the same as when somebody on the outside stops a friend from using the stuff. Either way, the person using the drugs is, in my eyes, the victim, and the person supplying them is just plain scum." Taylor said that he would not promise anything, but that he would think about it, and in any case, keep his eyes open.

Taylor was sure the other trustees assigned to the kitchen would know little or nothing about how the drugs got into the prison, but he was wrong. While cleaning a series of pots and pans, he started discussing the subject with the man working next to him. To his amazement, the man was quite well-informed, and he was surprised Taylor didn't know how the drugs were brought inside. The man, who admitted to being a user himself, told Taylor, "If you ever feel like trying some of the stuff, just ask George."

"George?" Taylor asked. "You mean the guard George?"

"Yup, that's the one," was the reply.

The next time Taylor saw George, he signaled him that he wanted to talk in private. "George, they're saying some pretty awful things about you. Do you know that?" George claimed to know nothing, and Taylor became more blunt. "I got some pretty reliable information that you smuggle drugs into this place." George claimed innocence, and blamed the rumors on inmates he had turned in for fighting.

"Bull, George. The ones telling me this have no grudges against you. On the contrary, they claim you supply them with the stuff."

George turned white as a sheet. "Taylor, are you going to turn me in? Hey, man, remember what I do for you. I always allow you extra time when you have visitors. You're not really going to turn me in, are you? Please, Taylor; please. I have a family that would suffer."

"George, what the hell is the matter with you? What were you thinking? How could you do something so stupid? You, as a guard, know the consequences when you get caught. And an ex-prison guard in jail won't live very long. So, if I turn you in, in effect I kill you. Shit, man, how the hell did you get into this fucking mess? Are you crazy or something?"

George collapsed like a bag of potatoes. He said nothing, and just sat there on one of the weight stations in the far corner of the weight room, where the two of them had gone so no one could hear them.

"Why, George, why?" Taylor kept on asking. "You, of all people; how could you do something so stupid?"

George recovered his composure enough to try and explain things to Taylor. "A guy like you won't understand," he began, but Taylor interrupted.

"Understand what, that you are a stupid-ass idiot to do such a thing?"

"You don't know what it's like," George continued. "From what I've heard, your family is loaded, so if you get out of here, you won't have to worry about money. For me it's different. I have five kids! On my salary we barely have enough for essentials. We can't afford braces for their teeth or home computers for their schoolwork, and all the extra equipment they need for sports. And then there's the problem of education; how in the hell can a guy on my salary afford to put five kids through college? They deserve an education, or else they won't get ahead in life. I want them to have a good life! Not like me, living from month to month, barely keeping up with the bills. So these people came around and offered me big money just to carry a couple of packages in.

"At first I said, 'Hell no,' but they kept on coming back and telling me how easy it would be, and that nobody would ever find out. Finally, I accepted. With the money they give me I can easily pay all our bills, give the kids the extras they never had, and put money away for their education. Now I no longer have to work overtime to earn a few extra bucks. Finally, I have enough time to go to night school to better myself."

Taylor interrupted him again. "And what, if I may ask, are you studying? How to become a better criminal?" he asked sarcastically.

"No, I'm studying law. I always wanted to become a lawyer."

Taylor couldn't hold back a chuckle at the thought. "Oh, man, don't you know that once you get mixed up in something like this, you can never become a lawyer? It would be impossible for you to be admitted to any state bar. Even if you managed to keep this mess a secret; too many people in here know about you. They would betray you to gain some favor from the authorities. George, you are in a real mess, and it will be impossible to get out of it without turning yourself in."

"No, I can't! Just think what it would do to my family."

"You should have thought about that before you got yourself into this stupid mess."

"Taylor, are you planning to turn me in?"

Taylor shook his head. "I can't, and I won't. As I told you, if I turn you in, I'm giving you a death sentence. You may be a stupid bastard, but for what you did, you don't deserve to die at the hands of some vengeful inmates."

"What are you saying? You expect me to voluntarily turn myself in? You're the one who's crazy! No way am I going to do that."

"You'll have to, but first you're going to talk to Father Flynn."

"I'm not Catholic; I don't go to confession."

"That doesn't matter. Father Flynn will help; you don't have to be Catholic for him to help you."

It took some heavy arm twisting, but George finally went to see Father Flynn. In the meantime, Taylor struggled with his own conscience. Now that he knew who brought in the drugs, was he obliged to tell the warden? He finally settled on waiting to hear what Father Flynn would advise George to do. The wait seemed like forever, but it was only a few days later when Father Flynn requested that Taylor be brought to the chapel.

"I brought you here so we could talk in private. First of all, you did the right thing; going straight to the warden would have resulted in punishment way too harsh for the crime George has committed. I think we've found a better solution.

"I put George in contact with a good lawyer, a friend of mine. This lawyer went to the DA, and without naming his client, asked if they could make a deal. His client could supply information about drugs being smuggled into the local penitentiary in exchange for a light sentence, maybe only probation. The DA was only too happy to accept the proposal. The warden had already contacted him about the drug problem. He had also been approached by Federal agents, who had been trying to infiltrate a ring of drug dealers. According to these Federal agents, these dealers were supplying the drugs that were being smuggled into countless prisons across the nation."

Father Flynn asked Taylor to keep everything he knew to himself until he heard further news from him. It was of the utmost importance that he avoid all contact with George.

For the longest time, Taylor heard nothing more, but finally Father Flynn came to him with the news that George and his entire family had entered the witness protection program. The Feds had been called in by the local DA. They persuaded George to continue what he was doing, but to wear a wire when dealing with his suppliers. George took some very risky steps, but managed to get to talk to some kingpins in the drug ring. He started by asking for more money. When told they would pay no more for what he was doing, George asked if they could give him some more important work. This led to talks with a man who operated higher up in the distribution chain. This man liked what George was willing to do, and he brought him to the ringleaders. After George supplied the Feds with all the evidence they needed to arrest the heads of a major drug syndicate, George and his family had to go into hiding for their own protection.

Taylor asked Father Flynn what would eventually happen to George and his family. Father Flynn smiled and said, "The irony of the whole thing is that by doing something incredibly stupid and illegal, George eventually secured the type of life he had wished for his family."

Chapter 31

Taylor had just started on the bench press when Isaiah entered the weight room.

"Taylor, sorry to interrupt your exercises, but I have to talk to you."

"Isaiah, what are you doing here at this time of day? You know you only have weight room privileges three times a week, and that has to be under supervision. You can get into big trouble coming here by yourself."

"No, no trouble. The guards know I'm here."

"How did you swing that?"

"Come on, man, you know you got a lot of pull around here. All I had to do was mention that I had to urgently see you, and the guards agreed to take me here. Two of them are right outside the door. They trust you; and the warden gave instructions that if inmates have some trouble and we want you to help, the guards should not interfere."

"Are you handing me some bullshit? Are you hiding from the guards?"

"No, man, that's the truth, and I really have to talk to you."

"What seems to be so urgent? Are you in trouble?"

"No, it's about Carlos Ortega. Do you know him?"

"No, not really."

"He's that tall Mexican dude, the one they call the knife fighter cause he stabbed someone to death during a drunken bar brawl. They were arguing over who was going to take the barmaid home, or something stupid like that."

"So, what's so important about this Carlos Ortega that you got special permission to come to the weight room to talk to me?"

"He's totally out of control. He's screaming and shouting in his cell that he has to get out of here. It all started when he had a visit from his son. The boy told him that his mother's latest boyfriend was physically abusing her, and he suspected bad things were happening to his younger sister. At the end of the visit, his son told him he had purchased a gun and was going to kill the guy. Carlos is going crazy; he wants to get out so he can stop his son from committing murder."

"Why doesn't he try to speak to the warden? Maybe he can help."

"You're kidding, right?"

"No, I'm not. The warden could call the local authorities and they could look into the situation."

"Man, are you for real? Carlos is a convicted murderer. You really think anyone is going to act to help a felon on a story he can't even prove is true? Besides, if the local police were contacted, they would probably just arrest the kid for illegal gun possession, and not do much about his accusation of the physical abuse of his mom by her boyfriend. The way Carlos tells it, the woman has never filed a complaint against the man."

"Why come to me? Why would Carlos want me to help if he doesn't even trust the warden to help him?"

"Look here, Taylor, everyone in this damned jail knows your family is very rich and well connected."

"Hey, hold on. If you're referring to the fact that my grandma is trying to get me out of here, just back off! She knows I'm not guilty of that rape and the murder they convicted me of, and it's perfectly legit for her to help me prove that."

"Cool it, man, nobody in this place believes you killed that woman. You're not the type. Besides, with your money and good looks, you could get any woman you wanted. Why would you rape her? No, none of us, not even the guards, believe you did it."

Taylor was surprised. He thought the inmates might be jealous of the special treatment he was getting here in the jail, and of all the help he was getting from his family in an attempt to overturn his conviction.

But Isaiah had not come to discuss Taylor's guilt or innocence. He pressed on. "I would like for you to talk to Carlos and see if you can help him."

"Like I said before, why would he trust me, and what could I do?"

"I know he'd trust you. You're different from all those rich dudes on the outside. You don't think of us poor guys as different from you. You don't think it's normal for us to get into trouble because we have no education. At times I can speak to you like you're one of us, like you understand. Oh, shit, I can't really explain it. You're not really like us, but I know he'll trust you."

The next day in the exercise yard, Taylor broke away from the inmates playing football and walked over to Carlos, who was standing by himself with his head pushed into the fence. "Carlos, I hear you got some troubles. Want to talk about it?"

Carlos turned around slowly, and Taylor was surprised to see the big red circles under the man's eyes. Carlos was not the type one would expect to cry. He didn't have an ounce of fat on his tall, skinny frame. Actually, he was too skinny. His elongated face, with its pronounced jaw and deep-set eyes, gave him a cruel look, and most people would find him scary.

"Who told you, and what's it to you, anyway?"

"Isaiah told me you could use some help."

"So, Isaiah went to get the fix-it man. Well, I don't need your help unless you have a magic wand and can wave me out of here." With that Carlos turned to face the fence again.

"Okay, have it your way," Taylor said, and he started to walk back towards the group playing football. When Taylor was about fifty feet away, Carlos turned around and called after him. "Hold on! I'm upset. I didn't mean to send you away." Taylor waited while Carlos walked up to him. "It's my son; I got to get out of here to stop him from fucking up his life forever."

"Want to tell me what's going on?"

Carlos hesitated, but then he began to talk. "My son, he's a really good kid. Regardless of all the shit that's going on at home, he has stayed out of trouble. He's a senior in high school, and if he can get a scholarship, he'll go to college. But the other day, when he came to visit, he told me he had bought a gun and was going to kill his mother's boyfriend. He tells me this guy beats up on his mother all the time, and he thinks bad things are happening to his little sister."

"Why doesn't he go to the police and report this?"

"He did. Actually, his coach did. You see, he hasn't been living with his mother for almost two years. He argued with her about all the men she was hanging around with, many of them staying at her house for longer or shorter periods. Hell, he's old enough to know that she was sleeping with every one of them. He finally moved out, and his high school track coach took him in. The coach has a son the same age, and the boys are best friends. Anyway, he told the coach about his mom getting beat up, and they went to the police together. The police investigated, but despite many bruises on her body, she denied any violence on the part of her boyfriend. They also questioned his sister, but she, too, insisted that all was fine. The police did nothing, and they won't go back to check."

Carlos' voice broke, and he stopped talking. He pushed his fingers through his long, straight hair and stood for a while, staring at his shoes. Taylor was surprised by how well-spoken Carlos was. Based on his appearance, he had underestimated this man.

"You obviously believe your son, but trying to get out of here is not a solution. They'll never allow you out based on that story, and even if they did, you going there wouldn't solve much. What were you planning on doing? Kill the guy instead of letting your son do it?" Taylor waited for a response, but all Carlos did was bow his head a little more.

When he looked up he cried out, "I got to stop him! God help me, I got to stop him!" With both hands he grabbed onto Taylor's shoulders and with tears in his eyes he sobbed, "Help me, please, help me! He's a good boy; we have to stop him!" If Taylor would have had a choice, he would rather have faced an angry Carlos threatening violence. Instead, here was this desperate father cowering in front of him, expressing his agony at not being able to stop his son from committing a serious crime.

"Carlos, as far as we know, nothing has happened yet; but I agree with you that we must act quickly. I'll help, but you must pull yourself together so we can see what can be done from here. Give me some more details. What is the coach's name, and how can we reach him?"

"I don't know," Carlos replied, barely audible.

"Okay, at least tell me the name of the high school your son attends."

"He goes to Montgomery High." Carlos was starting to respond. He finally had a glimmer of hope that something could be done.

"Where is Montgomery High? I mean, what state, what town?"

"It's in Wilkesville, about one hundred miles from here."

"Okay, now you try to stay calm and let me take it from here."

"Do you think you can stop my son from this crazy act?"

"Carlos, I don't know, but I promise it won't be from a lack of trying. Now, try your best to stay calm. Screaming and hollering you want to get out won't help."

Taylor left Carlos, who was looking a little bewildered, and headed straight for a couple of guards standing on the far side of the exercise yard. When he reached the guards he said, "I have an emergency. I have to see the warden as soon as possible."

"Sure," one of the guards replied. "And the warden is sitting in his office, waiting for you to come calling. Come on, Taylor, we know you're a privileged character around here, but now you're getting ridiculous."

"I'm not kidding, this is a real emergency."

"Cut it, Taylor. You know we can't just take you to see the warden for a so-called emergency declared by you."

"Just a minute," the other guard said. "What exactly is going on, Taylor?"

"I have real information that a kid on the outside is about to commit murder unless the warden gets a message to his coach."

"How in the hell would you get this information?" the first guard asked.

Before Taylor could answer, the other guard said, "Doug, this guy is a straight shooter. I don't think he'd try to hand us a load of bull. I'm willing to take a chance and take him to the warden."

Chapter 32

The telephone operator/receptionist ushered Taylor and the two guards into the warden's office. The warden was on the telephone. When he hung up he greeted the three with, "Well, and to what do I owe this unexpected visit?"

Pete, the guard who had agreed to bring Taylor to the warden, answered, "Sir, Trustee Taylor here told us he had an emergency. Considering his reputation, I agreed to bring him to see you without first asking your permission."

"I see. Well, Taylor, tell me what this emergency is all about."

"With all due respect for Officers Pete and Doug, I would like to speak to you about this matter in private. What I have to tell you was told to me in confidence, and I have to respect that confidence."

"I guess we can do that," the warden said. "Pete, why don't you wait in the outer office, and Doug, you can go back on patrol."

After the two guards left his office, the warden turned to Taylor. "Okay, go ahead. Tell me about this emergency."

"Sir, one of the inmates has been told by his son that he intends to kill the man who has been abusing his mother. The boy is presently staying with his high school coach. I'm here to ask you to try to contact this coach so he can talk some sense into this youngster's head."

"A kid making threats to kill someone does not necessarily mean he is actually planning to do it. He's probably just looking for attention."

"I don't think so, sir. According to what he told his father, he has already purchased a gun, and fully intends to go through with it."

"If that is so, why don't we call the local police and have them check it out?"

"Sir, that would just get the kid in trouble. It would not stop the abuse of the mother."

"You don't even know if the part about the abuse is true."

"That's right, but I'm told this is a trustworthy kid. The authorities should check into what's going on with his mother. In the meantime, I would like you to contact his coach so we can stop the kid from doing anything foolish."

"Taylor, if we have information that the kid illegally purchased a weapon, we are obliged to contact the local police and report it. Just tell me the kid's name and where he lives and I'll take care of it."

"Sorry, sir, I can't do that. In the first place, I don't know the kid's name."

The warden interrupted him. "Then give me the name of the inmate and I'll get it."

"With all due respect, sir, I cannot do that either. I was told about this in confidence, and I promised this man I would help him protect his son from ruining his life by taking matters into his own hands."

"Listen to me, Taylor. If we have reason to believe the kid has illegally bought a gun, we must inform the local authorities. Now give me the inmate's name."

"Sir, you know I have a lot of respect for you, but I will not divulge the father's name. I cannot honor my promise to help by turning the kid over to the police. Besides, I suspect the kid is smart enough to keep the gun well hidden. The police would probably come up empty-handed, giving the kid a chance to act at a later date."

"Taylor, I don't care if this was told to you in confidence. You are not a lawyer or a priest, so this is not privileged information. You must tell me the inmate's name so I can report it."

"I know this is not a very diplomatic answer, but this is not a court of law, and I do not have to give you his name. I came to you hoping you would respond in a less bureaucratic way, but since you will not try to contact the boy's coach, I must find another way to do so. Please try to understand my position. I hope there won't be any repercussions about our difference of opinion on this matter. Now, if I may be excused, I won't take up any more of your time. Thank you for seeing me on such short notice."

"Taylor, if it was anybody but you, I would put him in solitary until he gave me the name of that kid's father."

"No, sir, you wouldn't. You're too much of a stickler of the law to do that, and I respect you for that. You would never abuse your power to do that."

After his duties in the exercise yard assisting the lifers with their football games, Taylor normally had to return to the kitchen. While Pete escorted him from the warden's office to the kitchen, Taylor was thinking of a way to contact the coach in Wilkesville. He couldn't go to Father Flynn; he was away on a chaplain's conference and wouldn't be back for another week. If Father Flynn had been available, Taylor would have gone to him instead of the warden. He could ask one of the guards to call the coach, but he feared that if the warden heard about it, there would be disciplinary action against the guard. The only possible way was for him to make the call himself.

After lunch, all prisoners, including the trustees, were returned to their cells. Taylor took advantage of this break in his kitchen duties to request permission to make a personal call. The trustees were allowed one call per week to each member of their immediate family. This new rule had recently been instituted by the warden in an attempt to raise morale among the trustees.

One of the guards escorted Taylor to the visitors' room, which was used to make outside calls when there were no visitors in the building. There, another guard, on duty at the telephones, checked the log to see who Taylor was allowed to call. He saw that Taylor had called his grandmother two days before.

"Hey, you're not allowed any more calls this week; you called your grandmother two days ago. According to this list, she's the only person you are authorized to call."

"Yes, but I want to call my sister," Taylor replied.

"I don't see any sister listed on this list."

"That must be because she's my half-sister. You must have seen her. She's the dark-haired girl who often comes along with my grandmother to visit me."

"Yeah, I've seen her. She's the pretty one; but she's not on this list."

"They probably don't consider a half-sister a close enough relative, but it's real important that I call her. Two days ago, when I had my grandmother on the phone, she told me that my sister would receive an important award today from the medical school she's attending."

"She's going to medical school?"

"Yeah, she got all the brains I didn't get. I really would like to call her to congratulate her. This award is a very big honor, and I really should call her to let her know how thrilled I am she's getting this award. It's really a pretty big deal. And you know how much time she takes out of her studies to come see me. The least I can do is give her a call."

"Guess it wouldn't do any harm to let you make the call; here, give me the number so I can dial it for you. Go into booth three, and I'll connect you when the call is connected."

Before the guard could change his mind, Taylor handed him Maria's cell phone number. She had given him that number so she could be reached in case he was notified that something happened to his grandma.

The call really shook Maria. She anxiously asked, "Taylor, what's wrong, what happened?"

"Don't worry, there's nothing wrong. Grandma is fine, and I'm okay too. I'm calling because I need your help for someone else." Because the time allowed for a personal call was rather limited, Taylor quickly related, in a rapid monologue, what Carlos had told him. He didn't know who might be monitoring his call, so he was careful not to mention Carlos by name.

"Oh, that poor man! I can't even imagine the agony of having to stand by helplessly while knowing that your son is about to commit a serious crime."

Taylor could sense that the story was upsetting Maria, but he quickly continued. "I want you to try and contact the high school coach this kid is living with. He coaches at Montgomery High in Wilkesville. That's in this state, quite near to here. When you contact the coach, explain that it's vital he gets hold of the kid as soon as possible, and talks some sense into his head. I think he'll have enough influence over the boy to stop him from doing anything foolish. I also want you to ask him to come, together with the kid, here to the penitentiary, so his father and I can try to determine how true the story is that the kid told the father. It's possible we're dealing with a jealous young man competing with a bunch of strange men for his mother's affection. But I don't want to take a chance on that. I would rather overreact than take a chance on the kid actually shooting someone. If what he said is true, he might be able to give us some more information, which could help us persuade the police to reopen the investigation. In that event, we will also need the coach as our local contact with the police."

"I'll start calling information immediately to get the telephone number of the school. I'll also see if the school has a website listing the faculty members. Oh, Taylor, I pray the kid hasn't done anything yet."

"So do I, Maria, so do I. If he has actually shot someone, we could be in trouble for not reporting his purchase of a weapon. We can't deny having knowledge of that; the warden knows about it, and this conversation is probably being taped. What worries me even more is that if he has already gone after his mother's boyfriend, we, based on our knowledge, would have to finger him as the gunman."

Maria interrupted him. "I'm going to stay optimistic. Tell the father not to worry; I'll find the coach before the boy does anything crazy." Before he hung up, Taylor explained to Maria how to get a message to him so she could notify him as soon as she had spoken to the coach.

Chapter 33

The next morning, as soon as Taylor entered the exercise yard, Carlos came up to him to ask if he had any news. "Nothing yet, but I did make contact with someone on the outside. They're trying to contact your son's coach. Try to stay cool until we hear some more. I expect we'll get more information by tonight. In the meantime, why don't you tell me more about your son and daughter, so I can try to get a better understanding as to what's going on."

"The boy, Victor, is my son, but the girl, Gabrielle, is not my daughter. At least I don't think she is."

"Explain a little further."

"Okay, but if I tell you the whole grimy story, you probably won't want anything to do with me anymore."

"Look, I promised to help, so try me."

"I'm not proud of this, but here it goes. Victor's mother and I lived together for about four years. During that time Victor was born. We were never married, but all went well until the local carpet mill went out of business, and I lost my job maintaining the big looms. The carpet mill had been the major employer in the area, and jobs dried up quickly. With me being out of work, money was tight. Helga, that is Victor's mother's name, started to nag me about the fact that she could no longer buy the stylish clothes and expensive makeup she used to spend a lot of our money on. After several months, I noticed she was once again dressed in brand-new stylish outfits, and wearing her favorite makeup. When I questioned her about this, she become very angry and shouted that if I couldn't provide the money for the things she wanted, she knew how to get what she wanted. It didn't take long after that for me to find out she was putting out for money. I was deeply ashamed. You're a guy; I'm sure you can understand that if your woman was fucking other men for the money you couldn't give her, you could no longer face your friends or anyone else who knows you. So, I packed up and left town. I bummed around for a while. Eventually, I found a good-paying warehouse job here in this state.

"As time went by, I worried more and more about my son, and finally I decided to go back and see how he was doing. To my relief I found out my son was doing very well. She had taken excellent care of him, and I was surprised Helga was happy to see me. She invited me to stay for a few days so I could get reacquainted with my son. After the second day she told me she was tired of being a prostitute, and asked if we could get back together again. I told her I would have to think about it. I stayed for a week, and had a great time playing with my son. Helga and I got along better than ever. By that time my vacation time was up and I had to return to my job. Before I left, I asked Helga to come live with me. She was delighted, and looked forward to moving to a town where no one would know about her past. We agreed she and Victor would join me as soon as I could find a place suitable for the three of us to live. I had been quite frugal during the time I lived alone, so I was able to give Helga a substantial amount of money to tide her over until such time that she could join me. It took a while, but I found a nice house with a huge backyard, and I could easily afford the rent. I called Helga and told her all about the wonderful house I had found, and asked her to come as soon as possible. But she never came. It seems one of her more frequent clients made her an offer she couldn't refuse. He ditched his wife and she moved in with him. Me and my women; it seems like I never learn! After Helga shit on me for the second time, I hooked up with several other women, but each of them left me for another man. No, I have to correct that—one actually left me for another woman."

"The last woman I took up with, the one who got me into all this trouble, was named Bubbles. Her real name was Sonya, but she was a real bone-head. No matter what happened, she remained happy and bubbly at all times, so everybody called her Bubbles. Bubbles was a barmaid at a downtown honky-tonk. I used to hang out at that bar and I enjoyed her company. She was not beautiful or anything like that, but she managed to make the most of what she had. I was physically attracted to her, and she managed to turn me on by leaning all over me while I was sitting at the bar. Eventually I started dating her on a steady basis, and this led to me asking her to move in with me, which she did."

"Bubbles had the habit of flirting, in a light-hearted way, with all the men in the bar. It was perfectly innocent. Nobody took it seriously except for one guy, who developed a crush on her. He started hitting on her, and when his advances became too bothersome, she told him to lay off. She made it clear that she was not interested in him. Instead of leaving her alone, he started stalking her. It became so bad that I started picking her up from work so we could drive home together. The guy started following us to our house and parking his car in front of our driveway. I must have chased him away at least half a dozen times."

"Did you call the cops?" Taylor asked.

"Unfortunately, no. We thought he would get bored following Bubbles, and start paying attention to some other girl. He was not bad-looking, and some of the other girls at the club would have been more than willing to date him. Anyway, to continue, one night I went to the club to pick up Bubbles, but I was much too early. So I parked myself at the bar, waiting for her to finish her shift.

"I was bored, and had a few drinks too many. When I looked around the room, I saw what looked like this stalker guy accosting Bubbles. I went over to them and I got into an argument with him. He took a swing at me and I pushed back. He fell backwards over a table and knocked most of the glasses to the floor. The bouncer came over and escorted me back to my seat at the bar. I assumed the stalker had been thrown out because I no longer saw him in the bar. I looked around, but didn't see Bubbles anywhere. I got up to try and find her, but she was nowhere to be seen. I finally found the two of them outside in the parking lot. The stalker had Bubbles pushed backwards across the front fender of his car. Her short barmaid shirt was pulled up to her waist. He was bent over her and his pants were down around his ankles. I was looking right at his naked butt. I was sure Bubbles was being raped, so I pulled out my knife and raced towards them. Without stopping, I plunged my knife into his back, right between the shoulder blades. The rest is history."

"When the cops arrived, I was sitting on the ground next to his bleeding body. I still had the bloody knife in my hand. My lawyer said I didn't have a chance in hell to be found not guilty, and that I would have a good chance to wind up with a death sentence. So I pleaded guilty and got life in prison."

"Couldn't Bubbles testify on your behalf, and explain that she was being raped by the man you killed?"

"I told you about me and my women, and that I never learned. Bubbles was glad to testify about the stalking, but her story about the rape was quite different from mine. As she told it, this guy approached her in the bar that night, and when I thought he was accosting her, she claims he was making her the following proposition. She said he told her he would stop following her around if she agreed to let him fuck her just once. In her own happy way she believed him, and she thought this would solve her problem. So she agreed to follow him outside and get the deal over with quickly in the parking lot."

Taylor could hardly believe what he'd just heard, but that was not important. His only concern was Victor. "Carlos, does Victor know all this?"

"Hell, no!"

"What about Gabrielle and Helga, what do they know?"

"All any of them know is that I'm in jail because I stabbed a man to death during a bar room fight."

"That's good, let's keep it that way. I don't want any mention of what you just told me when Victor and his coach come to see us."

"Victor and the coach are coming here?"

"Hold on, not so fast! As I told you, I asked some-one on the outside to try and contact the coach, and have him speak to Victor. I have requested that the coach be asked to come here with Victor to talk to us. Presuming, of course, that we were lucky enough to reach the coach in time to persuade Victor not to take the law into his own hands."

That night, while he was still cleaning up in the kitchen, Taylor received a message from Maria which read, "Everything under control, the coach is terrific. He'll make arrangements for requested trip as soon as possible."

Chapter 34

T he next morning, Pete, the guard, came to take Taylor from his cell to the exercise yard to coach the inmates in football. That, in addition to his kitchen duties, had become Taylor's daily routine. To his surprise, Pete took him down the main corridor, which lead to the administrative offices. They should have gone through the double security doors, which would take them to the exercise yard in back of the main cell block.

"Hey, Pete, wake up! Remember, we're going to the exercise yard."

"No, not today. The warden wants to see you."

"Oh, shit. Someone told him about that message I received last night?"

"Any communication from the outside comes through the warden's office, and has to be approved by him or his deputy before it can be passed on to an inmate."

"I thought trustees would be exempt from that rule."

"You wish! You guys get a lot of privileges around here. More than in the federal penitentiary I used to work in. But you can't freely communicate with the outside."

"So, the warden knows I made a call the other night?"

"Hey, what am I, your information desk or something? We're going to see the warden; ask him yourself."

"Okay already, don't get all riled up. All I did was ask you a simple question."

When they got to the warden's office, they were shown right in. The warden was waiting for them, and he didn't waste any time on greetings.

"Looks like you were successful, Taylor. The coach and Carlos' boy will be here the day after tomorrow." Taylor looked at the warden in disbelief. "Don't stare at me like you lost your last penny. Of course I knew all about what was going on. You didn't really think you could keep me from finding out that it was Carlos who told you about his son, did you?"

"I was only trying to protect the boy, sir," Taylor stammered.

"I know, and I respect that. But it's my job to know everything that goes on in here. It wasn't very difficult for me to find out who asked you for help. All I had to do was ask Pete and Doug which prisoner you had been talking to just before you approached them and said you had an emergency and had to see me. Pete had a lot of trouble the day before trying to calm down Carlos. He was totally out of control and kept on yelling and screaming he had to get out.

When Pete saw you talking at length with Carlos, and you weren't paying attention to the men playing football, he was sure it had to do with Carlos' behavior the previous day. That's why he agreed to bring you to my office."

"If you found out so quickly that it was Carlos who told me about his son, why didn't you question him about his son so you could contact the police, like you told me you wanted to?"

"That's pretty simple, isn't it? You know as well as I do that Carlos would refuse to give me any information about his son out of fear of getting the kid in trouble with the police. We knew the kid visited him a few days before, but the name and address he registered under turned out to be that of his mother. No, I decided to let you go ahead and do it your way. I was convinced you would contact your grandmother and ask her to help in this matter. From my experience so far, that lady would have enough connections to get hold of the coach and get Carlos' problem resolved in a hurry. If she can reach all the way into this jail and have my superiors order me to keep you out of harm's way, keeping some confused kid from shooting his mother's boyfriend should be simple for her."

"What exactly do you mean, sir?" Taylor seemed troubled by what the warden had just said. "Did she call you about me?"

"No, no she didn't. Forget what I just said. What I meant to say is that I'm impressed by what that lady seems able to get done, and I thought that it would be a good idea for you to call her. Not knowing you had just spoken to her, I ordered the guard on duty at the telephones to expedite your call, and make sure he taped your conversation. When he saw in the log you had used your quota of calls to her for the week, he could hardly call me for permission to let you make the call anyway. That would have been too obvious, and he was happy you handed him an easy solution by giving him that story about your so-called sister. My guards are well-informed, and he knew very well what you told him wasn't true, but he knew I wanted you to make a call. He assumed you called that gal to ask her to call your grandmother. You're a bright fellow, Taylor, but you didn't realize the call you made to your friend's cell phone was not a collect call, as we require. The guard placed a regular call, and when she answered, he just connected you through like he usually does after the person being called accepts the charges."

"I suspected my conversation might be taped, but I didn't think you would find out about it so soon," Taylor said.

"I listened to the tape less than half an hour after you were returned to your cell, but I didn't call you in here today to explain all my actions. I called you to tell you that Carlos' son, with his coach, will be here the day after tomorrow. I will make arrangements for you and Carlos to meet with them in one of our rooms reserved for consultation with counsel. You can inform Carlos of this, but you must also tell him, whether he agrees or not, I will be present at the meeting. I want to be fully informed as to what happened to the gun the kid purchased."

Chapter 35

Victor, his coach, and the warden were already seated in one of the small conference rooms when Pete brought Taylor in. "Are they getting Carlos?" the warden asked Pete.

"Yes, sir, they'll be here any minute." Moments later Carlos arrived, accompanied by two guards. Taylor was surprised the warden allowed Carlos, who was not wearing either handcuffs or foot shackles, to freely go over to his son and give him a big hug. Victor seemed to be embarrassed by Carlos' emotional hug and pulled away.

"Pete can handle this by himself," the warden said to the two guards who'd brought Carlos in, and he dismissed them. Carlos was allowed to take a seat next to his son. Taylor had been placed on the opposite side of the conference table next to the coach.

"Carlos, this is Coach O'Neil, the gentleman in whose house your son has been living for the past two years."

The coach reached over the table to shake Carlos' hand. "I'm pleased to finally meet you, Mr. Ortega. Victor often speaks about you."

"Everybody just calls me Carlos. Please, no Mr. Ortega. Yeah, Victor told me he was living at your house. I owe you big for letting him stay with your family."

"I'll be glad to call you Carlos, but then you have to call me Jamal. You really don't owe us a thing. My wife and I love having Victor live with us. He's a fine young man, and a pleasure to have around the house. He's best friends with my son, Jason, and I think Jason has come to think of him as his brother."

The warden continued with his introductions. "Coach, the young man sitting next to you is Taylor Marx. He was instrumental in bringing you here. He enjoys trustee privileges, and was in a better position than Carlos to bring Victor's problem to your attention. Speaking of Victor's problem, I must start our discussion by asking what happened to the gun Victor supposedly purchased." The warden looked directly at Victor, but Victor evaded his look and looked down at his hands.

The coach quickly jumped in. "Maybe I should explain our gun policy at the school. That will clear up the matter for you. Whenever I, or any faculty member at our school, confiscates any type of firearm or unauthorized knife, we hand it over to the police. We have an agreement with the local precinct captain. We can do this 'no questions asked.' The police leave it to our discretion if any further action should be taken. The last time I confiscated a gun, I determined that no further action was necessary."

A slight trace of a smile came across the warden's face and he said, "I understand. Victor, you told your dad that your mother had some serious problems, and we're here at the request of your dad to see if we can help. I guess Coach has made it clear to you that you should not, and cannot, try to handle the situation by yourself."

Still looking down at his hands, Victor, in a soft voice, answered, "Yes, sir, he did."

The warden turned to Taylor. "Taylor, you requested that Coach and Victor come here as soon as possible. What exactly do you have in mind that could help Victor's mother?"

Taylor turned to Victor. "Victor, I want you to once more go over what you told your father, and, I assume also, to Coach. Only this time, go into as much detail as possible. I know you went to the police and they didn't do anything, but if you can give us some more details, maybe we can discover something that would make the police willing to reinvestigate."

Victor seemed very uncomfortable, and he continued to stare down at his hands. Carlos reached over and put his arm around his son's shoulder.

"I know you're scared to talk because I told them about the gun. You have to understand, I had to. You would have screwed up your whole life. Don't you see? You would have been like me. Do you want to spend the rest of your life in a place like this?"

Victor sat up in his chair and looked directly at Coach O'Neil as he spoke. "Yeah, I know. Coach explained all that." The coach nodded to confirm that he did, and that seemed to be a signal for Victor to start talking.

"About two years ago I moved out of my mom's house because we fought constantly about all the different men who came to stay with us. I did go back often to see how she was doing, and to check on my little sister, Gabrielle. Recently I noticed that my mom had a lot of bruises on her arms, and I asked her about it. She became very defensive, and told me it was nothing. She said she had been careless and bumped into things. When I asked my little sister, she told me our mom once again had a new boyfriend, but the man was not very nice to her. Gabrielle couldn't understand why mom didn't kick him out of the house.

"The next time I visited, Mom had a blue circle under her left eye, and her nose was swollen. Gabrielle told me Mom and her new boyfriend fought a lot and she, Gabrielle, was afraid of the man. That's when I went to the police and reported that this man was probably hitting my mother. As you know, the police did nothing about it.

"A week or so later, I went to her house again, but Mom wouldn't let me in. She told me I'd better mind my own business, and warned me that her boyfriend had threatened to kill me if I went to the police again. I tried to speak to Gabrielle, but Mom wouldn't let me. A few days later I came up here to visit my dad. Basically, I came to say good-bye. You already know why I was not expecting to see him again."

"When Gabrielle told you she was afraid of this man, did she tell you why?" Taylor asked.

"She told me a lot of nasty-looking people came to the house to see him. One time, when she saw him receive some money from one of those persons, he threatened to beat her up if she ever told anyone."

"Did you tell the police about this?" the warden asked.

"No, sir, I didn't."

"But you did tell your father you were not sure as to what was happening to your sister. Was that because of this man threatening to beat her up?" Taylor asked.

"Yes, and because Mom wouldn't let me talk to her the last time I went to the house." Taylor had the feeling there might be more, and he pressed Victor for more information, but Victor couldn't add anything else that might be significant.

The warden looked at Taylor. "Looks like we don't have much to go on."

Taylor agreed, but he had an idea. "If Victor's mom refuses to press charges, we can't get him for abuse, but there is a slim chance we could get him for selling drugs."

The coach caught on right away. "Yes; strangers coming to the house, and the exchange of money, indicate the man is probably dealing in narcotics. I suggest I have a talk with the captain at our local precinct, and see if we can't get the narcotics squad to stake out that house for a while."

Chapter 36

G abrielle Ortega cringed as she heard the footsteps approach her bedroom door. She pulled the bedcovers tightly over her head, hoping against hope that tonight it would not happen again. She had tried to lock her door, but he had broken the lock the first time he forced his way into her bedroom. The door swung open, and her whole body trembled as he stumbled towards her bed. When he ripped the covers out of her hands, she quickly curled up in the fetal position with her back towards him.

"Don't, please, don't!" she cried, as she fought to protect herself by rolling into a tight ball.

"Shut up, you bitch; you know you like it. Roll over before I take my knife and mess up that pretty face of yours."

She knew he was much too strong to fight off, but she tried protecting herself by tightly holding onto her knees, and tightening the ball she had rolled herself into. No matter how fiercely she held on, it didn't help. He grabbed her shoulder and rolled her over. Next he pried loose her hands and pushed her legs down. Holding her legs down with his body, he pushed her head into the pillows with one hand while ripping off her nightgown with the other. "Damn you, if you don't stop fighting I'll kill you."

She wanted to scream, but he had his mouth firmly over hers. Through her tightly closed lips she could taste the foul combination of alcohol and tobacco. She felt her panties being torn off and was overcome with fear knowing what would come next. The pain seared through her entire body as he forced himself into her. She held her breath, praying to God that it would be over soon. Finally he ejaculated, and she knew it was over. As soon as he stumbled out of the room, she ran for the bathroom and jumped into the bathtub. She let it fill with water as hot as she could possibly stand and lay there for a long time. As she had done before, she blessed the school nurse who had started giving her contraceptive pills when she turned thirteen.

Gabrielle knew she had to do something to stop the attacks by her mother's boyfriend, but she couldn't tell anyone about it. He had made it clear that if she reported him he would kill both her and her mother. She was aware her mother knew what was going on but would do nothing about it. Gabrielle had long known that her mother was totally dependent on her boyfriend to supply her with the drugs she craved. Besides telling her he would kill both Gabrielle and her son if she went to the police, he also withheld drugs when she would not obey him.

The members of the Narcotics Division, who had kept the house under surveillance for several days, had no idea what crime was being committed right under their nose. They did, however, pick up a suspected drug user just after she had left the house. It didn't take much to get the woman to admit she had gone to the house to purchase crack cocaine, and that she had done this at least half a dozen times in the last month. Based on that information, they decided to raid the house. A warrant was quickly sworn out, and two days later, just after ten at night, the narcotics squad raided the house. After they burst through the front door, they quickly searched the entire house, and were stunned by what they encountered in one of the upstairs bedrooms.

When they pushed open the door to Gabrielle's bedroom, her mother's boyfriend was still on top of her. Six foot six Agent Ward sprang into action and grabbed the rapist around the neck, dragging him half-naked down the stairs and into the assault van parked outside. On his way down the stairs Agent Ward instructed a female colleague to go to the small bedroom upstairs and tend to Gabrielle.

The newspapers and the TV news made quite a thing of what happened during a routine drug bust. Because of her age, Gabrielle's name was kept out of the news, and it was lucky for Victor and his sister that their mother still had her maiden name. No one ever mentioned the name Ortega. Gabrielle was placed in foster care and received extensive counseling, but it was left to Coach O'Neil and his wife to take care of Victor's emotional problems. Realizing the effect all this must be having on Carlos, the coach took the time to visit the prison to assure Carlos that

Victor would be okay, and he would see to it that Victor stuck to his plans to enter college upon graduating from high school.

Chapter 37

He knew the visitor waiting for him was John Phillips, but Taylor didn't recognize him when he saw him. Gone was the wavy brown hair. All that was left was a narrow ring along the sides of his head. John had put on quite a lot of weight, and looked older than his age. However, the deep, smoky voice remained unchanged. "Hello, Taylor. You look remarkably well considering the circumstances."

"Hi, John; or do I still call you Mr. Phillips?" Taylor said, as he took his place on the stool behind the glass panel.

John smiled. "John will do fine," he said.

"Grandma tells me you've been working hard on my appeal; do you really think I have a chance at a new trial?"

John had been told by Clair that Taylor had grown into a big, powerful man, but he was still surprised by Taylor's appearance. There was little resemblance to the scared young kid he remembered.

"Boy, you don't waste any time putting me on the spot, do you?" John laughed. "What happened to that scared youngster I last saw back home in Pentonville?"

"Not so young anymore, but believe me, I'm just as scared about my future, maybe even more so."

"You can never predict these things, but I believe we have a reasonable chance. We'll have to persuade the court that there were enough errors made in your original trial to warrant setting it aside and granting you a new trial."

"You know, John, when they convicted me, I was angry and frustrated that nobody would believe me. I was less concerned about the prospect of spending the rest of my life in jail than I was about the idea people could actually believe I had raped and killed that girl. But now I know I have something to live for—Maria and Grandma—and now I desperately want to get out of here. I hate being locked up in here, but I do feel good about having people on my side who believe in me."

"I have assembled what I believe to be the best team available to help me prepare your case. But these things take time; you must be patient."

"Was it you who had me moved and assigned to kitchen duty?"

"No, that was Dennis Anderson. Dennis is the senior partner of the law firm of Anderson, Parker, and Rodriquez. They are the top law firm in the county where you were convicted. I hired them to help review all the facts surrounding your case, and look into Lou McGregor's performance as your defense lawyer."

"I don't think Lou ever believed a word I told him. I think he was convinced from the start that I was guilty."

"From what I read so far, I tend to agree with you. But regardless of his personal feelings, he was required to defend you to the best of his ability. The record seems to indicate that he didn't."

"Have you met him?"

"No, but either Dennis or his partner Sam Rodriquez has already interviewed him."

"Did they like him?"

"I don't know, but I have to assume that he didn't like them. The man is retired, and I'm certain he didn't appreciate people coming to see him and checking if he did his job adequately in defending you."

Taylor was interested in hearing how the whole process surrounding his appeal would be put into play, and what the court would be looking for in order to set his conviction aside. Lawyers, unlike other visitors, were not limited to the amount of time they could spend with their clients, and John took Taylor step by step through the appeal process he and his defense team would follow.

After a while, the conversation drifted to more personal things. Taylor asked about his dog Ginger, whom he had given to John's six-year-old son Jake when he'd left for Florida.

"Jake and Ginger bonded amazingly fast. From the moment you dropped her off, Ginger seemed to sense that Jake was her new 'guy' and the two were inseparable from then on. We had a hard time persuading Jake that Ginger couldn't go to school with him. One summer, he even refused to go to camp because Ginger couldn't come along. When Ginger started losing her eyesight, Jake insisted there was nothing wrong with her and that she could see quite well. As time went on, Ginger became completely blind, and almost deaf as well. Jake refused to have us put her down. He tenderly nursed that dog, and she didn't seem to suffer from her dual handicap. Ginger was quite content as long as she could lie close enough to Jake to feel his presence. She finally died at the ripe old age of fifteen, with Jake clutching her in his arms. It took months for Jake to get over the loss of Ginger. To this day he refuses to have another dog. I'm not ashamed to tell you, I still get teary-eyed when I think of that kid holding his dog while she slowly fell asleep for the final time. He rocked her ever so gently, murmuring, 'Ginger, don't go, please don't go so soon.'" John took a deep breath and looked at Taylor, who was having a little difficulty too.

Before John left, he told Taylor that Dennis Anderson would come to talk to him. "Make sure you tell him everything you can remember that happened on the night before they arrested you; don't leave anything out. He'll also want to know all about the trial, and everything Lou McGregor and you discussed. He will be especially interested in how Lou prepared you before you took the stand to testify on your own behalf."

Chapter 38

Dennis Anderson looked more like a movie star than a defense lawyer. He was a tall man with a slim build. His wavy, blond hair was carefully styled to fall half-way over his ears. The most striking features were his baby-blue eyes set in an almost-too-perfect face. He was clearly not a man's man. Taylor could easily imagine women swooning over him, but hopefully this man would never have to spend time locked up in a men's prison.

Dennis had the reputation of being a great trial lawyer, and Taylor soon realized why. During what seemed like a nice, casual conversation, Dennis carefully drew out bits of information which Taylor had long forgotten, or thought to be unimportant to his case.

He must be murder on cross examination, Taylor thought. The more Taylor got to know Dennis, the more he realized that this man, with his soft-spoken voice and gentle appearance, was tough as nails, and all business when called upon to defend a client. All he cared about were the facts. He had no patience for emotions, and he was not interested in Taylor's theories about what happened during the trial. His piercing mind just sought out the facts. When Dennis was finished with his questioning and was about to leave, Taylor said he thought the DA was a close friend of the mayor's, and that was why they needed a speedy conviction.

Dennis looked at him with those baby-blue eyes and bluntly said, "The judges will not give a damn about what you think. All they'll be interested in are the facts. If we are granted a new trial, and I put you on the stand, all I'll want from you are the facts. Nobody cares what you think happened." Taylor was glad to have Dennis on his side. He would have been terrified to have to face this man during cross examination. He understood why John had selected him.

Chapter 39

It was not the only topic they discussed, but the appeal was certainly the main part of their conversation whenever Clair and Maria came to visit Taylor. The excitement mounted when the brief was finally submitted to the court. It seemed like ages before the court's decision finally came down. The three of them had high hopes, and they were stunned when told the appeal had been denied. The next time she came to visit, Maria couldn't stop crying.

It was Clair who finally had to rally the troops. "Look, you two," she said. "I want you both to pull yourself together. This was merely the first round. John told you that this would not be easy. It's going to be a long process, but eventually we will succeed." Clair spoke with such conviction that it was hard not to believe in what she said.

Clair's confidence was shared by Daniel Harris, the DNA expert John had hired. He flew in to explain to Taylor that he would try to get DNA samples from the semen the coroner had probably found on the victim's body. Once he had these samples, he would ask Taylor to have his DNA analyzed. He intended to show that the samples didn't match, and that the

DNA had to belong to a person, or even persons, other than Taylor.

Sam Rodriquez, Dennis Anderson's law partner, tried to get the coroner's office to supply a sample of the semen so it could be tested by the lab recommended by Daniel Harris. When the coroner's office refused to cooperate, he secured a subpoena to force them to comply with his request. This resulted in a drawn-out struggle. Finally the coroner's office admitted that during the autopsy, semen samples had been found, but they had either been misplaced or accidentally destroyed. In any case, they were not available for testing. Undaunted by this setback, Sam petitioned the court to have the body exhumed. The court held that because the case was closed, and the defendant had been found guilty and his appeal was denied, the semen was no longer needed as evidence. Sam persisted, and tried to get the victim's family to agree to have the body exhumed.

He tried to contact Mayor Frank Morgan, Kitty's father, but Frank Morgan refused to see Sam, or even take his telephone calls. Sam kept on trying, and, because Frank Morgan was still the mayor, he found a way to approach him. An associate attorney in the law office of Anderson, Parker, and Rodriquez had handled a case for the city, and knew the mayor quite well. This associate persuaded Frank to meet with Sam, just to hear what he had to say.

Sam went to see the mayor in his office in city hall. Frank Morgan greeted him in a hostile manner, and Sam feared his effort to persuade this man to have Kitty's body exhumed would be in vain.

"Mayor Morgan, I understand that you would not like to see the body of your daughter disturbed, but if there is a chance, no matter how small, that we convicted the wrong man, wouldn't you want us to search for the real killer?"

"Don't you worry, we got the right guy," was Frank's curt response. "That monster killed my daughter! You should be ashamed of yourself! I can't believe you're trying to get him freed!"

Sam didn't give up that easy. "If his DNA matches that of the DNA found on your daughter's body, you'll have the absolute assurance they caught the right man. Isn't that worth it?"

"To hell with you fancy lawyers and your DNA testing! To me that's just another way for you screaming liberals to get those bastards out of jail. They should have put that murderer to death. It was a mistake to only give him a life sentence. If the jury had done their job properly, you wouldn't be bothering me now about digging up my poor child's body. Now get the hell out of my office! I have heard enough." Sam knew he had reached a dead end.

Chapter 40

Once again, Taylor fell into deep despair. He was sure a DNA test had been his last chance to prove his innocence. Even John Phillips thought they had reached the end of the road. When everyone was ready to give up, it was the analytical Dennis Anderson who came up with their next line of attack. He told John Phillips he was going to find the man named Jim, the one who had told Taylor about Kitty's alleged drug habit.

"I want to get hold of that fellow, and see if he can give us any more clues as to who Kitty was with the night of the murder."

Finding Jim proved to be no easy task. He had been convicted of dealing in drugs, but by supplying the names of his sources he had managed to get a very light sentence, and he was out on parole. Ordinarily this would not have been a problem, and his whereabouts would have been known. But Jim skipped town and disappeared without a trace.

John Phillips hired Roberts and Associates, a detective agency, to help find Jim. The only clue they could give the agency was that Jim had no other vocation than drug dealer. Sooner or later he would wind up back in that business in order to support himself. Roberts and Associates started digging around the murky world of small-time dealers, but they had to admit that it was hard to scour the entire country looking for a small-time crook.

Dennis Anderson had a better idea. Based on the information that Jim had ratted on his suppliers, he contacted the prosecutor who had negotiated Jim's plea bargain. He found out who these suppliers were, and when they had been convicted. He went to see them in jail. As Dennis expected, these men were furious that Jim turned them in. They happily promised to have their contacts on the outside cooperate with Roberts and Associates in their efforts to find Jim. Dennis knew that once Jim had been found, no one could vouch for his safety, even if he was returned to jail quickly on his parole violation. Dennis didn't think that was his responsibly. He was hired to work on Taylor's case, and if that involved putting Jim in harm's way, so be it.

It took four months, but Jim was found. He was put into protective custody in a local police station in Michigan before being transported back to Texas to face sentencing for his parole violation. Dennis immediately traveled to Michigan to question Jim. He wanted the names of the persons Kitty had been getting her drugs from after Jim cut her off.

"She only dealt with two people: Jessica Moore and Alberto Perez," Jim told him. Jim wanted to know if, in exchange for this information, Dennis would help him fight extradition back to Texas.

Coldly Dennis replied, "Don't worry about it. Either way, you're probably a dead man. You won't last a month in jail."

Now the targets of their search had switched, and Roberts and Associates had to try to find either Jessica Moore or Alberto Perez. Dennis urged them to give priority to finding Perez, but it worked out differently. They struck pay dirt almost immediately; Jessica Moore had been arrested and jailed in Oklahoma.

Dennis wasted no time going to Oklahoma to speak to her. Jessica turned out to be very tight lipped. She claimed not to know who Kitty was, and never to have dealt drugs in Clear Valley. Dennis managed to get her to open up by promising to hire a local attorney to represent her. Jessica didn't admit to selling drugs to Kitty, but stated that she knew her. She confirmed that Kitty was a heavy user. She also volunteered that she had often seen the girl in the company of Alberto Perez during the week before she got herself killed. Dennis asked her to describe this Alberto fellow. He was not surprised to get the following description:

"He's between thirty and thirty-five years old, fairly tall, about six foot five I would say, and he is pretty muscular."

Before he rushed back to his office to work full-time on this new information, Dennis made good on his promise, and hired a local attorney to represent Jessica.

Sam Rodriquez wanted to go straight back to the judge and ask that, based on this new information, the judge would allow an inspection of the victim's body. Denis was opposed to that. He felt the information supplied by Jessica would not be sufficient to have the judge change his ruling. Dennis wanted more corroborating witnesses. He asked Roger Hicks, the investigator from Roberts and Associates assigned to Taylor's case, to go to Clear Valley, and find some more witnesses who had seen Perez in town around the time of the murder.

"If people knew that a man who also matched Maureen's description of the murderer had been hanging around with Kitty, why did they not speak up during the investigation?" Sam asked.

Dennis had thought about that and he explained, "Until the trial, the public didn't have any knowledge of Maureen's description of the man she saw running away. A description of the man was never circulated around town. It was lousy police work; they concentrated their entire investigation on Taylor. By the time Taylor was put on trial, they had the entire town convinced that he did it. No one even considered the possibility of another suspect."

It didn't take Roger Hicks long to find several people who knew Alberto Perez. The most detailed information came from the lady who ran the boarding house where Perez had been staying. She told him Perez had been living in her boarding house for about two years. He left town frequently, often staying away for long periods at a time. When Roger pushed her to remember when she had last seen him, she remembered he had left around the time of the murder, and never returned. She had not thought much of it; he always paid his rent three months ahead, and her boarders frequently left without notice. In addition to the landlady, Roger found two old classmates of Kitty who admitted occasionally buying drugs from Perez. They volunteered that it was Kitty who had introduced them to Perez.

When Roger Hicks reported back to the law firm, Sam Rodriquez was dispatched to Clear Valley to depose the three witnesses. Armed with their sworn depositions, and the evidence Jessica had supplied, Sam once again requested permission from the judge to exhume the body. This time it was granted.

Even though no one doubted the outcome, everybody celebrated when the DNA samples clearly showed that the semen found on the body was not Taylor's. This should have been enough to have the district attorney admit that they had convicted the wrong man. But instead of helping to get Taylor released, the DA took the position that even if Taylor's DNA was not found on the girl, that would not prove he didn't have sex with her and kill her. He even ventured the possibility that Kitty had sex with another man just before she met up with Taylor, and that Taylor later raped her while wearing a condom. Dennis attacked the ridiculous idea that a rapist would wear a condom, but the DA would not budge.

Dennis called a strategy meeting in his office to plan their next course of action. John Phillips, Roger Hicks, and Sam Rodriquez attended. They all agreed that Alberto Perez had to be found. In order to help

Roger search the country, they requested two more investigators from the agency. John Phillips approved the additional budget, and Dennis gave them specific instructions before they set out on their search for Perez.

When told about the new plan to find Perez, Taylor had his doubts they would succeed in finding him. If investigators working for his family couldn't find him in all those years, how did they presume to find *this* man?

Despite all the disappointments, Taylor's life in jail had become a lot more bearable. As a trustee he was allowed to be in the visitor's room to receive his visitors. He was now able to hug his grandma and kiss and hold Maria. The first time had been somewhat awkward, but they had been hoping for that moment for a long time, and soon it felt perfectly natural. One time, after the visitors had left and the inmates were being returned to their cells, a guard asked Taylor, "Do you want me to arrange conjugal visits for you and your gal?"

"That won't be necessary," Taylor replied curtly.

As Taylor had feared, it proved to be extremely difficult to find Perez, but Dennis directed the investigators as if he was conducting a military operation. Step by step, they tracked him down, and finally they found him in California. He had been arrested trying to smuggle drugs from Mexico into the United States. He was still awaiting trial when Roger, the detective, caught up with him. Dennis flew out to California to question Perez, but got nothing useful out of him.

Before Dennis left he instructed Roger to get a DNA sample from Perez.

Roger spent a lot of time visiting the local bars and restaurants. There he befriended one of the prison guards. He persuaded this man to help him get a DNA sample from Perez. "Isn't that illegal?" the guard wanted to know.

"Not as far as I know," Roger replied. "It may be considered somewhat unethical, because you won't be helping free this man. This is about another case."

Within a few days the guard supplied two cigarette butts and a plastic beaker, which he thought might have some traces of DNA of Perez on them. Daniel Harris had the items tested, and the DNA samples were a perfect match with the DNA found previously on Kitty's body.

"Now that we have the right man, how do we get Taylor out of jail?" Sam asked.

"I'll get the bastard to confess." Dennis sounded very sure of himself.

"Sure you will. You'll just ask him if he killed that girl and he'll say, 'Sure, Dennis, I did it. What else do you what to know?' You must be dreaming. That man is never going to implicate himself. Why should he?"

Dennis was sure he could get a confession, and once again he traveled to California to question Perez. Perez was as hostile as ever. "Why should I talk to you, Mr. Lawyer man? I have absolutely nothing to do with you. You get your fairy self out of here; I don't have to talk with you."

"Oh yes, you do. I have solid evidence you murdered that girl back in Clear Valley, and calling me names is not going to help you."

"You can't prove nothing!"

"Maybe not, but we found your semen on her body."

"Who the hell told you that was my semen?"

"Your DNA matched the samples found on the body."

"You're talking crazy. You don't have my DNA."

"Sorry, Alberto, but we do. We got it right off the cigarette butts and the beaker that were taken from your cell."

"Look here, I gave you nothing, and if you stole those things from me, you can't use them against me. You think I'm stupid enough not to know that?"

"Actually, I think you are very smart, and that is why you will want to tell me what happened between you and that girl. A guy like you can get all the pussy you want, right?"

"Oh, now you want to start dirty talk?"

"Not really, but I do think you're the type of guy who does not have to rape girls in order to have sex with them."

"You're damn right I don't."

"And you're not stupid enough to kill a client of yours who helps bring you customers. So, what the hell happened that night? How did she die?" Perez stared at him, and, for a moment, Dennis thought he was about to get hit.

Instead Perez asked, "How'd you figure it out?"

"I'm guessing you didn't kill her on purpose, but only you can tell me exactly what happened. Maybe if you tell me how she died, I can keep you from hanging for murder."

"If I tell you, will you help me?"

"I can't promise that. It depends on what you tell me. Either way, it has to be the truth. If you bullshit me, I'll make sure they throw the book at you, and that's a promise."

Perez started talking. In exchange for drugs, Kitty and he often had sex. On the night she died, Kitty had approached him for more drugs, but, as usual, she had no money. He took her to an abandoned warehouse and they had sex, right there on the bare floor. After he had given Kitty some crack cocaine, she wanted to play the choking game.

"You know, the thing they call the blackout game, or pass out game. She called it space monkey. I took off my belt and slipped it around her neck, and pulled it tight. I intended to let it loose just before she passed out, but something went wrong. She stopped breathing, and I couldn't revive her. She was dead. I panicked. I couldn't call an ambulance; they would know I had given her drugs. So I decided to dump her body in a place where they might think some passing truck driver had killed her. The next day I left town."

Dennis felt a surge of excitement knowing he had finally gotten what he needed to free Taylor. Outwardly he stayed perfectly calm. He proceeded to arrange for Perez to repeat his story in the form of a sworn statement. He promised Perez that someone from his office would come to see him to help with the drug smuggling charges against him, and also with the trial he could expect to face in Clear Valley.

On his return to his office, Dennis was treated like a conquering hero. There was a huge bouquet of flowers from Clair and Maria. John Phillips called to congratulate him, and even Peter Roberts, the president of Roberts and Associates, sent an e-mail singing his praise. To celebrate, Sam Rodriquez arranged a small dinner party for the three law partners. Sam and Jeff Parker brought their wives, and Dennis, who was single, came alone.

Sam was reminiscing about their past successes in some very difficult cases when he turned to Dennis. "Tell me, how were you so sure that Perez didn't rape the girl?"

Dennis laughed. "That was pretty simple. Jim told us."

"Jim told us?" Sam looked quizzical.

"Don't you remember? He told Taylor that the Morgan girl would exchange sex for drugs. Once we found out Perez was her dealer, we knew she willingly slept with him every time she needed a fix and had no money to pay for it. Why would he rape her? He already had complete control over her. As for the killing, you don't kill the goose that lays the golden egg. She brought him clients and put out for him. What more could he want?"

During the following week, Sam received a call from Frank Morgan.

"I owe you an apology," Frank said. "I acted rather stupidly."

"No you didn't," Sam responded. "You acted like a grieving father."

"My wife Nancy and I never even suspected that our Kitty was doing drugs. I know that doesn't say much for us as parents, but she even managed to hide it from her twin sister. After Kitty failed a grade and her sister moved on, those two had totally different groups of friends. Looking back, we probably paid more attention to Julie, her twin. Julie was the popular one; a bright girl, very popular at school, and always involved in lots of extra-curricular activities. Kitty, on the other hand, had few friends and mostly kept to herself. For the rest of our lives we'll have to live with the fact that we failed her."

Chapter 41

The press corps had been waiting for more than an hour in front of the main gate of the state penitentiary when Taylor finally appeared. Clair and Maria were on either side of him, holding tightly onto his arms.

They hurried to the waiting car, but were stopped on the way by the reporters shouting out their questions. "Taylor, how does it feel to finally be a free man again?"

"Did you ever give up hope?"

"Are you angry about the years spent in jail?"

Clair wanted to pull him along, but Taylor stopped to answer their questions. "Yes, I was frustrated and angry when no one would listen to me, but I'm one of the lucky ones. I'm blessed in having an incredible grandmother who believed in me and never gave up. I owe my freedom to her perseverance, and that of a very special young lady. I'm also grateful for having a brilliant group of lawyers who knew how to get at the truth. Without people like that fighting for me, I would still be in there."

As Taylor was about to duck into the backseat of the Lincoln Town Car, a photographer snapped one more picture and asked, "Is that beauty your gal?"

Taylor smiled as he slid in next to Maria; he leaned out of the open window and replied, "She sure is, and she stuck by me all the way."

News of Taylor's pending release had been picked up by the national press. A story about someone who has been wrongly convicted always draws public interest, and Taylor's case was no different. Clair was asked for interviews, but she refused to speak to the press. Dennis Anderson was more cooperative, and he was interviewed several times on television. Once out of prison, Taylor had several requests to appear on the nighttime talk shows. Clair was opposed; she was adamant that he refuse all interviews and not speak publicly about his case.

"All they're after is sensation, and you do not want the story about your statutory rape conviction all over the front pages, do you? It would be embarrassing for Maria!"

It was Clair's wish that Taylor would return to Pentonville and pick up the life which had been denied him many years before. She dreamed of his learning all about the factory, and someday taking her place as chairman. She realized his total lack of education would be a problem.

"Why don't you start by getting a GED, and we'll see from there," she suggested.

At first Taylor resisted. He was fearful of being placed in the same position his father had been. The factory, now called Van Beuren Manufacturing, was a thriving business, and he had visions of it once again failing, this time on his watch. But Clair insisted, and soon Taylor was put to work as sort of a super management trainee.

Sol Cohen, general manager of the factory, received the assignment from Clair to train Taylor. Sol had been with Clair from day one. She had recruited him to help her get the factory started, and, ever since, he had been in charge of daily operations. It didn't take long for Taylor to realize that Sol didn't particularly care for him. Knowing the great regard Clair had for Sol, he decided to keep this to himself, and deal with it the best he could.

He enrolled in a GED program and started getting himself reestablished in the community. Most of the kids he had gone to high school with had long since left town. At the time they graduated there had been little opportunity for employment in Pentonville, and they had gone to other places that offered better opportunities.

One of the few people from his past who was still around was his high school football coach. He ran into Coach Sam one day while picking up his dry cleaning. Coach Sam recognized him immediately, and invited him to come to the high school to see the new athletic fields, which had recently been built. Taylor was glad to meet up with someone from his past, and the two of them met later that week in the coach's office. It didn't take long before they started reminiscing about the time Taylor quarterbacked the team.

"Those were the days," Coach sighed. "I sure wish I had a team like that now." The coach went on to explain that for the past two seasons, his teams had gotten trounced by the competition. If he couldn't bring some improvement to the team's performance during the upcoming season, his job might possibly be on the line.

"Remember, football is big in this town. They expect a winning season."

Taylor told the coach about the football games Pat and he had organized in jail, and how they had managed to get a pretty good performance out of a group of guys who had not played football before. While listing to Taylor, Coach came up with the idea that maybe Taylor could help him improve the team's performance. As the star quarterback of the team that won a state championship, Taylor would have a positive influence on the team. Coach was sure that the players would respond well to him.

Taylor's presence during practice did have a positive effect. He spent a lot of time helping the players improve their mechanics. The fact that he always had encouraging words for each individual team member, including the bench players, helped boost morale. A "we can do it" attitude replaced the lackadaisical approach that had been prevalent among the players.

People in town hardly recognized the "fighting machine" that showed up on opening day of the new season. The success of the team was in no small part due to the return at quarterback of Ramon Martinez. Martinez had been kicked off the team in his sophomore year, when Coach Sam discovered he was using drugs.

Taylor heard about the Martinez kid while he was inspecting a new shipment in the factory's warehouse and Ramon's father approached him. "Excuse me, Mister Marx, can I speak to you for a second?" Estaban Martinez, Ramon's father, was rather timid, and it had taken some time before he tried to speak to Taylor about his son. His stooped-over posture and wiry frame belied the fact that he was actually quite tall.

"Come on, drop the Mister Marx," Taylor said, smiling. He stopped what he was doing and turned to talk to the man. "Just call me Taylor, okay?"

"Sure, sorry about that, Mister Taylor."

"I'd feel better if you just called me by my first name," Taylor responded. "If I'm correct, you're Estaban Martinez, right?" Estaban was impressed that Taylor knew who he was.

"What's up, Estaban? What you got for me?"

"It's about my boy, Ramon. He's a good kid, but he started hanging around with a pretty rough crowd after the coach threw him off the football team because he thought that Ramon was using drugs. Ramon keeps telling me that it is not true, and that the coach listens to too many stories. But I don't know for sure. Taylor, I trust Ramon, but he's changed. His grades have dropped, and he is constantly arguing with his mom. He never did that before."

"Sounds like Coach Sam might have been right," Taylor said.

"I'm afraid of that, and I was hoping you could help us."

"Be glad to, but how could I help?" Taylor asked.

Ramon should go back to football. He is a strong kid, and I tell you, he has a great throwing arm. He reminds me of you when I watched you win all those games for our high school."

"You remember me playing football?" Taylor was surprised.

"Of course, you were a big star. Everybody knew it was because of you we won the state championship. I was working for your dad at the time; he was so proud of you." Taylor had not realized that Martinez had worked for Van Beuren Textile before it failed, and he was pleased that Estaban spoke about his father without any trace of resentment.

"What is it you'd like me to do?"

"Just talk to him. If he's using drugs, maybe you could get him to stop."

"I'm not so sure he'd listen to me, but I'll be happy to talk to him."

The next day after football practice, Taylor brought up the subject with Coach Sam. "Coach, I'm not trying to interfere with the way you run this team, but would you mind if I try talking some sense into Ramon's head?"

"I would love to have him back. He's a gifted athlete, but I cannot tolerate the use of drugs among my players."

"I fully agree with you, but the least I can do for his dad is to talk to the kid. Can you ask him to meet with me?"

Chapter 42

Coach Sam arranged for Ramon to come out to the practice field, and Taylor started talking football with the kid. After practice was over, Taylor challenged Ramon to a little contest to see who could throw the most accurate pass. Ramon's dad hadn't exaggerated; the kid had a great arm.

"That's pretty good," Taylor complimented him. "Do you do any strength training to develop your arm further?" Ramon admitted that he did nothing in the way of exercise. Taylor asked if he would like to come to his health club to see if he liked weight lifting.

A few days later, the two of them went to Taylor's health club, where Taylor got Ramon a visitor's pass. Under Taylor's guidance, Ramon tried a few bench presses, and Taylor was impressed with the kid's strength.

"If you can press that much weight without practice, it's a shame not to develop your strength any further. From what I've seen, if you would give it half a try, my school football records would not be safe."

"Coach won't let me play," Ramon responded angrily.

"Nonsense. Coach would love to have you play, but you fucked up by using drugs. He had no choice. As long as you use that shit, he cannot have you on the team."

"You people always think you're better than us and that you can tell us what we can do." Ramon went storming out of the weight room.

"Wait!" Taylor shouted after him. When he caught up to Ramon, he said, "You're wrong. Is this outburst because you father is Mexican? That is pure bullshit and you know it. You're looking for excuses, but the fact is you use drugs, and it's your own stupid fault you got kicked off the team. It has nothing to do with the fact that your family happened to come from Mexico. I think you're a better athlete than anyone Coach Sam presently has on the team. You have a God-given talent, and I think it's a sin to throw that away." Ramon stopped and looked at Taylor.

Taylor continued, "Ramon, tell me straight, man to man—do you or don't you use drugs?"

Ramon looked down and almost inaudibly said, "You don't have to ask, you already know I do."

Taylor decided to push further. "I would love to help you regain the quarterback position, but you would have to lay off the drugs."

"Drugs aren't as bad as all of you think. All the others do it, and they don't have bad effects from it."

"Ramon, you know that's not true. It's only a small group in your school who use drugs, and you just don't want to see the effect that it has."

"If I stop, they'll think I'm just a jerk, kowtowing to you guys."

"If you stop, you'll regain the respect of a much larger group of kids; the kids you used to hang with, your old buddies, who are still playing football."

"Coach won't have me."

"You're wrong. I already told you he'd love to have you back, but, so far, you have made it impossible. Tell you what; lay off the drugs. Don't do it for Coach Sam, and certainly not for me, but do it for your dad. I had a dad once who was proud to see me play; I tell you, that's a good feeling. A lot better than any drug can give you. Ramon, you have that chance. Give your dad the respect he deserves; make him proud of you, like mine was of me."

Without getting any promises from Ramon, Taylor talked Coach Sam into letting him back on the team. Once back in practice, Ramon developed quickly. When the season opened, he was the starting quarterback. The issue of drugs was never discussed again. Taylor did notice that Ramon was again hanging around with the guys from the team, and that he had little to no contact with the group his father had warned him about.

They were halfway through the season and still unbeaten when Coach Sam asked Taylor to meet him in his office. "Taylor, you've done an incredible job with this team. The players worship the ground you walk on, and that makes it even harder for me to tell you what I have to."

"Come on, Coach, I'm just the assistant; you're the man."

"Taylor, this is a serious matter, and there is absolutely nothing I can do about it."

Taylor frowned. What was Coach Sam talking about? The season was going great; they couldn't still be after the coach's job?

"Taylor, the school board wants me to let you go. They don't want you to be my assistant coach any longer."

"Shit, I'm not taking any money out of their budget, so what's the beef?"

"No, no, it has nothing to do with money; they all know you don't get paid. It's about your previous conviction for statutory rape."

Taylor just about fell off his chair. "Who the hell brought that up, and what does that have to do with me helping you with the team?" he demanded.

"Mrs. Dubinsky checked the list of registered sex offenders in this area and discovered your name on it. She has persuaded the school board that it is not allowed to have you in a position that requires such close association with minors. Taylor, believe me, I tried reasoning with those people, but it was of no use. They say I have no say in such matters, and Mrs. Dubinsky holds firm that it's a matter of law."

Taylor had been aware his statuary rape conviction could someday come back to haunt him. When he was told the law required him to register, he went to see the local district attorney to ask what consequences that would have for him.

The DA told him it would be a handicap in matters of employment, but that many employers realized persons registered as sex offenders were often guilty of nothing more than sleeping with their high school sweetheart. "The law is pretty inflexible on that point. If a young couple decides to have sex, and he is over eighteen but she is not, it does not matter if it was consensual or not. If her parents decide to turn him in, the boy can be convicted, and will appear on the sex offenders list for the rest of his life."

"What if the girl is over eighteen and the boy isn't?"

"Come on, you know the answer. His father congratulates him."

Coach Sam told the team that Taylor had to stop coaching them because he was very busy at the factory, and all his spare time was taken up studying for his GED. Unfortunately, Mrs. Dubinsky had a big mouth, and one of the team members had already heard the true story from his mother.

Taylor withdrew from all social contact, and took to spending very long hours at the factory. What Taylor didn't know was that the members of the football team told Coach Sam that unless Taylor was brought back, they would start boycotting the team. Coach Sam approached the principal and asked if he could ask the school board to reconsider. The principal first investigated what exactly the law said about this. He found out that Mrs. Dubinsky had been wrong. Nothing prevented Coach Sam from asking Taylor to assist him on a voluntary basis. The school board might not be able to hire a person convicted of a sex offense, but in this case, they were not hiring Taylor for an official function. He was just a volunteer, and he was working under Coach Sam's supervision. As such, he didn't have unsupervised contact with minors.

The principal asked the school board to reconsider. He also brought up the matter of the boycott. In pleading his case, he found some strong allies among the members of the board. Two of the members had sons who played football for Coach Sam. The board voted overwhelmingly in favor of asking Taylor to continue assisting Coach Sam.

Taylor had trouble going back to coaching the team. He felt that by his past behavior he had let down Coach Sam, and that he couldn't be a role model for the players on the football team.

When Coach Sam called him, he declined to come back, saying, "What kind of a role model can I be for those youngsters when they know about my past?" Coach Sam insisted he was wrong, and that the kids had great respect for him, but Taylor would not give in.

Coach Sam realized that he must bring Taylor back, not only for the sake of the football team, but also for Taylor himself. He couldn't let Taylor hide for the rest of his life for something that was, in the coach's mind, no more than a stupid mistake.

Coach Sam enlisted the help of Ramon's father. He knew Ramon had broken down crying when he heard that Taylor would no longer be able to assist Coach Sam. The coach was aware that Ramon and his father had been very active in getting public support for Taylor.

This time, Estaban didn't wait for Taylor to come to the warehouse before approaching him. He marched right into the executive office suite and demanded to talk to Taylor. When questioned why, he responded, "Don't worry, he'll see me. Just tell him Estaban is here and wants to speak to him."

When Taylor came out to see him, Estaban wasted no time with polite greetings. "What's the matter with you? Those kids need you. They believe in you. You can't let them down." When Taylor protested that with his criminal record it was better for him not to go back to coaching, Estaban would have none of it.

"I think you're being selfish. Those kids worship the ground you walk on. Like it or not, you are their inspiration to achieve better. You motivate them to improve themselves. You have shown them how to believe in themselves, and now you want to run out on them? Taylor, they think that everything that happened to you in the past was a mistake. Both your convictions, and the fact you never got to play for Pentonville in your senior year, they think that was all one big mistake. And damn it, so do I. Taylor, you saved my boy. I can never repay you for that, but I need one more favor. Please don't throw it all away. I'm not embarrassed; I'll kneel in front of you, right here in the office, where everybody can see. Taylor, please go back."

Taylor put his arm around Estaban's shoulder and pulled him close. "I think you have just paid me back in spades," he whispered. "Tell Ramon I'll see him tomorrow."

Chapter 43

S ol Cohen asked Taylor to come to his office. "Did you authorize the purchase of the cloth for the Premium Warehouse rush order from a new vendor?"

"Yes, I did. Is that a problem?"

"They didn't follow our instructions, and sent it floor-loaded. The truck is sitting in one of our loading docks, and our warehouse guys are refusing to unload it. Why did you go to a new vendor?"

"Premium Warehouse placed that order unexpectedly. We had no idea those bathing suits were selling so well. It's a seasonal item, so they gave us a very short delivery time, and our sales people promised to have it done in ten days. Huntington Mills, our regular supplier for that type of cloth, was out of stock. Their earliest delivery time was three weeks. I contacted this new supplier, and they could deliver immediately."

"Well, it's here, but our guys won't unload the truck; the shipment is not on pallets. We still can't produce that order on time if we can't get that stuff unloaded. You'd better go and tell the chief on loading dock fifty to get his crew to unload that truck, or Premium Warehouse will be hopping mad. You know how unreasonable that young buyer of theirs is. He never bothers to check his stock position, and when he gets in trouble, he tries to put the blame on his suppliers."

Loading dock fifty was way over at the very end of the new warehouse that had recently been completed. Most of the warehouse crew working in that section were new. Taylor left the administration building by the back door, hopped on one of the yellow electric carts, and rode over to dock fifty. He went up to the dock chief and asked why the shipment had not been unloaded. The dock chief explained he had called the supplier and explained that all of Van Beuren's purchase orders specified that merchandise had to be loaded on pallets or delivery would be refused. He had asked the supplier to contact the trucking company and ask them to send over some part-time workers to unload the truck and put the merchandise on pallets. Because it was late in the day, the trucking company couldn't supply anyone till late the next afternoon. Taylor knew that would be too late.

"Jeff, you know the people in production will panic if they don't get that cloth tonight, or at the latest early in the morning."

"I know, Taylor, but these new guys go strictly by the rules, and they won't unload those heavy cloth bales by hand. We either get that stuff put onto pallets, or we have to refuse the shipment."

Taylor removed his coat and asked one of the hi-lo operators to bring him a stack of pallets. Without saying anything else, he calmly started unloading the truck by himself.

When the dock chief asked if he'd gone mad, he replied, "Don't worry about me. I'll have this baby unloaded by tomorrow morning." By the time he had loaded almost two full pallets, one of the warehouse crew joined him. Then, one by one, the others pitched in, and the truck was unloaded within three hours.

Taylor sat down; he was dirty, sweaty, and totally exhausted. Jeff, the dock chief, came over and sat next to him. He, too, had helped with the unloading. "Thanks, boss. I couldn't have solved this without you. Boy, I sure would have hated having to face Mister Sol if we had screwed up the Premium Warehouse order." As far as Taylor could recall, that was the first time anyone in the factory had addressed him as "boss."

Taylor arrived at the factory the next day to find Sol sitting in his office, waiting for him.

"To what do I owe this honor?" Taylor asked, not without some sarcasm.

"Take it easy. I've come to tell you I heard what you did yesterday, and I'm grateful. You prevented a huge problem with Premium Warehouse. They would be capable of canceling all remaining orders for the rest of the season if we were late on a critical order like this one. They really don't care that the order was placed much too late. I don't think I could have solved the problem myself. You really did a terrific job resolving the situation."

"Funny coming from you; you don't even like me." Taylor had not meant to say that, but it was out before he could help it.

"What makes you say that?" Sol asked.

Now that the truth was out, Taylor continued. "From the beginning you've been sort of hostile to me. You really don't like the fact that I came back to work in this factory."

Sol looked at Taylor for a while and then said, "You're right. At first I resented you, but I've changed my mind."

"How so?"

"Before you were freed, I was almost in complete charge here. Your grandma was the chairperson, but she was devoting much of her time to your cause. Actually, I had been making many of the strategic decisions long before they found you. So, naturally, I assumed that when it came time for your grandma to retire, I would be named chairman. Then you appeared on the scene, and it became very clear she wanted you to eventually succeed her. From those who knew you as a teenager, I heard you were a spoiled brat. Can you blame me for not being too happy about having to groom you to fill a job I had always thought would be mine?"

Taylor thought that over for a moment. "You say you changed your mind about me. When did that happen?"

"I got to know you better, and watched how you treated the people here. You are quite unassuming, and I have never seen you take advantage of the fact that you're Clair's grandson. That took away much of my fear that you would eventually want to push me out and run this company yourself."

"For God's sake, man, why would I push you out? I'm well aware of what you mean to this company, and my grandmother is not blind, either. She knows darn well what you have contributed to the success of this place. You must understand my grandma. Besides really liking you, she has deep respect for your knowledge, and your ability to run a company. When Grandma and you started this factory, you had a pretty good basis to operate on. Fay's brand gave you about ninety million in turnover, but that's nothing compared to the half a billion dollars in sales you project for the coming year. You might not realize it, but she selected you because you had the same background as my father."

Sol looked at him, confused.

"Just compare our last names, and you'll get the gist of what I'm saying," Taylor hinted.

"It didn't hurt any either that you were one of the top students at Wharton's Business School. She might have despised my grandfather for decisions he made later in life, but she admired him for building the company he did. He recruited my dad due to his belief that you folks are inherently better at financial matters. Having no other experience to guide her, she acquired this inverse prejudice from him."

Sol felt he had to correct the false impression Taylor's grandmother might have had that things had come easy to him. "If she only knew how I sweated getting through Wharton. Everybody seemed so much smarter. I had to study twice as hard to keep up."

"Maybe so," Taylor said, "but that's what she believed. We all know those ideas are rubbish, but that was reality to her, and she knew no better."

"I hope the years she's been involved in the business world have taught her that it's only a myth."

"I think it may have," Taylor said. "But that doesn't diminish the fact that she really values your input here in the factory. Believe me; she wants you to run this place as long as possible." Taylor knew quite well that his grandmother still wanted him to succeed her as chairman, but he thought a little white lie at this time wouldn't hurt. Besides, he had no illusions that he, with his limited education, would ever be able to run such a big factory. They both smiled, knowing what Taylor had said was not really the whole truth. So Taylor quickly added, "I, too, hope you'll be willing to manage this place for as long as possible, and allow me to help you in some position; for which I hopefully will become qualified."

"I appreciate what you're saying, but don't underestimate yourself. You have a way of treating people that I really admire."

"What makes you say that?" Taylor asked.

"That situation yesterday was a good example. You never lost your temper, and you never ordered any of the men to do something they didn't want to do, or that you would not be willing to do yourself."

"Yeah, but I have to admit—those bales of cloth were heavier than I expected. I doubt I could have finished the job all by myself," Taylor laughed.

"Probably not," Sol said. "But you certainly made an impression on the people in this company."

Chapter 44

After Taylor had been released from prison and returned to Pentonville, Maria resumed her studies at medical school. During her many visits while Taylor was in the penitentiary, she'd told him all about her years as an undergraduate. After two years in medical school, she had left school for a year to work in Argentina as a lab assistant in a local hospital. She explained her motivation for interrupting her education and going to work in Argentina as her way of giving back for all the benefits life had bestowed on her. It also gave her an opportunity to learn more about the land of her ancestors. Taylor was never told the real reason why Maria left school and went to Argentina.

During her undergraduate years, Maria had been involved in countless extracurricular activities. That, combined with her devotion to her studies, left little time for an active social life. She rarely went out on dates, and Taylor was always on her mind. This made her ill-prepared for all the attention she received from her male classmates when she entered medical school. Once again, she immersed herself in her studies, and tried as best she could to ignore any serious advances from the men around her. She couldn't be described as aloof; she was quite popular, and had many girl-friends. But among the males she was known as the "ice queen."

During her sophomore year, one of Maria's girl-friends, Julie, started dating Ryan Watson, a junior at the medical school. Ryan was known among the women as "The Catch," and he knew it. Ryan's father was the chief surgeon at the hospital that was associated with the medical school. His mother was the only daughter of the late Henry Clemens, the billionaire hotel owner. Ryan lived in his own townhouse, less than five miles from campus, and was often seen tooling around town in his Porsche Carrera. Ryan frequently gave parties in his townhouse, to which he invited most of his friends. Julie, Maria's girlfriend, urged Maria to come along to one of these parties, but Maria always begged off, claiming to have to catch up on her studies.

When classes ended for the year, Ryan invited a group of Julie's classmates to spend the weekend at his parents' beach house on Hilton Head Island. Julie kept pestering Maria to come along. "Come on, Maria, don't be such a deadbeat; it's going to be great fun. No more excuses; you have nothing to study right now. Besides, Ryan made a point of asking me to bring you along."

"I guess I do deserve a break," Maria said, as she finally gave in.

If Julie's classmates had expected a beach house, they must have been surprised when they arrived. Ryan's parents' beach house could better be described as a mansion on the water. On arrival they were greeted by Ryan, who had come a day early. He urged them to quickly change into their bathing suits and join him on the beach, where he had arranged for lunch to be served. Lunch included generous amounts of alcohol, and the drinking continued for most of the afternoon and into the evening. Julie, who shared a bedroom with Maria, was getting pretty high.

After dinner Maria said to her, "Why don't I take you to the room so you can lie down for a while?"

"Not on your life," Julie responded. "I'm having too much fun to quit now." Maria, who was a moderate drinker, felt uneasy as the party got more and more rowdy. Finally, when Julie got a little too wild and literally starting jumping all over Ryan, Maria once more offered, "Come, let me take you to the room so you can freshen up. Your makeup is starting to look a little goofy."

The last remark got Julie to cooperate, and she allowed Maria to gently guide her back to their room. Julie half-stumbled down the long hall, and Maria had to hold on tight to prevent her from falling. Once in the room, Maria told Julie to lie down on the bed for a moment before tending to her makeup. Before long Julie was fast asleep. Maria decided not to rejoin the party, and she walked onto the deck, which was adjacent to their room.

It was a beautiful night. Maria was sitting on the deck, enjoying the beautiful view of the ocean in the moonlight, when she heard a knock on the bedroom door. She tried to just ignore it, but when the knock was repeated with more urgency, she got up to see who it was. She went back into the bedroom and crossed over to the door. When she opened the door she found Ryan standing in the hall.

"How is Julie?" he inquired.

"Sound asleep," Maria told him.

"I was wondering why you two didn't return to the party. You sure she's okay?"

"She's fine," Maria assured him. "She just had a little too much to drink."

"How about you? Why are you still here in the room?"

"I wasn't in the room, I was out on the deck enjoying the beautiful view. It's really beautiful out there."

"Yeah, I love this place. Mind if I join you on the deck?" Maria didn't feel like letting Ryan into the room, but she couldn't think of an excuse to refuse letting him in.

"Sure, come on in," she said.

The two of them went out onto the deck, and sat in the elaborate swing set that faced the ocean.

"You're not much for parties," Ryan said.

"What makes you say that?" Maria asked.

"Well, you never came to any of the parties I gave back at school, and just now you were sitting here by yourself on this deck." Maria didn't have much of an answer, and choose to just remain silent.

"For a while I thought that maybe you were a lesbian, the way you avoided all the guys. But Julie assures me that is not the case."

"Me a lesbian? What gave you that idea? Just because I take my studies seriously and don't party should not lead to all kinds of conclusions."

"Sorry, I meant no offense."

"I'm not the least bit offended; being called a lesbian is no great shakes. It's just that I'm not."

"I'm happy you're not. You're very pretty, and I wouldn't mind going out with you sometime."

"What about Julie?" Maria asked him.

"Julie is a great kid, but our relationship is not such that I can't date other girls." As he said this, Ryan moved closer to Maria. Maria slid further into the corner of the swing set. Ryan followed. Before Maria could get up to go back to the room, Ryan reached over and tried to kiss her.

"No, Ryan, don't do that." She tried to push him away. Ryan persisted. "Ryan, please stop. I really don't want to." His face was within inches of hers, and she could smell the liquor on his breath. Before she could say another word, he pulled her body against his. She tried to pull loose, but he was too strong. She could feel his tongue pushing against her tightly closed teeth. Maria struggled to escape from his grip, but to no avail. He pushed her down into the pillows of the swing set and covered her with his body. Maria was in a complete panic. She tried to scream, but his mouth was tightly over hers; she could taste the alcohol. She could feel his left hand slide slowly down her shoulder and onto her breast. Roughly he ripped her blouse open, and his hand went inside her bra, his fingers toughing her nipples. Maria pounded with both her hands on his back, but it was of no use. Ryan was a big man, and she couldn't budge his two-hundred ninety-pound body. Maria could feel him press his erection into her crotch. She was sure he was about to rape her. Then, suddenly, she saw her chance. Ryan's hand moved from her breast to her waist in an attempt to pull down her shorts. This released the pressure of his body on hers just enough for her to quickly pull up one knee and push it into his groin. Ryan pulled up, and Maria had both hands free.

He screamed, "You know you want it, bitch!" Maria responded by poking her finger in his eye. Ryan cried out as he reached for his eye. Maria quickly rolled from under him and ran for the bedroom door. Once inside, she quickly closed the door and locked it. Next she raced to close and lock the windows. She walked into the bathroom, sat down on the floor, and broke down completely. Tears streamed down her face. She couldn't stop shaking. She finally calmed down enough to go back into the room and try to get ready for bed. Julie was still fast asleep, stretched out, fully dressed across her bed. Maria undressed and got into her bed, but sleep was impossible.

The next morning she told Julie she thought she was getting the flu, and it would be better for her to leave for home as soon as possible. Julie looked at her and said, "I think you're right; you look terrible. Are you well enough to travel?" She assured Julie she was, and left before the others got up for breakfast.

Clair was not expecting her when Maria burst into her house. "Maria, dear, what are you doing here in Pentonville?"

"Grandma, I just had to come see you. Something terrible has happened."

"Oh, no, not your parents or brothers? Maria, tell me quickly what happened," Clair said anxiously.

"No, nothing like that, they're fine. But, Grandma, a man tried to rape me!" Maria burst out in tears.

Clair rushed over to hold Maria. "Oh my God, you poor child! Come here and let me hold you."

With her head buried in Clair's shoulder, Maria told her what had happened at Hilton Head Island. "I should never have gone; I'm so ashamed!" Maria cried.

"You cut that out, right now! There is nothing for you to be one bit ashamed of. That bastard attacked you and you fought him off. I'll call John Phillips right now. We'll file a complaint against that man."

"No, Grandma, please don't do that. I don't want to press charges."

"Why not? What he did is criminal. We have to report him to the police."

"Grandma, you don't understand. They won't believe me. Ryan Watson is a big deal back at school. He can have any girl he wants, and they'd all love to have sex with him."

"That's their problem. But he attacked you, and that should be reported."

"Grandma, listen to me. Nobody will believe my story. He'll claim I'm jealous of Julie, and made up the story because he rejected my advances when he came to check on Julie. She was passed out on her bed. I don't understand why he came after me; he could have had any of those girls staying at the beach house that night. Why couldn't he wait for Julie to sober up? I know she had sex with him any time he wanted."

"He wanted you because he couldn't have you; that's the way those creeps are. The less interest in him you showed, the more desirable you became. But you can't let that spoiled little boy get away with it."

"Grandma, please, his father is the chief surgeon; he is very influential. I know they'll protect him. Julie and the others will surely side with him. They will ostracize me. I won't have a single friend left if I turn him in. Besides, I don't want everybody to know what happened. You are the only one I've told; I won't even tell my parents." Clair didn't fully agree. In her heart, she wanted to see Ryan punished for his actions, but she understood what Maria was saying. In the end, she agreed with Maria that it would be best if she transferred to another medical school.

Maria looked into transferring, but soon learned that she could possibly lose a year, and maybe even her high academic standing. If she had to lose a year anyway, she would rather take a year off and do something completely different. In the meantime, Ryan would have moved on to an internship—hopefully in a distant town—and her classmates would be a year ahead of her. That way, she could continue her studies at the same school without continually being confronted with memories of the incident at the beach house.

Maria had always wanted to learn more about Argentina, the country where both her parents grew up. She contacted her family in Argentina, and they arranged a job for her as an assistant lab technician in a local hospital. Her parents were pleased with the idea that she wanted to learn more about her Argentine heritage, and they didn't mind that she would interrupt her studies.

Her family in Argentina was delighted by her arrival, and her cousins went out of their way to introduce her to all their friends and acquaintances. One of their friends was Justin Simones, the Internet whiz. At the age of thirty he had already amassed a fortune from the five retail websites he owned. Justin's wife had died of cancer soon after their marriage, and he had been a widower for two years.

It didn't take long before Maria's family started playing matchmaker. Justin was not particularly handsome, but he had a great personality. Maria didn't mind having him show her around town. Justin had a Gulfstream corporate jet. Occasionally he would invite Maria along on his business trips to various cities in Argentina and Brazil. With the two pilots and several business associates traveling with them, Maria felt well chaperoned, even by strict South American standards.

Leandro, Maria's uncle, was getting a little pushy. He couldn't understand why Maria kept treating Justin more like a brother than a suitor.

"Maria, I do not understand you. You seem to like him well enough, but you continue to treat him like a friend instead of a boyfriend. Girl, it is clear the man is interested in you! I tell you, any girl in Argentina, I would even say any girl *anywhere*, would give anything to have a man like Justin court her. But you, you just continue to keep him at arm's length. Why?"

"Uncle Leandro, I do like Justin. He is great fun to be with, but I have a boyfriend."

"Come on, I know all about that. I spoke to your father, and he explained all about this Taylor you used to be so in love with. But, Maria, wake up, girl. It has been years since anyone heard from that fellow. If he loved you so much, why has he not contacted you?"

"He has his reasons, and it's really my fault he went away. Did my father explain that we falsely accused him of betraying my parents?"

"Yes, I know the entire story. You knew no better, and it was perfectly logical to suspect him. Maria, my child, life is too short to waste it like this."

"Uncle, I know you mean well, but please don't push me on this subject. I know you don't understand, and I can't explain it, but somewhere deep down I know we'll find him, and he'll come back to me."

In his own gentle way, Justin started pursuing Maria more seriously, and she started to like him more and more. Under the ever-curious eyes of her family, Maria started dating Justin on a steady basis. She had to admit to herself that her belief she would ever see Taylor again was more wishful thinking than reality. Just when she was about to abandon all hope, the seemingly impossible happened.

When she came home from her work at the hospital, Maria received a message that Clair had called from the United States. She immediately called back, and, even though there was only a one-hour time difference, she couldn't reach Clair at home. Urgently, she called Clair's cell phone. "Grandma, you called. What's the matter?"

"Great news, Maria! Sit down, because you are not going to believe this. We have found Taylor!"

"Oh my God! Is he okay?" Maria couldn't control her excitement.

"Yes, he's fine. John Phillips called this morning, and I'm on my way tomorrow to go see him."

"But how is he? Tell me all about it!" In her haste to find out more, Maria stumbled over her words.

"John tells me he's healthy, but there is a problem." Maria could feel her heart sink into her shoes. "Please, no; what is it?"

"Seems for some reason, John has not given me all the details, Taylor is in jail."

"Oh no, Grandma! Is he in big trouble?"

"I really don't know, my child, but don't worry, I'm going to see for myself. No matter what I'll get him out, I promise."

"Grandma, I'm coming home! I want to see him. I have to explain what happened."

"Why don't you wait till I have spoken to him? I'll call you as soon as I know more."

"No,   I'm coming home. I'm making arrangements immediately."

Chapter 45

I t was a festive night in Butlerville. The annual classic car show always drew a big crowd, and tonight was no exception. The large crowd cruised slowly through the downtown streets, admiring the cars lined up on either side of the road. This year the crowd was particularly drawn to the muscle cars. In the weeks prior to the show, Butlerville had advertised that no less than thirty nationally renowned muscle cars would be at the show.

Taylor wanted to go to the show to see if there would be a 1957 Chevrolet Bel Air convertible on exhibit. Maria had come in from medical school to visit for the weekend, and they drove over from Pentonville to see if there would be a car similar to the one so nostalgic to both of them. Arm in arm, they walked up and down the streets, admiring the beautifully restored cars, but mainly searching for a 1957 Chevrolet Bel Air convertible. Unfortunately, no one was showing one, but they did come across a Corvette very similar to the one Taylor had owned.

After they had been looking at cars for more than two and a half hours, they decided to stop for dinner. They selected a small restaurant on the corner of Main Street and Griswold. Over dinner, Taylor brought up a subject that had been bothering him for quite a while.

"You know, Grandma intends for me to eventually take over the management of the factory."

"Of course," Maria said. "Who else would she want to hand it over to?"

"I know that's what she wants, but I'm really not the least bit qualified to run a company of that size. An awful lot of people depend on our company for their livelihood, and I don't have the education or training to run the place successfully."

"You still have some time to learn. She's not retiring anytime soon, is she?"

"I don't know for sure, but I think it won't be too long."

"Well, you're smart, and I'm sure you can learn the ropes quickly. Besides, you'll have Sol Cohen to assist you."

"Sol assist *me*? Don't make me laugh. At the moment I'm barely able to assist *him*! He's the one who should succeed Grandma, not me."

"I don't think she'll go for that. I think it is, and maybe always was, her ambition to hand the factory over to you. And you can do it!" Maria said reassuringly.

Taylor shook his head. "I would never agree to that. Sol more than deserves to succeed her. Heck, he practically runs the place by himself now."

"Okay, then make everybody happy. He becomes president and CEO, but you make Grandma happy and take the title of chairman."

Again Taylor shook his head no. "Even if everybody could agree to that, there still would be a problem."

"And what is that?"

"The truth is, I really don't want to run the factory, not even with Sol in there to do the heavy lifting."

Maria was surprised at his answer. "What makes you say that?"

Taylor reached across the table and put his hand over Maria's. "If I tell you something in strict confidence, do you swear never to tell anyone?"

Maria laughed. "Hey, silly, it's me! Of course you can tell me something in confidence. Remember, we have no secrets from each other. Now, what's bothering you?"

Taylor looked like he was about to start crying. "A while back Sol asked me to take over the supervision of our HR department. He thinks I can handle personnel issues better than he can. He would love for me to be in charge of the entire HR department. I started working with Mark Parker, our HR manager. Once we got into the records of the individual employees, I discovered that Mark systematically refuses to check the papers of applicants. He does a superficial background check. If they don't have a criminal record or have not been fired for misconduct from a previous job, he okays them. He doesn't check at all on workers we get from temp agencies, or independent contractors."

"That's pretty negligent." The good mood Maria had been in was fading rapidly and she asked, "Are you upset because you have to fire Mark?"

Taylor looked at his plate, and slowly rotated his fork between his thumb and his fingers. "Yes, but it's much worse than that. I've already discovered that at least forty of our employees are aliens, without work permits. Maria, you know the problem. They're here illegally."

"Oh my God, you poor thing! It's happening to you again!" This time it was Maria who reached across to grab Taylor's hand. "What can you do?"

"It gets even worse. Two of our independent contractors, one which supplies cleaning services and the other IT workers, have refused to release any records on the people they employ. I suspect that most of the people who work for them are here illegally, and don't have the required work permits."

"Do you think Mark Parker knows all this?" Maria asked.

"He not only knows about this, he's a party to all of it. What I've discovered so far is that the illegals we employ directly actually pay members of our HR staff not to disclose their status. I also have a strong suspicion that the independent contractors have a secret agreement with Mark."

"That means you have to clean out the entire HR department. What will happen to those illegal immigrants if you can no longer employ them? Please don't tell me you have to turn them in to the authorities. Do you?" Maria was frightened at the prospect of Taylor having to decide the fate of the people who were illegally in the country. Flashes of the drama surrounding her parents' illegal status went through her head.

"The whole thing is a horrible mess. And if I had not learned a very hard lesson the last time I ran away, I would run away from this mess as fast as possible." Taylor pushed back in his chair and slowly starting explaining the problems that would arise.

"Obviously, Mark Parker and some other members of our HR department have to be fired. But it doesn't end there. They would probably face criminal charges for employing illegal immigrants, and even more serious charges for taking money to hide the fact. The company could be fined heavily for employing these people. That would mean Sol Cohen's neck would be in a noose. He might have to resign because of this mess. Then who would run the factory? It would be a big mess. The independent contractors would be in trouble, too. And then there's the problem we can identify with the most; what will happen to those folks who are illegally in this country?" Taylor stopped talking and looked at Maria, who looked about as miserable as he did.

"Will you tell all this to Grandma?" she asked.

"No, I can't. She'll feel responsible for not knowing what was going on. Sol's negligence in not double checking will just break her heart."

"Any chance Sol knew all along what was going on and he steered you to HR to get you involved in those practices?"

"I've thought of it, and I pray that it's not the case. I'm just not ready to give up on everybody. I sort of hate myself for having found out about all of this and having to expose it. In a way it's like being a traitor to Grandma. After all she's done for me, as payback, she gets a whistle blower."

"Taylor, you know that's pure nonsense. I have no idea as to what you have to do about all this, but in no way are you untrue to Grandma. In the end, you may save her from much worse things. If you go to the authorities, it might be better for the factory than if they discover it, and they try to implicate her."

"I hear you, but I really don't know what to do."

"I think the best thing would be to go to John Phillips and tell him all you know so far."

"You're right. I should go to him once again, and ask him to help us clean up another Van Beuren mess."

Chapter 46

Taylor looked over at Sol Cohen, who was sitting slumped over in the big leather chair in front of John Phillips' desk. Gone was the self-assured, almost cocky posture. He looked like the shadow of the broadly smiling man who had walked into John's office less than twenty minutes ago.

"I'll have to resign. I'll offer Clair my formal resignation in the morning," Sol said in an uncharacteristically soft voice.

"You'll do no such thing," Taylor said forcefully. "I don't care what that scum did behind your back. You can't watch every damned thing that goes on in a big place like this. Your only fault was that you tried to do too much. In your loyalty to Grandma and the company, you tried to take the whole place on your shoulders. That is just too much for one man!"

"I should have checked more closely on what Mark Parker was doing," Sol murmured.

"Maybe, in retrospect; but you had every right to trust Mark Parker. Sol, for God's sake, the man was your HR manager! For the salary we paid him, it's reasonable to expect he would be above such things. And let's be honest; you're the one who sent me over to HR. I don't know, but maybe deep down, you had a hunch something might be wrong. In any case, if you hadn't sent me over there, I would never have discovered the mess. And please stop that talk about resigning. We have enough problems without you leaving us."

"Taylor is right, Sol. None of us will hold this against you. By having the overall responsibility you were technically responsible for what happened within the HR department; that is true. But for that matter we could say that, as chairman, Clair also shares in the responsibility. Going even further, you could say that I, as corporate counsel and board member, should also share in the responsibility." Sol straightened a little in his chair as John continued. "I agree with Taylor that it was perfectly reasonable for you to rely on Mark Parker to do his work correctly, and not engage in criminal practices for his own benefit."

"But if this affair results in serious financial losses for the company, maybe even threatens its existence, I could never forgive myself for my negligence," Sol said.

"In this case it won't go that far. We'll be the ones who bring it to the attention of the authorities. At no time did management or the owners condone these practices, and they certainly didn't reap any personal benefit from them. At most, the authorities will try to levy some fines for having employed those illegal workers, and even that I'll fight."

"Where do we go from here?" Taylor wanted to know.

"I'm a good friend of our local DA, and we should try to get him to discuss this with the Federal authorities to see what we can work out with them," John said.

"Isn't it kind of risky to walk in and tell them exactly what happened within the company?" Taylor asked.

"I suspect it might be, so I suggest that I arrange for you, Taylor, to have a meeting with our DA. In that meeting, you'll hypothetically discuss a case of illegal immigrants working in a factory without management being aware of it. That way we can see how far he'll go in helping us, before we give him the actual details."

"He's not dumb," Sol said. "He'll know Taylor will be talking about real things that happened in our company."

"Of course he will," John replied. "But it's not unusual to do it this way. He'll understand, and he'll give you a chance to back out in the event he's not willing to help us. I hope we can make some sort of arrangement that falls outside the criminal sphere for all except those actually involved in the illegal transactions."

"Why me? Why do you think I'm the one who should talk to the DA?" Taylor wanted to know.

"Because, if I listened correctly to the two of you, Sol has recently put you in charge of HR," John replied with a grin on his face. He continued in a more serious manner. "I'll have to inform Clair and the other members of the board of directors."

Sol held up his hand as if to signal stop. "No, if you don't mind, I want to do that myself. I would rather have Clair hear this bad news directly from me. No matter what you say about who bears responsibility in this matter—and mind you, I very much appreciate your standpoint—I still feel I have to give Clair the option of keeping me or having me resign."

"Please don't be so noble, Sol. I for one will fight tooth and nail to keep you. The company can't run without you! If it comes to that, I would have to fight Grandma on this issue. But I'm not worried. My grandma is not so stupid as to let you go."

"You know something, Taylor? I'm getting to like you more and more each day. Not only because you flatter the hell out of me at a time when I'm really down and need your encouragement, but for discovering this fraud. The company, and I in particular, owe you a debt that will be hard to repay." While saying that, Sol got up and gave Taylor a huge bear hug.

Taylor turned to John. "I can guess Mark Parker and the rest of those crooks will probably be looking at some jail time, but what about the illegals working for us? What will happen to them?"

"Taylor, as a member of the bar, I cannot give you instructions as to what to do to protect those folks, but I think you can figure it out for yourself." For a moment Taylor looked at John with a questioning look on his face. Then he broke out in a broad smile and said, "Okay, I get it."

Clair took it very hard. Not for a moment did she blame Sol for what was going on in HR, but it was difficult for her to believe that Mark Parker could be so deceitful. She didn't know the others in the HR Department who were involved, nor did she personally know the two subcontractors, but she had always liked Mark.

"Sol, why would he do something like this? He certainly doesn't need the money."

"Clair, if I had any idea he was capable of doing what he did, I would have thrown him out long ago. But he seemed like a great guy—easy to work with, and seemingly always loyal to the company. As for the money, who knows? He has a very decent salary, certainly for this area. Maybe he has gambling debts or worse, maybe it's just greed. I really cannot guess what possessed him to do it. It's a real shame. He's a very bright fellow, and a real expert on all matters pertaining to HR."

The meeting with the DA was set for Monday morning. Taylor arrived early, and was talking to the receptionist when the DA arrived. Taylor knew the DA from the previous time he went to speak to him.

"Hi, Taylor, how have you been?" Douglas Bailey, the DA, was a relatively young man with a full head of prematurely grey hair that made him look very distinguished. "Come into my office and tell me what's on your mind."

It didn't take long before Douglas Bailey said, "Okay, we'll work on this together. Now, give me some more real details. Does John know what you're about to tell me?"

"Yes, sir, he does. He's the one who suggested I talk to you about this, and that's why he arranged for me to see you."

"If John knows what you're about to tell me, that's good enough for me. I'll work on a deal for you. Go ahead; give me some names and their position in your company."

Taylor started his story again, this time telling Douglas Bailey all the details, including the names of those involved.

When Taylor finished, Douglas said, "For someone new to HR, you certainly found out a lot in a relatively short time. Sol Cohen is pretty lucky you're working for him. I know Sol from the Golf Club and like him a lot. Over the years we've played quite a few rounds together. Tell Sol we'll try to work out something to hold the factory harmless, and tell John Phillips I'll need a week or so to contact some of my connections in several federal offices. I'll get back to you with some proposals. In the meantime, please keep everything under wraps. I don't want anyone prematurely tipped off that we're about to launch an investigation."

Douglas Bailey did move swiftly. In less than two weeks, Mark Parker and four members of his HR staff were arrested. Also arrested were several persons working for the two independent contractors. The case against all of them was pretty cut and dry. Thanks to the detailed information they'd received from Taylor, the authorities had all the proof they needed to convict them. Mark Parker received a stiff fine, a five-year jail sentence, and five years' probation. His staff members also received fines, five years' probation, and some community service. They didn't receive any jail time.

The heaviest sentences were given to the executives of the independent contractor companies. Their sentences ranged from five to ten years in jail.

Most of the illegal aliens working for the independent contractors were repatriated to their native country. When the federal agents pulled a surprise raid on Van Beuren Manufacturing, all the illegal aliens had mysteriously disappeared. Rumor had it that days before the federal agents raided the factory, someone tipped them off, and they quickly packed up and left town. By fully cooperating with the authorities, Van Beuren was not fined.

Chapter 47

S ol Cohen asked Taylor to sit in on the job interview with Pamela Nelson, a candidate for the HR
position previously held by Mark Parker.

"You want me to join you for the interview?"
Taylor was a little apprehensive.

"Yes, because you'll be her boss if we hire her."

"You're kidding! I read her resume. The lady has
an MBA, and she has specialized in HR for more than
ten years. You want me to be her boss?"

"Yes. If we hire her, she will report to you. She'll
have all the know-how and be the technician, but you'll
supervise the department. We have learned how vulnerable we are in HR. We cannot afford any more mis-
steps. The lady comes highly recommended, but so did
Mark Parker. I have no reason to think she is not one
hundred percent honest, but Mark Parker has made
me gun shy. You have proven yourself to be a smart
cookie, and I want you to keep an eye on that department. Besides, when you finish getting your GED,
your grandmother and I would like you to continue
your studies to eventually get a degree in HR."

They decided to hire Pamela Nelson as the new
HR manager. She would report to Taylor, who now

carried the title of vice president, directly reporting to Sol. When Taylor discussed hiring Pamela with Clair, he expressed his concern about having a person twenty years older than he, with much more education, reporting to him.

Clair smiled and said, "Deal with it. That's just one of the responsibilities that comes with being part of the Van Beuren family. But don't complain. It has a lot of advantages, too. Here, read this." She handed Taylor an advertisement for a car that had been auctioned off in a nearby town. Not knowing why she gave him the advertisement to read, he asked what her interest was in this car.

"Oh, it just reminds me of when I was a little younger."

Taylor read the advertisement:

1957 Corvette

Venetian Red

Red interior with Beige cove

Beige Soft Top and Red Hardtop

Fuel injection, 383 ci engine

4-speed manual

Single headlights.

"Wow," Taylor said when he finished reading the advertisement. "That sounds like one hell of a beautiful car. Certainly beats that Corvette I owned a while back."

"Yes, it does sound like a really nice car. They tell me it's totally restored, but that everything is authentic. Oh, by the way, I left a jacket in my car. Would you be kind enough to get it for me?"

Taylor went to the garage. When he opened the door he was shocked to see the red Corvette parked next to his grandmother's car. Like a little boy he ran back in the house and screamed, "Grandma, you're crazy! Did you really buy that car?"

"Yes, this grateful old lady bought that car for the man who saved the company."

Chapter 48

After Pamela Nelson was hired, Sol Cohen insisted Taylor move into the office previously occupied by Mark Parker. At first Taylor objected. He felt Pamela, as Mark's replacement, should have that office. but Sol pointed out that Taylor, as the new vice president, should have his office in the executive suite.

Taylor was sitting behind his brand-new glass and aluminum desk reading the morning papers when Pamela came into his office.

"Taylor, can we talk for a moment?"

"Sure, Pam. What's the matter? You look worried."

"I'm having trouble with Mortimer Barrett, my assistant HR manager. He insists we fire Evan Beltran, the cook in the cafeteria."

"You don't agree with him?"

"No, I don't, and he's quite angry about it. That's why I need your help in this."

"Why does he want Beltran fired?"

"It's a long story, but here is what I know. It seems that Mortimer's daughter and Beltran's son have been going steady for quite a while. The Barretts are opposed to this, and have been trying to break up the relationship. Now it seems the girl is pregnant, and the Barretts want her to have an abortion. As I understand it, the boy is opposed to aborting the child, and wants to marry the girl. Evan is backing his son. The whole thing has escalated into what amounts to a war between the families, which has spilled over into the work place. Mortimer is on a mission. He continually confronts Evan in the cafeteria and his loud, derogatory remarks are making everybody else uncomfortable.

"I have spoken to Mortimer about this and told him his behavior cannot be tolerated. But he is so convinced he's right that it's impossible to reason with him. Now he insists that if we fire Evan, the problem will be settled. I suspect he figures Evan will give in and have his son capitulate to the Barretts' demand for an abortion in order to save his father's job."

"Sounds to me like we would be firing the wrong guy."

"If it were only that simple! Mortimer's outrageous behavior has led to a whole lot of people taking sides, and this issue is threatening to become very disruptive within the company. We can't afford to have our employees divide into two camps. Abortion is already a hot-button issue in this area, and it has no business within our factory walls."

"Is this feud between these families based on religious beliefs?"

"I don't know, but my gut feeling tells me it has more to do with the economic and social disparity between the two families."

"Will it help if I try to reason with Mortimer, and try to persuade him to settle this matter in a civilized manner outside the company?"

"He won't listen. I tried to talk to Evan, but that did no good either; he is not the instigator of this fight. What I would like is for you to use your connections at the school, and try to talk to Barrett's daughter. It's important to know how she feels about this situation. She is eighteen, and the final decision on having this baby is up to her. Maybe if we find out what she wants, we'll better understand how to deal with this feud. You could call the guidance counselor or a religious leader to help mediate between the families."

"I agree that we can't let this create a problem within our company, but this is basically a private matter. To what extent do we have a right to interfere?"

"Since Mortimer has brought the problem into the workplace, it has become our business, and quite a few people who work around these two men are looking for us to help solve this problem. I hate to say it, but they're looking to you to step in and restore the peace around here."

"Me? Why?"

"They trust you, and most of them feel the company has to stick up for Evan. In his position he's no match for Mortimer."

It only took one call to the high school football coach for Taylor to arrange a meeting with Jennifer Barrett. They agreed to meet the next evening in the coach's office. The coach asked Ms. Doran, the girls' volleyball coach, to also attend.

Although he didn't participate in any of the school sports, Beltran's son, Mike, and the football coach were good friends. This made it possible, even before the meeting, for the coach to brief Taylor on many of the details of Mike's relationship with Jennifer. Mike was a junior, and a bright kid, but his grades were pretty mediocre because of a demanding after-school job. He was tall and had the graceful movements of a natural athlete. The coach would have loved having Mike on the football team, but Mike chose to work so he could afford a car and help support his family. His father had a steady job as a cook in the Van Beuren cafeteria, but he had a hard time keeping up with the expenses of five growing kids—three boys and two girls. Mike's mother had to quit working because of her crippling arthritis. Taylor was surprised to hear that Jennifer was one year ahead of Mike. She was in her senior year, and an honor student. She was the star of the high school volleyball team.

To everyone's surprise, Jennifer and Mike arrived together. Taylor, the coach, and Ms. Doran were already seated in the office when they walked in. Taylor wasn't sure if they should have Mike take part in this meeting, but he didn't mention it. He had a hard time visualizing Jennifer and Mike as a couple. Jennifer was about the same height as Mike, but she was very slim and her figure, as well as her face, was quite angular. She had a very fair complexion, and her dirty-blond hair was cut into a short bob. She was by no means pretty, but her large blue eyes and confident look signaled that she was not a timid girl.

As the coach had said, Mike had an athletic built, and he was dark and handsome, definitely a hunk.

The coach introduced Taylor to Jennifer and Mike. He told them he had asked Jennifer to come to his office to meet Mr. Marx, who was the VP of the factory where their respective fathers worked. Taylor took it from there. He explained that although he had asked to speak to Jennifer, now that Mike was also present, he would talk to both of them about the arguments between their fathers in the workplace. These arguments were extremely disruptive, and caused concern among the other employees. He added that it was no secret the feud was about Jennifer's pregnancy. It quickly became clear that Jennifer was the spokesperson for the two. She explained that yes, she was pregnant, and this disrupted her father's plans for her future. Her parents had always been extremely proud of her athletic and scholastic achievements, and they were ecstatic when Amherst offered her a volleyball scholarship. Since the baby was due next December, she would not be able to enter college in September, much less accept the scholarship. She was grateful Ms. Doran had gone to bat for her so she could graduate even if she was showing early. Jennifer hated the fact that by now the whole town knew of her pregnancy, and that her father wanted to force her to have an abortion so she could continue her plans to go to college.

"Mind you, I understand where he's coming from. Just when it looked like I was about to fulfill his dreams for my future, I informed him I was pregnant and planned to marry Mike right after my high school graduation."

"*His* dreams for your future?" Ms. Doran interrupted with a smile.

"Okay, I did dream of playing on a university volleyball team. I even talked about playing in the Olympics, and later coaching the volleyball team for a major university. But Coach Doran, you and I discussed that! And I explained that things have changed now."

"Yes, I think I understand how you feel, but why don't you go ahead and explain to Mr. Marx and Coach what made you change your mind."

"It started last summer. Mom, Dad, my younger sister, and I, had dinner in a restaurant to celebrate my mom's birthday. Mike works as a waiter in that restaurant, and he was our server. Mom and Dad kept mentioning what a nice young man he was. I didn't really know Mike, but I had seen him in school. When I mentioned this to my parents, Dad struck up a long conversation with him, and was surprised to learn that he knew Mike's father from work. Later, on the way home, both my parents kept raving about how wonderful Mike was, and how his serving at our table made the evening much more enjoyable. My sister put in her two cents by exclaiming how 'dreamy' he was. I admit, I too thought he was rather nice, but I didn't think much of it until we met again two weeks later.

"My best friend Kathy and I were at the beach when we bumped into Mike. Actually, we didn't really bump into him. It was Mike's day off and he was playing beach volleyball with some friends. Kathy spotted him and thought he looked pretty good in bathing trunks. I told her I had met him two weeks before in the restaurant where he works, and she suggested we go over to watch the game.

One of Mike's friends recognized Kathy and me as members of the school volleyball team and invited us to join the game. During the game, Mike paid a lot of attention to me. After his friends left, he invited Kathy and me to have a Coke in that little restaurant right on the beach. When Kathy said it was time for her to go home, Mike suggested that if I wanted to stay a while longer, he could drive me home. I don't remember what all we talked about, but we lost track of time, and were politely shooed out the door when the restaurant closed. After that we started dating, and by the time school started we were going steady. That's when my parents started objecting.

"Obviously, our relationship got more and more intense, and you know the result. But Mike and I want to be together. We want this baby, and we plan to get married as soon as I graduate. I no longer want to go to college. I just want to stay here and be with Mike. I certainly don't want to give up our baby."

The coach turned to Mike. "You're only a junior. How do you propose to get married and support a family? And how do you feel about Jennifer having this baby?"

"We talked a lot about it. One thing we completely agree on. No way are we going to give up our baby! Jennifer is not too happy that I plan to quit school and go to work full-time, but there's no other way. I have already talked to my boss at the restaurant about it. He has promised to take me on full-time. He says I can make enough so we can rent an apartment in town. He even promised my father a part-time job in the evenings, so I no longer have to contribute at home."

Taylor listened carefully while the youngsters explained their plans. *They're pretty naïve,* he thought, but it was clear that they really loved each other. He turned to Mike. "Do you really think it's a good idea to have a smart girl like Jennifer give up her plans to attend college?" Before Mike could answer, Taylor continued. "And what type of future do you think you can offer Jennifer and the baby if you quit school?"

It was Jennifer who jumped in. "You think I should get rid of the baby, don't you! You agree with my parents and you came here to tell us what to do!"

"No, Jennifer, I didn't come here to tell you what to do. Besides, my opinion is totally irrelevant. I asked to talk to the two of you to help find a solution to a problem which is causing a disturbance in our factory. I would like to mediate between your families, and help find a solution. To be quite frank, this situation is jeopardizing both your fathers' jobs."

Mike looked stunned. "You mean you would fire my dad because of this?"

"The company does not want to fire anyone, but we cannot allow a dispute between your fathers to make everyone else in the workplace uncomfortable.

I'd like to work with the two of you to see if we can come up with a solution that would be good for you and acceptable to both sets of parents."

"We'll try to cooperate, but we're not giving up the baby!" Jennifer said defiantly.

"Jennifer, I'm not the enemy. I can't and won't force a solution on you. I will speak with all concerned and see where we can find some common ground. You'll hear from me after I have spoken to your parents."

Chapter 49

A t the Monday morning staff meeting, two weeks after Taylor had met with Jennifer and Mike, Sol Cohen brought up the subject of the frequent quarrels between Barrett and Beltran.

Sol looked at Pamela Nelson to hear what steps she had taken to resolve the issue, but Pamela quickly deferred to Taylor. "I consulted with Taylor about two weeks ago, and he is looking into the situation."

Clair Van Beuren, who occasionally sat in on these staff meetings, also wanted to hear more about this quarrel among the employees. Clair turned to Taylor and asked for more details. "I'm hearing all sorts of rumors. People in town are saying the company is involved in forcing Barrett's daughter to have an abortion. Taylor, that surely must be a bunch of nonsense!"

"Yes, Grandma, that is pure nonsense. Let me explain what's going on."

Taylor briefly summarized his meeting with Jennifer and Mike in the coach's office. "I came away from the meeting with the feeling these two kids were determined to get married and have the baby. So I started looking for a solution that even the Barretts could agree to."

Sol interrupted by asking Taylor if this was really a company problem.

"Of course it is! Both fathers work for us. It's my understanding that if you work for Van Beuren, and you have a family problem, the company extends a helping hand. You certainly don't get fired so the company can get rid of the problem!" Taylor sounded slightly irritated.

"Touché, I deserved that. Please continue," Sol said, and Taylor noticed a quick smile of approval cross his grandmother's face.

"The first person I contacted was Evan Beltran. He agreed that getting married and becoming a father at such a young age would limit Mike's prospects. At the same time, he assured me that Mike is a level-headed kid, and he would back his son's decision no matter what. He told me he would be happy to work the extra hours at the restaurant in order to give Mike a little more financial flexibility.

"Next I went to see Walt Malloy, the owner of the restaurant, the one who promised Mike a full-time job. The man thinks the world of Mike, and said he would be delighted to give Mike a full-time job. However, he did warn me that there could be a problem. His partner, who was the head chef in the restaurant, wanted to retire, and was looking for someone to buy his share of the restaurant. Walt was worried he couldn't raise the money to buy out his partner, and he had no idea where to find a new head chef. I asked to give me some idea as to how much it would take to buy out his partner, and what type of qualifications a new head chef would need to have. I had an idea, and I asked Pamela to go over Beltran's personnel file with me.

"We have a lot of extra information in his personnel file because we had to make doubly sure, before we hired him, that Beltran was a US citizen. It seems Evan previously owned and operated a little restaurant in Crestwood. About six years ago, his wife became very ill with crippling arthritis. Besides the fact that she could no longer assist him in the restaurant, her medical bills forced Evan into bankruptcy. He lost everything, and considered himself lucky when he landed a job here in our cafeteria. The man is highly over-qualified for the job he does here, but he can't look elsewhere because he needs our medical coverage."

Sol Cohen stopped doodling and looked up. "I think I'm getting the gist of where you're going with this. You think you can solve the problem by buying into that restaurant on Evan's behalf. If you ask me, I don't think that's such a good idea."

By now Clair had also figured out what Taylor was planning to do. "Don't you think you're going a little too far by getting financially involved?"

"You two should talk!" Taylor couldn't help but laugh. "Sol, everyone in town knows that if you plan to raise money for charity, the first person you go to for a hefty personal and company donation is somebody called Sol Cohen. And you, Grandma, there is no reason for you to own a taxi company in the Dominican Republic, except for the fact you took a shine to a young woman you met on your very first visit there."

"Okay, so you know all about my little secret," Clair laughingly admitted, but then she continued on a more serious note. "Please explain to me how you envision helping Evan move to the restaurant if you tell us he can't leave here because he needs our medical coverage?"

"That's an excellent question, and, because of his wife's illness, I didn't know how to solve that problem. Luckily, Pamela is an expert on those things. Pam, why don't you explain how Evan can get medical coverage for his family?"

"As I told Taylor, it's not all that difficult. When we first hired Evan six years ago, his wife's preexisting condition prevented him from enrolling her in the company's medical plan. Luckily, the Health Insurance Portability and Accountability Act provides protection for people who have preexisting conditions, and the insurance company could only exclude her for twelve months. Mark Parker, my predecessor, persuaded Sol to have the company pay for Evan's wife's medical expenses for the first year. Now, the same HIPAA stipulation provides that the period for which coverage can be denied for a preexisting condition is eliminated if you were covered by a previous health insurance plan; which qualifies under HIPAA as 'creditable coverage.'

Obviously our plan qualifies! I spoke to our insurance agent, and he said it wouldn't be a problem to get an affordable health insurance plan for the restaurant. Under the umbrella of the local Chamber of Commerce he can arrange a group health insurance plan that would cover all employees of the restaurant and their dependents."

Clair was impressed that Taylor had carefully checked into this problem, and she nodded approvingly at him. "Go on; what do you plan to do next?"

"Now comes the really difficult part. I still have to speak to Jennifer's father." Taylor promised to have more information at the next staff meeting.

That same afternoon, Taylor asked Mortimer Barrett to come to his office. The conversation started badly.

"I know what you want to see me about, and I don't think it's any of your business!"

"Hi, Mort, nice to see you," Taylor replied, and he continued. "You made it my business when you went to Pamela and demanded that she fire Evan Beltran. It's also my business when you choose to make a scene in our cafeteria. Mort, why don't you sit down, take a deep breath, and listen to what I have to say? You may be surprised."

Mort sat down and looked defiantly at Taylor. "Jennifer has told me she thinks you agree with her, and that you will help her and that boy. You people just don't understand. She's throwing away her future! She's very bright. She's a great athlete! She can achieve so much! Now she wants to throw it all away. And for what? To marry that punk who'll divorce her and leave her single with a child and no future?"

"Mort, I completely understand that you're upset, and, if I believed the scenario you just sketched was true, I too would be upset. But I think the situation doesn't have to end like that. Mort, you're intelligent, and I have come to know you as a reasonable man. Even though you might not believe it at this moment, I do respect you. I would like you to return the compliment and listen to me! Your daughter is determined to have that baby, and you can't change her mind. She is eighteen, so you can't stop her. If you persist in your opposition to her having the baby, you'll drive a deep wedge between you and your daughter. I'm sure you'll regret that forever."

Barrett sat silently for a moment. He clenched his fists, and it was obvious he had trouble holding back the tears as he muttered, "Now my wife is also siding with Jennifer. She's desperately afraid that if we don't give in, Jennifer will leave home and turn her back on us." His voice broke, and Taylor could barely hear what he said. "I don't want to lose my daughter. Taylor, she's such a great person. It might sound strange, but I adore that kid." He stopped and took a deep breath. "Tell me why this had to happen? We had such high hopes for her, and it's so hard to give up our dreams for her future."

"Mort, your daughter fell in love. That's what happened! Jennifer fell in love with a great guy who really loves her! You might not be ready to admit it, but you really like Mike. Who wouldn't? From what I've heard and seen so far, any father would be happy to have a kid like that as a son-in-law. And just because she loves Mike, there's no reason for you to believe she has stopped loving you and your wife. There certainly is no reason to condemn those kids to a dismal future!"

Barrett sat up and seemed to be listing. "What are you trying to tell me?"

Taylor continued. "They're both bright kids, and they can go pretty far, if you're willing to support them. If you're willing, I'm also ready to help. Before you start protesting, please hear me out."

Barrett looked doubtful. "What possible good can come from this? Don't go putting the blame for this mess on my failure to go along with their plans!"

"Nobody is blaming you. Your reaction is very normal. But let me lay out the following plan for their future. First of all, both Jennifer and Mike finish high school. Jennifer lives at home until after she has the baby. When the baby is old enough to go into day care, Jennifer will start a full-time job here in the factory. As you know, we have excellent day care facilities. Mike continues his after-school job at the restaurant until after graduation, at which time he'll start working there on a full-time basis. *When* the two get married is completely up to them, but when Jennifer starts working full-time they should be able to rent an apartment in town.

"Before you agree to all this, they both have to promise you to finish their education. They do this by enrolling in one of the accredited universities which offers classes via the computer. Considering their intelligence and the ambition they have shown so far, you can set the bar pretty high for the level of education you want them to reach. It stands to reason that both fathers will have to contribute to their education. I'm not being presumptuous when I say you're in a position to do so, and I'll make it possible for Evan to do the same."

"Come on; how in the world do you expect Evan to help financially? As deputy HR manager I know exactly what he earns, and that is not very much!"

"You're right. I haven't spoken to Evan yet, but we can solve that situation."

"You're going to give him a big raise, and thereby upset the entire pay scale we worked out with the union?"

"No way. Pamela and you have enough of a problem keeping things together in the cafeteria, and complying with local food regulations. Besides, it wouldn't be good for all of you to be working for the same company; you never know what the future may bring. For Evan there is a much better opportunity. As you yourself have mentioned to me, Evan is way over-qualified for the job we have for him in our cafeteria. As luck would have it, he can buy a half-interest in the restaurant where Mike works, and become the head chef there."

"I'm sure he's capable of being head chef, but how on Earth could he come up with the money to buy into the place?"

"That's pretty simple; I'll lend it to him."

"You'll what!?"

"I'll lend it to him on soft terms so he and Mike can pay me back over time. Don't forget, this opportunity will make a sea change financially for both of them."

Barrett looked at Taylor as if he was sizing him up. "Why are you doing all this? I don't want to be rude, but why are you getting so involved in Jennifer's future?"

"That's simple; both you and Evan work for Van Beuren. And as one of our HR managers, you know that when one of our employees has a problem, the company does everything it can to help. Besides, those two kids are pretty special, and I really like them. They remind me of a young boy and girl who fell in love a long time ago in Florida. What do you think about this plan for their future?"

"You know I think she shouldn't give up the chance to go to Amherst, but let me think about it."

Two days later, Taylor received a phone call from Mortimer Barrett. "It's not exactly what my wife and I envisioned as Jennifer's future, but the way you spelled it out seems the best way to prepare them for the future they have chosen. It's hard, but it's time for me to face reality. I'm very grateful you stepped in before I alienated my daughter, and perhaps lost her forever. Thanks for waking me up! When do you intend to discuss this with Jennifer and Mike?"

"Oh, no, you're the centerpiece of this plan. Without your blessing, Jennifer will never be truly happy. You are her dad. You might not realize it, but in a way, she's still a little girl who looks to you for approval. After I talk to Evan, I hope you'll sit down with Jennifer and Mike to discuss this plan for their future with them. Remember, the plan has to be presented by you. Without your approval, the whole thing means nothing."

Four days later, Mortimer Barrett was back in Taylor's office. "Taylor, you have never seen two kids happier than Jennifer and Mike after I talked to them last night. Mike had already heard from his father about the arrangements at the restaurant, but when I told them about the plans for Jennifer and him, he nearly went berserk. Can't say I ever got kissed by a boy before, but I tell you, when that kid got me in a bear hug, I could hardly breathe. After that things got pretty emotional. Jennifer and I spent quite a while crying in each other's arms. The ironic thing in all this is now that my wife and I have stopped fighting Jennifer's decision, we're really looking forward to the birth of our first grandchild."

Chapter 50

The mystery surrounding the circumstances of Pat's wife's death kept bothering Taylor. Was his old cellmate and close friend a cold-blooded killer? Or did he get locked into a situation that was beyond his control? What did Father Flynn know that could shed some light on the extent of Pat's involvement in his wife's death? Not knowing the truth kept on haunting Taylor, and he finally decided to call Father Flynn and attempt to get more details out of him.

Father Flynn was delighted to hear from Taylor, but at first he was reluctant to discuss what Pat had revealed during his treatment. Taylor persisted, and finally Father Flynn reconsidered.

"Pat gave his unqualified consent to be injected with sodium pentothal, the so-called truth serum. What he revealed could clear him of any criminal act, rather than incriminate him. Since it was not a special confidence revealed to me as a priest, I guess I can discuss the story he told us." Besides relating Pat's version of what took place that fatal day on their balcony, Father Flynn went on to tell Taylor the story he had heard about Pat's wife's gambling addiction, and how Willie Baker, the bookie, had forced her to sleep with him. "Mind you, we have no way of knowing if this is the truth or not, but if it is true, this Willie Baker should be put behind bars, and Pat's reputation should be restored. All I know is what Pat told us, and what I learned from this bookie at the track named Jimmy Carson. I have always wanted to investigate if what I was told are the true facts, but I don't have the resources to do something like that. "

"But I do," Taylor said, without thinking about how he would handle such a project.

Father Flynn suggested, "If you could get those same investigators who helped solve your case to work with us on this case, I'm sure we could get at the truth." He was getting excited about the prospect of learning more about what really happened between Pat and his wife.

"I'll talk to our lawyers and see what we can arrange," Taylor said.

He wasted no time, and immediately contacted John Phillips. John let Taylor tell the whole story he had heard from Father Flynn before he asked Taylor to give him more details about the time he had shared a cell with Pat.

"So, from your personal knowledge of the man, you don't think he would be capable of killing his wife in cold blood?"

"He may have killed her, but I'm sure there must have been some mitigating circumstances. Except when playing football, Pat was a gentle giant. I would consider him incapable of premeditated murder."

"Then you think it's worthwhile hiring Roberts and Associates to investigate and find out if this bookie you call Willie Baker really exists?"

"Yes, I do," Taylor replied.

"They're not cheap. Do you intend to ask your grandmother to sponsor this operation?"

"No, I'll pay for it myself, out of my salary."

"Okay. I'll contact Roberts and Associates and see who they have available. I'll need all the details you can get for me, especially the town or city where Pat and his wife were living at the time of his arrest."

Taylor thought that would be easy. "Father Flynn should be able to get the entire dossier for us."

The investigators from Roberts and Associates quickly tracked down Willie Baker, the bookie. The man's real name was David Bennett. He had four other names he had gone by at various times. He had a police record, but was not under police surveillance; they considered him small fry, not worth bothering with. Keith Hill, the investigator from Roberts and Associates, came to Pentonville to report his findings to Taylor and John Phillips.

Keith fit the part of an investigator who unobtrusively goes around collecting information. He was of average height and weight. His dirty-blond hair was cut short and revealed a male-pattern bald spot in the back. His face had no outstanding features; he had that not easily recognizable face required in his profession. However, his deep baritone voice could blow his cover.

Taylor listened intently when Keith gave his report. "The guy is a one-man operation, and that made it very difficult to get the details on who he dealt with in the past. I asked around in several bars he likes to frequent, but the most I could get out of people who know him is that he makes book on almost anything, from horses to college football.

"Next, I tracked down several people who had known Pat and his wife. They told me Pat's wife played the horses and, over time, lost substantial amounts of money. I tried to verify this by visiting the local racetrack and throwing her name around to see who would remember her.

"On the third day of my visit, I finally hit pay dirt. A man who only identified himself as Buddy claimed to occasionally work with Willie Baker to cover large bets. He told me that apart from those large bets, he and Willie ran their own separate organizations, but he knew that in the past a man named Patrick Turner had paid large sums of money to Willie to cover his wife's debts. According to Buddy, Willie often bragged how he had this Patrick Turner's wife hooked on the horses, and how she was one of his favorite meal tickets."

When Keith Hill finished, John Phillips turned to Taylor and said, "I guess that wraps it up. We don't exactly know why Pat killed his wife, but we now know it probably had to do with her gambling."

"I still don't buy it," Taylor replied. "I got to know Pat pretty well when we were locked up together, and I don't think we have the story straight."

"Sorry, this is the best I could do," Keith said. "I couldn't discover anything that would tie Willie into Pat's wife's death."

"Taylor, do you think it's worthwhile pursuing this any further?" John Phillips asked. "I agree there's still a lot we don't know about the circumstances surrounding the death of Pat's wife, but I think it's clear the story Pat told when they gave him truth serum could have been a complete fabrication. He probably killed her out of anger because of her gambling."

Taylor protested; he didn't agree. "Keith, has Willie ever met you or physically seen you?" Taylor asked.

"No, why?" Keith was curious as to what Taylor was getting at.

"I have a plan," Taylor said. "I want you to continue your investigation, but this time I'm coming with you."

"Oh, no, you won't!" John Phillips sounded very determined. "This has gone far enough. In the first place, you are not a trained investigator like Keith. And secondly, you certainly won't discover anything he couldn't. But more importantly, this Willie character may not have done what Father Flynn told you, but that doesn't mean he's harmless. You will not put yourself in harm's way just to prove some theory of yours. Just accept the facts, Taylor. Pat confessed to killing his wife for the simple reason that he did it."

Taylor got up and started pacing around the room. He asked Keith to leave John and him alone for a while so he could discuss something very personal with John.

When Keith had left the room, Taylor turned to John Phillips. "John, you have no idea how hard it is for me to disagree with you on this matter. From the time I was in high school I have looked up to you as a giant. You have continued to be that giant in my life. Even now, your influence looms over me stronger than ever. I don't want to have a disagreement with you, so please try to understand why I must pursue this. When I was in jail, being locked up was not the worst part. It was the fact people believed I killed that girl. Nobody would listen to me when I tried to explain I was not guilty. Then along came one person who believed me, and fought for me. That was my grandma. I know Pat is dead—dead at his own hands. But I truly believe he was not the brutal murderer the world labeled him to be. I believe him! What he said under the influence of that truth serum is the truth. If we can find out the true circumstances surrounding his wife's death, it will show us that Pat was not a murderer. His family and friends, who hate the person they think he was, should not keep that image as their memory of him. They should be told who Pat really was, and cherish, rather than despise, his memory. It may sound silly to you, but I think I wound up in a cell with him for a reason. I, of all people, can understand how important it is for people to know the truth. Pat, in his own mind, might have felt he was guilty, but his loved ones deserve to know the truth for the sake of his memory. And I, just like Grandma, have the means to find the truth."

John Phillips didn't respond immediately. He sat at his desk drawing doodles on the paper pad in front of him. The silence made Taylor feel uneasy. Finally John spoke. "I won't even presume to say if you were or were not placed in that cell by some divine intervention. The spiritual thing is that you interpret it as such, and you feel you have a debt to repay. Yes, your grandma never doubted you. You were lucky she had the means to help. That was given to you, and now you feel you have to give back. I can understand that. I do have great difficulty with you pursuing this case because I do not share your firm belief that Pat was a good person. However, you have proven to have good insight into people's character, and I'll respect your judgment. I will help explain this mission to your grandma, but only under the condition that you promise to follow Keith's judgment on matters affecting your personal safety. You'll have to explain your feelings to Maria."

Chapter 51

As part of Taylor's plan, Keith and he checked into the most expensive suite in one of the fancy hotels in town. Soon after their arrival, they went down to the bar and started asking about the night life in town. Was there a casino where they could go to gamble? They got a list of the most popular bars and clubs, but, unfortunately, the town didn't have a casino. The town did have a very well-known racetrack. They would have to go to the track, because there was no official off-track betting.

Taylor winked at the bartender and said, "Maybe you can help us with that." The bartender smiled, nodded affirmatively, and gave them the names of several bookies in town. He also told them where these bookies could be found. After they made it pretty clear they were in town to have a good time and do some serious gambling, they left for one of the bars Keith had identified in his earlier visit as one of Willie's regular haunts.

Seated at the bar within earshot of the bartender, they started discussing what a shame it was they didn't have time to visit the racetrack. When the bartender came over to ask if they wanted a refill, Taylor asked her, "The bartender at the Claremont Hotel told us to contact a guy named Willie Baker about placing some bets. Do you know him?"

"Sure do," she replied. "Let me check if he's here tonight."

"That would be great," Taylor said, flashing a twenty dollar bill.

After a while the bartender returned. "Sorry, it seems Willie isn't here tonight, but I can get a message to him if you like."

"Yes, please tell him to contact us at the Claremont Hotel, we're in suite 1212." Laughing, he added, "Almost forgot, my name is Taylor, and this is Keith. We're visiting here for a few days." Another twenty dollar bill changed hands.

Back in their suite, Keith asked, "Do you think this scheme of yours to trap Willie will really work?"

"Yes, I'm sure it will. We'll place a couple of large bets with him and continue to spread the word that we have the money to spend for a good time. Once guys like that smell money, they lose all caution. That's when we suggest he get some girls for us." Taylor had hardly finished speaking when the phone rang. Taylor let it ring a while before he picked it up.

"Yes, this is Taylor, who's calling? Willie Baker? Yes, we asked the bartender in the Silver Moon to have you call us. Yeah, that's right. Can you bring us some racing forms tomorrow, so we can place a few bets? Yes, we'd like that. Do you have any maximums? Okay, so you can arrange that for us. Of course we'll give you some advance notice. Fine, we'll see you tomorrow. Call from the reception desk and I'll come down to get you, because all floors above the tenth can only be accessed with the room key. Thank you. You, too, have a nice evening."

When Taylor hung up the phone, Keith just shook his head. "That guy is nuts! He has no idea who we are, and without carefully checking, he agrees to take our bets."

"I told you, when these guys smell money, they become reckless. Now let's get on the computer and check the website of that local racetrack. We don't want to look like a set of country bumpkins when he shows up tomorrow."

As agreed, Willie Baker showed up the next day at the Claremont Hotel. Taylor went down to the lobby to meet him, and he brought him up to the suite. Willie was a short, skinny guy with jet-black hair which he combed straight back. His pale, white face belied the fact he spent many hours at the racetrack. His pinstriped suit needed pressing. Willie was duly impressed by the suite and the luxury throughout the Claremont Hotel. They sat down to go over the racing forms Willie had brought. Keith ordered drinks from room service.

"What do you guys do for a living that you can afford all this?" Willie asked. Taylor looked him straight in the eye and, as coldly as he could, replied, "For a professional, you ask too many questions."

"Okay, you're right of course, but you don't have to get so huffy about it. I was just making social talk.

Actually, I don't give a damn what you do to get your loot."

Taylor and Keith placed bets totaling $5,000 each, and Willie was obviously pleased. They agreed he would come back the next day with the race results and any payoff.

After Willie left, Taylor sat back and laughed at the bets they had placed. "Based on what we learned yesterday from that website, we really picked ourselves a few stinkers. I'll be surprised if we manage even a few hundred bucks in winnings." But the next day brought a big surprise; two of the horses they bet on unexpectedly placed and brought them seven thousand dollars in winnings. This reduced Willie's total take to just over two thousand dollars. Taylor wanted to tempt Willie with bigger bets, and the next day he asked to place a ten thousand dollar bet on Enterprise.

"To place or what?" Willie asked.

"A straight bet to win," Taylor replied. "We met one of the owners of Enterprise, and she really spoke highly of her horse. Besides, it might bring her luck if we bet on him to win."

"Let me see what the racing forms give for odds." Willie took out the forms he had brought along and quickly found Enterprise.

"They list him as five to one; is that the odds you're looking for?"

"Too steep for you?"

"No, that won't be a problem, but I'll have to make a few calls to get an associate of mine to partner on this bet."

"That's fine, just let me know. If the odds change before post time, both sides can reconsider, right?"

"That's a little unusual, but okay."

"Hell, that's in your favor, so be glad."

"I also want to place a couple of bets," Keith reminded Willie.

If Taylor and Keith had done their homework correctly, Willie stood to make a clear profit of almost fifteen thousand dollars on the bets they had placed with him. Their research of the website made them pretty sure Enterprise would be a sure winner for Willie and his partner. According to the information they had gotten from the Web and the local newspapers, the horse had run badly in his last race, and the odds makers had overrated his potential.

The race went more or less as expected. Enterprise placed seventh. Keith didn't do much better. He won six hundred dollars on bets totaling five thousand.

When Willie showed up the next day he was full of smiles. "You guys ready to win back some of that loot?"

"We're taking a day off from betting," Taylor told him.

Willie was visibly disappointed. "What's the matter? You lost faith in the horses?"

"It's not that, but we have other plans for tonight. How about you finding me some female companionship for tonight?"

"You mean an escort, like a date? Or the other type?"

"What you call the other type. A date for games right here in this suite, not a night on the town. Keith has a business appointment, and I don't intend to spend the evening watching television by myself."

"I'll call an escort service for you; they'll fix you up real nice."

"Oh, no, no escort service for this boy. They record names and keep records, even if they pretend to keep it anonymous. That's not for me. Besides, I don't care for the professional type. I prefer the amateurs; you know, the bored housewife type."

Willie needed a moment to digest the request. If he told Taylor he was not the right guy for such an errand, they would most likely ask the bartender downstairs; he would have no problem filling the request. However, the bartender could steer them to another bookie for their next bets. In exchange, that bookie would give the bartender a piece of the action.

"Okay, I think I can arrange that for you, but it'll cost you."

"How much?" Taylor asked.

"Well, I know the high-class escort service here in town charges twenty-five hundred and up, depending on the girl you choose. I'll give you a break; I'll find you a real amateur housewife and only charge you that minimum of twenty-five hundred. Deal?"

"You got yourself a deal," Taylor replied. "Here, take this room key so the gal can come straight up to this suite. Tell her to be here around eight."

"Boy, he took the bait rather easily," Keith said after Willie had left. "You may actually trap him in the web you're spinning. At first I thought your idea was really crazy, but I'm starting to change my mind."

"You just wait and see. We'll catch the bastard red-handed." Taylor sounded like he had never doubted the outcome of his plan.

At exactly eight o'clock, there was a timid knock on the door. Taylor went to open it. He didn't bother to ask who it was; he just opened the door. "Hi, come on in."

She stood in the open doorway, shoulders slightly stooped. Her scared eyes looked past Taylor into the suite. When she saw Keith her hand flew to her mouth and she cried out, "Oh my God, there are two of you!" This was followed by a sob. "No, no, I can't do this." She quickly turned and headed back to the elevator. In a few steps Taylor caught up to her.

"Leave me alone!" she sobbed, and pushed the elevator button to go down. Not to scare her too much, Taylor stopped at a distance. As she stood waiting for the elevator to come up, she pressed her head against the wall. Her sobbing increased, and Taylor was worried people in nearby rooms might hear her.

"If I promise not to come any closer, will you listen to me for a moment?"

She looked up. "I'm not the type of girl you think I am. I'm so sorry, but this has nothing to do with you. I just can't do this type of thing."

"I understand," Taylor said.

"No, you have no idea; please, I beg you, just let me go quietly."

The elevator arrived, but before she could get in, Taylor said, "That might not be a good idea. How will you explain it to Willie?" She stopped and took a step back. The elevator door closed. She started crying again, her chest heaving up and down with each sob.

"Really, I can't do this, but I don't know what to do."

"Will it help if I told you we have absolutely no intention of having sex with you?"

She stopped crying and turned to look at him in disbelief. "Who are you? What are you saying?"

"I'm telling you we never planned to have sex with you. We know how Willie forces women to pay off their gambling debts, and we hate him for it. Please help us to stop him from doing that again."

"You didn't agree with Willie that I would come up here to your hotel to have sex with you?"

"Yes, as far as Willie knows, that was our agreement. But what we really want is for you to help us put Willie behind bars." She seemed to relax just a little, but it was obvious she couldn't comprehend what exactly Taylor wanted, or if she could really trust him. What were his real intentions?

"Me, help you? You must be kidding. Willie will kill my kids if he thinks I crossed him."

"If I don't make sure you're protected, he may well do that." That caught her attention.

"How can you protect me? I don't even know who or what you are."

"Here out in the hall is no place to discuss this any further. I appreciate the fact that it's scary for you to trust me, but it must be scarier to go back to Willie and have to explain nothing happened between you and me. I suggest you take a chance on me, and come into my suite, so I can explain why I asked Willie to arrange for you to come here."

She took a deep breath and looked Taylor straight in his eyes. What she saw must have given her some sense of comfort, because she shrugged her shoulders and followed Taylor back into the suite.

Keith walked up to her and extended his hand. "Hi, I'm Keith, and you already sort of met Taylor in the hall. May I ask your name? You don't have to tell me if you're not ready to do so."

Without hesitation she responded, "I'm Dorothy. And if you guys are for real, I'm probably the most relieved person in the whole wide world." Dorothy was a tall girl, and even though she still looked very scared, they could tell she was very cute. Her long brown hair hung loosely over her shoulders; the color matched her big brown eyes. She was dressed very modestly, and looked extremely vulnerable standing there in the middle of the room with her handbag clutched to her chest. She must have been in her late thirties. It wasn't difficult to imagine that a guy like Willie would try to take advantage of her.

Taylor smiled at her remark. "Dorothy, why don't you sit over there next to the telephone? If at any time you feel threatened, just dial the operator and ask for security." He paused for a moment while Dorothy sat down and he continued. "I think we can all use a drink to calm our nerves a little. What can I order for you?"

"A double vodka on the rocks, please." Dorothy seemed all too eager to get a drink

Keith called room service to order their drinks. Taylor started explaining to Dorothy that they were trying to contact women who had lost money gambling, and owed Willie a gambling debt they couldn't pay. He carefully inquired, and got Dorothy to admit she owed Willie a substantial amount of money.

"When we asked Willie to arrange a gal for us, we suspected he might force someone with a gambling debt into coming up here. You just confirmed that for us. Now, if you're willing to tell us why you owe him a bundle, and what threats he used to persuade you to come up here, we can help break the hold he apparently has over you."

"Sounds great, but why should I trust you? I still don't really know who you are and why you would want to help me."

"Fair enough. I think you're a straight shooter, so I'll start by giving you some information about us. We're here because we believe Willie was instrumental in the death of the wife of a close friend of ours."

"That's pretty heavy. I know the bastard is capable of some nasty things. Yes, he could kill."

"Hold on, I didn't say or mean to imply that Willie murdered anyone. I said he may have been instrumental in causing her death; somewhat in the same way he used the debt you owe him to persuade you to come here and have sex with me."

When the drinks arrived, Dorothy quickly took a big gulp, and Taylor knowingly glanced at Keith, who nodded to signify that he, too, had noticed.

Taylor turned to Dorothy. "Tell us how you got involved with Willie, and how he got you to come up here."

Dorothy sat back in her chair and took a deep breath. "It's a long story, but I'll keep it short. My husband and I have been married for fourteen years. We met when he was an intern at Holy Mount Hospital, and I was a waitress in a café right around the corner from the hospital. When I was single and waitressing, some of my coworkers from the café and I used to go to the track a lot for entertainment. At the track we met Willie, and we started placing our bets with him. Later, he would come by the café and collect our bets.

"After I got married, I stopped going to the track, and rarely placed a bet with Willie. When our first child was born, I quit working and lost all contact with Willie and my former colleagues from the café. When our kids, we now have two, got a little older, we enrolled them in day care. Without the kids at home I had little to do. Out of boredom I started visiting the track again. There I bumped into Willie, and once again started placing my bets with him.

"At first I was winning quite often, and it was a lot of fun. I increased the size of my bets, and I continued winning. I became a little too daring, and the bets I placed became rather large. Before I knew it, I owed Willie quite a bit. My husband makes good money, and I had the money to pay my debts, but I felt guilty losing all that money and I tried to win it back. That didn't work. My losses increased. At present, I owe Willie more than twenty thousand dollars. I don't dare tell my husband about it, and it's too much to cover out of my household money.

"Then, early this morning, Willie called and said he had a proposal. If I did him a small favor, he would be willing to forgive a large part of my debt to him. When he explained what it was, I told him absolutely no. He threatened to tell my husband about my gambling debts if I didn't agree to his proposal. I told him I would take that chance before agreeing to be unfaithful to my husband. He upped the threat by telling me he knew where my kids' day care was, and he could not vouch for their safety if I didn't agree to sleep with this business associate of his. He promised it would be for just one time. He was very insistent, promising to forgive more than half my debt, and to give me as long as I needed to pay the rest. He also stressed I should not gamble with my kids' safety."

Dorothy abruptly stopped talking. She brought both hands in front of her face and her head went down towards her legs. Her cry sounded like the screech of an animal wounded in the wild.

Taylor jumped up to console her, but Keith held up his hand and waved him off. "No, don't touch her. The last thing she needs is a strange man's arm around her."

As Taylor backed away, they heard Dorothy sob. "God help me, how could I? I agreed to sleep with a stranger to pay a lousy debt. Why did I do it? Why did I agree to such a foul thing? I never meant to hurt John; I love him so much. How could I even think to do it?" Taylor and Keith sat silently while Dorothy quietly wept.

When she finally regained her composure, she looked up and asked, "Can I please have another drink?"

"I think you'd better lay off the juice for a while, young lady," Keith said. "I'll get you a drink of water if you'd like, but I strongly suggest you watch the alcohol from now on. If I guess correctly, it has a lot to do with that gambling of yours."

The expected denial about drinking too much never came. Instead Dorothy looked at Keith and nodded. "Yes. You're right, I drink a lot. But so do all our friends. Even John, my husband, drinks a lot. It doesn't seem to trouble any of them."

"Maybe so," Taylor chimed in, "but apparently they can control it better than you. We're not here to criticize your drinking. We only suggest that maybe you would have less trouble with gambling if you get some help with your drinking. But let's get back to why we asked Willie to set you up with us. We know we're guilty of putting you in a horrible position. However, based on Willie's past behavior, your large debt to him would've put you in jeopardy for something similar to this, or even worse, at some time in the future. Sooner or later he most probably would've forced himself on you by threatening to expose your gambling debts. That's what he did to our friend's wife."

"What exactly do you want me to do, and how do you plan to stop Willie from taking revenge on me when he finds out this was a setup?"

"Your part will be simple. When Willie comes to see us tomorrow, I'll report that everything was perfect; you were the best lay I had in a long time. We'll continue to place our bets with him until we find one more witness. Then we'll call on you to give a statement to the police about his threats. Don't worry, you won't be in danger. By that time we'll make sure Willie is in police custody. Your husband will never know more than that you had a gambling debt and you helped set a trap for the bookie. He'll be told you knew about the scheme from the beginning, and there was never a possibility of you sleeping with one of us."

"What do you want me to tell Willie?"

"You just tell him mission accomplished. You can add that you hated it and despise him for making you do it. Tell him you'll pay off the rest of your debt as soon as possible, and that in the meantime he is to leave you alone. We'll keep him busy. Don't worry; he won't bother you for a while. I hope you trust us enough to let us know how and where we can reach you when the time comes to give your statement to the police."

Dorothy was so glad at the way things turned out that she happily gave Taylor and Keith her full name, cell phone, and even added her home phone. Without being pressured, she assured them she would tell her husband she had a gambling problem and ask for help. After she left, Keith said, "Damn it, she still has our key."

"Don't worry," Taylor said. "She won't use it to do anything bad. I trust her. She is completely on our side. Actually, she's lucky. If we hadn't shown up, she would have wound up exactly like Pat's wife."

"Yeah, I agree," Keith said. "That's one down. But do you think it will be that easy to get another witness?"

Taylor laughed. "Piece of cake, Mr. Investigator. We just continue to place a few more lucrative bets with our friend Willie, and then you'll tell him you're jealous. You also want to get laid by one of those lonely housewives."

Early the next morning, Willie came to their hotel room to collect his money. "Tell me, how did you like that broad I sent up here last night? She's pretty, isn't she? Was she any good?"

From the smirk on Willie's face, Taylor guessed Willie wanted to hear all the details. "I couldn't have asked for anything better. I swear, from the way she acted it must have been the first time she slept with someone other than her husband. I could see she was scared stiff; she shook like a leaf when she undressed, and she had no idea how to get started with me. She didn't even know how to give a decent blow job! But when I showed her, she was a real fast learner. Once we got started, she was terrific. I loved it when she wrapped those long legs of hers around me."

Willie laughed. He was happy Dorothy had performed well. "You see, you can always depend on

Willie to supply the best. I should charge you a lot more than the twenty-five hundred bucks I promised. You got yourself a real bargain."

"Tell you what; you reserve that chick for me, and don't let her fool around with anyone else, that includes you. And the next time I come to town I'll pay you an extra two thousand to fix me up with her."

"You got yourself a deal."

For the next couple of days, things went pretty much the way Taylor had planned. On the third day, they placed a few modest bets, which didn't make Willie very happy.

As Willie was about to leave, Keith said, "Hey, Willie, that gal you got for Taylor; can you do the same for me?"

"Sure, you want the same one?"

"No, remember you promised Taylor to reserve her services for him. Besides, Taylor and I like to have different experiences so we can compare later. That's half the fun."

"I'll see what I can do. Taylor got his very cheap; can I get three thousand from you?"

"Sure, three thousand will be fine, but I expect her to be at least as good, or even better, than that chick you got for Taylor."

Willie turned out to be a resourceful man, and at a little past eight there was a knock on the door. This time the knock was anything but timid. When Taylor opened the door, he was amazed to see the bartender from the Silver Moon standing in front of him.

Noticing his surprise, she said, "Who the hell did you expect, the man in the moon? Yes, it's me, the very same gal who contacted Willie for you a while back." She stepped into the room and saw Keith. "Oh, shit, he didn't say I would have to fuck both of you."

Both Taylor and Keith realized they were on thin ice. They never expected this type of development. There was no way they could use this gal to testify against Willie. Worse than that, if they didn't play their cards right, she might smell a rat and expose their scheme to Willie.

Keith signaled to Taylor to come closer, and when they were standing next to each other he whispered very softly, "Lay low, and let me handle this. This broad is dangerous. She's probably a pro, and if we don't play this right, she's likely to blow our cover."

"Why the hell are you two standing there like a couple of school boys about to have sex for the first time? I should hope that at your age you've done it before. Okay, who's going to be first, 'cause I'm not about to have group sex with you guys."

Keith quickly took charge of the rather awkward situation. "Actually, I'm the one who asked Willie to arrange for you to come up here, it'll only be me."

"Well that's a relief. Which bedroom is yours so we can get this over with?" Keith pointed to the bedroom to the right of the big living room in which they were standing. "Let's go." She marched right past Taylor into the bedroom Keith had pointed out. Keith followed and closed the door behind him.

Taylor sat down on the couch, wondering how Keith was planning to get rid of this gal without alerting Willie as to who they really were.

As soon as Keith closed the door behind him, she took off her shirt and bra and was about to pull down her skirt when Keith said, "You don't have to undress." She looked at him in surprise. Cupping her small but firm breasts in her hands, she said, "What's the matter, my tits too small for you?" Keith had to admit that they looked tempting, but he reminded himself that he was on a professional assignment.

"No, they're beautiful, but Willie had promised to hook me up with some bored housewife, or some other type of amateur. I specifically told him I didn't want a professional lady."

"Do I look like a professional whore to you?" She sounded angry.

"Calm down, I didn't mean it as an insult, and, no, you do not look like a prostitute. I just assumed you might be."

"And what gave you that idea?"

"Well, sort of from the way you came into the suite, and the matter-of-fact way you marched into this room."

"You can put your mind at ease; I don't normally do this type of thing. It took all the courage I could muster to step into this room with you. If you must know I'm scared stiff, and I'm only doing this as a favor to Willie."

"Let me understand this. You're not getting paid, and you say this scares you, but you're willing to do this strictly as a favor to Willie?"

"Damn you, don't ask so many questions! You got what you wanted, a total amateur. So let's get this over with! It's all I can do not to go to pieces right here in front of you, or maybe that would add to the thrill you're looking for?"

"Come on, sis, I wasn't born yesterday. You really want me to believe you're doing this against your will, strictly as a favor to Willie?"

Tears started coming to her eyes. "I'd better just leave; you're just having fun torturing me with your stupid questions." She put her bra back on and hastily tried to button her blouse.

"Of course you're free to leave," Keith said gently, "but I think you're either a gal in real trouble or a very good liar. Either way, I expect Willie will be more than a little upset with you when he hears you walked out."

"Look, why I'm doing this is really none of your business. Can't we just get this over with so I can tell Willie I did what he asked? That I'm scared should be an added attraction for you. You'll really feel you're fucking an amateur."

"Getting a little vulgar probably gives you a little extra courage, but let me assure you, I have no intention of having sex with you. Sleeping with women against their will is not what I'm about. How would you feel if I told you we could solve this without Willie getting mad at you?"

She looked at him, and her face was one big question mark. "What the hell are you talking about?"

"If we go back to the other room, we can sit down and calmly discuss how we can get you out of this unfortunate situation you have gotten yourself involved in."

Taylor jumped up from the couch; he was surprised the two of them came back into the room so quickly. He really didn't know what to expect. No way could Keith have had sex with her that quickly, but what was he up to?

Keith realized Taylor had no idea as to what was going on, so he explained. "We're all going to sit down and be a little more honest with each other. It's time for us to admit that we're not really into sex tonight. If this young lady cares to tell us what exactly is going on between her and Willie, I can assure her he'll never find out from us what happened, or rather, what *didn't* happen here tonight. To start with, maybe we should introduce ourselves. All we know about you is that you're the bartender we met at the Silver Moon, and somehow Willie got you to come up here to have sex with one of us."

"Yes, I'm Lorrie, and if I remember correctly from the other night, he's Taylor and you're Keith."

"Excellent memory," Keith said admiringly. Then, to their great relief, Lorrie said, "Look, I'll be honest with you guys. I don't do this type of thing merely as a favor to Willie. I owe our friend Willie a bundle, and he sort of forced me into this. Please don't tell him I told you this."

"Don't worry; he won't hear anything from us other than that you performed better than expected. Once again, let me assure you, you are not here to have sex with either of us."

"Now you're talking gibberish. You plan to tell him I did when, in truth, I didn't. Look, no offense. I'm delighted not to have to have sex with the two of you, but why would you tell him we did?"

This time it was Taylor who took the initiative. "Lorrie, we're asking you to trust us, and tell us why you owe Willie so much money that he could force you, against your will, to come up here to have sex with one of us."

"So now you want to know why I owe him the money, and how he got me to come up here? Okay, gentlemen, sit back. Here comes the whole fricking story." Lorrie seated herself in the same big easy chair Dorothy had sat in. Taylor looked at her, thinking how very different these two women were. Lorrie was by no means short, but Dorothy must have been at least half a foot taller. In contrast to Dorothy's slim body, Lorrie had a rather full, but very good figure, which she didn't hide under her tight skirt and low-cut blouse. Her short blond hair was brushed back in a ducks tail, and if you didn't mind the cold blue eyes, you could consider her rather pretty.

Noticing that she caught him staring at her, Taylor quickly said, "Before you get started, let me offer you a drink. What can I order for you?"

"Believe it or not, this bartender does not care much for liquor. A Coke would be great."

After room service had served the drinks, Lorrie sat back and told her story. "My girlfriend and I have always enjoyed betting on the horses and other sports events. By the way, you might as well know everything about me; my girlfriend is my steady live-in companion. We're lesbians.

"My gambling was always just for fun. But a while back, I started placing more and more bets. Willie always seemed to be around just in time to persuade me to place yet another big bet. It was fun until I started losing large amounts. In an attempt to win back some of my losses, I got deeper and deeper in debt. When I couldn't pay up, Willie went to my girlfriend and forced her to pay. Stupidly, I continued to bet and lose money. When neither of us had enough cash to pay, Willie started demanding sex from us. He always demanded that we do a so-called trio with him. That was really disgusting! The whole thing has caused serious friction between me and my girlfriend. She has told me if she is forced to do the trio bit once more, she'll leave me. So I jumped at the offer when Willie called this morning. He offered to cut my debt by a substantial amount if I was willing to have sex with you. If I would do it, he promised he would no longer force us to have sex with him."

"If we were to turn Willie in to the police, would you be willing to testify as to what he made you do?"

"I would castrate the bastard if I could, and I know a lot of gals who would be glad to help me."

"You know others who are involved with Willie?"

"Sure, as a bartender you hear all kinds of things. Liquor loosens tongues."

"Could you give us some of those names?"

"Absolutely. Did you know that he also dabbles in narcotics?" Taylor and Keith could hardly believe their ears. Not only had Lorrie completely dispelled their fear that she might expose their scheme to Willie, but she turned out to be a fountain of information that could be used against him.

Before Lorrie left it was agreed that Taylor and Keith would contact the proper authorities. They would also arrange that Lorrie and her girlfriend would be fully protected after they gave evidence against Willie. Once more, Lorrie assured them she would supply a complete list of persons who had been threatened and blackmailed in some way by Willie Baker.

The next day, Keith called his office to have Roberts and Associates set up a meeting with the proper authorities so he could report what they had uncovered about Willie Baker. By early afternoon he got a call back. The head of the local vice squad, which dealt with prostitution, would handle the initial interview. That same evening, Captain Lewis and Detective Harrison came to their hotel suite to talk to Taylor and Keith. Taylor almost broke out laughing when the two introduced themselves. They looked almost exactly like Starsky and Hutch from the popular TV show. It took the better part of two hours for Taylor and Keith to brief the captain and the detective on all the details they had collected.

When they finished, the captain assured them he had enough to go after Willie, and hopefully to put him away for a long time. Detective Harrison promised Taylor to do his best to find out if Willie had forced Pat's wife to have sex with him.

***

Taylor had been back in Pentonville for more than three weeks when he finally received a call from Captain Lewis. The captain reported that the district attorney had charged Willie with a long list of crimes: blackmail, conspiring to solicit for prostitution, illegal gambling, selling crack cocaine, forcing persons to commit lewd and salacious acts, including sexual acts against their will, threatening to commit bodily harm upon two minors and, for good measure, he had thrown in tax evasion. Willie had been taken into custody and was in jail pending his trial. Because of his repeated threats of violence, the judge had refused bail. The best news came from Detective Harrison. He reported that, after repeatedly questioning Willie about Pat's wife, he finally admitted that, in exchange for the gambling debts she owed him, he forced her to have sex with him. He even admitted he had secretly filmed himself having sex with Pat's wife. Later, when Pat's wife refused to have anything further to do with him, he threatened to send this videotape to Pat unless she once again gave in to his demands. To Taylor's relief, Detective Harrison told him the tape had been confiscated and destroyed.

It would not be needed as evidence, since they had Willie's signed confession.

Immediately after receiving this news, Taylor called Father Flynn, who was ecstatic.

"Father, I would like you to be the one to visit Pat's family, especially his wife's parents, and tell them what really happened. This revelation will change their entire view of Pat and erase all the hatred they have for him."

"Taylor, bless you for what you did for your friend. This is truly a gift of grace. It will be the most rewarding mission of my life. Taylor, bless you for once again strengthening my faith in mankind and showing me there can be true, unselfish friendship among my flock."

Chapter 52

Maria successfully completed her internship, and before she started her residency, she and Taylor decided it was time to become officially engaged. It was hard to tell who was more excited, Maria or Clair. Clair insisted on buying the engagement ring.

When Taylor demurred at the size of the diamond she selected, she said, "I have only one granddaughter, and she deserves the best because she is the best. You know I adore that child, so grant me this pleasure." The setting she selected, a large diamond flanked by two rubies, was very tasteful. And after he saw how happy it made Maria, Taylor was happy, too.

To celebrate the couple's engagement, Maria's parents threw a huge party. Taylor and his grandmother went to Florida for the festivities. Maria had invited most of her friends from college and medical school. She tracked down some of their classmates from high school, and she invited them, also. Two of the young doctors who had done their internship with Maria also attended. Except for their friends from high school, none of her other friends had ever met Taylor. Every one of them dying to meet this guy Maria had waited so long for.

Maria was more than a little tickled when one of her college friends came up to her and said, "You told us he was good-looking, but I didn't expect him to be that handsome."

Another friend chimed in, "What do you mean, handsome? The guy is drop-dead gorgeous. No wonder you waited for that hunk!"

Maria's father monopolized most of Taylor's time by taking him around and proudly introducing him to all his friends and relatives. Taylor had a hard time breaking away in order to spend some time with the group from their high school. He enjoyed hearing what had become of the people he'd known. He particularly enjoyed hearing the gossip about the infamous sons of the football coach. One of Coach Nielsen's twin sons, Abe, the quarterback, never made it big in college football, and was dropped from the team in his senior year. His twin, Charley, didn't do too badly playing football, but academically he couldn't keep up. He left college before his junior year ended.

The party kept going till late in the evening. Taylor and his grandmother didn't get back to the motel they were staying at till well after midnight.

At a little past two in the morning, Taylor was awakened by a knock on his door. He wondered who it could be, and was surprised to find Maria standing at his door.

"What's the matter? What happened?" he asked.

"Don't worry, nothing happened. I couldn't sleep and wanted to see you."

"Come in."

Maria came into the room and sat down in one of the big arm chairs at the far end of the room. "I have to talk to you," she said.

"Sure, what's up?"

"Are you marrying me because you love me, or do you feel obligated because I waited so long for you?"

The question really threw Taylor. "Maria, how could you possibly doubt that I love you? I'm crazy about you."

"I still worry that maybe deep down you can't forgive me for my stupid behavior, and by not believing in you I chased you away. I know Grandma wants us to get married, but you don't have to do it because of that. I love that lady with all my heart. I would not like to break her heart, but I don't want you to marry me because of that."

Taylor rushed over to where she was sitting and pulled her up into his arms.

"Maria, my darling, stop this foolish talk. The moment I saw you again, standing behind that big glass wall, all I hoped and prayed for was that you had not gotten married, and that I had not lost you forever. It was I who was stupid to run away, but it was really my grandfather I was running from. Baby, I love you so much. Please don't talk like that."

Maria buried her head in his shoulder, and with tears in her eyes asked, "Then why haven't you touched me during all this time we've been back together? We kiss, and that's all. It's not natural for you not to want me. I want you."

Taylor held her tight. "Maria, darling, things happened while I was on the road. There were girls. I—"

She didn't let him finish. "I don't need or want to hear about that. As long as you tell me you didn't fall in love with any girl you did...it...or whatever with, it doesn't affect me. Remember, I promised you the first time you would do it out of love would be with me, and as long as that can be true, I'm happy."

"Maria, I swear I've never loved anyone but you."

"Then don't just kiss me, you big goof! You are no longer the schoolboy who got in trouble for wanting to touch my breasts." With that, she pulled him against her body as tight as she could. They kissed long and hard, and finally Taylor's hand reached down to stroke her breasts. Maria responded quickly and unbuttoned her blouse.

"I've been praying for your lips to caress my nipples. My daydreams always go back to that night we got caught on Lover's Lane. Only in my dreams we didn't get caught; we made beautiful love in the back of your car."

Taylor was only wearing his bathrobe, which he had quickly pulled on over his pajamas to the open the door. While he was struggling with her bra, Maria pulled the robe loose and pushed it from his shoulders. It fell on the floor. She held him tightly for a moment, and then pushed him back so she could finish undressing. Before she pulled her panties down, she took off his pajama top and once again held him tightly. She kissed him so hard it almost hurt, and her breathing became very rapid. Although her body was pressed against his, she managed to push his pajama bottoms to the floor. When she felt his erection press against her, she stepped back and took off her panties. She took his hand and led him to the bed.

"Not so fast; let me look at you." Taylor's breath was coming even faster than hers. He took both her hands and spread her arms wide and looked at her admiringly. Her well-shaped breasts were much sexier than Betty's man-made beauties he had admired in Galveston. Maria's beautiful face was natural, not at all like that all-too-perfect artificial mask of Betty. Her body was truly magnificent, even better than Betty's. Or was that because he loved this girl so deeply?

He picked her up in his strong arms and very gently laid her on the bed. Carefully he stretched his powerful body across her naked body. For a long time they just laid there, kissing, and gratefully absorbing the warm feeling of each other's body. Then Maria moved her legs so he fit in between them. His erection gently caressed her lower lips as he moved slowly up and down. He could feel her responding, and when her hand took hold of him to help him enter her, he was so anxious that he pushed a little too hard.

She winced. "Go slow; remember, this is my first time." Then she murmured, "Okay," and wrapped her legs around him. Where Betty had squirmed underneath him and made rapid, jerky movements with her hips and thrashed around violently when she came, often sinking her teeth into Taylor's shoulders, Maria made very gentle moves with her hips and just held him tightly, and kept telling him how much she loved him. Maria murmured softly when she climaxed just before Taylor did. She held him very tightly when his whole body began to quiver, and she continued to whisper in his ear how much she loved him. She had kept her promise. The first time he really made love, it was great! Was it better than the sex he'd had with the women he'd met along the way? Or was it great because this was finally Maria, the girl he had always loved?

The next morning, while everyone thought they were asleep in their respective rooms, they slipped out to make a sentimental visit to Bayside Beach, where the parking lot was known to them as Lover's Lane. Taylor's stodgy rented car was a poor substitute for the flashy Chevy convertible he drove that night so long ago, but the fire in their embrace had not diminished.

Chapter 53

It had been half a year since Maria had started her residency at Johns Hopkins in Baltimore. Originally she had planned to enter a residency program in a hospital a little closer to Pentonville, so she and Taylor could see each other more often. But when she was offered a residency at Johns Hopkins, she jumped at the opportunity to work under the supervision of the famous Johns Hopkins's surgeons. She did, however, spend as much time as she possibly could commuting back and forth Pentonville. Taylor, in turn, flew out to Baltimore whenever he could. Their commuting trips were short, often only for the weekend. Plans called for the couple to get married right after Maria finished her residency. After that she planned to associate herself with Pentonville General, the large regional hospital located less than five miles from downtown Pentonville.

Late that summer, a fierce hurricane, with winds up to one hundred thirty miles an hour, slammed into the coastal region of Belize. It wiped out many fishing villages, and devastated almost fifteen percent of the country. Aid poured in from all over the world.

Maria, together with several other young doctors and nurses from Johns Hopkins, volunteered to join one of the medical groups sent out by the US State Department.

Communication with the stricken area was difficult, but Maria managed to call Taylor a few times on one of the Red Cross satellite phones. She reported unbelievable human suffering throughout the stricken area, and that their work was seriously hampered by the lack of medical supplies. The US Army had recently dispatched four more helicopters to the area she was working in, and she hoped that would speed up bringing in additional supplies.

It was eleven thirty in the evening. Taylor had just turned off the late news when he received the call. It was Maria's father; they had just been notified by an official from the State Department that Maria had been involved in a serious car accident. Taylor could feel the blood drain from his head.

"Oh my God, how is she?" he screamed into the telephone.

"We don't know, but I'm afraid it's serious."

"How did it happen?"

"Apparently they were on their way to a small seaside village when a big tanker truck, carrying fresh drinking water to the same area, hit their SUV."

Maria's father tried his best to stay calm while talking to Taylor, but his emotions got the best of him, and he burst out crying.

"Do you have any more information; did they tell you where she is now?"

377

Maria's father recovered enough to give Taylor the name of the person who'd contacted them, and the number he had been given to call for updated information. Taylor promised he would try to find out more about her condition, and exactly where she was.

After he hung up, Taylor immediately called the number Maria's father had given him. An operator answered, and quickly connected him through to the person who had called Maria's family.

"Fredericks here, can I help you?"

"Yes, I'm Taylor Marx, Maria Valera's fiancé. You called her family to report that she was in an accident in Belize. Can you give me more information on her condition?"

"I'm sorry, that is all the information we have at present."

"How can I find out how she is?"

"I promise you, as soon as we receive additional information about the accident we will contact you."

"You mean there's no way I can find out now how she is, and what exactly happened?"

"I'm sorry. I know this uncertainty must be hard for you, but I can't do anything until we receive more information from the agencies on the scene."

"What agencies are on the scene?"

"I assume representatives of the Red Cross will be there to coordinate operations of the volunteer medical teams."

"You mean to tell me there's no one there you can put me in contact with?"

"I'm sorry, but we have to wait until—"

Taylor interrupted him. "Is that the American Red Cross or what?"

"I believe the International Red Cross is in charge of the medical relief effort."

Realizing he was getting no place fast, Taylor said, "If you hear anything further, please add me to the people to call. I'll give you my number."

Taylor remembered that Maria had mentioned US helicopters had been sent to the scene. On a whim, he called the Pentagon. Staff Sergeant Kelly was on duty at the switchboard.

"Sergeant Kelly, please help me. I'm desperate. My fiancée has been injured in a car accident in Belize, and I'm trying to find out if she has been seriously injured."

"I can imagine you're upset, but how can I help?"

"She's part of a US State Department medical relief team, and the US Army has recently dispatched several helicopters to the area."

"Yes, the Belize disaster. We've sent a large contingent to help, and that included several helicopters. I can find out in what area they are presently operating. It's highly irregular for me to try and contact that helicopter unit, but I understand your worry; let me see what I can do." Sergeant Kelly promised to call Taylor back as soon as she had some more information for him.

All Taylor could do was sit and wait, and hope either Mr. Fredericks or Sergeant Kelly would call back. In the meantime, he woke up Clair to tell her what happened. In retrospect this was not such a good idea. Clair, who was always so level-headed and able to take charge in emergencies, couldn't handle the uncertainty. Not knowing what had happened to Maria caused her to go completely to pieces. Even though it was the middle of the night, Taylor was forced to call Dr. Morton to get her some sedatives. Dr. Morton was an old friend of the family, and he came right over to tend to Clair.

When Dr. Morton left and Clair, under heavy sedation, was resting upstairs, Taylor sat down, staring at the phone, hoping he could wish it into ringing. He had to wait till six in the morning when finally the phone rang.

"Hello, is this Mr. Taylor?"

"Yes, it's me," he hastily answered.

"Hi, this is Sergeant Kelly. I have some information for you. One of our choppers was operating in the vicinity of the town of Dangriga when they received a call for assistance. Some US nationals were injured in a motor vehicle accident and had to be transported to the hospital in Belize City."

"Did you get any names of the people involved, or if it was a medical group that was involved in the accident?"

"Unfortunately no, but it's my guess we're talking about the accident your fiancée was involved in, and she's probably in the hospital in Belize City by now. I really hope her injuries are not serious."

Taylor thanked her profusely for her efforts and immediately called the airlines. He couldn't get a direct flight to Belize City that day. But after numerous calls, he did secure a flight later that afternoon via Cancun to Belize City.

Due to the stopover in Cancun it wasn't until the next morning before Taylor arrived in Belize City. Luckily there was only one major hospital. He took a cab to get there. The main entrance to the hospital led directly into a large lobby, which was very crowded. Taylor had no idea where to go to get information about patients. He started asking, and was happily surprised that quite a few people spoke English. He was directed to a long counter at the back of the lobby area. There, an older man sitting behind a computer told him that four seriously wounded Americans had arrived by helicopter days before.

"Do you have their names?" Taylor wanted to know.

"No, I don't have that."

"Where are they?"

"Three of them are upstairs in intensive care on the fifth floor. Unfortunately the fourth one, a girl, died this morning."

Taylor felt his legs grow weak underneath him. He closed his eyes and silently prayed, "Please God, not her, don't let it be her." He turned and ran for the elevators. A uniformed guard was standing in front of the elevators checking the people getting on. When the guard challenged Taylor and asked for his pass or ID badge, Taylor pushed the man aside, and quickly disappeared into one of the elevators. On the fifth floor he started wildly running from one room to the other, checking quickly to see who was inside. He had already looked into twelve rooms when a nurse tried to stop him.

"What are you doing here?" she asked in fluent English. "These people are critically ill; you can't go around disturbing them."

"I beg you, have you seen a young woman, very pretty, dark hair?"

The nurse saw that Taylor was in bad shape, and on the verge of bursting into tears. She felt sorry for him and decided to help. "Follow me," she said. At the end of the hall, she opened a door and pointed inside, "Is that her?" she asked.

Anxiously Taylor looked inside, but the young girl lying there, attached to several machines, was not Maria.

"No, no, that's not her. Please, is there another patient here who looks a little like that?"

By now tears were coming down his cheeks. The nurse took him by the arm and pushed him into another room where a heavily bandaged patient lay with her head turned away. Taylor ran up to look and fell to his knees next to the bed; it was Maria. Badly wounded, but alive! Taylor didn't dare touch her, and with his head resting on the edge of the bed, he silently sat there crying while the nurse stood at the door watching. After a while, the nurse came over to the bed and placed her hand on his shoulder.

Taylor looked up at her and asked, "How bad is it?"

"Come, I'll take you to the doctor who's in charge of her case." She led him down several hallways to Doctor Barillio's office. Doctor Barillio was a short, pudgy man with a kind, round face sporting a thin mustache. He looked up at them when they entered his office. Taylor hastily explained to the doctor who he was, and that he had just flown in from the United States to find out what happened to Maria.

"What's her condition?" Taylor asked.

"To be honest with you, it is very serious. We've been able to stabilize her, but I'm afraid we can't save her left leg, and the right one looks doubtful too."

Taylor didn't respond. He stood silently, tightly gripping the hand of the nurse who was still standing next to him.

"Her life, is her life in danger?" he finally blurted out. He didn't seem to understand what the doctor had said about her legs.

"If we act quickly and amputate her left leg before the gangrene spreads and poisons her blood-stream, we can save her life. We'll do our best and try to save her right leg, but I fear gangrene is starting to set in there also."

The news was devastating, but at least she was alive, and the doctor said she would not die of her injuries.

"Can I see her the next time she wakes up?"

"Absolutely. She is under heavy sedation, but wakes up occasionally. Nurse, please inform the staff that Mr. Marx can stay in her room as long as he wishes."

Taylor was sitting next to her bed, holding her hand, when Maria opened her eyes. It took a moment for her to realize he was there, and then she cried out, "Taylor, darling, you're here!" She tried to reach out to him, but Taylor quickly bent over her and made sure she didn't try to move.

He kissed her softly on the forehead and said, "Don't try to move. Yes, I'm here, sweetheart, and I'm going to take care of you."

"Taylor, I hurt. My legs, they hurt so much."

"Yes, I know, darling. Lie still, and I'll ask the nurse to give you some more pain killers."

"Taylor, help me, help me. I'm so scared!"

"I'm here now, darling; it's going to be okay. I'm here to take care of you." Taylor rang for the nurse, who came in and gave Maria another shot of morphine to help kill the pain.

When the pain subsided a little, Maria became extremely agitated. She tried to sit up and grabbed Taylor with both hands. "Taylor, my legs; they're going to cut off my legs!"

"No, no, baby. No one is going to touch you unless I say so. I won't have them amputate your legs."

"Yes they will!" she cried. "They said they have to or else I will die. They made me sign permission to do it."

Taylor held her tightly and tried to calm her down. "Maria, trust me. I'll take care of you. I won't let anything happen to you that you don't want." The strong morphine injection took further effect, and Maria dozed off again.

Taylor got up and asked one of the nurses where the nearest hotel was located. They told him the Grand Palace was right next to the hospital. After he made sure Maria would stay asleep for quite a while, he decided to go over to the hotel and get a room. He asked the nurses to call him immediately in case Maria woke up before he returned.

Taylor called Johns Hopkins in Baltimore the moment he got into his hotel room. He got past the switchboard to surgery, but when he asked for Dr. Minsky, the surgeon who was Maria's supervisor, he got nowhere fast.

"I'll take a message. I think Dr. Minsky will be here in the morning," the nurse on duty told him. Taylor was not about to wait.

"This cannot wait. I must speak to Dr. Minsky immediately. Please tell me how I can reach him."

"Sorry, sir, I cannot do that. I'll be glad to take a message though."

"Let me speak with the head nurse."

"Sorry, sir, I cannot do that. Please just let me take a message." Taylor knew he had to do this for Maria; he couldn't give up.

"Nurse, please don't make me threaten you, but this concerns one of your doctors. It's a matter of life or death. Now get the head nurse on the phone, or I'll report you to the chief of staff."

"Just a moment."

It seemed like an endless wait, but finally the head nurse was on the other end of the line.

"Which one of our doctors are you calling about?"

"Maria Valera, she's a resident."

"Oh yes, Maria, I know her. What is the matter with her?" Taylor explained about the accident. She was in the hospital in Belize, and the doctors were about to amputate her legs. The head nurse responded quickly. She gave Taylor Dr. Minsky's secret cell phone number, the one that could only be used in case of emergencies, and told him if he didn't get through to Dr. Minsky, to call her back so she could help find him.

Luckily, Dr. Minsky answered his cell phone on the first ring. Maria had become one of his favorites at the hospital, and he was very upset when Taylor told him what happened.

"I'd fly out immediately, but I wouldn't have the proper facilities to help her out there."

"No, stay where you are, I'll bring her to you."

"How could you do that?"

"I'll fly her in. Just tell me what to do in order to prevent the doctors here from amputating her legs, and how to prevent the gangrene from spreading before I can get her to you."

"Tell the doctors to cut away as much of the dead flesh as possible, and give her the strongest anti-infection drug they have available. Pack her legs in ice if necessary. If they object, have them call me on this cell phone. I'll tell them I'm willing to take the risk that you can get her here before blood poisoning sets in. You have to hurry. From what you told me, we don't have much time."

When Taylor got off the phone with Dr. Minsky, he called Clair. He had great difficulty persuading her not to take the first available flight to Belize to be with Maria.

"Grandma, calm down! I need you as my contact in the US. For Maria's sake, take a deep breath, and do the following immediately. Call MedjetAssist; here is my member number. I don't think Maria is a member, but tell them we'll pay. Tell them we need a hospital plane, with medical personnel, as soon as possible to transport Maria from Belize to Baltimore. Explain the condition of her legs, and that time is of the essence. Next, you have to arrange an ambulance to meet the plane at Baltimore/Washington airport to transport Maria immediately to Johns Hopkins. Call Dr. Minsky on his cell phone, I'll give you the number, and give him the expected time of arrival at the hospital, so he can arrange to have her rushed right into surgery. And yes, don't forget to call the Valeras and tell them to meet us at Johns Hopkins."

Clair was instantly back to being her efficient self. She carefully noted down the telephone numbers, and repeated the instructions Taylor had given her. In a firm, determined voice she said, "Consider this taken care of. Taylor, you do whatever it takes down there to protect our Maria. I'm trusting you with the life of my little girl."

"Don't worry, Grandma. She's not going to slip away from us."

The doctors at Belize City Hospital were not at all convinced it was advisable to transport Maria to Baltimore without first amputating her left leg. But Taylor was not to be moved. He had them talk to Dr. Minsky at least twice before he finally convinced them to release Maria for the flight to the USA.

When the MedjetAssist plane landed at Belize International Airport, Taylor had the ambulance with Maria waiting on the tarmac. After a short delay to refuel the plane, they were ready for the direct flight to Baltimore. The nurses on the plane made Maria as comfortable as possible, but she insisted on holding onto Taylor during the entire flight.

"Do you think they'll be able to save my legs?" she asked.

"Baby, you told me Dr. Minsky was the best surgeon in the world. Of course he can!" They both knew this might be wishful thinking, but she needed to have him convince her that everything would be okay.

Clair had arranged everything perfectly! When the plane stopped at its designated parking place, an ambulance was waiting to rush Maria to Johns Hopkins. When the ambulance left the airport grounds, a motorcycle policeman signaled the ambulance to follow him. With sirens screaming, he led the ambulance at breakneck speed to the hospital.

Upon arrival at Johns Hopkins, Maria was rushed straight into surgery, where Dr. Minsky and a team of six other surgeons stood ready to examine her legs.

Chapter 54

For three grueling days, Taylor, Clair, and the Valeras hovered around Maria's bed. They anxiously waited to hear from Dr. Minsky how her body was reacting to the eight-hour operation, and the massive amounts of drugs they were giving her to prevent further infection. Finally, on the fourth day, Dr. Minsky could give a concrete assessment of her situation.

He came into the room and stood next to Maria's bed. "Maria, I don't think I'm being too optimistic if I tell you that you'll be able to keep those legs of yours."

"Both of them?" she cried out.

"Yes, both."

Maria reached for Dr. Minsky and pulled him towards her in order to give him a big hug, and place a kiss on both his cheeks.

"Thank you, thank you!" She wept for joy.

"Don't thank me," Dr. Minsky replied. Pointing at Taylor he said, "You can thank that persistent young man over there. I don't know how he did it, but he got you to our hospital in the nick of time. If you'd gotten to us just one day later, there would have been little we could've done for you." Taylor blushed and stared at the floor as Clair and Maria's mother pounced on him. They all competed in trying to give him a hug.

Raising her head as far as she could, Maria called from her bed, "Hey, what about me? When do I get to kiss him?"

Taylor stopped to look at his grandmother. "Without your help, I couldn't have done it!"

Several days later, Taylor bumped into Dr. Minsky in the hall.

"Taylor, under normal circumstances I would have to tell you that Maria will never walk again. But I have gotten to know you, and I think you'll go through a brick wall for that girl. With a lot of patience and continued hard therapy, there is a slight chance, and I must emphasize *slight*, that she could regain some degree of mobility in her legs. It will require total dedication on your part to help her through long, difficult years of physical therapy."

Maria was hospitalized for two more months. She had to endure five more operations before she was well enough to leave the hospital. Clair persuaded her to come to Pentonville, where she could receive all the medical care and physical therapy the doctors recommended. In Pentonville, Maria could take all the time she needed to regain her strength. As one would expect, Clair left no stone unturned to make sure Maria would be as comfortable as possible during her extended stay at her house. The guest suite was converted into a hospital room, complete with a special hospital bed. All the apparatus needed to move Maria around, and the latest physical therapy equipment were installed.

As soon as Maria's legs had healed sufficiently to be exercised, Taylor arranged for a therapist from the local hospital to come to the house twice a day to carefully start moving her legs. The first movements were extremely painful. Maria would cry out in pain each time the therapist would try even the slightest movement. Gradually, the therapist would increase the movements, and each incremental increase would bring renewed pain to Maria.

After several months, Maria got very depressed. She became less cooperative with the therapist. Taylor noticed the therapist had stopped pushing Maria as hard as he had done in the beginning. Taylor talked to the therapist about this, and discovered that the therapist felt Maria's legs would not get much better. The therapist told Taylor it was not productive to put Maria through more extensive exercises when the mobility of her legs couldn't improve any further. Taylor didn't argue the point; he just called the hospital and asked for another therapist.

Misty, the new therapist, was quite different from her predecessor. She responded to Taylor's determination that Maria's legs would improve, and she agreed to train Taylor so he could take over the morning exercises.

Taylor was much stricter with Maria than either of the therapists had been. He encouraged her every step of the way, and when she balked at an exercise, he would keep telling her, "We're getting better each day, I can see it!"

By this time, Maria was able to leave her bed, and, unlike Misty, Taylor could easily carry her to the exercise machines. Maria would often joke that the best part of her day was being carried in Taylor's strong arms. The interaction between Maria and Taylor was so good that pretty soon Taylor became the main therapist. Misty only supplied professional advice and training. Maria accepted Taylor's strict training regimen without question. The few times she objected, he would take the time to sit and discuss with her that Dr. Minsky had said she could walk again, but they would have a hard road to follow together in order to get there. He would always stress the *together*. When Maria seemed to give up all hope she would be able to walk or even stand by herself, Taylor would gently, but very firmly, admonish her, and remind her it would take a long time, but in the end they would be successful. Maria knew very well that the doctors had given her little hope she would ever walk again, but somehow, when Taylor said it with such certainty, she believed him.

Misty made no bones about the fact she really liked Taylor. She freely complimented his muscular build and movie-star looks. Taylor didn't take it too seriously, but one day, when Misty made a flirty remark, Maria overheard her. When Misty left, Maria said to Taylor, "You might as well take her up on it, because I'm no good anymore."

"What the hell are you talking about?" Taylor asked her.

"I mean you might as well take her up on her offer to sleep with you. I'm certainly of no use to you in this condition. All I can do is just lie there; I can't even wrap my legs around you."

Maria had never really seen Taylor angry, but this time he nearly exploded with anger. "Is that all that this has been about? All we've been through together just comes down to sex? Is that it?" Maria was shocked at his reaction, but even more shocked that she had said what she did.

"Oh my God, Taylor, I didn't mean it. But I feel so hopeless! It's been months, and I can't move a muscle in either leg. I'm so jealous of that pretty young girl with her long legs she can move at will." Taylor calmed down once he realized Maria only spoke out of desperation about her condition. He took her out of the wheelchair she was sitting in and, supporting her under her elbows, held her as if she was standing in front of him.

"Maria, look at me. Someday you'll be standing just like this without me holding your elbows. Maria, trust me! When we get married, you will walk down the aisle without support. You have promised to marry me, and I now promise to help you walk down the aisle."

Chapter 55

C lair kept asking, Maria's mother kept asking; it seemed like everyone kept asking—when were Maria and Taylor finally getting married? They had always planned to get married after Maria finished her residency, when she planned to start her medical career in Pentonville. Now that she could get around in a wheelchair, Maria could resume her residency at Johns Hopkins, but she would have to switch to another specialization; not being able to stand made it impossible for her to become a surgeon. Taylor didn't agree. He wanted Maria to fully concentrate on her physical therapy, and not forsake their dream that she would someday walk again. Maria suggested a compromise. She could switch her residency to Pentonville General Hospital. That way she could continue her physical therapy with Taylor's help.

Just about the time they were considering this option, Maria noticed an improvement in her left leg. This was very encouraging, considering this was the leg that had the worst injuries, the one the doctors in Belize had given up on. Taylor grabbed hold of this new development as an opportunity to push Maria even harder.

One day, when he had brought her to the parallel bars and she was moving across slowly, dragging her legs across the floor, he told her to stop.

"This should not only be an exercise to develop your arm strength. Move your hands back so your left leg is under you, vertical to the floor. Now try to put some weight on it by relaxing your left arm a little."

"Stop it! You know I can't. I'll fall."

"No, you won't. I'll stand right here to catch you."

"I can't do it! Just leave me alone and let me do my arm exercises." Taylor moved over and put his hand under Maria's right armpit.

"Now do it!" he said.

Maria shouted at him, "I can't!" But she put a little weight on her left leg and to her surprise, it held.

"Taylor, Taylor, it's not buckling! I can feel my weight on it!"

"Go slow. I'll hold you. Now, try if you can, and let go with your left hand. Be careful; do it very slowly."

Very hesitantly, Maria removed her left hand from the bar.

"Taylor, I'm standing! Really, I'm standing!"

Taylor could feel almost her full weight on his arm, but he had to encourage her. "You did it, baby! You stood."

From then on, Maria's determination to push on matched Taylor's. They decided to go to Baltimore to have Dr. Minsky and the staff at Johns Hopkins test the muscles in her legs.

What they found was more than just a little encouraging. Dr. Minsky was delighted, and told them the bone grafts had taken much better than they had expected, and her leg bones had healed beautifully. Her muscles were starting to develop, and the nerves appeared to be regenerating.

"If you can keep up whatever magic you're doing, pretty soon you'll be able to stand all by yourself. Maybe even to walk with support. Don't give up on that dream of yours of being a surgeon. You'll be good at it, and we need young doctors like you."

After their trip to Baltimore, Taylor was more determined than ever that Maria would walk again. Between his work at the company and working with Maria twice a day on her exercises, he still found time to surf the Web, hoping to learn about new treatments for Maria's disability.

Late one night, he hit pay dirt. He found an article about a clinic in Switzerland where they used electrical impulses to stimulate nerve and muscle growth after injuries similar to Maria's. He discussed this with Maria, and she agreed to let him take her to this clinic to see if their treatment could help her.

In order not to raise false hopes, they decided not to disclose the purpose of their trip to Switzerland to their friends and family. Maria arranged to start her residency at Pentonville General in the fall, and they announced they would get married at the end of October, just before she would start her residency. Their announcement that they would finally get married caused tremendous excitement. Clair and Maria's mother threw themselves into the planning with great gusto. The two of them worked together on making the arrangements. Maria's mother was over-joyed when the young couple agreed to be married in Florida, in her church.

Maria and Taylor had carefully selected their wedding date less than a week before Maria was to start her residency. This made it easy to explain their unusual plan to take an extended honeymoon in Switzerland before the wedding. A few friends voiced the opinion that this would bring bad luck. Most everybody else thought it was a great idea, after all the emotions of the previous years, for them to take a long vacation together to a place neither of them had been before.

Chapter 56

The Swiss clinic arranged a car and driver to meet them at the airport. They were driven to Lausanne, where the clinic occupied a beautiful villa in the mountains above the city. They were welcomed by Dr. Baumann, a slender young man with short, curly brown hair and striking blue eyes.

His English was flawless. "I hope you had a pleasant trip and that the flight wasn't too tiring for you, Ms. Valera." Maria assured him she felt fine, and he volunteered to give them a tour of the facility. The outside of the villa was deceiving; a passerby would not expect that the inside housed an ultra-modern medical clinic with the latest equipment.

"Dr. Hans-Ruedi Meier and I will be your doctors. We'll take care of you while you are here at the clinic." He went on to explain, "Dr. Ueli Brunner is the chief of staff. He'll lead the team that will evaluate the status of your legs, and develop a therapy program for you." After he had finished their extensive tour of the clinic, he took them to his office to introduce them to his colleague, Dr. Meier.

Dr. Meier was concerned that it had been a long trip for Maria, and he wanted her to have something to eat and drink to recover her strength. Maria protested that she was fine, but Dr. Meier ordered coffee and pastry.

"Food is not only good for your physical strength, but it makes you feel better, too," he said. When the food arrived, Taylor understood what he meant by making you feel better. The small Swiss pastries were incredible; it was hard to choose which one to try first. The strong coffee, laced with whipped cream, made them feel comfortable in their new surroundings.

Dr. Meier continued, "Most of our patients stay with us here at the villa. But you, Ms. Valera, are quite ambulant, and you have Mr. Marx to help you get around. So there is no need to keep you cooped up here with us. I have taken the liberty to arrange a cozy little hotel for you two in Ouchy. Ouchy was once a fishing village, but is now part of Lausanne. It is a beautiful resort on the shore of what we call Lac Leman, but is better known as Lake Geneva. The hotel is within a short commute from here, so you can spend most of the day working here with us."

Taylor was worried that staying off the premises would take away from the time spent on Maria's therapy. "That is very kind of you, but wouldn't it be more convenient if she stayed here in the clinic?"

"As I said, it is a very short ride from here, and we really don't exercise our patients all day long. No, I want her to spend the time we are not working with her not in these clinical surroundings, but there, by that beautiful lake in that cozy little hotel. You must understand, we need this young lady to feel happy, to completely be the beautiful young woman she is, and to stop thinking all the time about her handicap and her legs. That way it is easier for us to try and get her brain talking once again to the muscles and nerves in those legs. Please excuse me for explaining it in layman's terms, but the more relaxed she is, the better." Dr. Meier looked like a little cherub sitting in his huge leather desk chair explaining the logic of having them stay in Ouchy.

Maria couldn't get over her excitement when they checked into the little hotel on the waterfront in Ouchy.

"Taylor, this is a fairytale. It's beyond cozy; this is just perfect!" she exclaimed. Her happiness knew no bounds when later that evening they took a stroll along the lake. Taylor pushed her wheelchair slowly along the waterfront. Maria looked at the sun setting over the water and said, "Taylor, let's just stay here forever."

The next day, bright and early, they were at the clinic to face Dr. Ueli Brunner and his staff. The examination of Maria's legs took the better part of the morning. She was alternately strapped to some device that measured reactions to impulses, or she was taken for an x-ray from yet another angle. When the exam was finished, they were told to go back to their hotel and enjoy the rest of the day.

"Take a nice boat ride," Dr. Meier advised. He also recommended a small fish restaurant which was one of his favorites.

They had a wonderful afternoon and evening, but couldn't shake off the tension they felt, wondering what the prognosis would be.

After a restless night, they left early for the clinic. Maria squeezed Taylor's hand tightly as they entered Dr. Brunner's office to hear the results from the tests of the previous day.

"Good morning. You two are nice and early." Unlike the rest of his staff, Dr. Brunner spoke with a heavy accent. Taylor could feel Maria shivering as Dr. Brunner started to explain what he and his staff had found out about the condition of her legs.

"We have carefully studied all the medical records you forwarded to us, and the ones you brought with you. From the initial x-rays taken in Belize, showing the damage to your legs from the accident, and from what we saw yesterday, we are in awe at what the doctors at Johns Hopkins managed to do. They literally put one totally and one partially destroyed leg together again. You are indeed a very lucky lady to have wound up in the hands of the very best. It's close to a miracle that they were able to save your legs. Now the wonderful news. Judging from the responses to the various tests we ran yesterday, it is not unlikely that we can get you out of that wheelchair in a few weeks."

It took a split-second to sink in, but then the emotion overcame them both at the same time, and both Maria and Taylor burst out in tears of joy. Dr. Brunner sat silently to let them experience this overpowering feeling of happiness.

Finally, Maria looked at him and, almost in disbelief asked, "You mean I'll be able to walk?"

"Yes. Unless we run into some unforeseen problems, we feel we can further develop those muscles and nerves so they will be able to support your weight. They responded amazingly well to our tests. As we speak, you should already have enough feeling in your legs to create some movement."

Taylor was overwhelmed. All he could do was reach out to Maria and tell her over and over, "Baby, you'll walk. You'll be able to stand by yourself. You'll be a surgeon!"

When all the emotions had somewhat subsided, Taylor said to Dr. Brunner, "We should have come here much sooner; all that time we wasted trying to do it ourselves."

"You are wrong, very wrong," Dr. Brunner responded. "As I said, we found that her leg muscles and nerves had regenerated enough to respond to our tests. The fact that the doctors at Johns Hopkins put those legs together again is, like I said, a miracle. But it is also a wonder the muscles grew back, and the nerves they tried to repair actually regenerated. That, my friend, is not normal; that can only be the result of hours and hours of therapy, and the dedication of someone who took this as a mission. If, as I assume, that someone is you, I would love to have you here in my clinic to work some of your magic on my other patients. Many of them start out in far better condition than Ms. Valera, but they'll never learn to walk again because they don't have someone like you to refute medical science. Your love for this girl must be very strong." Dr. Brunner's eyes teared up as he complimented Taylor on his unwavering dedication to Maria.

Maria reached over from her wheelchair, pulled Taylor's hand to her lips, and kissed it tenderly. "Thank you, my darling. Thank you for being you."

Chapter 57

They were supposed to arrive in Florida a week before the wedding, but because of an airline strike and a subsequent mix-up in their flight reservations, they arrived only two days before the wedding. Maria's mother was a basket case, and it took all of Clair's persuasive powers to assure her that Taylor would find a way to get them to the wedding on time. In the end, two days proved more than enough to complete any last-minute arrangements.

Maria's mother and Clair had arranged everything in such detail that there was actually nothing left to be done, and on the morning of the wedding, everything proceeded smoothly. Taylor, accompanied by John Phillips, whom he had asked to be his best man, arrived early at the church. Maria's two younger brothers were already there, and Clair and the other members of the wedding party arrived soon after.

The church was packed that morning, and everyone was anxiously awaiting the arrival of Maria and her father. As the organ started playing, the doors at the back of the church opened and Maria, on the arm of her father, proceeded slowly up the aisle. She looked truly radiant in the beautiful dress her mother had helped design. With one hand she leaned on her father's arm, and the other hand rested on a short crutch, which reached up to her elbow. One of the bridesmaids walked right behind her to make sure the crutch would not get caught in the bridal gown. For all those who had not seen Maria stand since her accident, this was quite a surprise, and there was a ripple of applause from the guests. Maria and her father proceeded slowly up the aisle. Taylor and the wedding party stood waiting for them at the altar. Unexpectedly, Maria pushed her crutch away. She leaned over, pulled up her veil, and kissed her father. Then, to his amazement, she let go of his arm, and slowly started walking up the aisle. When the people realized she was walking by herself, pandemonium broke out. Everybody was shouting and cheering at the same time.

One of Maria's brothers couldn't contain himself and he started shouting: "She's walking! She's walking by herself! It's a miracle! Thank you, God, thank you!"

When Maria reached Taylor, she smiled up at him and said softly, "Thank you, my darling, for giving me this day." This time it was Taylor who had kept his promise.

Also by Harold Fischel
ANTHONY
ISBN 1494851210

Amid a series of interesting twists that keep the pages turning, topics like schoolyard bullying are covered with a straightforward pragmatism that helps the moral message stand out clearly. ... [In] *Anthony*, Harold J. Fischel chronicles the life of the title character as he grows from being a troubled but well-intentioned boy to a responsible and understanding parent. The story is full of rich, engaging characters and surprising twists. Anthony is an enjoyable and easy read. ...[T]he book attracts attention with its own strengths that keep readers involved to the end."

ForeWord Reviews *ClarionReview*

Harold J. Fischel's coming of age story, Anthony, is inspiring and heartwarming. Anthony's life is turned upside down by his mother's illness, but the adults he comes in contact with as he grows up help make his life story a triumphant one. Yuni's friend, Aunt Rita, is a marvelous character as are Kay and her parents. Anthony's progression from a withdrawn, small and chubby kid into a confident, caring and ethical young man is wonderful to watch. Fischel's writing style is accomplished and smooth, and I quickly became immersed in this athletic and ethical story of triumph over adversity. Anthony is a marvelous book and is highly recommended reading

Reviewed By Jack Magnus for Readers' Favorite

Harold J. Fischel's book Anthony is as meaningful as it is simple. A simple story, with a normal plot, but the depth and the meaning within is so much more It's not often that I find a book that truly moves me, but Anthony may have just been it. Anthony is so real...such a realistic and poignant character. He is bitter, confused, sad, angry, and while his experience is not necessarily the norm of a typical young adult, you can easily relate to him. What a transformation. Anthony goes from a scared and weak child to a fierce, understanding, and competent young man. I loved seeing the way that other people had an effect on him. Usually you see characters change because of events that happen, but Anthony really changed based on his perception of himself vs. the perception that others have of him. Fischel writes with skill and craftsmanship that is a joy to read. I would read anything else he has to offer in a heartbeat.

Reviewed By Katelyn Hensel for Readers' Favorite

Anthony by Harold J. Fischel is a wonderful coming of age novel. I loved the story of Anthony, but it didn't seem to follow one plot line. There were lots of smaller stories crammed in the book, although they all revolved around Anthony. It was okay but everything happened too fast; there was conflict after conflict so that it felt like there was no real climax and the ending seemed abrupt. On the other hand, I welcomed all the surprises and I loved all the characters. Anthony was resilient and strong, even when he was still a kid. Everything he experienced growing up only made him stronger, some of the things that happened to him even made me cry. Aunt Rita was a really nice person who just made some mistakes. Kay was persistent and supportive in all that Anthony does. All the supporting characters also played big roles in Anthony's success. Overall, a good book with great characters.

Reviewed By Lorena Sanqui for Readers' Favorite

The story evokes poignant feelings and it is wonderfully narrated. All the characters have important roles that have been portrayed well. Anthony's growing up and leaving behind a troubled childhood, to finally becoming a responsible husband and father has been developed well. His leaving behind the stigma of being an illegitimate son and then holding down an important job position is true to the times and resonates well with readers. The language is simple as it targets young adults. The story line is fascinating, which will make it difficult for readers to put the book down. On the whole, it is a very interesting book.

Reviewed By Mamta Madhavan for Readers' Favorite

I truly enjoyed the book and felt that it told a terrific story. You portrayed Anthony's younger years with warmth and compassion and provided him with many opportunities to rise above his circumstances. As he grew up and began the relationship with Rita, it was portrayed naturally and innocently in its own way and, again, provided opportunity for Anthony to grow, mature and understand himself. I really appreciate the way you allow Anthony to restrain himself in so many different situations and not 'go with the flow' – do what everyone else is doing because of peer pressure. It is also important later in the story as his daughter is intimidated by her fear of how others will react to her, so Anthony's experiences are a good background from which he can provide understanding and guidance.

Reviewed By Melinda Hills for Readers' Favorite

ANTHONY by Harold J. Fischel is a novel that takes the reader on a life journey with characters they can really care about. This is a story of strength, growth, and courage.

Reviewed By Judge, 22nd Annual Writer's Digest Self-Published Book.